THE
REVENANT SERIES
BOOK I

THE REVENANT'S BARGAIN

MOLLY ADAZA

THE REVENANT'S BARGAIN

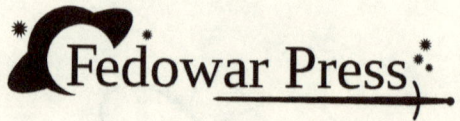

www.FedowarPress.com

ISBN-13 (Digital): 978-1-956492-25-5
ISBN-13 (Paperback): 978-1-956492-26-2
ISBN-13 (Hardcover): 978-1-956492-27-9

Edited by B.K. Bass & Renée Gendron
Cover Design by MiblArt
Interior Design by D.W. Hitz

THE REVENANT'S BARGAIN

MOLLY ADAZA

DEDICATION

To the little girl who thought being a published author was as much a fairytale as riding a dragon.

CHAPTER
I

I WAS FIVE WHEN I KILLED MY MOTHER.

My pursuers' jeers chased me like a wolf upon the scent of a limping rabbit. Her plea for my life was a single, shrill note in the otherwise rumbling stampede of footsteps and threats.

She told me to run.

I ran as fast and far as I could, ignoring the ache in my legs and burning in my chest, even as the sun chased me from the horizon on its ascent, casting my shadow as a beacon to aid their hunt.

When I fell, scraping my knee against the bark of a fallen tree or scuffing my palms against the ragged rocks of the stream I waded through, her demands echoed in my head. To keep going. To put the rising sun in my path. Run until I found a town. Not more tents. A town with cobbled streets and towering brick buildings. Like in the stories she told before the sun bathed our camp in life.

When morning dew wrinkled my toes and soaked the hem of my pants.

When the stars twinkled above, so near. If I were taller, I could have plucked one from the midnight sea and hid it away in the cupboard with me. So, even in the darkness of the days, I'd have something more than my dingy blanket, lumpy pillow, and poorly sewn dolls.

But she told me to run.

The echo of her wail followed me into the thickest sections of the forest. I never heard those noises from her, nor from anyone who entered our tent. Those, I didn't understand.

But the voices — I'd know those anywhere. They stalked me in my nightmares.

A shadow blocked the sun.

I cut sharply, bare feet slipping in the mud, as mother taught me to do when someone bigger and stronger found me. The bark of the branch I spun myself around cut deeper into my already blood-soaked palm. A red handprint remained as a new beacon.

The underbrush cleared and the tree line thinned. Soon, rolling hills with towering grass would blanket the horizon. Mother said never to cross it in the sun's warmth.

My toes dragged on a moss coated log, and though I tucked as I rolled, I slammed into another tree. The world spun, though the cool of the wet leaves beneath my fingers and the metallic sting between my lips remained.

I stifled the heavy tears with a bloodied hand over my mouth. Their boots were too close. They splintered sticks. They snapped low-hanging branches.

They neared.

I squirmed, as my body could do little else as pain radiated with every blink and breath, until the fallen tree obscured me in shadows. Still in the open. Still exposed to the jeers and taunts I'd only heard through the cupboard's walls.

I closed my eyes. The chill of the damp ground soaked through trousers already soddened by my fear. It froze around my locked joints, spearing inwards to the rumbling in my gut.

A shadow passed over my hiding place, and I hid my face in my billowing sleeves.

The sky lit with blaring light and then softened into darkness;

still, I dared not to leave the moist leaves and chilled shadows.

Nights were worse.

More bad males would come. They always did, lumbering with the stench of what mother had called *bad tea*. Swords would clatter to the floor. They would curse. They would bark commands at mother.

As they brought my nightmares to life.

Mother said nights were the safest for crossing the open fields.

When I left her behind.

The trees dwindled until only the starlight and the crescent moon illuminated my path to the next grove.

There, on the horizon, a line of emerald.

Shaking from more than the cold, I stepped from the safety of the tree line. Swaying grass tickled my chin. Every blade's brush filled my nose with agitating sniffles. They returned to scratch my exposed hands and catch on the tatters of my clothes.

I ran.

Wings flapped above me. The moon cast my pursuer's shadow across my path. I cut left. Then right. The flap of wings remained over my shoulder. The grass slicked my steps.

Tender hands swept me far into the night sky until only the moon rivaled my height.

His grin and the whites of his eyes glowed, though the steady rock of his wing's flap was as lulling as mother's arms.

I thrashed.

Like mother said to, I fought against the iron. I thrashed and kicked and punched with all I had, meeting armor more often than not.

"What's your name?" He smelled of lavender.

Mother said to fight, but I was tired. My teeth chattered and my fists ached where they'd struck his armor.

"My name is Amaury. "His grip softened.

My arms and legs refused to lift for another blow. I only wanted to rest, to be back in my cupboard, sleeping through the noises, snuggled within the blankets smelling of mildew.

"What is your name?"

If I could just sleep.

"Kacela."

When Amaury spoke, he didn't smell like bad tea. "Where is your mother?"

A sob ruptured my breath.

She said to fight.

But I couldn't.

"*Better to fight as long as you can than let them take you,*" she whispered into my hair the first night I'd almost been seen, nearly a year ago. Needing to pee, I stumbled from my cupboard. He didn't see me, or hear me over his grunts, but mother saw me. She lifted her head from where it laid on the pillow, her hair strewn across it like a jagged halo. Terror filled her eyes then.

The same terror I saw in her eyes before she told me to run.

"I want my mom," I said through another sob. "Go get her!"

He held me closer to his chest. "Hold on to my neck."

"I want my mom." I shrieked and thrashed.

"Kacela." He ignored my hands, shoving at his cheek and shoulder. His wings arched, only his arm keeping me from plummeting back to the field. "I'm going to take you somewhere safe, okay? Away from here. Where no one will ever hurt you, understand?"

I pressed my nose into his neck, my wails for my mother lost in the wind.

CHAPTER 2

Seven years later

THE WOODEN BLADE'S thud on the training mat echoed like my onlookers' chuckles. I scooped it up before it stopped rattling and gripped the one-handed blade in two.

"Eyes on your enemy, Kacela." Lord Tait's training master was hardly a warrior, more a scholar of war. He moved as if his arms were made of the same oak as the chairs in the library.

Across the grounds, boys my age stepped through patterns similar to mine. They moved together, their comrades on either side like mirrors. A soldier in black leathers shouted orders at their every action, his voice a drum to guide their movements and disrupt mine.

"Kacela," the training master snapped, "eyes on your enemy."

I stepped through the series of spins again, dragging my knee through the dirt to duck beneath an invisible attack and skewer my blade through the assailant's chest. On the upward spiral, I stuttered and plunged my sword's tip into the dirt.

Dust glittered on polished boots. Behind them, soldiers fell silent.

"That would have been impressive," a familiar voice said, "if your opponent were the ground."

I bit my tongue.

"Master Wylan, I trust you have been advising my ward with more than insults." Amaury covered me with his shadow and offered his hand, but I rose without taking it. I stepped from the cover of the one who'd scooped me from the field, outfitted me in the finest of clothing, and saw to my daily training, squaring my shoulders as he did.

He wore the raven black of the king, his tunic outlined in ruby red. The shine of the sun through the ruby on the pommel of his longsword gave his cheeks a peachy blush.

Master Wylan hinged slightly at his waist. "Royal Commander Amaury, your ward is wasting time. She is easily distracted—"

"By boys?" Amaury clasped my shoulder. "Hardly, Wylan. If she's watching them, she's devising a dozen ways to defeat each."

"If they'd fight me." I glared at the backs of their heads.

"Her balance—"

Amaury held up a hand to cut off Wylan, then observed me and the scrapes through the dirt. "Speed is not always your ally, Kacela. A sprinted stumble—"

"Is a rush to death." I twirled the blade, but a splinter snuck from it into my palm. I yelped, then dropped it.

Amaury waved away the scholar. "Dismissed." He grabbed my blade from the ground and fit it back into my grip.

I prepared my stance. Amaury pulled his longsword from his belt and mirrored me from the side. "Patience, Kacy. You are a soldier, not a child with a blade."

The dirt crumbled beneath my shifting toes.

Amaury's instructions guided my movements alongside his. We swept through the patterns like the boys across the training field did, as one, spying one another's movements through peripherals to stay synchronous.

I wobbled, but my sword leveled and only boot marks marred the training ring in the end.

"He's an awful instructor," I told Amaury between sips of water after the first pattern.

"You say that about everyone who isn't me."

"I do not."

He swept his stringy locks back into their leather binding. "Your dance instructor?"

"She said my feet are too big."

"That's not it." Amaury snagged the wooden sword from my hand, replacing it with his longsword. "You don't like to be led."

I heaved the blade up to point its tip at his chest. "I am a soldier. Soldiers are led by their commanders into war to save their kingdoms."

His brows furrowed and their shadows brushed away the warmth from his hazel eyes. "Again."

My movements faltered and struggled to gain the momentum necessary to wield the longsword's weight with deadly accuracy. Dust muddled the air at my every stumble until its grime caked my cheeks and itched at my palms.

"A good soldier knows how to follow," he said over the scuff of my steps. "A great soldier is brains and brawn. A great soldier does not blindly rush to death."

I stopped. The sword swung in my grip, knocking into my padded knee. A tinge shot up my thigh. "I will serve Kadea on the front lines, until glory or death."

He held my gaze with a blank stare. "Again."

Amaury took his blade back after I'd gone through three more patterns. He motioned toward the doors leading inside. "Come."

"I have another hour—"

"We have more pressing matter, Kacela. Come."

The Tait Estate, overlooking the northern bluffs, was decorated as if the black waves crested into its halls. In many rooms, tiles gave way to glass, revealing the ocean-battered, jagged outcrops at the cliff base. Glittering black stones lined the windows overlooking the blue horizon.

Salt-saturated breaths clogged my lungs with their pricks.

Wind howling through open windows swallowed our footsteps in the halls nearing the grand office Kadea's King, Griffin Quillon, made his during visits to the Tait Estate.

Amaury knocked once, then shoved the door open.

"Enter," Griffin grumbled without looking up from where his quill scrapped parchment. The curtains tied at either side of the arching window at his back allowed the dull, clouded sun rays to glow within the tips of his crooked, obsidian crown. Raven black hair stuck from it like a spider's legs. "Sit."

I took the nearest chair and dug my nails into the underside of the cushion. Amaury stood beside me, hand on the backrest.

"The Sacrament ends soon," Griffin said, still looking downwards. "A Blessing Ceremony will be held in Virian for dozens of clans. We will be in attendance."

"No," Amaury barked, his grip causing the chair to tilt back. My heart jolted and hands fumbled to steady on the armrests.

The quill came to a stop with a sharp creak. Griffin raised his raging, ocean-blue eyes. The planes of his face were rigid, his chin slightly turned up like a glaive. "No?"

Amaury eased the chair back to its four legs. "Kacela is not stepping foot back into a Forterian camp, especially not the one of her birth."

"She has not returned since you took her from it."

"Because I wish for her to live."

Quill forgotten, Griffin straightened. A jet of sparkling black magic from his flicked finger righted the skew of his crown. "She returns as your ward and under my protection, not as a dead courtesan's runaway daughter. Whether they recognize her as one of their own or not, action against her is treason."

"There is no reason other than curiosity for her to accompany us if you wish to observe the ceremony, Griffin."

"Sometimes curiosity is the only reason I need." He winked at me.

I bounced, rattling the wooden chair on the tiled floor. "I want to go."

Amaury kept his gaze on our king. He heaved a breath, as if to object, before releasing a heavy sigh. "It will cause questions with the lords and ladies if we bring her. My reputation sways by the day with the Altuns. Bringing my ward to a Forterian camp, on their most sacred day, will not paint her in any positive light. Questions of her heritage, ones we are not ready to answer, will arise."

"Her heritage has been questioned since you brought her to Kadea. The lords and ladies have and will believe what I tell them to."

"Which is?" Amaury seethed.

Griffin raised a brow. "It is on the way to Kadea. We'll be returning home immediately after."

"I want to go." I tugged on Amaury's sleeve. "I'll stay behind you, out of sight. I won't say anything."

Amaury swatted away my hand. "Bring her home, then visit Virian."

"A waste of time and energy," Griffin stated.

I tugged Amaury's sleeve again.

"Her presence may be seen as an insult to the ceremony. The Forterians are preoccupied fighting one another; do not turn their attention to you."

Griffin ruffled the papers together. "I will leave you to explain the Blessing Ceremony's events to her. Careful where you speak."

After we stepped out of the office, a sweep of Griffin's magic slammed the doors closed.

Amaury's gaze swung to me.

I perked up. "I want to go."

He steered me away with a hand on my shoulder. We trekked back through the halls to a library in the southern wing of the fortress. The two-story tall shelves of dusty books were interrupted only by windows at the far side. Before us, a white capped mountain jutted from the crosshatching of rolling hills and dense forest at its base.

"Sacrament Land," he said, pointing. "Currently, hundreds

of young Forterian males fight on the mountainside to survive. Three days from now, when the full moon rises, those who are alive will emerge and be blessed with magic."

"I want to see the ceremony. I'm Forterian."

He squatted before me. His chestnut hair fell in stringy clumps to his brow, some curling and others fraying. "You are part Forterian, Kacela," there was a rasp to his admission, "and you are part Altun. Two races of fae which do not mix lightly. Here, as an Altun, you can learn any skill you wish."

"I want to fight."

His laughter was thunderous. "I know. You can, here, as an Altun. If you return to your life as a Forterian, you cannot fight. Forterian females do not fight. They cook and clean and take care of the children."

I wrinkled my nose and looked past him at the mountain — the perfect arena for a warrior.

"Virian has nothing for you except memories. Painful memories."

I looked at my boots, studying the scuffs of dirt across them and the untied lace on the left one.

"If Griffin believes you should attend, who am I to speak against the king?" Amaury sighed, engulfing both my hands in his. "No Forterian has innate magic, as you do, as any Altun may have. Survivors have magic carved into them by the Oracle — "

"Who smells of feet."

He squinted at me.

"With a black blade. It has magic within it and enhances the abilities of whoever is blessed. You are blessed with wings to fly, so it carved wings into your back. A thinker is blessed with brains and has a line of swirls and dots over their brow. Then there's the stamina, who have rivers carved into their backs, and brutes who have many of their muscles outlined. Feline claws on the hands and feet of stealths. A gross beast on the chest of shapeshifters."

I waited for his scrunched features to brighten with pride. They did not. He quirked his head slightly.

"There are books about Forterians." I wiggled my fingers in his grip.

"I had them moved to—"

"The top shelf in Griffin's office." I mirror his raised brow. "If you let me train more, I'd have less time to climb."

His chin dropped to his rumbling chest. When his gaze met mine, a renewed sparkling lightened the hazel irises. Amaury adjusted his shoulders. Wings unfurled from the slits in his armor, nearly golden, as if a torch hummed within each feather.

I reached for the left wing and flicked a feather.

His hand, still encasing one of mine, gave a gentle tug. "Do you know who blesses the Forterians? Who they worship?"

"The goddess of war."

"*Their* goddess of war, Kacela. Not yours. You do not need another's magic, you have your own. You are part Altun, and you have more in common with the Altuns than you do with the Forterians."

I nodded, still staring at his wings. How they adjusted to the slight draft in the library, where they swept across the ground, the frill of every feather at the bristle of his shoulders. I knew how fast they could fly and the feeling of wind battering my face while soaring through a cloud.

The wings folded, then disappeared back beneath the armor and into his black tattooed blessing.

I met his gaze.

"You don't draw more attention than your presence already will. Understand?"

"Understood."

Remembering Virian was like trying to cup water in my hands. The memory of the stars peeking between the trees and the melody of my mother's voice dribbled from my grasp first. The rest, the worst, remained in the creases of my palms and dripped from my wrists. Her screams and pleas to save herself, to save me. The smell of mildew and rotten wood of the cabinet. The insults hurled at her like stones.

The very same they tossed at me now.

I tugged at the sleeves of my fur-lined coat and pressed to Amaury's side.

"She is not welcomed here!" the nearest warrior snapped. His wings, on display instead of hidden within the magic-laced tattoo on his back, reached past his flung-out arms.

Others mumbled agreements.

I peeked around the hazel wings tucked against Amaury's back. They reached toward the rising sun, as tall as any others. He fluffed them regularly, as if warning those advancing to consider their next step.

Warriors packed the field, caged to our presence within the circle of pines. Blood splattered faces as it did the snow. Patches of it gathered in boot prints. It's metallic scent, tangled in the dry breeze, burned my nose.

"Forterians have no laws barring females or Altuns from Blessing Ceremonies. Prejudices," Griffin smirked, readjusting his crown with a flick of magic, "there are many."

Because this was his land and defeated armies don't make demands. Griffin allowing Forterians autonomy within their clans was a leniency they pressed daily.

I leaned a bit further, stopped by Amaury's arm.

The first accuser's glare found my staggered steps. His nostrils flared and grip went to the twin blades on his hips. Those flanking him, one whose brow was marred with the swirls and dots of a thinker blessing and the other with the black lines of a strength blessing spearing from beneath his leathers, matched his stance. Others, some with obvious blessings and others without, filled the grove with their snarls.

"We mean no disrespect, Chief Daviat," Amaury huffed. Whispers of traitor, aimed at him, wrapped around the echo of his words. "We come from the north, passing through, and felt inclined to enjoy the glories of your Blessing Ceremony ourselves."

I gripped his arm where it crossed before my shoulders.

Jitters knocked my knees and my throat refused to close around a swallow. I scoured the field for something, knowing not what it was, only that I needed it for my next breath.

Sweat stuck my sleeves to my palms. It plastered my shirt to every curve of my back. I squirmed. The sense of something missing remained like a second skin, locking my joints, as if my body would only allow my next movement to be toward it.

The source of my thundering heart.

Amaury peeked down, and his eyes widened at whatever he assessed on my face. I fought the guide of his palm flattened to my shoulder, attempting to tuck me further behind him.

"Kacela," he hissed, "stop."

I couldn't.

Something rumbled from deep in my gut, where warmth billowed like smoke from a fire.

Somewhere within the fields.

Waiting.

Griffin's voice was a knife in my belly, rupturing the intrusive urge which narrowed my focus. "However, we are well versed in knowing when we are not welcomed."

Too soon. We were leaving too soon. I hadn't found it. Needed to find it.

I scoured, taking another step against Amaury's unrelenting grasp.

Somewhere. It was here, and I'd rather lose my every breath than leave without knowing what called to me like a victorious horn bringing soldiers home.

There!

Across the field. A face splattered in blood and scars. Brushy eyebrows high. Cocoa curls crusted in a rusty red.

Relief swaddled me like a blanket warmed by coals.

I took a step.

My chest ached at the desperate shout of my pulse, squished by the sensation of Griffin's magic taking us from the field.

From him.

CHAPTER 3

Thirteen years later

"BIRTHDAYS ARE A GOOD REASON for a break." Amaury rested a hand on the decorative rapier at his belt. "Twenty-fifth birthdays even more so. You have trained obsessively for years to be the best of your age. One party will not deplete your strength nor skills."

My pins in my blond hairs picked at my scalp. I craned to see how each curl cascaded over the tulle overlay of the ballgown. Rubies sparkled within the red bodice where the sheer fabric did very little to hide the breadth of my shoulders and only achieved an annoying itch where it sleeved down to my wrists.

Drastic makeup masked the burns on my cheeks from an afternoon beneath the blistering sun, training until my gloved fingers bled. The scabs and calluses scraped with every jitter.

I accepted the steady rhythm of the servant's work and settled into myself in preparation for the night ahead, to leash the spark of temper Amaury claimed I inherited in my Forterian blood.

The bold makeup was like a visor pulled over the face of a solider trudging into battle. I steeled myself, settling into that space King Griffin Quillon dominated more than any other. The courting and cleverness where he reigned as deity instead of merely king. The hell of waltzing on black tiles reflecting every insecurity and imperfection for my inspection, taunting me with the click of heels when I was better suited for the clang of blades.

I steeled myself into a place not entirely mine, yet part of me surged forward, eager to free itself from the confinement of training gear. The courtier lurking within, adorned in jewels and wit.

Amaury, the ever-present smile of a proud father plastered on his tight lips, paused as I stood from the vanity. The tiny wrinkles around each eye, the only clue of his age, molded into one large crease. He wore a black suit with red detailing, including the embroidered symbol of his Forterian clan, the same as mine, on his left breast: A mink wound around a sword, holding a rabbit in its canines. "You look beautiful."

"Is it not too dark?"

"You should see the ballroom." His voice was dry.

"Twenty-five is a happy year."

Amaury held up a necklace of black sapphires arranged in the outline of a raven. I scrunched up my ringlets, much to the dismay of the servants.

"In Forterian culture, it is. The last year to be in the Sacrament, and those who have already been blessed settle back into life and perhaps consider starting a family..." He laid the gems around my neck and clasped the red chain.

The jewel's icy bite sent a shiver to my jaw.

Amaury continued, "if there is no war looming."

"If you find your mate," I added, though the words sprang from a chink in the armor I kept concealed. War was looming and fantasizing of inconsequential love only wasted training time. Time also wasted by extravagant parties when death could march from the west and scouts brought in daily reports of nightmares leaking from cracks in the fabric between realms.

His chuckle told me he knew where my mind ran. "Do not allow fate to shackle you, Kacy."

The conversation stalled there, as it always did. Once, he'd explained how my frequent, abrupt, and annoying moments of desperation to seek out my fated mate would fade in time. Normal, for my age, to feel the unquenchable need of a mate bond, for the one my soul called to above any other.

As normal as a young soldier's urge to run to the front lines in a quest for glory.

He never mentioned, though, what might happen if I found my mate. Some days I wondered if he'd forgotten about mates entirely after his century and a half of war. He treated the subject like that of me fighting on the front lines — with a glare and silence.

"I hate these parties," Amaury muttered. He escorted me through the winding, obsidian hallways. We passed portraits of royalty, commanders, war heroes, and estate heads, all mocking my stumbling with their elegantly craned poise. I stared ahead, feeling as if the stares of the dead peeked through them, harboring the hatred of my heritage. The closer we walked to the entry, the scarcer the portraits became and larger the windows overlooking the western gardens grew.

A red runner cascaded down the grand stairs into the foyer. At its end, Amaury would trade me to an unlucky estate heir.

Though I shared no blood with Amaury, a marriage to me, the Royal Commander's ward, would provide a line of access currently unparalleled by any social standing. On my eighteenth birthday, the requests for my attention fluttered in.

I hated their eyes on me. Spoiled brats with decorative blades and unbloodied hands. Those who half-assed trained and viewed ladies on their arms in the same light as the swords clipped to their belts.

"None of the boys would fight me this week." They'd gladly fought one another, spending hours monopolizing the training mats, yet I'd been barred by glares.

Amaury patted my hand nestled in the crook of his elbow. "Smart lads."

"Cowards."

"Pay them no mind." He patted my hand again. The veins of his neck bulged, but his tone remained light. "These boys will not know the blood of the front lines, and neither will you."

"With Beaddeon looking to move east—"

"Beaddeon is not currently of concern." Amaury pinched my hand.

"Then why is Griffin planning a visit there?"

He stopped before the maze of halls gave to the grand staircase and courtier's probing stares. "There are more pressing issues than Beaddeon. The visit is a courtesy."

I stepped before him. "What pressing issues?"

He bowed slightly to meet my gaze. "If you're going to nag me about the demon rifts once more, I'll tell Griffin you fell violently ill and could not attend."

I was silent a moment, then cracked a wide smile. "Tell me about the demon rift."

"No, no." His chuckle rumbled like marching boots. When he shook out his hair, bits of it fell from the caked-on gel attempting to mat down the stringy locks. "You are not avoiding your own party."

I smoothed back the free lock spilling over his brow. "Today isn't even my birthday."

He took my shoulders in his oversized grip, turned me back toward the stairs, and offered his arm. "The day I plucked you from the field seems like as good as any to celebrate."

Carved obsidian ravens interwove with the dark-stained wooden banister, and as I touched one, magic ruffled its feathers. It squawked out an announcement, though no courtiers littered the entryway at the base of the staircase to acknowledge it. Then, it returned to stone.

"No escort?" I asked.

"Perhaps the lad is running late." Amaury guided me down the staircase, taking extra care of my dress's dragging tulle.

I pinched as much tulle as I could without yanking it up to my thighs, missing the sturdiness of my boots and training pants.

Grand oak doors, carved with the scene of a conspiracy of ravens descending on a battlefield, muffled the roar of the courtiers already indulging in Kadea's wealth.

I'd wanted a smaller party of those I considered family, only the Royal Inner Council. Those who raised me and saw to my training and tutoring, instead of outsiders poking for a way in. However, Griffin insisted on gathering every estate in Kadea. There'd been no further discussion.

"I'm sure he'll be along shortly." Amaury stopped me at center of the entryway. "You are a soldier, Kacela. Do not let these pompous lords and ladies squish you beneath their boots. Understand?"

I cast a glance toward the rumbling of voices. "Understood."

He kissed my brow. "I am so proud of you."

Once Amaury was hidden behind the closed doors of the ballroom, I reached beneath my dress to tighten the brace of knives on my thigh. It held five throwing blades as thin as paper. If he'd seen, he would've left me weaponless.

"Armed for war?" a voice, like the first breeze of winter, asked.

I turned on him, one blade half pulled.

"Killing your escort would be a terrible start to the night." With his hands in his pockets, Lord Tait's heir apparent leaned against the wall, concealed in shadows beside a tapestry depicting the arrival of the Quillon Monarchy to the continent. Their ships, triple the size of any sailing now, broke through the surf of the fabled Aqualtin, the fae of the sea.

He glided to me as if propelled on the same tide.

"Nalin," I greeted, curtseying. My small, quivering breath did very little to keep my smile simple and shoulders from caving.

He nodded.

Nalin's hair was as dark as the shadows he moved between, and his voice as airy. A glint in his leaden eyes was like the flash of light off a hidden blade seen too late. He wore all black except for the silver crest of a stalking leopard embroidered on his left breast pocket. He'd won the rapier on his belt in the previous year's tournament between the male heirs of estates. The ruby in the mouth of a cawing raven on its pommel was larger than any I'd ever worn.

I took his offered arm.

Servants rushed to the doors and waited for my permission to reveal my jitters to the entire kingdom. I took another breath before falling back into the thunder of battle, then nodded. The doors unveiled hundreds of eyes absorbing every detail to tuck in their back pockets for another time. Leverage. As if the king's secrets were tattooed across my cheeks.

Nalin took the first step into the ballroom, and with my courtly smile plastered in place, I allowed him to guide me through the crescendoing applause.

The colors of each estate swam in the sea of black.

I picked out individuals noted in my briefing with Griffin the previous week. Lord and Lady Jukes were dressed in black with sea-foam green accents. Lord Bilks, patting the left breast where Griffin's family emblem sparkled in rhinestones, gritted gold covered teeth. The faint hint of tobacco coated Lady Fortuna's upturned, blackened lips. Beside her, Lady Messalia ran a white gloved hand down the wrinkled cheeks of her knobby lord.

There were more. An ocean worth of painted lips varnished in the rakish spoils of wealth. All those who scrutinized my place within the castle. My place on Nalin's arm. For what Altun lord would allow his son to escort the ward of a Forterian? No matter that Forterian's favor with the king.

Only upon reaching the dance floor did my lungs clear of their perfume veiled indulgences.

If I heard the first tap of the conductor's baton as a call to war, my stomach would settle.

Nalin's finger curled around my hip and mine wrinkled the silk shoulder of his jacket.

With a sword in my hand, I was elegant and stunning. The slight elevation in my heels made me a lame deer.

The first dance was ours. Then the garish rainbow sea crested around us. The courtiers were excited to show their obedience to the traditional dances, where spins and lifts were as clean as fighting patterns.

"Our king does not dance," Nalin said, then twirled me away to snap me back to his stern frame.

I cast a glance, when not being yanked through steps like a hound on a leash, at the king. He threw his hands around while conversing with Lord Tait, Nalin's father. Beside her husband, stoic Lady Tait met my glance. Both were ghostly white and dressed in midnight black.

"He has no partner," was all I could offer. There was no queen, not in his dozens of years of reign. A travesty, or weakness. It was the constant chink in his armor that a fae more powerful than any seen on the continent could not find his fated mate. That he ruled alone.

As much as it bothered the lords and ladies, it bothered me even more that he could wait a hundred years for his mate and I could not.

Nalin took an hour of my time before the narrowed glares of others forced him to pass me along. Then to the next, and the next, as if I were a jug of wine. Each heir of an estate filling a dance with more information and pleas for resources than Nalin had offered all night.

"Our people are not meant for battle," one said. Another claimed they could provide more soldiers for the army if only their goods were exported at higher rates. They weighed down every dance with their needs and offering, as if I were only a mule meant to transport their words.

More. They all wanted more.

I didn't admit to any how little Griffin listen to my reports the morning after parties. Often, I was sure he did it for my entertainment instead of his own need.

Still, I listened. I nodded. I gave them my time, and when appropriate, I reminded them that when war comes, all must answer the raven's call to defend Kadea.

I tucked away the information they did not even know they gave. The slightest notions of tension and the insecurities tucked behind boasting. I knew it would only take one piece to show Griffin I was more than a ward to be married off.

When my ears ached as much as my feet, I bid my own party an early leave.

The servants, with a flick of their wrists and without touching the doors, cracked them enough for me to slink through. I slipped from my shoes and eased aching feet onto glassy floors.

In the entry, I could hear the grand bell in the eastern tower signal midnight.

"Leaving so soon?"

I pivoted like a soldier readying for a new enemy. My fingers twitched at where my short sword would be. Instead, I held my heels. My knives were tucked too far beneath the tulle to slip free.

It was only Nalin.

My polite smile morphed into a glare. "You're missing the party out here by yourself."

"Merely taking a moment to avoid the stream of beautiful dance partners." His chin dipped and brows masked his eyes in shadows.

"If you'll excuse me." I turned, but Nalin's smirk appeared before me.

He'd skipped, pinched the fabric of our world together and cleaved a portal to step through. While moving food or water within the castle could be done by servants harboring drops of magical power, skipping oneself around the numerous wards took an extremely strong or wildly clever magic wielder.

I'd seen Nalin be both.

"It'd be rude of me not to escort a lady to her room." His half grin caused the wine in my gut to churn.

The words of the heirs slipped off my shoulders. Him being my escort and finding me when I tried to sneak away were far from being coincidences. The night reeked of Griffin's tactics. He needed the Taits for their army and the obsidian they mined off their northern coast. For their command of the Forterian clans on their land.

"That is extremely kind of you."

Once, I'd yearned for his offered hand to find mine beneath the dining table or within the throngs of dance partners. No longer. My skin prickled where he clasped his hand atop mine in the crook of his elbow.

Squishing the folds of my dress between my palm and shoes, I took the first step to force Nalin to follow in stride.

"Which lords and ladies sent their boys to you tonight?"

I hitched my skirt higher. My knuckles skimmed the tip of a throwing knife sheathed to my thigh. "Many."

"Pressing matters?"

"As pressing as they always are. You have your own matters to whisper in our king's ear, do you not?"

The hand atop mine tightened. Trapped, I kept my gaze forward, determined to disguise the unease in my stomach at our slow pace.

"Your visits have grown sparse. I'd hoped you would accompany the royal commander during his army inspection last month."

I gave my most innocent smile. "Amaury is far more competent at assessing your lines. I, however, am still learning. Often, I ask more questions than Amaury has time to answer."

Nerves jumped beneath the squeeze of his hand. "I would have made ample time to advise you on such matters."

The offer was like a cell with the door half ajar, as if I had a choice in the matter. Not if Griffin decided. By his whim, my next visit to the Tait Estate may be to move my things instead of teeter along beside Amaury. "I'd be honored, then, to accompany Amaury on his next visit."

"Delightful."

My chest tightened with every step down the hallway to my wing.

We stopped before my door.

Nalin turned and captured my hand in both of his. "Has your

room been properly searched? The crowds make easy work for those wishing you harm."

I held his calculating gaze as a smirk slid across his lips. "Perhaps there are guests who wish ill against me, however, my room has its own security measures."

He stepped closer, head dipping. His berry-tinged breath tickled my lips. "It would be rude of me—"

I turned to my door, disentangling my hand from his. "To keep many lovely dancing partners waiting. I assure you, Nalin, I am safe. Please, enjoy the remainder of the party."

"Without you, it will be a challenge."

I eased the door open enough to slip through. "You are quite fond of those."

CHAPTER 4

THE NEXT MORNING, I sulked to the door of the parlor, back itching under midnight blue ruffles. Cascading from a high neckline, they threatened to trip my every step.

The echo of chatter from within the parlor dashed my hopes of disappearing within the lines of bookshelves unnoticed. I preferred the parlor echoing the pluck of strings instead of slander and hearsay.

The gossip welcomed me to the gathering of courtiers with jutting nods.

Lord Garnell's daughter, Jacinth, babbled on about dance partners while others hung half off their seats toward her. Oceane, Lady Taggart's heir presumptive, stared past the curved wall of windows into the northern water garden where overlaying planks replicated the deck of a ship.

Some heirs and courtiers strolled the shelves with their fingers tracing titles. Others mingled and spoke in hushed whispers, foreheads pressed together. Another filled the library with a harp's melody.

I greeted each with a nod before dashing into the maze of

shelves.

"Oh Kacela, come back. Please, we are discussing your party," Jacinth called in her sickly sweet hum.

"In a moment. I have a title in my head and if I do not find it now, I may lose it forever." I ran my finger down the row of books with enough effort to be forgotten.

"I danced with Jocast, Lord Compton's nephew, who was wonderful," Jacinth continued, "and Commander Vance Allerick's son, Valor. And Nalin, of course. Oh, we had the loveliest conversation about the paintings father is commissioning of the fields in the summer. Oceane, you must come see them!"

"Yes." Oceane's voice fluttered away like the breeze. Tucking back wild black hair, she continued, "and you must come see the ocean in the summer. The silence before a storm is worthy of such art."

Jacinth lowered her chin. "Lady Taggart is very lenient with the Forterians, is she not?"

I snatched a random book before taking a chair in a shadowed section, near enough to input, "They're our strongest allies in war."

"Bred barbarians, best for dying in the front lines," Jacinth snubbed. "I've heard they kidnap females from nearby towns when they cannot find their mates."

Oceane returned her gaze to the trickling water outside. "That's not true. I know someone whose mate is Forterian. She's happy—"

"She looks happy, but they'd kill her if she said otherwise." Jacinth leaned toward the courtier on her other side. "They cannot use magic until it's carved into them. If it were up to me—"

"It's not," I reminded her with a pointed glare.

"Well, if it were," Jacinth said, voice as sharp as a blade, "I'd have them exterminated. Wipe their mountain from the map for northern trade routes and stop their barbaric Sacrament."

"We'd lose half the army," I muttered. "Then, it would be our soldiers dying on the front lines instead of theirs."

"We'd destroy an enemy." Jacinth, despite her courtly ways, could have dominated a battlefield. Her father would have been wise to name her heir instead of her dull brother, who was as quick with a sword as he was with his wit. She'd inherited the Garnell traits of a narrowing face, wide-set eyes, and lips so thin they disappeared when she snarled. Her father's land, in the middle of Kadea, was little more than fields of corn and potatoes and wheat. His wealth and heavy exports made her the favored suitor for most heirs. That, and she hadn't spent years training the softness from her curves.

A spate of knocks on the library door stopped my retort short.

It swung open, revealing Nalin with his finest courtier manners. He wore a simple black tunic, drab in comparison to the ruby-hilted rapier on his waist. I met his amusement-tipped smile with my own simple grin. He glided toward us, his steps as silent as shadows.

He stopped before me. "May I have a word?"

"We are in the middle of a conversation. May I find you afterwards?" I gestured to the ladies gawking at me. Jacinth, in particular, narrowed her eyes to slits.

"I'd prefer now." His voice left no room for argument, and neither did his outstretched hand.

I glanced at Jacinth again. I knew she fancied him and the power of being his lady. She'd told me as much the year prior and made a habit of reminding me during her visits.

Nalin pulled me from the warmth of the midday sun flittering through the expansive windows into the bitter stone hallways. The door swung closed at my back. His gaze nailed me to the spot.

"There are rumors."

The clicks of his polished shoes echoed down the hall in his haste to catch me. I'd nearly made it to the corner when the aura of his magic, smelling of tart cherries, encased me in the same steering grip as his hand on my elbow.

"Rumors are tricky," I wheezed, and the magic swelled.

"I've heard many as well, though I find most hold a warped sliver of truth."

His magic choked the next witty line from my grasp. Nalin ignored my gasp for breath and knocked on a dull door leading to an even duller room. No paintings adorned the stone walls, and only a couch with a thin sheen of dust decorated the insipid interior.

Nalin snapped shut the wooden blinds across each of the four windows with a flick of his wrist. I stared at the speckles of magical silver mist illuminated in the slits of sun.

My curiosity about his mastery of magic did not overshadow the pounding of my heart. I grasped at my skirt where my short sword should have hung, as if I could've hidden a blade within its ruffles.

Alone.

I stilled my shaking knees and held my mask of indifference. My slow breaths were full of reminders that this was not the same study I'd found myself alone with him in a year prior. Though his magic raged with the same anger, no smashed bottle littered the floors as a reminder of my mistake and his resentment.

His jacket scrunched and crinkled at his shoulders. "Which weakling?"

I straightened my shoulders and let a smile slide across my face. Never mind that I did not know of what he spoke. "Are you jealous, Lordling, of another and his access to my time?"

Nalin pivoted on the balls of his feet and closed the distance, allowing me a breath from the stifle of his magic. "No."

"You are." I roused and pressed to my toes to mingle our breaths. Slipping into my courtier demeanor, I raised a hand to trace the lines of his suit up his chest. I thought I might've heard his breath snag or felt hesitation as our knees nearly knocked.

I locked when his fingers ran over a ruffle at my waist. "Who?"

"You do not own my time, Nalin. I can converse with whomever I fancy."

He gripped the ruffles. I already could hardly breathe against the spines of the corset hidden beneath them. With his grip pinching as it did, I forced shallow breaths.

"I know we've had our," he clicked his tongue, "disagreements in the past. I'll not allow you to make a fool of me with your flirting and entertaining of others."

I broke his grip on my dress, but then it was on my wrist, holding it against his chest. "Let me go, Nalin."

His magic, a glittering snowstorm, encased us. It plucked at my hair, darted through the dress's ruffles, and itched at my brow. Flittering around my mind, his magic tested my mental barriers, designed to block even a magic-wielder as powerful as Nalin from entering my mind.

I wheezed against his encasing power.

He dipped his head, yet still towered over me. The crane of his neck gave him the appearance of a vulture eyeing a carcass.

Again, his magic skimmed the mental barriers protecting my consciousness, and I threw effort into fortifying them.

"You're still hoping to fight." He released my hand, and I clenched it against my chest. His laughter filled the room like his magic, rattling the wooden blinds and disrupting the dust on the sofa.

I stumbled back. "I've trained! I'm not a mere courtier."

His laughter floated off. "No." He dropped his chin and shadows masked his eyes. "A proper courtier would know when to shut their mouth. And you're not a soldier. What are you, Kacela?"

I gritted my teeth. "I've trained to fight like any other in the army. There is no reason I cannot fight."

If his magic hadn't claimed my fear, I may have shivered at the trace of his fingers up the curve of my shoulder, onto my neck. He pinched my chin between finger and thumb, guiding my gaze back to his.

Trapped.

Like an animal in a cage she'd walked herself into. Not even my heart understood my command. He'd seeped into my mind through cracks unbeknownst to me and seized my breath without breaking a sweat. I couldn't escape the tang of his magic clouding my senses, drowning the rebellious thoughts, and dulling the urge to fight.

"If you were a commoner, but you are not. You are a lady and the Royal Commander's ward. You cannot continue this delusion of being a soldier any longer, Kacela. It's as childish as the flirting. I speak with the king this afternoon. It may not be premature of you to discard your weapons and begin packing your things."

His kiss on my cheek released the clench of his magic. His chuckle left me numb, staring at the walls with the lingering tartness of spoiled cherries stinging my tongue.

When I met Nalin's gaze at dinner that night, the bite of his magic burrowed from where it hid in my memory and surged up my throat like steam from a rolling boil. A reminder. A cruel one that brewed my hatred for him and his scheming father, Griffin's tactics to secure estate's loyalties, and Amaury's resistance to me fighting.

It spoiled the sweet, jelly-filled pastries I'd filled my plate with, so they remained untouched.

Jacinth leaned onto her armrest toward me. "Would you be inclined to continue our conversation from earlier?"

"My apologies, but I am not feeling up to such discussions."

She leaned away, propping her cheek on her fist. "Yes, I see you have hardly touched your deserts. It couldn't have anything to do with why you left the library earlier? Certain rumors?"

I clenched my hand around the skirts of my dress to keep myself from showing any surprise. A rumor needed a source, and Jacinth had more than enough reasons to tarnish my reputation further.

She raised a slim brow. "You should be more preoccupied with your health, Kacela." From my plate, she picked a pastry and nibbled enough to release the cherry jelly within. "With so little magic, it'd only take a harsh storm or foul illness to bring about your deathbed."

Across the table, Nalin turned his attention to us, chin propped on his hand. I held his gaze and willed the terror in my gut to stay rumbling there. If I begged, he may have come to my rescue, deflecting the conversation or pulling Jacinth's rancid attention from me.

However, that would admit I needed him for anything.

Returning to Jacinth, I gave her hand a squeeze. "I appreciate your concern. Perhaps I shall retire early. A few extra hours of sleep may be all I need."

Her other hand landed atop mine. A musty smell, like rotting potatoes, drowned out the scent of berry-flavored wine and warm pastries. From her palm, magic flaked onto my skin and darted beneath my sleeve. Like a centipede with needles for legs, it trekked up my arm to my shoulder. "Sleep well, Kacela."

Once in the safety of my room, I peeled off my dress, but no rusty brown magic marred my skin. Again and again, I checked in the mirror, feeling it beneath my skin like a thousand needle pricks.

A knock on the door brought me from scratching at my arms and shoulders. I wrapped myself in a robe and padded across the overlapping rugs to crack the door open.

Amaury dropped his hand to his side.

I motioned for the couches by the fire.

He stayed in the doorway. "I wanted to say goodbye. I leave with Griffin in the morning for Beaddeon."

A burning began in the hand Jacinth had touched and spread up my veins like fire across an explosive's fuse. A drop of sweat rolled down my spine. "How long will you be gone?"

"A week at most."

I nodded. "Safe travels."

The burning leeched into my neck, and I fought the twitch threatening my composure.

He opened his mouth as if to say more, then pulled the

leather binding from his hair, which fell before his eyes like a curtain. "Behave. Understand?"

"Understood," I said, and he closed the door.

Without a moment to guess at why he'd really come by, I sprinted to the bathroom, tearing off the robe to stare at the unmarred skin hiding a burn which felt like fire ants burrowed beneath it.

The magic needed to skip water into the tub sapped the rest of my energy. I hauled myself into its frozen grasp, feet flipping over the rim. Water splashed over the edge, then settled around my quivering body.

Jacinth's warning that I'd crossed a line faded into the water, and from my fingertips, rusty magic seeped. It leeched across the surface until the entire tub was the color of muddied blood and smelt of rotting potatoes.

I couldn't skip it away, not after I'd used so much energy to fill the tub, so it remained, as did I, staining the porcelain.

I stared at the ceiling. A steady drip of water on tile echoed.

A year prior, I'd dodged a sure-fire marriage to Nalin at the expense of both our reputations. At the time, certainty had been a double-edged sword, slicing me with either decision. It'd been hope of fighting and, annoyingly, of finding my mate that'd led to Nalin's hatred. And my resentment, but not regret.

Never regret.

I still had a few months to prove myself more than a ward to be married off. To prove myself a soldier and an asset, even if my magic rivaled only the servants of the castle.

Even if I was truly just an unblessed Forterian.

CHAPTER 5

A WEEK AFTER GRIFFIN left for Beaddeon and the estates slinked home, I woke to a castle beset by chaos. I wandered halls where streams of black and red curtains and banners fluttered behind sprinting servants. Magic swept bits of dirt from every room. All ten chandeliers within the entry hall sprang to life, and three servants hauled a grand chair rivaling Griffin's from the depths of the castle toward the ballroom, a chair none had seen since his mother's passing.

I stared at the chair in the ballroom after the servants left, one almost knocking me over. The black bib hanging over its top rail was embroidered with a golden kraken wrapped around a sinking ship. I stared at it longer, as if memorizing the details would jog a memory as to which estate or powerful family had a kraken as its emblem. None came to mind.

A raven at the top of the banister cawed, then another further down, and those scattered throughout the ballroom. All of them, made of the same obsidian and bundled in Griffin's magic, joined in the announcement.

The king had returned.

I dashed to the grand ballroom doors as they opened, revealing their black spiked exterior. A draft littered with the first fallen leaves of autumn guided in a low, melodic voice praising the grand architecture. "And the northern gardens?"

"Trapped in eternal summer, and a maze so large I've had to skip lost servants from within it."

First, I saw the hair, like ribbons of low-burning fire, swinging as her attention did. She appraised the tapestry of the Aqualtin, and then the portrait beside it. Griffin's grandfather, who'd first landed on the eastern shores and brought peace to a continent submerged in war, wore the obsidian crown now askew on Griffin's head. They were near twins, the Quillon traits perfectly passed from father to son, twice.

I stepped from the ballroom, knowing Griffin had already spotted me.

"Please," he guided her from beneath the tapestry. Black tendrils swept from his back, his magic's tangible form. The female reaching for his arm stared at them with a childlike curiosity.

Her billowing satin, olive green dress danced as if the wind swept through it. It settled upon her soft and plump curves. Flushed skin folded over itself around her exposed waist, giving a sensual arch to the otherwise shapeless drapes clasped at her shoulders and waist with golden hoops.

Her lips were the color of autumn leaves, and when she smiled at me, I felt the same warmth radiating from the still opened doors.

"You must be Kacela." She shot forward to hug me, and I scrambled to not trap my wrists in her dress's fabric. "Griffin has told me everything about you."

Where she held me, more warmth prickled from her fingertips.

"It's an honor to meet you," I forced out against the cage of her embrace. I eyed Griffin over her shoulder, but he only had eyes for her.

"Oh, no formalities, Kacela, please. I've come from a court of strict manners. I prefer less," she said, head bouncing with her words.

"My mate," Griffin said proudly, "is from Beaddeon. She hails from the northern Isles of Mortring."

I blinked away my surprise. Mate? Griffin's mate! The future queen. The female he'd searched the continent for since assuming his title. One we all speculated had yet to be born or had long since died.

The continent seemed to shift beneath my feet. What the announcement of a royal wedding meant for me would've landed me on my rear if the king's mate didn't have an iron grip on my shoulders.

"Deianeira, but please, call me Neira."

Griffin led her away, into the depths of the castle, and any hoping to meet the queen-to-be scurried after them until only Amaury and I remained.

"How are you?" He cupped my cheeks. His warm hands felt like a blanket despite the scratch of calluses on his palms and the pads of his fingers. His greasy chestnut locks hung over his flattened cheeks. "I know you didn't ask for this life, nor were you born into it."

I placed my hand over one of his. "I'm fine."

"I wish there was another way, Kacy. All we've done is necessary to give you the best life possible."

He marched away, leaving me alone to feel cold abandonment which was soon overcome by a furious burn. But like a candle with a short wick soaked in wax, the fury fizzled and died in the next breath, leaving me with nothing but the ice of his words.

In the following week, when Griffin and Amaury disappeared into the royal office and locked the door, Neira insisted I tour her around the castle, show her how inept I was with the harp and lute, and listen to her prattle on about the chill of the castle and how a few rugs and drapes would turn the fortress into a home.

Then, there were the estate visits for all to meet their future queen and for Amaury to assess army strengths for the upcoming war he'd all but shut up about.

It left little to no time to train, and my calluses began to soften.

A week after her arrival, Neira woke me by ripping open my curtains, basking my bed in soft morning rays.

She braided back my hair and picked a lilac dress from my closet, all while humming an old tune my memories sang with. I surveyed her reflection in the mirror, wondering where the servants ran off to and how her fingers so delicately wove my hair like strands of silk.

Her copper hair, braided into a crown atop her head, left the black, sheer material of her sleeves to accent the glow of her pale shoulders. She'd painted her lips the same green as her dress, giving her the appearance of a withering rose.

Her arm slinked through mine as we walked the eastern gardens, which smelled of lilac and peonies sprouting from the hedges.

"This war, what are your thoughts?" she asked, staring at a status of an Altun in full armor with a longsword readied for onslaught. If she noticed my lurching surprise, she said nothing of it. We'd spoken of their wedding, estate visits, her home in Beaddeon, and my upbringing. Never this.

"The demon rift?"

"Yes." She dawdled her fingers through the tulle ruffles protruding from my sleeves. I clenched my fist to keep myself from brushing away the itch.

"I don't entertain the term war. Wars last years. They consume generations. If this is not a single battle, we'll be overrun before winter freezes the northern lakes."

Neira appraised me as if I were another garden decoration. "Do you not have faith in your king's magic?"

"Griffin is the nearest being to an unbound god on the continent, but he is not limitless. Even if he can fight dozens, how many will escape? If it is merely a matter of closing the rifts as he claims, why has he not done so already?"

Neira patted my hand. "There are always reasons beyond our understanding for the actions of others. Just as we own our intents and defend our beliefs."

"I would defend this kingdom with my life, if Amaury and Griffin would allow me to fight in the lines."

Her laugh fluttered from her, but nails pricked at my forearm. "Wars are not all won on the front lines, dear. There are less brutish methods of victory, more sophisticated blades to wield than those made of steel."

"Let others be courtly. I've trained to fight."

"If politicking bores you, then you are not the might I believe you to be." She dragged me further into the gardens. "If you wish to prove your ability to hold a line, very well. I will speak to Griffin."

I grasped her arm. "You will?"

"You are an adult. I see no reason to treat you like a child when you are intent on making mistakes. If it's how you will learn, very well. It is how my father raised me, and how I have allowed others to waste their potential."

Even the bite of her words could not leech the bundling excitement from my gut.

We reached the heaviest congregation of statues. Some were of soldiers, others of courtiers in elegant dress. All of them towered above the blooming flowers obscuring the width of their bases.

"War is not constant, and soldiers are not always needed. Shouting your wishes at another will only diminish your influence, which of current you hold very little. You could climb the ranks quickly, Kacela, if you willed it. I want to help you do so."

Neira steered us to a female courtier, hands gracefully clenched before her billowing skirts, nose upturned to the north.

"I do not enjoy politicking. I do not have enough magic to be a powerful lady of an estate," I said through gritted teeth. The wind wrapped my dress around my legs, tangling at the knees.

"On the lines, I could fight. I could be of use."

The castle loomed, statues towering like the spikes of a walls intent on keeping me within its grasp.

"I prefer a steel blade."

Neira's voice, as still as the statues, snaked down my spine. "Then who am I to keep you from war?"

I baited my opponent with a sloppy pull of my sword. There was no need to feign exhaustion to make the final blow any more appetizing. I saw the victory in his eyes in the moments he pulled his attention away from the fight to begin crafting his lecture.

Amaury spun the axe around his head as if it were a toothpick and hooked it around my blade. As he did, I twirled. The change in momentum snapped the weapon from his grip.

We stared at one another, chests heaving and shoulders sagging. Between us, the axe rattled on the ground.

"Tricky." Amaury grinned. "Who taught you that?"

"Not you." I raised my blade to his throat.

"Obviously not. I would never show my opponent any vulnerability."

Weapons discarded, we headed for water.

In between gulps, I said, "Griffin says to win at whatever cost."

Amaury nodded, but I could see the thought weighed heavier on him than it should've. He'd trained me in honorable fighting against a single opponent. Gimmicks and tricks were for last moments of a fight when life hung in the balance.

"I am not going to the Tait Estate with you." Amaury muttered. "The Forterians have requested my presence."

"Why?"

He capped his water skin with a snap. "Griffin has ordered them to prepare for war. They convene to discuss tactics."

"Convene?" I prodded.

His shoulders fell further, crinkling the forest green, long-sleeve shirt he wore. "Relations between clans are not peaceful. If they are called upon to fight as one, new agreements must be made."

"All the chiefs are meeting?" I asked.

"You are not coming."

I crossed my arms. "Give me a better reason than no."

"Give me a reason you should go." Already, his attention drifted between the soldiers drilling in wall defense tactics on the far side of the rooftop training fields and commanders speaking in hushed voices with heads pressed together.

I grabbed his arm before he could take a second step from me. "I could help prove females should be trained. If they saw my ability to fight, even if they believe me to be an Altun, they may change their reception of your demands for equality."

He lowered his gaze so the shadows made his irises look more ebony than hazel. It was not the first time I'd suggested it, and it would not be the first time Amaury feigned consideration to stop my prattling.

Amaury shook off my grip. "I have spent decades encouraging Forterians to train their females. They have fought with our lines and seen the equal mix of males and females in our armies. It will take more than an Altun example of a female soldier for them to change."

"There must be some way I can help."

He shook his head.

"Are you afraid they'll recognize me?" I continued. "If any knew my mother, do I look like her enough to be recognized?"

Amaury turned to face me, his scowl morphing into an appraising glare. "It is not a risk I am willing to take, not with your life."

"I am your ward. It would not be unusual for me to accompany you to Forterian clans as I do to Altun estates."

He ran both scarred hands through his stringy hair. "Your very presence would be seen as overstepping. You were young when you last visited. You may not remember how many would have gladly killed you for intruding at the Blessing Ceremony. Do you believe your presence will be any more welcome at a war council?"

I cooled the retort on my tongue with a sigh. "No."

"The Forterians are necessary to defend Kadea. We cannot threaten their wavering alliance for your curiosity."

"Would they rebel? They're sworn by treaty to live under Altun rule."

Amaury stepped closer, feigning reaching for my water skin. His whisper was raspy and eyes darting. "They have threatened war for years. The new generation sees Altun rule as tyranny. I do not know, if war claimed the kingdom, who would survive."

The water skin shook as I raised it to my lips to cover my words, "I am Forterian."

"By blood."

"By training traditions." My moment of victory at his rolled eyes was short-lived. I could have convinced him the continent's survival depended on me attending one war council, and he'd have left me in my room to watch the world burn.

He tapped my nose, leaving behind a wrinkle of grime. "I'll only be gone while you are. You'll have your hands full with Lady Tait and Neira."

"The queen-to-be would let me fight."

His features sharpened, and his falling hand stopped. He hinged to put our gazes on the same plane. Even then, he stared down his crooked nose at me. "You are not fighting in a single battle of any war, and if I hear more about it, I'll leave you here."

I stuttered back a step from the anger tensing his shoulders. "You promised to take me."

"I promised to take you as far as the war camp to learn about planning an attack, not to partake in one. Understood?"

"Neira—"

"I will not send you to be another corpse on the line!"

"I'm twenty-five. Your ability to command my life is slipping."

"Blooding your hands is unnecessary to gain influence,

Kacela. This kingdom, and the world, needs strategists as well as soldiers. Even the Forterians value their thinkers as well as their brutes."

"I want to fight."

"You are not fighting. Understand?"

In my gut, something cracked like the first chink in armor or a stone falling loose from a dam. From it, energy leaked. First, only a few shocks of power that chattered my teeth, then it sloshed against my every breath.

"Understand?" Amaury demanded. I met his glare. The magic surged. Only a speck, enough to put a charred taste in my mouth and raise the hairs on the back of my neck. I let it, eager and curious for its embrace. After a few breaths, once Amaury softened his brows, it settled back into a tide threatening to rise at the smallest ripple.

"Understood."

CHAPTER 6

THE TAIT ESTATE HELD sweetened memories and soured smiles. Overlooking the northern bluffs, my usual room was as cold as the white-capped waves wearing away the jagged outcrops at the base of the cliff. It bore only a simple bed with black covers and pillows, a vanity of black jade, a darkly stained dresser, and a white-tiled bathroom.

A servant set my bag on the bed, giving me only a passing glance when metal clanked within it. I said nothing, preferring to stare out at the ocean and the brewing storm. To the east, thunderous clouds rolled onto the bluffs, drowning them in its haze. Lightning struck, and part of me surged with the same excitement.

The servant straightened, as if a hand gripped the back of her tunic, and left the room. The door shut. Then opened.

I turned on Nalin, wishing I'd had another minute to uncover the knives and short sword from within the depths of my bag. He eased the door closed.

"Nalin," I said, my back stiff and unmoving.

"Welcome." He prowled across the room like the leopard on his family's crest, proudly embroidered in black on his white tunic. At his side, the belt he'd won in the tournament hung uselessly. An equally ornate dagger was strapped to the other side. He'd styled back his hair except for one strand arching over his brow. "I trust your travels were well."

I walked to my bag, but before I could untie it, a string of silver magic batted my hands away. My clothing floated across the room and into the dresser. His efforts left a tart ting on my tongue.

"Thank you." My words were as clipped as his glance toward the weapons hidden in the folds of my undergarments.

"Always looking for a battle," he muttered, shaking out his brushed back hair. More strands fell. He still looked as polished as the frigid room. "I hope soon you'll think of me as your ally instead of an enemy."

"Enlighten me, Lordling, as to what will cause the shift?"

The glint in his eyes made me feel as if I'd set off a trap.

I pulled the thigh sheath from the bag and strapped it beneath my dress, then slid four thin knives into it.

Nalin gave a flat look toward the sword.

I motioned to the powder blue silk gown that made my torso look like a vase, as if to ask him where I should strap it. He took it from the bag, walked to the bed, and stuffed it under the mattress.

"I'll instruct the maids to leave your bed alone for your stay." He offered his arm without another glance at the weapons. "We have other guests for this visit."

I touched the sheath through my dress to ensure he hadn't magically removed my blades, then slid my hand high on his bicep to keep his short sleeve as a barrier between our skin.

"When Lord Garnell and Lady Messalia heard the king found his mate, they insisted on being amongst the first to meet the future queen."

The tide bashed against the maw of rocks in its wake, spraying the wall of windows we walked by at a crawling pace. I stared out at the rainbows dancing in the mist, relying on Nalin to keep me walking forward. I'd spent hours seated beside these windows when I visited as a child, watching the mountain goats scale the vertical cliffs and winged Forterians catch the ocean breeze in their ruffling feathers.

I slowed where the windows gave way to black marble, and Nalin paused for me to soak up the last bits of sunlight erupting in white caps before the storm overtook the brilliance. I wished it was upon us, battering the fortress with all its might and lighting the rooms with its brilliant strikes.

"Jacinth is here," he said beneath his breath.

I smiled up at him. "Splendid."

He reached for my cheek, but I pulled away. He curled a strand of my hair between his fingers. "Kacela, if she tries to hurt you —"

My smile dropped in the wake of a shuttered breath. The memory of her magic stung. The residue on my arm still half a shade darker than my skin. "Jacinth and I are friends, Nalin."

"Kacy." He dropped his hand to mine, and I yanked it back before I could fight the instinct.

Nalin stopped, shoulders slumped.

"Am I in danger within your estate?" I asked, angling my head. "What shadows chase me here?"

He cleared his throat. Trapped between Nalin and the wall of windows, I was reminded how small I was. He towered over me, as did the fortress, each threatening a different shackle.

"None, darling. Where would you be safer than with me?"

The study was as stoic as the leopards carved from white jade outside it. Their black eyes seemed to watch us as we approached, and I felt the weight of magic in their gaze.

Lady Messalia sat by a harp, plucking its strings in a seemingly random array while staring at the window at the fields leading to the snow-laden Sacrament Mountain, the sacred mountain of the Forterians. I'd spent more time here than anywhere else in the fortress growing up, reading beside the wall of windows and wondering why they'd built them to frame the mountain, as if honoring it.

Lady Garnell sat with Jacinth, speaking in hushed tones

behind her red-gloved hand. Nalin's mother, so pale she looked as if they'd pulled her from the surf, sat farthest from the windows. At our entrance, she eased to her feet and took the length of the library in stammered steps.

She greeted her son with a kiss to his cheek, but I seemed to be to her no more than a speck of dirt on his sleeve.

Then Nalin left, and Jacinth excused herself from her mother.

"Jacinth," I greeted with a bowed head. "A pleasure."

She stared down her nose at me. "I hope you have given serious thought to your health, Kacela. You are looking as ill as you were at your party." She smiled, revealing small, perfectly white teeth. They, along with the narrowness of her eyes, gave her the appearance of a bat.

I gripped my stained arm. "Kadea has been busy. There is much to be done for the queen-to-be."

She followed me into the stacks of book, nearly stepping on my gown with every stride. The ladies paid us no heed, as if we were truly friends losing ourselves in the massive library to giggle about boys and parties.

"Yes, of course. Kadea may host two marriages this year."

I turned to her tilted head with a snarl stretching her lips to thin lines. Magic, like dust, fell from her clenching fists. The realization of Nalin's words was like stepping on ice. I was stuck in her glare, unable to deny it or throw it in her face.

She stepped closer. "You are not strong enough to be lady of this estate."

I gritted my teeth. The dam in my gut, steadily leaking magic through a minute crack, ached with a surge of fury. It transversed the leak, and I was in a sea of it, drowning in the unknown power boiling in my gut. Each spark of it emitted a rich, sweet scent.

"I don't want to be lady of this estate." Each word was like a clap of thunder.

Jacinth's nostrils flared. She grabbed my forearm and sunk her nails into the skin above my wrist. Her magic, before pin pricks, speared through my arm and up the veins to my neck.

"You don't deserve him."

I clenched my fists, but my magic was surging out of my control no matter how hard I pushed it back down. It latched onto my anger and soared with it, twisting around it to escape the dam. It hummed in the nerves of my fingertips.

I shoved at her hand and lunged toward the back of the library, but her grip was a shackle.

"Let go," I pleaded.

Jacinth's glared dropped to my hands. She dropped my wrist and stumbled back. "Stop." Fear cracked at her words.

Static filled the air, sparked on my tongue and between my fingers. Strands of Jacinth's hair rose around her.

I took two steps toward the corner before the magic robbed me of movement and burst from the puddle in my gut like a geyser.

Blinding gold encased the bookshelves and Jacinth, with me at its apex. I shrieked against the cage within. As if it'd also break the one they tried to shove me in. Its shattered remains crumbled at my feet along with the unsalvageable remnants of my reputation.

Someone screeched, and the stomp of shoes moved both toward and away from the ball of golden light expanding from my outstretched hands. I felt the pulses of others in the room through the tips of my magic. Books fell around me, turned to ash in the halo of gold wrapped around me. The smell of vanilla bloomed, clouding my senses.

Two hands grasped my forearms. Peace flooded through my skin where nails pricked like thorns. Wrenched by black vines and buried in an earthy scent, my magic slipped from my grasp in waves.

A face of white jade came into view. Lady Tait kneeled before me, hands capturing mine and face close enough I could count the speckles of ash freckling it. Behind her, Lady Garnell held her daughter's head to her chest and whispered into her hair.

The doors to the library burst open. What sounded like an

army marched toward us, and Lady Tait only had a moment to hiss in my ear before her husband pulled her from the ground.

"Who are you?"

The question trailed me through the fortress for the remainder of our visit. Griffin excused it as normal, that most magic wielders either gained their magic gradually or all at once in a grand display. But his demeanor changed, as if he'd uncovered a secret.

Nalin trailed me as the nagging repercussions of my outburst did. I told myself it was to ensure I didn't have another, that he'd been assigned to do so, as he'd been assigned to entertain me when I was growing up to keep me from the darkest shadows of the fortress or from wandering off the cliffs.

There were more meetings, ones I was barred from, and tension-laced dinners seated across from Jacinth after my magic had singed off half her hair. Griffin had grown it back with a flick of magic.

I was most unnerved by Lady Tait's icy stare following my every move, as if she were desperate to know what I would do next. If I would show more magical strength, or if it was a onetime explosion.

I wondered the same, feeling the phantom limb of my magic but unable to coax it from its hiding place.

The morning after returning to the castle, I sat in Griffin's office, watching him scribble across the piles of papers on his desk. He stacked them and skipped them away with a flurry of his fingers. Ash from his magic fell onto his desk, and he swiped it away as easily.

I thought of telling him about what Lady Tait had said. That her question plagued me. That I maybe didn't know who I was, not any more than Amaury had when he'd plucked me from the fields outside Virian, the Forterian clan of my birth. Or that Jacinth's words and magic had spurred the outburst. That it'd been a moment of fury, and I hadn't felt chaos brewing in my gut since.

Griffin cleared his throat and laced his fingers together on the desk. He'd forgone his usual black tunic for a red, airy blouse with ruffles down the sleeves. His raven hair fell across his forehead and over his ears like a mophead. "I've neglected training your magic because I did not see this potential. Your Altun father passed along a considerable amount. I'd like to train you in espionage."

I perked up.

He raised a knobby finger. "On one condition."

"Yes, of course." I nearly toppled from the chair. "What is it?"

"You will marry Nalin Tait."

Griffin's words sucked the excitement from my rapid pulse, as if he'd thrown a bucket of ice water across me. I buried my hands in my skirt to stop their shaking.

"Why?" My voice was like a trickle.

"You told Neira you were not strong enough to be the lady of an estate," he said. "You've showed you are. I know you wish to prove you are not useless, Kacela, and you now have the chance to be one of the most powerful ladies of my kingdom."

His words, laced with such promises, made me feel as if I were a child stealing sweets, that the promises would flutter away with the next breeze and I'd be left as the shut-in wife of a lord. My muscles and fighting skills withering away with my freedom.

"The Taits have agreed on the condition I train your magic over the next year." Griffin stood and rounded the desk to lean on the front. "Give up the dream of fighting, Kacy. Take this one instead."

My next breath shook across my lips. I ducked my head, allowing the curtain of my hair to block the king's gaze. His eyes had sparkled with hope, as I wished mine would. If he'd been foolish enough to expect me to jump at his bargain, he hid his disappointment behind a soft smile.

"Please, Kacela."

At my command, the minute swirls of my magic testing their boundaries burrowed away.

It made me more than a bride. More than a courtier passed between dance partners.

My magic made me a weapon.

It made me someone else's blade.

CHAPTER 7

WINTER CRAWLED TOWARD US, and news of war captured every street corner until Kadea buzzed. Daily, Griffin smoothed away my soldier exterior to mold the courtier lurking beneath. I strengthened my mental barriers and broke through others. I morphed with the shadows of the castle and became as unnoticed as a breeze. Still, the warmth of my magic's golden light remained just out of grasp.

I wore myself out with training, yearning to feel something more than exhaustion as I lay in bed, staring at the flimsy, forest green curtains hanging around my bedposts. They swayed as I did, letting the wind take me further from the battlefield.

Then the world crumbled around me.

Amaury woke me in the moon's light. "Get dressed. Your leathers and weapons."

I stood in the entrance hall alone with a bag packed and foot tapping.

Guards sprinted around me, muttering of war. A crack within the Valley of Ulyerse had opened some time after dinner and demons poured from it to bash against its encompassing peaks. The steep ridges delayed the nightmares, as did the Forterians and Altuns who called the valley in the south home.

Armies, marching for the past few days, abandoned sleep to reach the valley in time. Griffin dropped Neira and I within the camp before skipping away to meet Lord Tait's army at the front lines to close the crack.

The west-facing camp, high enough on the slopes to overlook the surging demons ripping through lines of soldiers, spanned half the mountain ridge. Tents erected in circles created a bull-seye around a blood red pavilion. Forterian shelters blended so well into the bland rubble I couldn't tell them from the outcrops.

I stared at the fabric of Griffin's tent, woven with magic. It buzzed, and I knew one of Griffin's most trusted and powerful magic-wielders was either within or nearby, fueling the shield.

If the demons reached the peaks, the shield would hold long enough for the courtiers, those who had come to see the king save the continent, within to skip to safety.

Altun soldiers and Forterian warriors scurried around us with shields and weapons clattering in their hands. Some barked order and some stared south at what might become their deaths.

I gawked alongside them.

Suspended at the base of the mountain, the crack shimmered between pulses of black. Groveling shapes plummeted into our world from it and broke into a wretched sprint through the soiled valley.

Demons.

Shadowy creatures of another world, intent on devouring ours. What little information we had on them was gathered by those brave enough to extend their minds into the forming cracks. Those whose minds came back unharmed reported icy bites, poison tipped claws, unsatisfiable appetites. Some never came back, their bodies reduced to empty shells.

"Don't wander," Griffin commanded Neira and I before skipping away.

"*Don't wander,*" she said in a voice eerily similar to the king's. "Where would we wander to? Battle?"

The idea had crossed my mind with every breath since Amaury woke me. If I were to don a helmet, kept my visor down, and carry a shield, I'd blend into the crowd of soldiers corralled to the front lines.

One chance to prove myself before the approaching marriage and prove my use in battle.

Neira's knowing sneer snagged me.

From her sleeve, she produced a roll of paper. "I snuck it from Griffin's office," she slid it into my dumbstruck grip. "His seal and all. Give it to any commander."

I shoved it into my sleeve. "Thank you."

"Find your blade," she said and waltzed into the blood red tent to join the other courtiers.

I slipped between two soldiers of similar height, spear in one hand and shield on the other, into a line marching out to support the holding back the tide of demons. Heavy plates covering my body tugged at my shoulders and bruised my hips, clanging as I matched my boots to my line commander's count.

I craned over the edge of my shield to peer through my helmet's visor at the waves of bronze, black, white, and blond wings carrying black armored Forterians into their favorite arena. They were a swelling wave of metallic, each a scale of armor of the finest blacksmithery.

Amaury once filled my nighttime stories with heroic tales of winged, often himself, flying from the front lines unscathed and victorious. The strongest, fasted, deadliest, and bravest survivors of the Sacrament. Each a weapon divinely crafted for this arena.

Guilt accompanied the first thud of bodies against shields, still far enough off to keep the bit of food in my stomach from churning. I'd picked my platoon, my line commander, and my role within this war.

Those before me were assigned to sacrifice their lives.

A cloud of writhing black limbs obscured the sun. Their unworldly shrieks and the command of seasoned war veterans rained down as I battled to keep my shield at proper height.

"Hold," went through the lines. The flurry of arrows did nothing to pin back the chill of the beast slipping through the wall of shields. It slithered beneath my armor, itching in my sweat-soaked shirt.

My magic hummed within me. It coiled my muscles.

Our march progressed as the front lines fell, one by one, until the shadowy bodies of demons came into view over the tops of only a few rows. Their claws sliced through the air like an executioner's blade. Their shrieks grounded me to the weight of my sword on my belt, the breath of my line mates, and the glory of walking from the field soaked in bloody victory.

An entire platoon of winged Forterians caught the moon's light in their feathers. Demons, with their own wings unfurling from sickly, seemingly broken figures, rose to meet them. Their colliding bodies sounding like the squish of mud.

Another line fell. Black forms of jutting limbs slithered over one another. White teeth gleamed within the gnashing maw, blood-soaked talons slashed craters in the valley. They rolled toward us like a black storm cloud.

Their shifting forms paled in comparison to the icy, haunting bite radiating in my bones. The soldier on my left tremored against my shoulder.

My shield slipped.

I let it fall a bit further and searched my line mates' expressions to gauge if they, too, would forsake the battle.

Then regret, as suffocating as the demon's stinging presence, burst through the hastily constructed barrier of courage anchoring me within my line. I raised my shield to protect my line mates.

Another command spurred us into action. Our shields leveled to close the gaps in the front line, battering back the demons from the crack Griffin was fashionably late in closing.

"Don't falter," the soldier on my left commanded. Fevered

blood splattered my visor. The demon sliced through another's armor, then tossed the two halves back into the growing wave of surging shadows.

The soldier before me shifted to close the gap. A space in the line before me beckoned.

With my heart jammed in my throat, I stepped forward.

I held my shield. In the moonlight, it seemed so flimsy. Against talons and fangs, it was a leaf. As flimsy as the shield crushed by a crashing demon four soldiers to my left. Beneath it, a soldier shrieked one last time. Their comrades fell upon the feasting beast, but then another died, and more marched to plug the gap.

A demon soared past four lines and crushed into my line mate's shield. I threw my weight to her side. The nauseating smell of rotten eggs and spoiled meat cannoned into us.

Tearing at the edges of our shields, the demon threw its entirety into the squawk of anguish rattling our heads. A splitting ache began in my jaw. It speared through to my forehead.

"Don't...let...it...through," my partner grunted.

"On my count," our command yelled. "One, two, three, heave!"

The line, as one, shoved.

"Attack."

My spear shot from the gap created by my line mate. I struck the demon's eye and lurched back before black blood squirted through the wall of metal.

We shoved, retreated, held, and speared. We stepped in to fill the spots of fallen soldiers. The cycle continued until the morning rays gleamed in the slick blood coating the field and the crimson coating our armor.

I saw more than my share of demons breach the lines and toss soldiers into the pits of swelling shadows, then return, famished for more. Their blood joined the puddles at my feet. Their screams remained in my ears long past when my commander's orders died with him. Their deaths were as heavy as the plated armor digging into my hips and shoulders.

Salt rolled off my brow and stung my eyes. I raised my visor with my forearm to see the carnage and met the empty pits of a demon's gaze.

Its head lolled one way, then another. It clinked its jagged teeth together.

My throat clogged with the power throbbing from the rift between realms.

A victorious cry rang through the winged Forterians and broke my captured stare.

I didn't recognize anyone in my line, and what the Forterians celebrated in the high noon sun, we remained ignorant to.

Every glorious story of battle and war shared over desserts and a glass of wine fell beneath my bloodied boots.

The demon tipped its head back and released a baritone shriek. It reared, crashing upon me. Teeth gleaming like the moon snapped at my shield, nearly tearing it from my grasp as talons raked against my front leg. The leather strap snapped and the plate skidded away.

Fire radiated from my shin to my knee.

I crutched into my line mate. She shoved me off, and I nearly sprawled into the mud, a perfect snack for a lucky nightmare. Scrambling to stand, I watched the demon turn on her. Shadows licked across its maw.

She screamed.

It struck.

I turned from her death, unable to do any more than wait for her replacement.

This bloody, messy, push for every step and watch others die hoping not to be next war took more than willpower to continue to fight.

It took pure fear of dying.

I knew I toed the line of death with every step my line pushed.

The burn in my shoulder increased with every attack, and my spear missed more than it hit. My line mates fell like leaves in an autumn grove. Soldiers surged to plug the gaps and relieve others to tend to their wounds. But not my line. We were too deep in the sea of battle to find.

There, for Kadea's victory, we became more causalities marked on a note and bodies buried in a mass grave.

There, I met my blade.

The demons diverted, and I took a breath to glare right at the setting sun. Bright as blood.

Through its mocking, something with wings tumbled and spun until it crashed into the ground between me and the line behind me.

I pivoted to face what could be my death.

He held no weapons, though his leather-coated hands and platted knees were caked in black blood. One white wing prepared to launch into the sky, but the other was crooked and tucked against his back. Beneath a red speckled helm, widened green eyes snatched the breath from my burning lungs.

The ghost of a feeling of need prickled my memory. A failed search. Something marred and bloody.

Death barreled through my back and sent me tumbling into the Forterian. My helmet clanked off my head. My shield and spear fell from my grasp. My hair spewed from its braid and matted itself across my face.

His gaze locked on mine.

Chaos and desperate screams overtook my line but I couldn't tear my gaze from him.

The Forterian's left arm jutted at an odd angle and a large tear through his right leg grounded him as well as the broken wing. He brushed the hair from my lips with shaking fingers.

He couldn't run, couldn't fly, and couldn't fight.

Spurred by something deeper than the fear of dying, I stood to protect him. I dislodged his lurching grasp on my arm and pivoted to come face to face with a demon shaking a disemboweled soldier in its maw.

I unsheathed my sword. The demon flipped the torso of the soldier for one of its kin to scoop up.

The demon was a rigid figure of jutting joints. Its knees bent back, even when on all fours. Its skull long like a hound's, with a neck craned like a vulture. Slimy black arms sliced at me. Drool puddled in snapping jaws and rolled over a slippery tongue that snaked out to snag my fear from the air.

I slashed at the extending black nail, striking through the middle. Its wail turned my head into a raging inferno. I shuddered.

It scraped a talon through my exposed shin.

Fire retook its claim within me.

The nightmare wildly swung at my head, forcing me to stumble across the soiled field and away from the Forterian.

On all fours, it darted for him.

Panic squeezed my every breath.

The shifting shadows of its talons speared for him, and I wouldn't make it. I couldn't intercept his death, not even with my own. My feet dragged and my knees knocked. I floundered to the blood-soaked ground a sword's length short of his death blow.

My chest caved in on itself, choking around the swelling scream. It blasted from me like a victorious horn.

The battle slowed. Scrapes of claws against shields faded along with the dying wails of my fallen comrades. Even the blood dripping through my armor seeped away, as if the world were sucked between me and the demon.

It craned its head toward me, and the shadows left, as if whisked by the breeze, to reveal its eyes.

Yellow eyes.

Something familiar spanned its features, the bone white of the leathery flesh beneath. Whiffs of rotten skin and the chill of a riverbed congested the battlefield. My limbs swam, suspended in the weight of its gaze.

As the green eyes called to a part of me, the yellow roused another. Swirling power hidden in deep recesses leaked forth, frothing like a rabid dog.

The Forterian's scream shattered the slowed seconds as if they were glass.

My sword found its mark in the demon's outstretched claw. I pared away another and brought my blade up in a long stroke to slice the demon's arm at the joint.

It bellowed and reared with its maw aimed at the faint moon. I plunged my sword through its lower jaw and into its mouth, to explode from its left eye. Black blood from the gash raced down my blade onto my hands.

They shook as the tangy thick goop coated me. My vision deluged with a thrashing sea of pain.

I met the demon's retreating steps with a staggered lunge. Too close. I'd gotten too close. I was within its wild swings and noxious breath.

Its talons streaked forward.

I heard the echo of another's scream.

Releasing the rising desperation from my gut, I propelled my sword up into the demon's neck. Gold arcs of lighting streaked from my hands, across my blade, and up through the monster's maw.

Instead of rows of jagged teeth sinking into my neck to take my head, only black dust fluttered across my cheeks.

The demon's skull rolled to my feet, jagged and hollow, draped in a black veil of mist. Then, it was gone.

I fumbled my blade. Adrenaline gave to exhaustion, and my legs went along with it. The plates of my back clanged against the Forterian's chest, and his arm wrapped around my waist.

The pounding of blood in my ears drowned out his commands. Black armored Forterians sprinted to his call.

My heart clenched. Breath refused to fill my aching lungs. My skin burned as if the demon breathed from within it. He adjusted me across his lap, clanking my armor against his as he turned me to face him.

The world around me, blackened and unmoving, crumbled until only his gaze remained. His eyes were green as the pine forests to the north, with a ring of sapphire around the irises.

They darkened as my eyes refused to hold them. His lips moved, but his demands fell on deaf ears.

I reached for his cheek and scraped a speck of blood from a scar peeking from beneath his beard.

Then, darkness reached for me, and I collapsed within it.

CHAPTER 8

I SPRANG UP. Not dead.

A calloused hand cupped my cheek.

I screamed, jumping away, but a hand on my hip proved stronger than my startled movements. Warmth flooded me as his hands caressed my skin, a calming tenderness I wanted to fold myself into.

Those green eyes looked down at me, emerald encased in blue as if the ocean itself were trapped within his gaze.

"Breathe," a honey sweet voice said. "You're safe. The battle is over." His hand on my cheek scraped at the sensitive skin. His warm breath smoothed the chill of the night air.

My breathing settled. He eased away without removing his hands, as if I'd vanish the moment he stopped touching me.

The thing that had snapped inside of me, further down than I thought anything could be, screamed against my being. It demanded the same thing it had years ago. It was a ghost of a memory I'd shoved aside at Amaury's demand, a search I'd been forced to abandon, a call I'd been too young to understand.

Mate.

My hand moved on its own to feel the stubble of a messily

shaved beard on his cheek. He leaned into my touch, lashes fluttering.

He took my hand from his cheek and pressed my palm to his lips.

Thin, cracked lips.

My mate.

With his broad frame, he was the Forterian all described, nearly identical to the statues in the eastern garden. Unlike the smooth muscle of lordlings, hidden under slim fitting jackets, his bulky frame demanded to be noticed with every breath. He bore a square jawline racked with white scars, heavily hooded eyes, a crooked nose, and flat cheeks. His brunette hair was matted down with wisps of curls hugging his ears.

He was like the first breath of spring, or the first morning rays peeking through a dense canopy. Warmth only rivaled by a fire.

"Did we win?" My voice broke.

A small smile lit his face, and the warmth trickling from him curled my toes. The air changed, an awakening of magic laced with pine, wrapped around us. Then, his wings replaced it. White, speckled black, grand feathered wings like those of a hawk appeared from the blessing on his back and curved to blot out the rest of the world.

It was not a cage nor a fortress, but a cocoon to narrow the universe to us, to where his thumb scratched down my cheek. His other hand rested on my leg, thumb in the bare crease of my thigh.

"Yes," he whispered, "we won."

The ache in my shoulder relented and the memory of battle was barricaded by the warmth radiating within my magic's embrace.

Giving to the itch, I dropped a finger to trace across his collarbone and onto his sternum, to feel the rise of his chest and the steady drum of his heart.

His forehead dropped to mine, and in the wake of my finger wandering to the scars overlaying his abs, he released a low groan. He squeezed my thigh. His fingers curled into the muscle beneath my hip. "Mountain be damned."

A crash outside the tent broke the stifling heat encasing us. He snarled, exposing slightly stained teeth. Then, he was out of bed and across to the tent flaps in a blink. The black tattoo of wings on his back morphed, retracting the feathered appendages within the ink.

I'd never seen the transition so close, and its beauty left me grasping for a breath.

The flaps closed behind him, allowing me only a glimpse of the midnight-veiled camp and dying embers in the nearest fire.

I took the stark cold of his absence to assess my surroundings. The interrupt was like the shattering of a mirror, turning the reflection of us, of that moment others spoke of in celebration, into scattered remains.

I'd found my mate.

The soul destined for mine.

While betrothed to another.

I pulled the blanket around my shivering shoulders, wishing I could clutch as tight to him as I did to it. Wishing to stay in the euphoria of his wings a bit longer despite the call of the breeze rolling from the northern bluffs.

The bed, covered in furs and pillows, meant he wasn't a low-ranking warrior. His helmet, with fanned wings over each ear, marked a general. His armor and the burned remains of mine were piled beside a small bucket of soiled water with red-tinged rags on the rim. Dual blades leaned against a rack nearby.

I eased off the cot. My knees buckled. I scrambled for the tub as one leg knocked into the other. I was wearing a long gray shirt, whose collar fell nearly off my shoulders, reeked of pine, and draped over a pair of loose shorts. No, not shorts. His underwear.

Accusations flew outside the tent.

I stumbled toward my mate's voice.

Then I heard it, the voice I dreaded the most. My heart

twinged at the thought of Amaury seeing me in such a state. The disappointment in his eyes the last time he'd caught me sneaking from another's room made the resulting scolding all the more harrowing.

"Where is she?"

"Who?" my mate demanded.

"You took her from the battlefield."

Amaury's face ranged from relieved to furious as he saw me emerge from the tent, lacking armor and with a blanket wrapped around my shoulders.

My mate instantly stepped between us, his expression impassible.

"Leave," he commanded Amaury with a voice that shook my knees. Amaury didn't take his stare from me. "This is not your clan. You have no authority here."

Amaury's eyes slid from me to him. "You've made an awful mistake."

A growl ripped through my mate's chest. I felt the same growl rising in mine. "Try to take—"

I lunged under my mate's outstretched arm to push some space between them. "I'm fine." He stared at my mate, who tugged on the back of my blanket. "There was—"

"I heard the report from your line mates. You could have died." Amaury's stale voice only spurred me further.

I reached out to push his chest, to get him to listen to me, when my mate snagged my arm and hauled me behind him. The warmth of his touch and the overwhelming smell of pine threatened to lull me from the chaos drawing a full crowd.

"Leave," my mate demanded again.

I searched the gathering crowd, but all were Forterians. None would step between them, not if my mate was as high ranking as I assumed him to be. Not if he was making demands and willing to step against Amaury, the Royal Commander.

"Easton," Amaury seethed, "move."

Easton. My mate, Easton.

I threw off his arm and pushed back between the two. "Stop

it!"

"Amaury," a silky smooth voice brushed through the crowd, "perhaps we take this discussion inside." Griffin slid through the Forterian warriors lined up in the small space between the shelters. He waved a hand toward the tent. He was commanding, not offering.

My mate's arm wrapped around my waist, steering me back into the space I'd unceremoniously barged from. Amaury stomped behind him, Griffin on his tail.

"This is interesting," Griffin purred. He'd forgone the armor of war, back to his sleek tunic and sharp obsidian crown.

"You are both trespassing." Easton's arm tightened. I nearly followed the guiding curl of his fingers to bend myself into his embrace. "This land belongs to the Virian War Clan, not you, King. If Chief Daviat finds out—"

"You've kidnapped my ward," Amaury snapped, baring his teeth.

"He didn't—"

Amaury's glare shut me up.

"I didn't kidnap her," Easton continued. The guiding hand yanked and our chests met. I couldn't pull from the urgency in his gaze, even if his hand wasn't cupping my cheek. "She was injured on the battlefield," he choked, and his throat bobbed around the words. "If I had not saved her, she'd likely have succumbed to her wounds."

I covered his hand with my own, my fingers falling in between his to skim my own cheek. "You fell."

A growl rumbled through Easton's chest. The warmth in his eyes faded with that of his smile. "You won't be fighting anymore. You're safe with me."

I broke his grasp on my waist, nostrils flaring as I rounded on him. He spied my clenched fists and smirked, as if convinced I wouldn't or couldn't put fury behind my strike. As if I hadn't saved him from being a demon's next meal. "I've trained—"

"You don't need to anymore," he said, as if stating a fact to a child. He reached for me, and the tent narrowed to the foot of space I'd put between us.

I seethed. "I never needed to. I *wanted* to."

My mate's posture tightened and his fists turn white. His gaze jumped between Griffin and Amaury. I felt both their breaths at my back, close enough to reach for me before Easton could.

Easton shrugged, but the veins on his forearms popped and his knees bent. "It's not your place to fight," he said.

I felt the tension coiling his muscles as if they were my own. "Then what is my place?" I forced out between clenched teeth.

He pursed his lips. "You're my mate. Your place is to keep the tent, cook, and eventually breed."

A crackling frenzy of power lurched through my gut and rode my pulse to my fingertips. "*Breed?* Like some dispensable wife?"

Amaury and Griffin snatched my arms. I felt the pinch of skipping. The ash-tinged air tightened around my chest before releasing.

The absence of Easton's presence ripped the ground from beneath me, and I all but collapsed at Griffin's feet on a different tent's floor. My next breath, void of Easton's pine scent, burned my lungs.

I stared at my hands, aware but uncaring of Griffin's presence next to me and Amaury stomping from the tent. Then, the flaps moved again, and another walked in.

"Go," Neira commanded.

Blood stained my hands up to my elbows, a tone darker than that of my skin, akin to the stain left from Jacinth's magic. I scratched it. Rusty flakes rained down between my knees. I scratched harder until red streaks cut apart the stains.

Another hand appeared before me, easing my nails away from my red-striped forearms. "Come," she whispered, then dragged me to my feet. Once she'd tucked my legs beneath the blankets of the bed, Neira left. She returned with a water flask.

I grasped for it, missing with my first reach and cradling

it with the next. The water slopped over my lips. It dribbled down my neck onto Easton's shirt's collar. I continued to chug, despite the subtle taste of valerian, an herb often used to aid sleep.

"Careful." She ran a hand across my tattered braid, then untied the leather thong and released my hair. Her fingers worked through the knots and dirt clumps, snagging once only.

I mumbled, "I was going to die."

She hummed in response.

"I'm not weak. I killed the demon."

Neira stopped. She twirled the ends of my hair around her finger, observed them for a moment, and then yanked. Our faces nearly smashed, but her other hand grasped my chin. Her nails squeezed like a beast's claws. "For what, Kacela? What did you prove?"

I snatched my braid and chin from her. One nail nicked my jaw, and I felt warmth swelling from it.

She yanked the flask from my hands. Her green eyes were no longer warm. They'd become a forest fire with a burning, all-consuming demand within them. "Tell me of the front lines, Kacela. Of how you toyed with death so you could prove your-self *better* than a courtier. Were the lives lost worth your pride?"

I hung my head, but my shoulders could not take any more weight. They caved around the answer sitting rotten on my tongue.

"You chose your usefulness, your blade," she muttered, tearing the remaining knots from my hair. "Who will die next because of your mistakes?"

The valerian begged, but I did not sleep. It's earthy residue coating my tongue was like sandpaper against my every breath.

Still in my mate's shirt, I held it above my nose to smother myself in his scent. Pine, like the northern forests. Every bit of me he'd touched, from my cheek to my thigh, itched. I fought the cascade of tears, as if they'd wash away the memory of his touch.

Lowering my mental shields, I reached with my mind for him across the mate bond. The thin thread of magic between us was as fickle as a spider's web. It would grow, if we let it.

He was in the furthest Forterian camp, awake and pacing within his tent.

I pushed deeper.

"You didn't have to say her purpose was to breed." The male sitting on the ground against the bed had his arm in a sling and a long cut over his left eye. His skin was pale olive and blond hair was matted to his skull like a helmet. Every muscle had been outlined in black blessing ink. A brute.

"She could've died!" My mate walked the length of the tent again.

Another, lanky and with hair like matted, black spiderwebs sat on the bed. The thinker blessing on his brow was only a shade darker than his skin.

"She's a fighter."

I felt my mate's growl as if it vibrated through my own chest.

"I don't want her fighting. How would I live if she'd have died on that field? She was there, below me! I should've gotten her away from it before the demon broke through the lines."

I felt it there, beneath the frustration and fury: worry. An abundance of worry with my face plastered over it. Every question he hadn't asked me, every detail he yearned to know.

He didn't even know my name.

"She saved your life," the blond brute quipped.

Easton let out another growl and paced the tent. "If Barin would've held the line like I instructed, I wouldn't have taken that bite to my wing."

The brute held up his hands in surrender. "If she single-handedly killed a demon, maybe she's not meant for tent-tending. Did you think about that?"

My mate hadn't. He'd been so focused on losing me that his mind had gone territorial. Defensive.

"And now you can't find her?"

"I know exactly where she is, but with Altun guards and the king's magic protecting her, she might as well be on another continent."

The thinker whistled. "That is high security."

"Amaury claimed her as his ward."

The thinker stopped his sharpening of an arrowhead. "The one our sources say is being married off to ensure loyalties with estates?"

My stomach sank. Forterian camps and Altun cities traded rumors like goods. If others learned, soon the Taits would too, and the wedding would be canceled, along with my magic lessons with Griffin.

Easton snatched the stool and ripped a leg from it. "She's my mate!"

I stumbled out of his mind, back into the pitch-black tent. Into the empty bed and the shadows of guards, standing nearly shoulder to shoulder outside my tent.

I pulled his shirt back over my nose. The pine scent was both a lullaby and stab of pain in my gut.

I closed my eyes.

I tried not to think about tomorrow. It could wait.

CHAPTER 9

I REGRETTED DISCARDING EASTON'S shirt and blanket the next morning in a fit of rage. Despite the echo of his demands for me to be subservient, his scent had lulled me to sleep as the moans of the dying and injured reverberated through the camp long into the morning. It might've dulled the stabs of pain pulsing across the mate bond in the days following our return to the obsidian castle, which was leaked of its pre-war warmth like the hollow echo of my boots in the halls.

Amaury visited the Forterian chiefs who'd lost warriors in the battle. Griffin locked himself away in his office. Guards barred me from the training field and pointed me toward the gardens from where Neira planned the victory ball. I listened to her prattle about color schemes and seating arrangements until the sound of her breath set me on edge.

Then, I retreated to the solitude of my room to bear the pain of my mate's absence in secrecy and shame. My chest ached at the constant thundering of my heart. My head pounded from the energy needed to reinforce the block on my side of the mate bond and keep his emotions away.

The ghost of Easton's scent lingered in my dreams, a haunting reminder that the day we didn't speak about had come. Every skirted conservation with Amaury about whether I met my mate returned with prodding questions and the gut feeling they'd planned for this without my knowledge. Other courtiers married their mates. Griffin waited over a century for his mate and would have waited longer.

Was it foolish to believe I might have a future with mine?

As deep as Easton's absence cut me, his words cut deeper. His demands for me to live beneath his will as a silent wife boiled my magic and fury. I dreamed of being back on the battlefield, stepping aside to allow the demon past and hearing Easton's pleases for help. If released from the castle, I might've returned to him only to prove us equals by besting him in battle or kill him to silence the mate bond's begging pull.

The day Amaury returned, I was summoned to Griffin's office. Two guards with crossbows escorted me. Drapes covered all the windows, leaving white torches to bask the hallways in icy light.

The office doors swung open after a single knock.

They revealed Amaury first, glancing left as often as he adjusted his grip on his blade.

Then Griffin, seated behind his desk, hands folded before him and eyes appraising my steps. His obsidian crown seemed to suck in the light, at odds with his eyes as clear as shallow bays.

Neira stood beside him. Her ruby red nails scratched at the shoulder of his suit. She'd forgone her embellished outfits for a black dress void of ruffles or gems.

"Sit," Griffin commanded.

My steps faltered where rugs cushioned the unrelenting stone floors. A slap of blistering chill, as harrowing as the demon's glare, shackled my breath. I lurched against it with sparks of my magic, only for Griffin's wards protecting the castle to smack that from my grasp as well.

Stumbling to the chair, I plopped into it. A headache began at the base of my skull. Easton's concern dashed across the mate bond. I held back the two tides demanding access to my consciousness. One of my mate's fear and the other of the king's annoyance.

Griffin tapped the desk. "If we act quickly, we can turn your mistake into a tactic to win back the loyalty of the Tait Estate. You saw their lines marching and worried of the strength of them. You joined, not to prove yourself, but to ensure as many of their soldiers returned home as possible."

My tongue was heavy with questions, but I bit it.

Dozens of lives were shredded for my naivety. Soldiers trained or forced into the lines and taken from their families and livelihoods, farmers who'd swapped their hoe for a sword, and shopkeepers who'd locked up their goods and hugged their family for the last time.

"The soldiers will see you as strong and selfless. The Taits will allow the narrative in favor of having your magic within their bloodline." Griffin beamed.

"My mate—"

"We can remedy that now."

My shoulders and neck cried, but I raised my head to meet the king's gaze. Fear fueled my white knuckled grip on the armrests. "How?"

Neira swept a hand toward the darkened corner to Amaury's left. The shadows shifted, curved, and surrendered to a cloaked pillar.

It raised its hooded head.

The wood of the armrest groaned in my grip. A chip of it splintered into my palm.

Pale white, sunken cheeks rose from the veiled black, giving way to porcelain skin and irises as bright as ripened cherries. No hair peeked from the hood, no brows, only skin taught over knobby bone. Blue-tinted lips curved in a feline snarl.

The being emerged from the shadows leaching to its back. Wisps of black remained beneath its chin and across the back of its hands, swirling as Griffin's magic often did, as if night itself lived within her.

Amaury's faced screwed in disgust, as did mine. A putrid taste choked its way down my throat and rimmed my eyes with hot tears.

"This is Pila," Neira announced, "a priestess of the Old Faith in Beaddeon. She has experience breaking bonds."

My hand instinctively covered my gut where Easton's concerned frothed across our connection. "A bonk?" I'd only heard legends of the priestess who partook in self-mutilation, bloody sacrifices, and the worshipping of gods thought to long be buried beneath the advances of the continent.

Pila glided past Amaury, cherry eyes seemed to drink in my palpable fear. Above her brow, the shadows continued to shift. They danced for me, and I lost myself in the trance of their spirals.

Griffin's mind knocked at my mental walls. He shattered them with a flick of his magic. I gasped around its loss, at the naked vulnerability.

The depth of his prodding curled my toes. Within my gut, he plucked the thin magic-laced thread to my mate.

A second presence followed his, rotten and slippery. It oozed across the mate bond and suckled in time with my pulse, tighter and tighter. Pila's grasp pinched the bond where it anchored to me.

I stood. My retreat knocked the chair over, and I crashed to the floor beside it.

Pila took my mate bond, as if it were a branch, and bent it until it splintered. Pain laced my every breath.

Fire bubbled in the base of my skull and plunged upward, accompanied by a crackling laugh reverberating only between where I clasped my hands over my ears.

The sparks of my magic rumbled.

A burst of blinding light cleared the cackle.

I was too warm, feeling as if my skin could melt off.

Then, darkness, like being plunged beneath the ice.

Only I remained within my head. Pila's ooze and Griffin's demands of submission faded beneath the heaving of other's breaths. I filled my aching chest with a breath and let the cool of the air fall over the heat of Easton's fear.

Hands pinched my shoulders. Amaury's scrunched features were blurred by my pouring tears.

"It's for the best." He caged me within his arms. "He is Forterian. There is nothing for you there."

The conflict within me was icy hot, like a flame slicing me in two. The mate bond and Easton's emotions stabbed into me, demanding more than I would give for it. It infected the part of me begging for love and acceptance promised in tandem with a mate bond.

I drew the stiff seams of Amaury's uniform into my grasp.

No love was worth my freedom or my power. I would not sacrifice my years of training and my potential for the warmth I'd felt within his caress.

Amaury cupped my cheeks in his hands. The stringy brown locks tickled my forehead. "It is going to hurt, but then it'll be better, and you can return to training."

I fastened myself together with the hope of normalcy.

Pila resumed her prowl, assessing me as a hunter does a buck. She screeched down my bond, her magic like a nail on metal.

It snagged, and Easton jolted from the other side.

"Wait!" I cried, breaking from Amaury's embrace. The words left my lips on impulse, spoken by the part of me desperate for love and spurred by Easton's turmoil flooding across the bond.

I felt the swords in Easton's hands drop as if I'd released them. I felt his wings spread as if they stemmed from my own back and his feet leaving the ground. Wind loosened the curls matted to his brow with sweat.

Griffin's pause nailed me to my conviction. I had his curiosity, more precious than gold. Retreating now would show weakness.

I met Amaury's stare and an inkling of a plan began to form.

Pila straightened. Then she continued her smooth stalking. The shadows I thought I'd left on the battlefield crept from the corners and speared with a frigid bite.

"I can get the Forterians to train the females," I declared, meeting her gaze, then Griffin's "You've attempted diplomacy and reason. You've avoided outright ordering them to keep the peace. Now let me try. I can use his station as a general to our advantage."

Amaury reached to reel me back in.

Pila took another step but was stalled by Griffin's raised hand. I caught my breath as she obeyed.

Neira clawed Griffin's shoulder with red-tipped talons.

Griffin narrowed his gaze and titled his head. Five breaths went unanswered before he gave a wave of his hand. "How?"

"A bargain." I turned to Amaury. "You said they would need more than an Altun example of a female soldier. I can use their arrogance about his strength to corner them into a deal, sealed with magic, to train their females if I beat him."

Amaury gripped my shoulder. "He is a superior fighter. You cannot beat him."

"Train me to. You sparred against him when visiting Virian, have you not? You could go again, learn his technique and his weaknesses, then help me." I looked to Griffin, his brow raised and lips pursed. "I can do this. I can beat him."

Griffin tapped the desk. "And if you cannot?"

I straightened and stepped from Amaury's side. My next break sunk in my gut like a rock and my mouth dried as I said, "I'll kill him."

I braided my hair and applied a light layer of makeup. Putting on my courtier mask had never churned my stomach as much as it did in preparation to see my mate. There was no settling into the politicking arena, forgoing the rhythm of battle. Today, I'd be both the alluring courtier and the trained fighter, a cross of two worlds I'd kept veiled from one another to preserve myself.

For the equality of Forterian females, to remove the boots

from their necks, I'd have to be willing to do anything. Risk anything. Even myself. Even my mate.

"Are you ready?" Amaury asked, leading Griffin into my room. His voice sounded like my inner voice: unsure, quiet, and scared. He wore full armor, the plates on his back like a hunchback to allow the wings to unfurl.

I pulled at my sleeves, eyeing the blades Amaury held out to me. Forterian blades, the very ones he'd gifted me on my eighteenth birthday. Their pommels and guards were decorated with a looping design, far more intricate than those given to Forterian warriors on their eighteenth, the first year of eligibility to earn their blessed magic by surviving the Sacrament.

He turned to his king, brow creased. "If she doesn't win, I will not leave her—"

"There is more than one way to end a bond." Griffin took the blades from Amaury and offered them to me. His crown gleamed. "Kacela is aware of what she must do if she loses."

I took the blades from him and slid them into their sheaths on either hip. They were heavier than I remembered. I dug my nails into their grips.

"Ready?" Griffin asked, placing a hand on my shoulder. His fingers pinched, not too hard, but enough. A warning and reminder.

He'd get me there. My strength had to be saved for what I was about to do.

I nodded.

The squeezing feeling of skipping started in my gut and spread across my limbs until I couldn't breathe. Then it released. We landed at the edge of the camp, where sparing circles were filled with young boys. Their wrestling matches stopped. Jokes half told hung between training partners. An old warrior cut short his correction of a boy's form, moving to shield them from us. They couldn't have been older than I was when Amaury took me twenty years ago.

When they killed my mother.

A call went ahead of us through the camp. I fought away

the urge to smile at mothers gathering their children into their tents. I was a soldier with a battle-hardened sneer, not a girl returned home to my mother's grave or a desperate mate longing for love.

We reached the center of the camp where a host of warriors awaited. Chief Daviat stood at the center. He wore the forest green of his camp, a sword on each hip, with a crooked-toothed snarl and his gray hair in a matted bun on the back of his neck.

Beside him, my mate spoke in hushed tones to his thinker friend with the bushy black hair.

Griffin raised his arms like soaring wings. "Is this how you welcome your king?"

Easton's mouth stilled and the lines of his brow creased. His cheeks looked hollowed, not flat. When he surveyed me, he straightened. The corner of his lip curled. Then, his glare returned and chin dipped. He stared at me, and I stared back.

"I see she's gained some sense." Chief Daviat scrutinized me as his general had, and his triumphant smirk curved downwards. "You've come to mock us."

Griffin shrugged. "Not necessarily."

Easton followed his chief's approach, but his eyes did not leave my unmoving snarl. I wouldn't give him any inclination of how the bond tormented me with its insistent demands. I wouldn't show him the sliver of me, like the magic of the mate bond, excited by our proximity.

"We've come with an offer." Griffin cocked his muse to Easton. "You want your mate," then he returned it to Chief Daviat, "and we want equality."

A roar went through Virian and the crowd surged in.

"An offer?" The chief turned to his advisors. He nudged one with his elbow. "Not a command?"

I wanted to roll my eyes. They were children, as Griffin often said, still throwing tantrums over a war their ancestors lost.

"A friendly wager," Griffin continued, "on a fight between mates."

Their attention returned.

I reeled it in. "You say my gender makes me inferior, yet it was I who saved your general from certain death. How many of your warriors were devoured by demons while I cut one down single-handedly?"

"State your wager," the thinker beside Chief Daviat barked. The sun gleamed off a thick sheen of sweat on his bald head and washed out the blond of his brows.

Mutters chorused around us.

I felt their stares stalking me. "If I win, you abolish all laws and forsake any tradition creating inequality. You will train all children together. And when they come of age, any willing youth will be given their birthright of the Sacrament and, if earned, their blessings."

Easton stepped past his chief, shaking off the grasp of his thinker friend. "And if I win?"

"I will assume my place here, with you, as your mate." The words were thick as they crawled up my throat.

The pale scars on my mate's chin stretched to accommodate his quirked smile, and I once again felt as if the morning rays of sun beamed across me.

I grounded my teeth together. I would leave here today, either a victor or no longer plagued by the bond's nagging, having instilled equality or relieved Virian Clan of a general.

"Our wives are not warriors. Our daughters will not be trained to die in your lines," Chief Daviat said, shouldering past Easton. "If his mate remains a whore, they are plenty others willing to take her place in his tent. This offer is laughable."

I set my hands on my blades, a Forterian gesture promising bloodshed. "Scared?"

The walls of my crafted cage closed around the chief. He could publicly refute the offer and add doubt to his superiority or allow the fight. Allow a risk I may best his general and stake the Virian Clan as the flagship for female equality.

Chief Daviat gripped Easton's shoulders, clapped one, then shoved him toward the fighting ring. "Be blessed with strength now, boy."

Easton nodded, the twinkle obscured by the darkness of a fighter's resolve.

"How do we know this is fair?" Easton's other friend, the blond brute with biceps as thick as my skull, handed my mate practice blades. "She has magic to give her an advantage."

"I can make wards," Griffin flurried his hands. "Those commonly used in healing circles to ensure the ailing warrior isn't under a spell worsening his condition, and your healer can check them."

Chief Daviat sent a young boy to find a healer.

Griffin stepped beside me. Amaury flanked my other side. "As much as I'd like to take you at your word, today it won't be enough."

"It is an insult to claim a Forterian would not stay bound to his oath," Easton grumbled.

"Insulting as it may be, a deal must be shaken upon." Griffin gestured for Amaury to approach Chief Daviat.

The chief studied Amaury's outstretched hand. He clasped his forearm, and Griffin's head dipped. The crown teetered with it.

From beneath Amaury's sleeve, a stream of black slithered across their conjoined grasps.

"What is this?" Chief Daviat demanded, throwing off his grip. Magical bargains were fused in ink, similar to their blessings. Above both their wrists, the Quillon family symbol of a raven cawing at the waning moon held each to their oath.

"A bond," Griffin mused. "If either party fails to uphold their end of the bargain, including obeying the laws of a clean fight, the bond will fail. It takes a life as payment."

Chief Daviat prodded at it, then scratched.

Easton's gaze snapped to mine. "If I win and you don't come fulfill your role as my mate."

"My life will be forfeit," Amaury intervened. "And if Kacela wins, but you fail to uphold your end of the deal, your chief's life will be forfeit." He turned to Chief Daviat. "The bond will then transfer to your next of kin and onward until it has fulfillment."

"This is trickery. "The chief covered the bargain from his advisor's glance.

Amaury's hand went to the longsword on his hip. He revealed the gleam of metal. "Watch how you speak to our king."

Chief Daviat's hands fell from his own blades. "My apologies, My King."

"All is forgiven. Please, we are ruining a wonderful day for a fight." He waved his hand and around one of the sparring circles, a complex mix of ruins appeared, interlocking with one another.

The healer, an old female with tanned, wrinkled skin and downturned eyes, inspected the marks. She nodded once to Chief Daviat. "They will prevent any magical interference."

Amaury turned to me and squeezed my shoulder. My stomach convulsed. I avoided Easton's gaze. The hope in his eyes may have undone the restraints on my emotions. Might have dulled my strikes.

Sliding the two swords from their sheaths on my hips, I handed them to Amaury and took the practice swords a Forterian all but shoved into my chest.

I stepped into the circle.

The loss of magic was jarring, as if my breath had been forced out, and no air came to replace it.

Each breath came shorter than the one before, each step staggered.

Easton had rolled up his sleeves to his elbows. The veins in his forearms pulsed with each practice swing.

I drew my gaze from the strain of fabric against his arms to an already curling smirk. The clouds covered the sun, and the shadows darkened Easton's glare. I didn't feel the warmth of spring in them. They were like the first snowfall gathering on dying grass.

I shut out the part of me aching to be in his arms. This was another fight to prove to all I wasn't the same little girl running

from her mother's murder. Not the same girl who woke scream-
ing with nightmares. Not another girl to be married off.

I was a fighter. A lethal blade.

Defeat was not a thought I could afford.

Easton stepped forward and raised his swords to cross before
his face.

It was identical to what Amaury had described from his visits
back to Virian. In the weeks prior when he'd returned to Virian
to assess their losses during the war, he'd analyzed Easton's
technique and scoured for weaknesses. We'd then trained until
no combination of his attacks could surprise me.

I'd have one opportunity to clench victory. One misstep was
all I needed.

I mirrored his stance.

When his brows rose, I flashed wink.

Easton recomposed himself with a shake of his curls, but I
grinned at the pause of his stance. A taste of triumph.

Easton attacked first, as expected. I ducked from the blades
and weaved around from one jutting out to catch my retreat. His
fifth attack finally connected with my blade. The blow should
have shaken my core and toppled my stance, but he'd pulled it.

He was treating me as his mate and treating this fight as
anything but continent altering.

Channeling my frustration into my fighting, I threw my
weight into the blows. I delayed my evasion to avoid his swing
by a half breath.

I giggled.

Easton's jabs became more erratic as those around the circle
muttered speculations. If a small girl treated the fight like a
performance, who else might be able to topple the general?
Who could challenge him?

He struck with speed and strength matching his reputation.
The clang of blades rattled my teeth. I held strong, met his lean
with my own, and waited for him to step into the fray before
spinning away with my blades tucked.

His momentum carried him past me and into the ground.

I gave another wink.

Easton beat his swords into the ground, and when he turned, I saw no speckle of hope in his eyes. No trace of spring warmth. Gone was the lover whose bed I'd woken in, replaced by a general on the front lines.

I lost myself for a moment, despite the blocked mate bond. The strength of his blows rang through my arms and into my gut. It fueled the curiosity until my mind clouded with only him and the pine musk rolling from his glistening brow.

I could outline every muscle in his exposed forearms and neck along with each bead of sweat tracing them if I wished to. I knew him as if he were a portrait within the castle halls, and I hated myself for it.

He was sharp with his attacks, working at a pace I hardly kept with. The strengths of every sparring partner I'd tested my abilities against combined into this bred warrior hellbent on my concession.

I waited, counting the steps and keeping a keen eye on his feet as they shuffled effortlessly.

Then it happened, the moment I'd been waiting over three dozen moves for. He swung around on his left side, aiming at my neck. I ducked, and the warrior, true to his training, switched his momentum to bring both swords down upon my head.

But his feet, sweeping and tip toeing, crossed for a split second. With my shoulder lifted and head ducked, I sprang from my squared position into his open chest. My blades speared through the space between his head and arms before breaking them apart.

My knees came up into his chest and arms down upon his at the elbows.

His blades soared.

I landed on his chest, my knees pinning his biceps to the ground and blades crossed over his neck.

The dust churned up by the crash of our bodies settled around us.

His brows raised. He looked at his pinned arms, then at the cross of my blades over his throat, licking his lips as he did.

My mate's face slipped into the shadows as his eyes fell from my face, down my heaving chest, and lower. Then lower still.

When his gaze returned to mine, a new warmth billowed within the vibrant green.

"I concede." His words, like the clang of a gong, sent the crowd into roaring chaos.

The markings around the ring disappeared, and I moved before he could, dropping my blades to place a hand on his chest.

I skipped us away.

Amaury had marked a place I could easily skip to and back without fail, and I tested the distance nearly a dozen times in various spots around Kadea.

I missed the landing, opening the pinched fabric of reality at waist height. We toppled through and crashed into red, damp leaves, then rolled apart.

My stomach heaved as the scattered autumn leaves seeped their chill through my pants. They clumped to my palms, crumbly and sticky.

A hand grasped my neck, thumb pressing at my chin to raise my gaze.

Thoughts of bloody battle seeped away.

Easton's stare flittered down as my breath stuttered between parted lips. Three breaths passed, his chest heaving in time with mine.

I licked the itch from my lips. His stare kept me suspended in time with one hand near my hip, close enough to grab him or my dagger. I crunched the leaves stuck to my palm. My chest heaved as I fought the warring halves, one spurred by the mate bond and the other riled by his demands.

His mouth crashed against mine. The mate bond drowned all thoughts of attacking until it was only him and his grasp tugging at my hair. Fingers ran up through the braid. Strands fell around as our lips fought like clashing armies.

The pinch of his fingers curling around my hip pulled me from the mate bond's allure.

I shoved at his shoulders, skittering back through his grasping hands.

Easton lurched toward my retreated steps. His chest smacked mine. The rough bark of the oak dug into my shoulder blades.

His foot stomped between mine, his thigh pinning me at the core. Callus-padded fingers traced from my chin to temple and speared into my hair. Their threading yanked my head back. He captured my feeble gasp with his inhale.

"Easton—"

His mouth was there again, holding me within his clutches and scrambling the sane thoughts in my head until any inkling of plan melted into a puddle along with me.

I wrestled with his belt, then the restraints of his pants. They gathered where his leg pinned mine.

His hand trailed down my thigh then shoved his pants past our molded legs.

His first moan reformed my plan, like a waterfall freshly thawed in the spring, crashing over my nerves.

This, his pleasure, was my role within the camp. A wife, mother, and home tender.

I ran my hands over the brawn of his abdomen, around his hips, and searched upward, to the sprout of his wings. His shoulders adjusted, giving me ample room beneath his shirt to explore.

His groan told me I'd found the right spot. The sensitive blessed tattoo was bundled with nerves and excited by war and lust.

Within a few strokes of my fingers across the blessing, he came apart against me in jolted groans. His tightened grip in my hair dragged my head back and his lips fell to my pulse with a string of nips.

Each one was a spark threatening to burn us down, and for a breath-turned-gasp at the next scrape of his teeth over my pulse, I wanted to let him. To watch the world turn to ash from the middle of the inferno, with him as my flare.

He yanked my shirt from my pants and walked his fingers up my ribs, as if he were counting each. I arched into his grasp. His hand slipped to the small of my back, where my muscles tensed at his beckoning. "Mountain be damned," he grunted, moving as if he wished to grind me into the tree bark.

The pain, like water, doused the flames threatening to ignite my plan.

I snapped my eyes open and stared past his shoulder toward the snow-capped mountain peak in the heart of Sacrament Land, barely visible over the treetops.

I skipped us back to Virian War Camp. Only for a second. Enough to deposit him like a used rag.

Then I was gone.

CHAPTER 10

NO TALK OF MY MATE or marriage penetrated the renewed feeling of home within the castle. Griffin continued our magic lessons, focusing on how to break into a mind, then control it.

My free time was spent with Neira, planning the ball to celebrate victory over the demons, even as reports of new cracks to their world arrived every few days.

It was during those moments I allowed a bit of the premonition about my future to slip in.

I was busy, annoyingly so. Too busy to wander down the mate bond to see if the ball of fury that was Easton had cooled. Too busy to train with Amaury. Too busy for a moment to myself.

In the moments between meetings and training, something soured in my stomach like an overripe fruit, the edges leaching off and fetid muck underneath worsening by the moment.

It stuck with me, a nagging thought in the back of my head, as if I were missing something.

A larger piece of the puzzle.

The feeling intensified whenever I spotted Pila's black robes drifting through the hallways. Shadow to my every move. Death lurking within.

Lords and ladies arrived for the victory ball a day prior. The servants were in a panic as they attempted to prepare the castle to Neira's wishes. It was a tall order to clip every leaf to the same length, rid all rooms of every speck of dust, and polish the floors as if we were to eat off them.

It was a production like those Amaury used to take me to in the theater district of Kadea, where colors were as vibrant and varied as the spring bloom.

With the excitement of the castle, I took refuge in my room to heal from a grueling few days of training with Griffin. My absence wasn't questioned. I didn't take it well. The billowing worries of what occurred outside my quiet wing had my magic poking its head out of its hiding place. What other talk of marriage, heirs, and my position at court occurred without my input or knowledge?

The morning of the ball, I stared at the dark bags beneath my cheeks and the width of my shoulders, so slender compared to my birthday ball. The full picture came to me like a portrait being drawn. I saw the grand scheme, then the brushstrokes of the maneuvers I'd made, thinking I'd done them myself.

But it was Griffin's hand holding the paintbrush, and I was a mere spectator waiting for the final reveal. Still waiting.

Servants bustled into my room as music floated through the castle, a quiet hum perfect for conversation.

They scrubbed me clean and set me in the chair before the vanity as if I were a doll.

Neira waltzed into the room, the train of her satin grown like a trail of blood behind her. "Hello," she sang, sweeping her curled, copper hair over her shoulder. It rippled back, stopping only where a diadem was woven within her braids. "How excited are we today?"

"Very," I forced out with a gulp she either didn't notice or ignored.

With a hand on my shoulders, she appraised us in the mirror. Her green eyes burned once again, as if embers lived within her irises. "We've won the war," she boasted, "but that does not mean the fighting is over."

I turned in my chair away from the mirror so the servant could begin her work on my hair. Neira lounged on my bed, still unmade.

"We've been very selective of who is aware of your actions within Virian." She looked at her nails. "The Taits, however, are aware of all your post-war actions." Her words were as putrid as the perfume she wore, jasmine and berries. They pricked like the pins in my hair.

"Are they aware it was not some random general?"

She righted her diadem in the mirror, looking over my head. "There should be no secrets between husband and wife. Battle brings out emotions in all of us, dear. Better to let the kingdom believe you've continued your promiscuous run with a barbarian instead of being mated to one."

I felt the mate bond. The steady beat of Easton's heart traversed it, even if his emotions did not.

The servant finished my hair, having curled the bottom portion and staked the rest to the top of my head as golden roses. I might've loved it and shown my gratitude if my jaw were not clenched to keep away a grimace.

Still, Neira watched me with hawk-like eyes.

Unlike the previous balls, my natural features shown through the light makeup and pink blush. The servant speckled gold across my eyelids. Even my lips, usually painted blood red, were pale pink.

"It's a shame," Neira said from the bed, where she picked at a tray of scones, "a lady didn't take more of a hand in your previous ball outfits. The harsh makeup and dresses make our light beauty cold and wicked. Soft souls need soft hands and silks."

The joyous smile I'd seen in the gardens or while making wedding preparations spread across her lips. "I have a gift."

She hopped from the bed, her silk robe floating around her as if suspended in water. Her feet made no noise in her haste to reach a servant holding a dress bag.

Neira slipped a baby blue gown from the cover and held it up.

I studied the garment more closely as the servants snugged me into it. Pink, gold, and white flowers obscured the corset lines in the front of the sweetheart neckline. A single string of flowers stitched in lace ran up the right shoulder and spread across the back, otherwise leaving my chest bare. From the waist, the dress hung loosely with tulle and more flowers stitched into swirling patterns of green embroidery made to look like vines.

I twirled back and forth in the mirror to observe how it flowed with me.

"What do you think?" Neira asked, gesturing for another twirl.

"I love it." I smiled, happy to begin a night of politicking with an absolute truth.

She studied me, one brow raised, and nodded her approval, face as staunch as that of a general preparing for war.

Neira and the servants had been gone for nearly an hour before another knocked at my door. I'd spent the time searching for my sheath and throwing knives, only to find my many hidden armories cleaned out.

"Come in." I could already feel the mellow of his magic. A sense I'd have to get used to.

Nalin cleared his throat, but I took my time securing the straps on my heels. Another few breaths to settle into my new identity as a courtier. A soon-to-be lady.

Not the mate of a Forterian general.

Not a general or line commander.

Not a soldier.

"You look ravishing," Nalin said, the glint in his eyes always the same. He wore a black jacket, fitted like a second skin. The detailing of it and the seams of his pants were silver, as was the embroidered leopard on his breast pocket. The gel in his hair seemed to be a shade darker, making his flesh seem as pale as a skeleton reaching from the darkness encasing him.

His hand touched mine, and anger as bright as my magic flashed down the mate bond. The clipped compliment I'd intended soiled on my tongue, then disappeared.

I nodded my thanks.

He titled my chin up with the brush of his finger. "Are you alright?"

"Nerves," I dragged my face from his touch. "Shall we?"

There was no grand entrance for me, no moment where I was the most interesting one in the room, only a servant opening the doors to the ballroom and a handful of widened gazes.

"How many know?" I muttered to Nalin.

He patted my hand, though it felt more like a slap to my wrist. "You barged from a tent half naked. Did you believe none would know?"

"Yet our marriage stands."

"Careful." His nails dug into the back of my hand. "The announcement hasn't been made."

The lords and ladies had been partying long before the ball began, and many were already leaning against one another like pillars of a toppled temple. The ballroom was slashes of red, and while Neira wanted it to be satin tides, I thought it looked like a corpse's ribcage.

I sent away servants with wine and picked at the crumbs on my plate well into the night, preferring to watch the sloppy storm of dancing than allow Nalin to drag me into its hold. He sat beside me, arm strewn out across the back of my chair.

"Why don't you go?" I asked, nodding to the crowd.

"Kacy—"

"This may be your last party without a wife on your arm.

Go."

He did, and another took his place.

Amaury. The medals adorning his chest looked like fish scales. He wore the raven black of our king, but the details of his suit were forest green instead of royal red. The longer I watched the wine swirl in his glass, the thicker it looked.

My stomach heaved.

"He's a good lad," Amaury said. "Lord and Lady Tait are elated to have you as their daughter."

I didn't respond. I couldn't let him know the pain of breathing past the anger lurching from the mate bond. If I did, I didn't know how long until Griffin ordered Easton's death to keep word of my Forterian mate from the wrong ears.

Across the ballroom, Jacinth enticed Nalin to a dance with a flair of her skirt. He smiled, and she led him into the throng. The mixture of their feigned innocence and blissful charade set my teeth grinding.

I wanted it, I realized.

I wanted back the years I'd spent adamant that politicking and forming connections with other courtiers was secondary to the necessity of fighting. To have someone to giggle about boys with. Someone I could unload the weight on my shoulders to.

More than an ally. More than someone watching my back in the heat of battle.

I wanted a friend.

A guard approached Amaury's other side and whispered to him, too low for me to hear.

His face stilled into the calculating mask of the royal commander. He pulled me from my chair with a tight grip on my elbow. "Go," he urged.

I strode toward the main doors. Amaury clung to my side as if the moment he stepped from me, I'd vanish.

I'd nearly reached the doors, my nerves on edge, when they swung open. The pine scent washed over me first, then blazing green, hooded eyes attempted not to widen as we blinked at one another.

Easton.

Amaury tightened his grip on my elbow, causing a wince. Easton's nostrils flared.

"Be a shame to miss such a party," the blond brute beside Easton said, hooking his thumbs into the waist of his beige trousers. On his other side, the thinker with skin as dark as Griffin's crown surveyed the party. His hair was twisted in coils as thick as my fingers, all held in a chunky bun on the crown of his head.

The music crumbled, a fiddle attempting to hold on despite the silence of the dancers.

I held my breath as my mate scanned me. With a satisfied nod, Easton turned back to the partygoers as they shifted apart.

Griffin appeared at the front of the crowd, Neira clinging to his arm. "Finally!" He flung out his arms. "I'd begun to think our Forterian representatives had gotten lost in the mountains."

The crowd roared.

Easton's shoulders loosened and the breath he held fell past his lips. I stared at those lips longer than I should've, remembering their fever against mine.

I snapped my gaze back to his to find him still watching me. Before either of us could move, the crowd surged like a tide.

It yanked the Forterians into the pit of dancing bodies and shoved wine into their hands. The blond brute went willing, throwing back two glasses as he did. The thinker gave to Lady Fallan steering him through the crowd.

Leaving only Easton to shrug off their grasping hands. He inched toward me.

"Royal Commander." He raised his right fist over his heart in the Forterian salute.

"Not a dancer?" Amaury used my arm as a rudder to steer me away.

"To the right music." His lip quirked up, and the hunch of his shoulders softened. "With the right partner."

I calmed my face, feigning boredom at his words. I had to. Stone. I'd be the stone he saw on the battlefield, not the girl he'd kissed in a field away from prying eyes.

I banished the memory of his hands before it sprung a crimson blush to my cheeks. "There are plenty here who would be thrilled to dance with a winged Forterian."

Easton's gaze never left mine. "Leaving so soon?"

"No," I said before Amaury could stop me.

Easton's cheeks brightened. "If you'll excuse me, I'd like a drink. Long day of flying." He disappeared into the crowd. I could feel his lingering gaze threatening to brand itself on my every action.

Amaury's reddened face turned on me. The stringy bits of hair had fallen out from behind his ears. They swung wildly before his darkening gaze. "Kacela—"

"I'm not hiding in my room for the best party this castle has seen in decades because he's here. I'll keep my distance."

After speaking with Griffin, he relented on letting me stay, with one requirement.

As soon as Nalin's hand touched my waist, repulsion rocked through me, and Easton went rigid from his spot beside the fireplace. I managed one dance with Nalin, forced by Neira's glare, before escaping the heated mess of the dance floor for my chair. Nalin's muttered complaints followed me.

Easton's attention to my every move was as heavy as plated armor. Anger sprinted across the mate bond, a ring of red around my sight.

I followed it back, winding up the rage as if it were unraveled yarn, and smothering it in cool reassurances.

Despite the beauty of those who grasped his hand, Jacinth included, Easton parried their advances. Jealousy reared, and I gave a breath to the traitorous emotions threatening to pull me from my courtier semblance.

I reached out with my mind, hoping Griffin was too far away or too preoccupied to shove me back inside my head. Moving past Nalin's steel walls, I peered through the crowd and avoided the minds unveiled by wine.

My mate's unguarded consciousness welcomed me as a part

of it.

I gave him the small nudge he needed.

Then, I felt another presence like an intruder on my back, following the wisps of my magic across the ballroom to my mate.

I yanked back from Easton and closed myself into my own head.

Nalin's dark, calculating eyes turned from me to the dance floor and then back. Something, perhaps realization, flashed behind them.

I held Nalin's gaze, my expression bland.

Nalin's will slammed at my mental barriers. My body locked, the magic in my gut frozen mid tide. The walls around me crumbled as if they were straw. I waited for him to attack, to drop me like a sack of potatoes across the festivities and retreat as if I'd died of my own embarrassment, to rid himself of another's mate.

His voice floated through my mind as a breeze does a forest. *It wasn't a coincidence you walked out of his tent.*

I held my silence.

The Forterian is your mate. The king, he didn't say —

"I believe it would be rude of me not to ask the warrior who saved my life for a dance." Easton stood before us, his black jacket, detailed with the forest green of his war clan, wrapped around his sculpted muscles. He'd slicked back the thick curls so they gathered at the base of his neck. In the shadow of his collar, I spied the tips of tattooed wings.

Silver flurries of Nalin's magic tickled where they landed on my neck and cheeks.

Easton grinned at my escort. "Just one."

I was out of my chair before Nalin could protest, around the side of the table, and taking his hand.

We fled into the jumble of bodies, his clutch unyielding. Heat seeped between our interlocked grip and rose in my gut.

"Do you know how to dance?" I guided his right arm around my back, molding my body to his. I arched my fingers in the curls at the base of his neck, crinkling whatever gel caked them.

The music crescendoed.

I pressed against his hand holding mine. "It's an eight count—"

Easton stepped in sync with the other dancers, his body guiding mine without a hitch, as it had in the forest. He shot me a wink.

Blood thundered through me.

We spun along with the crowd, pressed together in one moment and twirling apart in the next, always coming back chest to chest with one another in time with the beat. I'd never gripped a hand so tightly, even when stumbling through waltzes.

But his, I needed as if he were my weapon and the jumble of dancers my death.

The next song started, and without hesitation, we continued.

Three more songs passed until I couldn't ignore the curl of Easton's fingers into my waist any longer. Need and desire pulsed between us, the mate bond blinding like a single torch beneath a starless sky.

Chest to chest. Noses inches apart. Breaths fanning. I pressed into his chest, shoulders arching around his hand sliding up my back.

His eyes danced with delight, putting the most dazzling emeralds to shame. He ducked his head. Our noses brushed.

I reared back, as if the graze of his lips against mine was a spark and I was coal ready to be set aflame.

Easton met my every retreating step with a prowl. He reached for me again, fingers skimming my skirt.

I ran.

CHAPTER 11

THE SANCTUARY of the northern water gardens called to my wayward thoughts. From the dimly lit parlor, I emerged onto the thin planks spanning ponds of multicolored koi. They danced as the drunken courtiers did, swirling in the currents like leaves. Past them was a maze as expansive as the castle, so intricate I'd never found its end.

Planks creaked beneath my search for a haven to drown out the party's thunder. I'd almost reached where they gave to the first stone of the maze when the flap of wings brought my attention skywards.

Easton spun me by my arm into his grasp.

Desperation flooded the mate bond, sticky like molasses. It coated his every gaze, every movement. He fumbled to hold my cheeks, so gentle as if he feared to bruise me.

"A wild chase?"

I shook him away and continued. The music's echoes bounced from the ponds, a tunnel of pestering stomps and plucked strings in which I begged to hear only my own breath.

Easton landed before me again, blocking the exit from the small bridge with outstretched, white wings.

"Why?" I demanded, fists lost within the tulle of my dress.

He stared down at me. His hands opened and brow scrunched. "You are my mate."

"I made my intentions clear—"

"You used our bond and my Forterian arrogance to maneuver me into a no-win position. You left me with my pants around my ankles and climax on my legs in front of every warrior I'd trained with for my entire life. I was the camp joke for the last few weeks." His grimace spread into a grin. "I have nothing but pride for you."

I glared at the stupid smirk. "Has Daviat held to the bargain?"

"He is alive, isn't he?"

I sighed.

Easton rolled his eyes and eased onto his heels. "The oldest have relented to learning self-defense. The adolescent girls have been smoothly integrated with the boys, and the teenage girls are being given their own lessons."

I put a step between us, but Easton met it with one of his own. His legs twice the length of mine, he closed the gap.

"And the Sacrament?" I asked.

"You fly for the moon, Kacela."

I retreated, searching for another plank to lead me into the maze and away from the party's ringing. "The Sacrament is every Forterian's birthright."

"It's their birthright to train for it," he sighed, reaching for my skirt. "Not even all Forterian males qualify for the Sacrament. It's for the strongest of our kind."

"A female could be that." I leaped across the planks, but Easton followed with a bound.

The moon caught the scrunch of his cheeks. "Could, if she were as tenacious and skilled as you."

I stopped him from advancing, palm on his chest. His hand clasped over mine and heat scorched at the contact. Beneath my touch, his heart sang for me. It called to the magic in my gut, sloshing it back and forth so it rose higher with every pulse.

Traitorous words readied themselves on my tongue. To let

him in, tell him my plan, and betray my kingdom for a lovesick smolder.

"I left you on that field because I am not a wife to tend the tent, Easton. You should not have come."

His lip quirked and his hand tightened against mine. One moment, my straightened arm separated us, then his nose brushed my temple and my lashes raced down his cheek. He swung a hand lazily down to the high slit of my dress.

"Don't run from me, love." Pristine white wings ruffled, the black dots in them like holes to the midnight sky. They extended outward, then around, shepherding me into his embrace. Light glistened down on his head, creating a darkened halo within the chocolate curls. His nose looked twice as crooked in the shadows of his brow. "I want you."

His fingers walked across my chin and cheekbone. They slipped back across my neck, his touch as light as his feathers. He twirled a handful of curls into his grip, guiding my chin up and away. He pressed his lips to my neck.

I swallowed back the rebellious moan. Scarred hands, knowing of death, coaxed a renewed breath from me where they stroked the top of my thigh, as if he were the musician and I the harp.

If I let him hold me any longer, he'd strum it all from me. He'd end me, and I'd willingly crumble to be remolded by him.

The first kiss left a searing mark, amplified by another. He trailed his mouth up to the underside of my jaw. Every stroke of his finger through my hair, every breathless kiss, set my skin aflame. They were brands left on the mate bond. Tattooed claims so deep I felt the quake of each in my bone.

I pressed a palm to his collarbone, bending my fingers over his shoulders. The blessing on his black hummed with greasy magic. Touching it was like running a finger across coals, a streak left on my skin.

Soft feathers brushed my back, feeling as heavy and silky as I imagined them to be.

His knuckles skimmed my cheek. "Kacela," he whispered,

voice as weak as I felt. "I do not run from battles. I do not surrender. My soul has allied with yours. I will not lose you."

The mate bond, the magical thread telling us our souls were made for one another, that we were made for one another, swelled in our proximity. It glowed like embers, taking each kiss and touch as another thread to weave. To strengthen.

My magic spiraled upwards to encase it. It cracked, a strike of lightning curling my toes.

His mouth hovered over mine. I could taste the wine on his breath.

A raven croaked, and ash coated my parted lips.

"It's futile to entertain this," I managed, tone even, "that we could be together."

He growled, "Why?"

I skipped out of his grasp to another plank, putting a pond of cobalt koi between us. His scowl snapped to me and his grip fisted the air I'd just occupied.

"It doesn't matter," I told him through a tightened chest.

His wings spread, as if they meant to propel him to my plank. "Kacela—"

"I don't want you." My magic thrashed against the lie, higher and higher, calling for what it knew was home.

I let it billow to the surface in search of him, then, as his wings flapped, funneled it to skip to my room. The wards of the castle raked my skin. I landed near my bed, cheeks stinging.

Shattered hope beamed down the mate bond.

I locked it out, letting it gather against my mental barriers.

Stone.

To him, I had to be stone.

But alone in my room, I crumbled.

Someone knocked. I muffled a scream behind my hand and clenched my shirt near my navel to calm my erratic breaths.

"Kacela?" Amaury called through the door.

I eased it open enough to cover myself from the waist down. I'd been crawling into bed, dressed in only a loose shirt and underwear.

Seeing me, Amaury sighed. His cheeks were flushed and eyes drooping. He raised an arm to lean it against the door. Missing, the commander staggered into my room.

I caught his shoulders. He smelled of ale.

"You should go to bed."

He heaved back. "I wanted to ensure you were safe." Amaury looked past me, hand on the decorative blade on his hip.

I squeezed his shoulders. "No one is here."

He cupped my cheeks and dipped his head so his squinted gaze was level with mine. His thumb scraped a crusty tear track from my cheek. "The Taits will keep you safe, even when I cannot."

I broke his grip to turn, hiding the tremble of my lip. Amaury wore the same forest green as Easton and his friends. The green of Virian, of our birth clan.

"What would have become of me if you had left me in Virian after my mother's murder?" I'd wondered for far too long, had never believed it was more than a theoretical question until Easton came along.

Amaury grounded his teeth. "Kacy—"

I rebuffed his outstretched hand. "Tell me why marrying me off for stronger alliances is better than allowing them to groom me into my mother's replacement."

He put a hand to his gut, as if I'd plunged a knife there. "Kacela, those are not the same. You do not know the atrocities your mother faced."

"I heard them. Every night." The memories surfaced. The smell of mildew and the grunts of warriors. The orders they gave. Each was like a scab I couldn't stop picking. "You ask why I want to fight; it is because I know what evil does to the innocent when left unchecked. No one protected my mother. Not one protected me."

"I protected you."

"To ship me off to another?" I held up a hand, stopping his counter as if it were a thrown knife. A single flash of gold traveled from my pointer to middle finger. "I will continue to fight for every female in those camps that could have been me. If I cannot save the kingdom from the front lines, I will do it on another battlefield."

Amaury's hand wrapped around mine. He curled it, as if that would ball up my magic. His medals clanked together like warning bells. "Let this go, Kacela. Break the bond with Easton and marry Nalin. Stop fighting for another. Fight for yourself."

A shock of my magic danced through our clasped hands. A warning reflected in his widening eyes. "I won't. Understand?"

He left.

CHAPTER 12

THE ESTATES LEFT after the week of festivities. I'd been shackled to Nalin for its entirety, through the tournament and parties, to be released only in the eyes of gossiping ladies and courtiers, all who gave me a wide berth in wake of Jacinth's recounting of my explosion in the Tait library.

Easton and his friends left without a grand goodbye, having stayed to advise the estates on their trade routes through Forterian clans.

Then the estates, each parading through the castle as they had on arrival.

Nalin pulled me from the grand entry with a wave of his hand. He didn't offer me his arm as he led me away from pestering spies.

"You found your mate," he said, staring past my head toward the entry.

I straightened my ruffled skirt. "It matters not."

Nalin's glare dropped to me. "It does."

I let the masked smile fall, then shook my head. "Not to the king. Not to your father."

My chest tightened. The small hallway we stood in squeezed

in like a grasping fist, closer and closer, pressing me to a husband reluctant to accept me as his wife. The corset of my dress cut into my ribs at every staccato breath. I put a hand to its binding to convince myself someone wasn't lacing it tighter.

"Kacy." Black irises, so raven I could hardly distinguish them from the pupils, were too close. Nalin gripped my hands where they hung limply at my sides.

"If you tell your father—"

"No." His fingers wove between mine. "If it does not matter to him, then it does not matter to me. You are safe with me, Kacela, until my dying breath."

I needed to snap the mate bond.

In the nights between parties, I'd tried. I'd concentrated on the thin stream of magic stalled between us and imagined breaking it like one does a large branch over their knee. Like Pila has tried to.

Those efforts left me sobbing, curled in on myself. Crawling for the cool tile of bathroom and tucked beside the tub until the shivers relented.

I sought out Griffin in his office. Amaury was already there, discussing trade routes and an unfeasible budget. I took a seat on a chair pressed against the full-wall bookshelf.

I stared at the empty sheath on my leg, a reminder I hadn't located any of my weapons in weeks. Even the blades gifted to me over various birthdays. All gone.

The door creaked open. I spun, nails digging into the wooden armrests, but instead of Pila's oily presence slipping through, the royal spymaster entered and took a seat before the king's desk.

Ronan was slender, surprisingly so for how well he wielded a longsword. His skin was the color of amber. His chin-length hair was like oak bark, both in color and texture. He wore a tight, black tunic with deeper black detailing, ideal for slipping away into the shadows.

Griffin looked up. "You have a report?"

"The Forterians are not mobilizing. It seems their appearance was an isolated incident. Chief Daviat had very little knowledge of his general's whereabouts."

"You're certain?" Amaury asked.

Ronan nodded with a frown and tapped a quick beat across the armrest with his gaunt fingers. "My sources say the camp has been in a bit of a frenzy."

"Forterians have their own traditions when returning from war," Amaury said. "Those celebrations and mourning are now being put on hold to ensure Daviat doesn't lose his life to this bargain. With winter approaching and the daylight lessening, they scramble to prepare and train the females."

"What would you suggest?" Griffin rifled through papers.

Amaury leaned onto his knees. "Give them time. They will sort themselves out, eventually. These are allies, not children to be ordered about."

"Sometimes they act like it," Griffin muttered with a flurried wave of his hand. "My father dealt with their antics for the entirety of his reign. The quelling of a rebellious clan should remind them who stood victorious after the Great War."

Amaury stiffened, as did I.

"A month," Griffin continued, "then we'll go for a report on our way to close the crack."

Amaury lurched to his feet. "A month to wait to close the crack? If it splits, there are Forterian war camps within attack distance of it. It is on their Sacrament Land."

Griffin nodded, as if waiting for Amaury to say something that mattered.

The royal commander continued. "If Sacrament Land is attacked by demons, the clans will revolt. You'll lose an army and gain an enemy."

"As I said, extinguishing one rebellious clan will be enough to quiet the treasonous."

The wood of the armrests creaked beneath Amaury's grip.

Griffin leaned back, hands folding over his stomach. The late afternoon light streamed through the window, catching on his disheveled hair. The shadows were like thorns on his cheeks. "Is there a chance Virian will rebel?"

"Not with War Chief Daviat," Amaury said. "Proud, but levelheaded."

"What about clans nearby?"

"I have no news of unease in any," Ronan said.

Griffin scoured his desk for a note or letter within its clutter. "What of mutiny? If Chief Daviat were to be killed?"

Amaury stood. He gripped the king's ornate desk. "You cannot dispatch a chief without turning every Forterian against you."

"If he were killed," Griffin continued, "would his successor threaten rebellion? Would the youth who saw their mates ripped away by Kacy's win flock to him?"

The Demon War had not been enough spilled Forterian blood. The king hungered for more.

Amaury fell back to his chair. "Yes."

"You need to relax," Griffin instructed.

My hand stretched toward the desk. I saw it move in my head, willed it to happen, but lacked the grasp on my magic to send my desires into a tangible outcome.

"You're too tense. Magic flows freely, like a stream. It may stumble upon the rocks and branches in its path, but on the other side, it is smooth as silk."

I dropped my arm to my side and slumped back into the chair. "What if I go back to the book?"

"You can make that fly across the room. Repeating easy tasks will not make you any stronger."

"Griffin, what if I could help close the cracks?"

He smiled softly. "Even when you have full control over your magic, I fear you will not be strong enough to close a crack."

I nodded, stood, and raised my hand again, willing the desk to hover off the ground. It tremored and raised to eye-level, then fell.

Using magic was like wrapping strings around an object and ordering them to brace enough to raise it. My shoulders ached at the strain.

"That's better."

"You said you couldn't reach all the cracks because you would burn out. If I could funnel my magic into you, could you close the cracks faster?"

Griffin eyed me, leaning against the shelves beneath the window, arms crossed over his chest and hair falling across his brow. The Obsidian crown sat beside him, its points twinkling like starlight. "Why such an interest in closing the cracks?"

I raised my hands, floating the desk back to eye-level. The veins in my forearms bulged and my breath became ragged. "I saw war, the worst of it, on the front lines with the highest casualties. I never want to see Altun death in such abundance again. If I can do anything to help prevent it, I want to."

He stared through the windows toward the torches atop the castle walls. "This has nothing to do with seeing your mate?"

"I'll go to Pila tomorrow to have her snap the bond."

He considered the desk again. "It may be worth exploring, funneling your magic."

A grin broke out. "You think so?"

"I must admit, I had the idea years ago when the cracks first formed. It was my mistake not to close each of them as soon as they appeared. Curiosity delayed me. I now see how foolish I was to think we might explore a new realm without its beasts escaping into ours."

I raised the desk above my head.

"I'm leaving tomorrow morning to close a crack near Lady Taggart's borders. When I return, we'll look into funneling magic. We can start the training for it now if you're too eager to wait."

I grinned, and the desk shot to the ceiling. Griffin caught it with a web of black moments before it shattered into the decorative chandelier, then lowered it back to the floor.

"Your magic is like your consciousness. It spreads out from you," the black tendrils of his magic swirled around him, "if you will it to. You can utilize it as you please." The tendrils became a shield on his back. Then a ball on the desk. Finally, a sword in his hand.

I tried for the remainder of the night to present my magic to him, each attempt bleaker than the last. And as I left, he held the door slightly ajar with magic. "Kacela, do not visit Pila tomorrow. I fear snapping the bond will affect your magic, and we do not have time for you to recover."

I held my grin until I returned to my room and flopped onto my bed, the leach of Pila's magic squirming away once more. The mate bond squirmed as if it also knew I'd spared it another few days or weeks, and Easton's pulse on the other side crushed my excitement of closing the cracks. I threw up more barriers to silence the bond.

Every night until Griffin returned, I imagined my magic, the same gold as my hair and less opaque than Griffin's tendrils, spreading out around me. I lifted books, picturing the ropes of energy reaching for and tossing them into the air like hands juggling. The fretting of their leather spines tickled where they landed in its hold. Pages slipped through its trembling touch.

Every scrape of the fore-edge, itching through my magic to my thumbs. I couldn't still my breath with the anticipation of opening my eyes to sparkling evocations. The very same from the battlefield and to prevent Pila's grime from tainting my mate bond.

A flicker was all I needed. A single spark in the darkened room.

Yet when I ventured a peek, I saw only the rug squished between my toes.

My tears didn't fall, sloshed away by a jerk of my wrist.

It was safer to let Griffin down, to fail at presenting my magic to him, so I would not tag along to Virian. Yet, I could think of nothing else, and only when recalling my mate's smile did my magic rear its head from its hiding place deep in my gut.

I didn't want to see Easton, but my magic needed to. I needed to.

We met on the roof training field with Amaury the day the king returned. I thought of my mate, of the warmth of his feathers caging me to his chest and the brush of his fingers through my hair. The heat of his lips on my neck. My magic surged with my excitement. It spun from me and followed my consciousness to Griffin. To Amaury, I might've looked ready to soil my pants, my face squished and hands fisted in my sleeves.

Griffin, though, allowed a section of his walls to fall, sucking my magic through. His black tendrils strengthened, a thread of gold weaving in them and burning with light.

Amaury stepped forward to reach for the nearest black tendril, allowing it to wrap around his fingers and down to his forearm. I watched my magic taking tangible form as golden shadows bloomed through the night air, words unable to describe the bubbling in my gut.

Instead, I laughed.

I laughed while Griffin spun around shadowy tendrils laced with my gold, grasping at weapons and nearly knocking Amaury into the stands. Laughed as they stitched together into a black dome swirling with wisps of gold like stars in a clear night sky.

A tether connected my chest to Griffin's movements, each speckle of gold like a nerve ending. Each movement tugged harder than the last, until I felt the direct connection, as if I, too, could spin our combined power to my own will.

Griffin let the display wither away.

I forced away the gag at the vanilla-tinged ash clogging my throat.

He stared to where the last speckle of gold fluttered into the stars. "Pack your things. We leave for Virian tomorrow."

CHAPTER 13

VIRIAN WAR CAMP had not changed since I'd beaten Easton. Reminders of that day littered the camps, where elders of both genders hung laundry and girls smacked at practice dummies with wooden swords. Females my age wore aprons and skirts to train, stumbling in their folds. Their glares were sourer than those of the warriors who escorted us through camp.

Chief Daviat emerged from his tent. His thinker and brute advisors, along with Easton, trailed him. I avoided my mate to stare at the chief. Amaury stepped before me to meet their approach, and once more, I was a young girl peering over his shoulder at the spectacle.

"It is an honor, my King," Chief Daviat said through pursed lips.

"The honor is ours," Griffin purred.

"Amaury had sent word you would be visiting, though he failed to mention why."

"We have business to attend to on Sacrament—"

"The crack," the thinker said. He was silenced by Amaury's growl.

Griffin eased him back with a warning hand on his shoulder. "We'll have it closed tomorrow."

"I was about to send word. A demon slipped through yesterday. Our scouts killed it. One casualty. We hope other cracks are not widening as quickly as ours."

Griffin laid a hand on the decorative dagger at his belt. Amaury stiffened, as did I. Touching one's blade, in Forterian culture, was an act of war. I eyed every warrior within attacking distance, my hands creeping toward the sword at my hip.

"Unfortunately," Griffin said, "the cracks all differ in magnitude. We have eyes on each to monitor their pace. We believe their activity is dependent on the size of the horde pressing against them. As a crack widens, more demons flock to it."

Chief Daviat waved toward his tent. "Please, let us discuss the matter in private."

We followed.

Easton and the other generals stepped aside to let us through. I felt his stare on the back of my neck. I'd intentionally worn old leathers, pulled my hair into a simple bun, and forgone any makeup.

This was business between us, despite how the mate bond sang in our proximity. My fingers twitched to reach for him as they did for my blade, as if the slightest brush of his hand might quench the bond's unrelenting yearn.

One hesitant step and his front would collide with my back. His breath would graze my neck. He might even steady me with a callused grip. Overwhelming pine scent chipped at my control and called forth roaring blood in my ears until there was only him and the trivial space between us.

Then he was gone, putting the table between us.

I met his stare, shoulders back and head angled.

My breath wouldn't come, as if he'd snared me in a trap. He held me there in his gaze like a lame deer staring down death and hoping it would turn away. Because I couldn't. The longer we stared, the more intense the prickling of other's glances on my entranced features became.

"The crack is here," Chief Daviat said, "on Sacrament Land."

Easton's attention shifted to the map, and I was left with hollow abandonment. I rasped my fingers on the dagger strapped to my thigh and thought to loosen its clasp, as if that might release the tension coiling my lungs.

"Four months until the Sacrament," the thinker muttered. He touched the tattoo of swirls and spikes above his brow. Against his olive skin, the black seemed to be shadowed. It faded near his ears. "Only a portion of those who enter return. It will be even less so if they are to contend with demons."

"You'll need permission to enter Sacrament Land," Chief Daviat continued, his finger drawing the line on the map of where it began, "from all war chiefs, and then perhaps your presence will be permitted."

Griffin pursed his lips. "That will not be necessary."

"It is our sacred land," Chief Daviat pressed. "Only those participating in the Sacrament are allowed. There is powerful magic protecting it."

"Do you suggest we allow the crack to become large enough for demons to slip through as they did during the war?" The table creaked where Griffin leaned.

Amaury said, "In the time it'll take to gain the approval of fifty-two war chiefs, you'll have a demon horde devouring Virian and every other nearby clan."

I surveyed Chief Daviat, then the brute on his left and the thinker on his right, and finally to Easton. Their nostrils flared at every word of defiance from Griffin.

Hands clenched near their twin blades, but not on them. They eased them further from the pommels beneath Amaury's stare.

"There are provisions within the treaty," I added, "allowing the king and any personnel he deems necessary to cross Sacrament Land for the security of the kingdom. The current circumstances allow that provision to be invoked."

The thinker gripped his left blade. Easton flinched.

"Is her presence necessary?"

I held his glare and rested my hand on my own, larger sword. I eased it from the sheath. "I'm needed to help close the cracks. Without me, they might threaten your little warriors in their games of ego."

Others reached for their swords, including my mate, but his eyes were not on me.

Easton stared at his chief. He raised his blades from their sheaths enough for the steel to catch a lantern's light.

"Enough," Griffin commanded, his voice woven with his shadowed magic, and the resulting hint of ash tickled my nose.

Chief Daviat released his weapons. "Very well. You wish to cross Sacrament Lands, but my warriors will not escort you. You'll find your own way through the barrier. I'll have every war clan know—"

"That while your king dealt with a lethal problem on your lands, you sat in your tents like cowards," I mused.

Another puff of magic and ash itched my lips. A warning not to press further.

Easton pulled his swords a bit higher.

"Will you be staying long?" Chief Daviat surveyed the map.

Griffin rapped a knuckle against the wood. "Only the night."

The chief nodded, a dismissal as good as any other, and we turned to leave.

Only then did Easton release his blades.

My mate volunteered to show us around camp to see the bargain's fulfillment.

He walked a step behind Griffin and Amaury, who prowled the tents in search of training circles not overcrowded with males.

"We have them training further away from the others for their safety and comfort."

The females trained in a hastily cleared area at the northern edge of the camp. Rocks, leaves, and patches of upturned grass challenged their every step.

Many lounged in the shade beyond where a young, blessed warrior halfheartedly guided them through stances. Only a few wore ill-fitting training pants. Instead, they fought against their skirts, aprons, and loose, long sleeves. The flaps of aprons fluttered around simple footwork.

Easton continued, "All children under the age of ten are training together. We've given any of childbearing age or older the choice to train but have required basic self-defense. Here are the remainder."

"We've heard of disagreements about chores and duties around camp," I said over my shoulder.

"With any change comes resistance," Easton shrugged. "We're preparing for other clans to object, and we've settled disputes here effectively."

Amaury looked pleased. "Other camps will realize the benefits of having twice as many warriors."

The trainees noticed us, many of them dropping their blades to their sides. Some surveyed, others glared.

I licked the sweat from my upper lip. These may have been my peers, girls I could've shared chores and chased boys with.

I'd been born an outsider, and I returned an enemy.

Easton placed a hand on my sagging shoulders. "Some feel that you have taken their purpose in life from them. They value taking care of their husbands and children. They feel this has squandered that dream."

"They can still rear children and do household chores," I gritted through my teeth loud enough for them to hear. "Taking care of their family can extend to the battlefield, to saving their lives instead of ensuring they have clean underwear."

Some dropped their gazes. They returned to mirroring the stances and steps of their instructor. Others remained with broad shoulders, staring me down as I stared down my sparring opponents.

I grinned at their staunch resolve.

Easton excused himself from afternoon meetings I hadn't been invited to. Since he was the only one in camp not glaring at me, I trailed him toward the training fields.

He quirked a smile over his shoulder before allowing me to catch up. "I want to show you something."

We cut through the tents, past those doing chores, and emerged into a small clearing where boys and girls between the ages of three and six sparred.

I spied a blond girl with blue eyes and the same chubby cheeks I hadn't outgrown until age ten. I never asked Amaury if camp whores lived in proximity to their extended family, if I might spy my cousins or grandparents milling around Virian. I turned from the girl before I could recognize any more familial traits.

"You want a girl who'll make it through the Sacrament." His breath trickled across my turned cheek. He pointed to a little girl with kinky black hair held back into two small buns. Her swords swung in wide arches into her opponent's arms. He tumbled.

Blades forgotten, she fell upon him with open-hand smacks.

"Isn't the fight over?" I asked.

"He hasn't conceded."

I sprawled my hands. "There's no honor in beating a cowering opponent."

His hand snuck to my lower back. The tingle of heat from his palm dropped the tension from my stance. "There is no honor between children. Until they learn to value it, we discourage mercy."

The boy scrambled out of the small sparring ring. "I concede!"

At Easton's call, the girl's barred teeth widened into a grin, and she reached us in three bounding strides.

"Kacela, this is Trinity. She has four older brothers, all blessed, but no winged."

"I'll be the first," she gloated.

"How many have you beaten today?" Easton asked.

"Six."

"All boys?"

"And Ines."

Easton's hand dipped lower. His thumb skimmed the top of my pants. "Ines may also be ready for the Sacrament when she's old enough."

I followed Easton's other hand, pointing toward a blond in another circle.

"It's just a start," Easton said after Trinity picked a new opponent, "and it's satisfying the bargain."

I jolted as his hand attempted to steer me away, turning toward the main training area to hide my blush. "It is about more than simply preserving Chief Daviat's life."

He jogged to catch up.

I eyed the chief's tent as we returned to the sparring circles.

"They're discussing Sacrament preparations. Chief Daviat believed it'd take the afternoon."

"Did he send you to distract me?"

"I offered."

I picked a circle and stabbed my blade into the ground beside it. "You show your hand too easily, general."

"Perhaps you don't know the game, milady." His eyes, dancing with threats and promises, set a fire roaring up my throat to my cheeks.

"You think you can out politick me?" We toed a dangerous game with Griffin and Amaury only a flimsy panel of canvas away. Threatening the safety of hearts and the bond if our words and tones fluttered into the wrong ears. Threatening my marriage.

"I'd like to try." He offered practice swords to me. I gripped the hilts, and he yanked on his hold. Our chests almost touched, separated by the lengths of my forearms. His breath fanned across my face. I was forced to hold his gaze or relent and steal mine away. "Though I'm more persuasive in," his tongue darted to the bow of his upper lip, "other realms."

I wrangled the swords from him. "That's unnecessary, Easton."

"No tricks this time." He winked.

The crisp of winter had yet to touch so far inland, even if the northern bluffs reported scattered blizzards. Sweat pooled on my brow and lower back. I stripped the leather armor, revealing a tightly fitted black shirt beneath.

Easton's gaze dipped and returned to mine.

I sank into his warming gaze like plopping into a bath. "Are you insinuating you didn't enjoy it?"

A very dangerous game.

Easton leaned the blades against his leg and held my gaze. He loosened the ties of his armor to release the leather panels from his shoulders. Still, our gazes held. His armor fell into a pile. His shirt fluttered atop it. Retaking his swords in each hand with ostentation spins, Easton stepped into the circle.

I gulped away the blush rising like the high tide. To keep my emotions down and eyes from scanning the breadth of his shoulders, the definition of his torso, and the scars littering his skin.

He leaned close. "I thought you didn't want me, Kacela."

"I don't."

Any humiliation I'd dealt Easton left with the summer heat. Hushed whispers clogged the air around us. The warriors training in the nearest circles slowed their fights, attention on us.

Gone was the fury of the warrior I'd humbled, replaced by elated chuckles and far too many swings aimed at my backside. He worked in diversified patterns, feet never once crossing as they had. Twirls of his blades forced me to expose my back far more often than I'd care to admit, each time receiving a wallop of his sword against my butt. Then, he was gone, twisting away before I could bring my sword in a full arc to beat him back.

I spied the fleeing edge of his smirk through the hair loosed from my braid.

Kicked-up dirt obscured our graceful feet, knee slides, fallen blades, and outlandish swings. Every pass of breaths in our waltz, every heaved chest and lingering gaze, pushed the tide within me higher and higher. The mate bond sang its symphonies in our heavy breaths.

We'd drawn a crowd by our first water break and halted all training by the second. Mutters followed our flourished moves, useless in war.

I envied his swords for how tightly he held them. Envied the water he splashed over his chest. Hated every word from his mouth that was not my name.

The clearing of a gruff throat stilled Easton mid-swing. I tensed for the smack to my thighs that never came.

His glare flashed to the intruders of the fight. His blades fell to his sides.

"I hope she didn't beat you again." Chief Daviat's voice jerked the semblance of bliss from my grasp.

My toes dug holes where they pivoted to face my judge and jury. Amaury's chest nearly reached his chin before he released his irritation in a breeze-disrupting huff. Griffin pondered, lips even and head quirked.

I forced a laugh. "We'll call it a draw."

"A new training style?" Chief Daviat asked over his shoulder to Amaury. The squint of his glare brought decades' worth of wrinkles to his brow. "Wasting my general's time with antics?"

I couldn't hold in the snort of amusement, dropped my blades, and slapped my hand over my burning cheeks.

Chief Daviat's head cocked, then he marched forward until my neck ached to level my gaze with his. "Are you mocking me, child?"

"Step back," Easton said.

I didn't dare break my glare from Daviat to peer at my mate. His arm lifted, raising the hairs on mine where they brushed. He pressed the blade's wooden tip to Chief Daviat's chest.

"You're giving me order now, general?" Chief Daviat's chuckle shook my bones. "For an ungrateful mate who shamed you?"

"Step back," he repeated.

"That's a practice sword, boy."

Easton shielded me with his outstretched arm. "She is my mate. You will not harm her."

The air shifted as if a cold-front move through the camp. Black tendrils slithered from Griffin's outstretched hand across the training field. Shadow-flittering magic overturned rocks and toyed with the soles of our boots.

They crept up Chief Daviat's calves.

Easton dropped his practice sword in favor of gripping my arm. He stepped before me. A tendril slapped at his knee.

Screams of horror frenzied in the camp caged by Griffin's demands for submission.

I evaded my mate's grasp, stepped to his side, and unclasped the dagger on my thigh. "We came peacefully, without intention of a fight." My mouth was full of ash, but I would rather have swallowed mountains of dirt than break first.

"Chief Daviat." Griffin's tendrils climbed higher up his legs. "Move away from Kacela. To threaten her is to threaten me." His voice held the command of the king. Not even a chief could ignore his aura, plastering itself to every living being within the camp in its search for obedience.

Babies wailed, and I longed to join them.

Easton gripped my wrist. He broke through my barrier on the mate bond, and his desperation sloshed across, salty and stale.

Chief Daviat's panicked eyes surveyed the tendrils toying with the inseams of his pants. One reached the buckle at his waist and gave it a flick.

With hands raised, he pivoted around Easton and I, took two steps, unfurled his grey wings, and sprang into the air, heading north.

Griffin's magic slinked back to his outstretched palm.

I sucked in a clean breath

"Back to training," Amaury huffed. I turned to retrieve my blades, aware of the daggers he stared into my back.

CHAPTER 14

"I'M GIL." The blond brute's outstretched hand and arm was entirely marred in lines as wide as my little finger. He gripped my forearm as if I were a delicate flower he could crush with a breath.

The thinker gave no such consideration in his greeting. "Berel."

Easton's glanced between them and me, his eyes narrowed as if considering whether he needed to defend his territory.

I sat with my bowl of stew at the fire between their three tents, though Amaury glowered at my refusal of Griffin's dinner invitation. Such a public act toed the line Pila waited for me to cross. Waiting so she could retake the bond in her oily fingers.

"I've been telling him how idiotic he was," Gil explained through a mouthful of stew. "When you find your mate fighting in a war, she won't take well to being told to tend the tent."

I nearly spat my own food out. Easton aimed for his head with a toss of a wooden spoon and only struck wispy blond locks. "I didn't say that," he grumbled into his bowl.

"You did." I'd meant it dryly, only for the words to sound more like a sword thrust.

"I like her," Gil beamed.

Easton cracked a smile and nodded as he reached out, beckoning for the return of his spoon.

I'd seen Easton after battle, seen him threatening to kill, seen him dancing, and seen him trying to tear my clothing off. But this Easton, the carefree friend, I liked him the most. I fought the flutters in my stomach at his every smile and laugh. At how he skimmed a thumb against the back of my hand when he believed neither of his friends were watching. At his smile, wide enough to crease the scars into their own grins.

Gil took advantage of dinner to indulge me in Easton's childhood antics, while Berel grumbled details between bites. Easton broke his arm attempting to jump from an oak and scare Gil. The scar above his brow marked where a girl whipped a thorn branch into his awaiting kiss. He nearly skinned his arm in his first successful flight.

I drank in every story, even as the last glimmer of light faded, and tossed log after log onto our fire.

The other fires went out, leaving only ours, when Amaury appeared in its glow. "Your tent is there," he nodded away.

If I rolled my eyes, giving to the scorn of innocent affection. I'd be no different than the lord's daughters who dropped the hand of a general's son at their father's approach. But for once, I didn't mind.

Amaury's gaze sliced through me.

Easton stood as I did. "I'll walk you —"

"I can find my own way." I didn't wait to see the pain on his face. It hummed down the mate bond despite my blocks. With a pulse of magic, I volleyed it back to him.

I brushed past Amaury toward my tent, smaller than the others, where it sat nestled between his and Griffin's with a fire on the open side.

"No guards in the tent?" I asked with a sour tone.

"Go to bed. You need to rest for tomorrow."

The defiance must've rung in my eyes, swelling until it threatened to manifest into words. Amaury gripped my upper arm in an almost painful pinch. He dipped low, lips skimming my ear.

"I did not save your life for you to return as a Forterian's maid. Do not mistake this day for a future with the warrior he is not. This clan killed your mother. Do you wish to be its next victim?"

I swallowed my retort. Amaury's words watered the doubt seeded in the hours after the war. The stabbing pain of blocking the mate bond returned, splitting me in two. I curled my nails into my palm and gritted my teeth through its fiery rebuke.

"Go to bed," he repeated, grip softening.

I shoved aside the flaps of my tent and sank into the tiny bed covered in furs.

Despite the wind's whistle, the tent flaps were like stone.

I chucked a pillow at them, and a wall of magic shimmered where it struck.

Stretching my arms out on the bed, I was dismayed by how easily I touched both sides of the tent. The jitters of the mate bond, awakened by our proximity, was a rattle against the cage of my tiny tent.

I swiped my mind against every seam, connection with the ground, and hole repaired with a brown patch.

Perfectly sealed within the bubble of magic.

Again and again, I tested the barrier. Eyes closed. Eyes opened. Hands against the magic. Hands clenched into white-knuckled fists. The shield blocking me from the camp of my birth refused to yield. It snickered at me with its occasional flicker of black ash within the seams.

"Damn you," I grunted, smashing my fist into the magic. It shimmered. Crackles of gold snatched up dark pebbles and razed them from within.

I struck again, and more webs of gold cleared the ash.

The crack speared for the ground and fizzled out where dirt smothered it.

There, the wind whistled through, and my magic pounced. Temptation yanked me by the gut. I skipped, heaving at the pressure of not only sliding through the thin slice in the fabric of our world but also the seemingly inconsequential crack in Griffin's magic.

I appeared in Easton's tent, half a meter from the ground. My bare feet thudded into crinkly rug. A wisp of ginger floated from the tub.

The barest light seeped through patched holes in his tent, speckling Easton's face. My eyes adjusted. Black corners softened to a desk and chair, another to a dresser. Outlines of armor became detailed craftsmanship.

My mate, idle on his bed with one hand thrown over his eyes and the other clenching the patchy blanket over his waist, rolled toward me.

I held my breath. If he woke, I didn't know if I could pull myself from his arms once more. If he kissed me—

His head jerked the other way and fist raised the blankets to his chin.

I raced down the bond to his fretful nightmares. Across his face, his wrinkles and scars collided like the tides of an irate storm.

Again, the mate bond tugged, and again I answered with my own stumbling mistakes. I clambered onto the bed and him. The graze of my fingers against the scar on his right cheek snapped his eyes to life.

My word tumbled. My back hit the mattress and the blankets folded around me.

Fingers scraped up the column of my neck, stalling my breath.

I whispered his name, as my mother had whispered mine when waking me from the cupboard.

"Kacela?" he snapped.

"You were having a nightmare." I craned my neck to keep our noses from brushing.

They did anyway. Then his lashes, like a blizzard rolling in, crashed into my cheek.

His fingers flexed over the flutter of my pulse. I scratched at the blankets, squished my toes to feel the cool of the breeze, and pursed my lips. Nothing pulled my awareness from my mate's warm breath cascading over my cheeks and throat.

His nose skimmed mine again. I yearned to itch away the tickle his beard left across my cheek and jaw.

My hand collided with his sternum. "Easton. Stop."

Fluttering, closed eyes snapped back open. "What do you want?"

"I said, you were having a—"

"Not that," he muttered. His fist creased the pillow, causing my head to sink toward it. "What do you want with me?"

I blinked.

"You ran from me, Kacela." His fingers trailed to my sternum. "You left me not knowing where you went, if you were safe, or who'd taken you. You soiled my reputation by treating my home as a trial. And now you insist on remaining in my life despite repeatedly telling me you do not want me. If you are so damned insistent on forgetting me, reject the bond."

My lips floundered.

His fingers rode the line of my collarbone to peek beneath my shirt's collar. "Is it a jaunt for you Altun high lords and ladies to play with your subjects?"

The roll of his eyes froze my sour retort in wintry bitterness.

"And you wonder why we remain in our homes instead of mucking your pristine palace halls with our splendors."

I shoved his caress from my throat and lurched to meet his glare with one of my own. We kneeled, knee to knee, chests only a heave away from colliding. I hoped he felt the fury in my gaze. "Your splendors are to oppress half your population."

"Ironic," he jeered, "for an Altun to speak against oppression." Easton straightened, and no longer were our noses nearly brushing. I could snarl at his chin and glare at his nose. I had to crane to look up my nose at his gloating sneer.

"The Forterians lost the Great War. The Quillon Regime was merciful in allowing Forterians to continue their religious offerings to a vulgar deity."

Easton howled with laughter. He slumped onto his heels, and once more we were glare to smirk. "Allows us? As he has allowed his magic to scour the mountain and seep from within, soiling our holy land."

I stared at his accusing lips, but I wouldn't give doubt to Griffin's actions. Not to a Forterian general. "Your ancestors lost the war."

"What do you know of war, love? You saw one battle and soiled your pants."

"You lost one fight and did the same."

The laughter in his tone faded. Even his tussled hair, kinked at multiple angles, could not soften his glowering manner. "You are a court lady. Fate was cruel to lump me with such an arrogant lady-in-wait—"

"Fate was cruel to shackle me to a brute—"

His wings rustled. They reeked of him and whatever dirt he'd rolled them in. "I am not a brute." His tone resonated like a gong.

"A thug then," I snapped, "who attempted to keep me from fighting before he knew my name."

I flinched at the rush of wings snapping wide. One hand jolted to protect my face and the other reached to where my knife should have been on my thigh. I stared at his bared, berry-stained teeth past my outstretched hand.

Easton swatted it out of his face.

"I nearly watched you die, Kacela! Our best healers said you needed Altun magic, but none would come to our camps. I begged for their help." His snarl slid across the words as if they were the ice growing in my gut. "I would have traded my life for yours in that moment. And I would trade every moment since to keep you from risking your life in another war."

I tried to wet the cracks of my lips. "That is not your choice to make."

"I am your mate," he argued.

I jolted when his hands cupped my shoulders. They smoothed the collar of my shirt in their trek to my neck. Warmth flooded from his touch, pooled in my gut, and pattered at my fingertips.

Wings glowed with the faint light flurrying through the tent flaps with the breeze, illuminating him in a full-bodied halo. They twitched around me.

His fingers angled my glare up.

I burned beneath his gaze, willingly.

"If you never see me nearly die in your arms, you will not understand. You are my mate. You are mine to protect."

"Yours to keep?" I dared.

His fingers curled into my skin. "I'll do what I have to do to protect you."

I couldn't get away from his grasp fast enough. His attempt to capture my shoulders spun me into the cocoon of blankets.

They wrapped around my bent knees. They constricted my ankles. They locked me onto my mate's bed when swords lay within grasp. They were the same shackling threats as marriage.

"Kacela—"

"Stop!" I slammed into the scratchy rug. It tore at my loosened hair. My legs, still encumbered in blanket, squirmed behind my dragging arms. I grasped his sword and rolled to defend myself, only to meet bulging eyes and stiff limbs.

Easton stared at me from his spot on the bed, frozen as he'd been when reaching for me.

Only then did I feel my grip on his consciousness as I felt it on the sword. He jostled and screamed against my magic's hold, yet not a sound rattled the tent.

I dropped him and the blade. "I'm sorry," I blurted. "I didn't mean to."

Easton lurched onto his hands. His chest heaved and stomach rolled. "Altun magic. Born, not earned." He spat. "You are a plague on my kind. There is no peace. There will never be peace. We've lived with your king's throne on our backs for too many generations. The Great Blunder may have wiped our names from history, but it did not defeat our warriors."

I untangled my legs from the blankets.

"It gave us a taste for Altun blood." He lifted his scowl. "And we want more."

CHAPTER 15

OUR FEET CRUNCHED GRASS. Griffin snatched my arm to prevent my tumble.

"Long night?" he asked, lips quirked.

I'd skipped from Easton's tent in the wake of his continent shattering declaration, yet the echo of his threat rattled my dreams. Our armies, drenched in blood, ran from the might of Forterians. War chants promised death. Blades disemboweled. Forterians cackled at our pleas.

Amaury dismissed my jolt awake as nerves. I didn't tell him nor Griffin at breakfast that my lack of appetite stemmed from where the murderous Easton in my dream plunged a sword through my gut.

We left before the sun broke the horizon and my mate woke.

I arched my back, satisfied at the crack and release of the ache from my spine. "The tent felt a bit small."

"Smaller tents are easier to protect," Griffin said.

We reached the edge of Sacrament Land, and though I saw no barrier, I felt the hum of the magic surrounding it.

I raised a hand to it. The barrier swaddled my fingers in warmth. It eased me back. Not a rebuke, but a parry. As if to say, not yet. "They said only Forterians in the Sacrament can enter."

Griffin placed a hand on the barrier. "There are always exceptions with magic, Kacy. "It shimmered beneath his touch. A pulse of black spread through the air like spider webs. Still, his hand remained raised in the air, same as mine.

He tried again. The black webs dissipated a breath after they appeared.

I reached for my magic. The stench of Easton's disgust at my innate, Altun magic rolled through me. It lurched forward, as if to escape, and tested itself against the barrier.

My hand fell through, then his. I looked to my king, but there was no celebration on his lips. Only contemplation.

We entered Sacrament Land, the sacred land of the Forterian soldiers, where they fought one another to the death to prove their feral dedication to their goddess of war and earned their blessings. Thirty-eight days on the mountain side, exposed to the elements, equipped with only the leather armor they wore. No weapons. No food.

At the center, a mountain with a single peak loomed over four different terrains: desert in the south, rolling hills on the east, jungle in the north, and swamp in the west. Where we entered within the grassy hills, the nearby jungle's humidity licked at my skin. The divides between ecosystems were as staunch here as they were on a map. A thick wall of vines, saturated in magic to keep the climates nearly separated, hung from towering trees, blocking the light from the jungle floor.

Griffin nodded forward. I fell into step behind him.

He skipped us short distances until our boots hit snow high up the mountain, but the warmth of the jungle remained within the pooling sweat on my lower back.

We walked for another hour, Griffin allowing his magic to guide us around the mountain toward the crack. It slinked ahead. In its wake, a path of ash.

The crack within the Valley of Ulyerse had rippled darkness, distorting the demon-soiled land. It'd been as cold as the snow leaking through my boots. Promised death with every pulsed release of contorted, black demons.

In comparison to the world-shattering rift, this was merely a slice. It hummed instead of screamed with otherworldly presences. It was cold, but not frigid, like the first fall breeze fluttering through yellow- and orange-tinged leaves.

A child's prod instead of soldier's clamor.

I willed my mind toward it. It met my curiosity with its own, inspecting me as I inspected it. Shadows fluttering from the crack intensified in their tangles. Opaquer than Griffin's tendrils of magic, they waved in the gale rolling up the mountain. They weaved between my fingers.

I inched toward it, guided by a pull on my hand.

Griffin grasped my shoulder. "It yearns for death."

It drew me further and further toward it, laying out a path for me to plunge deep within the demonic realm.

I felt life in the bleeding rift. I felt the pain and regret of a soldier left to die.

But "yes" was all I said. The crack scrambled for me like a child reaching for its mother's hand. "Why didn't we skip directly here?"

"Sacrament Land holds too much magic. I couldn't track it to an exact location due to the interference." He turned back to rift. "Are you ready?"

My magic gathered without my command, hammering at my walls to be released. I presented it to him.

Black tendrils shimmering with golden twirls crept toward the crack.

He slapped at it. Gold, ash, and wisps of shadows collided in sparks. A surge of power struck back, sending a ping through my magic and back to me, like a bee sting in my chest.

It awoke something within me, something humming with desperation. I sank into myself to find it.

Whatever it was, it ached for the mountains eagerly as it had yearned for Easton, and with the same dread it'd shuddered with beneath the gaze of yellow eyes.

Nearby, a cave screamed for me. A small speckle of black within the flurry. A line tethered me to it, yanking at my core.

A blizzard ruptured the clear sky, as if conjured. Snow pelted us. The winds howled and whipped the trees in the jungle at the base of the mountain like weeds.

I fell to my knees and clutched my hands over my ears to block out the mountain's wail.

The same curiosity of the crack raced from the cave to shred through my grasp on my magic. It crashed over me like the tide and dragged my consciousness with it as it receded back to the depths of the mountain.

Griffin grabbed my shoulders and screamed through the wind.

I fumbled to follow his voice, my consciousness nearly at the cave mouth. It blared in my mind like a warning horn. Its mouth swallowed me whole and gulped me into the grasping shadows of its bowels.

Accusations screamed at me. I swam in their stone-like faces. Their lips and hands drowned me within their fury.

I threw my head back and shrieked with them.

Blinding light, flaring from where their pain and sorrow prodded at my gut, mangled the shadows into squirming shards of black.

The wind died. The thrashing clouds dissipated.

Griffin eased my hands from my ears and stroked soft circles on the backs of them. My breath dropped in juts.

"This place reeks of rabid magic," he whispered with a light-hearted chuckle. "Freak storms are bound to happen. Perhaps the goddess is not pleased with this blemish on her mountain."

I looked past his shoulder at the cave. A shadow moved through it, snaring my attention. Then, it disappeared before I could betray its presence to Griffin.

"Kacela, are you alright?" He held me at arm's length and surveyed me. Taking an extra second on my face where my hair was plastered to it with sweat.

Spurred by Griffin's gaze following mine to the cave, I

evened my breathing and grounded myself in the crease of his sleeves in my grip.

I squeezed his arm. Blue, curious eyes flickered back to me. "I thought I saw something in the cave."

A wisp of ash tickled my nose. A black tendril, thin as a spider's web, shot from his outstretched hand and rode the dying winds up to the cave. It disappeared within, and Griffin closed his eyes. His grip on my arms slackened.

"What is—"

His eyes snapped open. His lips curled and he stared at the cave for another moment. "Magic should not live so wildly, Kacy. It is meant to be controlled." The string of his magic dissipated.

"Did you find something?" I asked.

Griffin shook his head. "We are safe." He appraised me, giving my arms another squeeze. "If you're done or too tired, tell me. I have the strength to close this on my own."

Trying to decipher the lies from his expression, I shook him off and reformed my magic around him, though it came with dragging feet. "No, I'm here to help."

Griffin stitched the slice closed with our entwined power, starting at the top and working his way down until the seams were airtight and it shimmered out of existence. He brushed his tendrils back through it to check. The air around us didn't ripple. The curiosity disappeared, and I felt, much to my surprise, unsettled by loss.

He'd done it, and made it seem so easily.

My magic refilled the warmth in my gut. I collected it like it was the first rain after a drought and I hadn't drunk in weeks.

"There are two more cracks within skipping distance, off Sacrament Land. Do you have the energy to close them, or shall I return you to Virian?"

I tore my eyes away from the cave. The promise of a warm bed tempted, but Easton's accusing glare threatened to unravel my conquests today. Past that, my mistakes on the battlefield demanded atonement.

"I can do it."

We skipped from Sacrament Land.

I landed on my knees before the second crack. Griffin hauled me to my feet, arm strict beneath mine. Then, he was less gentle with the third crack, nearly impatient. He yanked at my magic at the first hint of a whisper of gold. He spun it from me like thread from a spindle.

He clutched my magic despite the pain I fell limp to. I weathered this test of my resilience silently, gritting my teeth through the wintry tingles beginning in my toes and traveling through my veins until the warmth seeped away. Coldness washed over me like I'd been dunked in an icy river.

Burnout. I felt it dragging me to the riverbed.

I tumbled to my hands and knees. "Stop," I managed, my voice a raspy cough.

Griffin spoke, but the words blew away like ash in the wind. Gold freckled my cheeks.

My elbows gave out, and I pitched to my side. I watched him, between the slits of my fingers, stitch closed the crack with gold and black tendrils.

My magic slinked back, attempting to fill the hole in my chest where the warmth had been.

I rolled my face into the prick of pine needles scattered on the forest floor. Griffin's boot prodded my shoulder before it rolled my unblinking gaze to the sky.

The black veil of Griffin's magic fell over my consciousness, and through it I saw the cave again and felt Griffin's curiosity like a hound on a scent.

"Like calls to like," Griffin mused, his breath a jolt to my cheeks. I blinked away the numbness enough to see the king's blaring blue eyes gazing up at the cloudless sky.

We skipped. The warmth of a bath startled the frigid cage around my breath, only for it to settle back, a constricting net and suffocating gag.

Amaury crept into my room the next morning. His usual stringy hair was matted down, as if he'd spent the day running his hands through it. His clothing was slightly ajar, shirt untucked and belt too loose, so his sword swung against his hustle.

I folded into his chest with my remaining energy.

"I'm proud of you, Kacy, as is Griffin." he said, despite my tears. Instead of bragging, a sob seeped out of my brittle lips. He flicked a tear away with his thumb.

The warmth in my chest faded with the sunset. By the next morning, the dull ache disappeared as well. Like an empty tomb I continued down into the pits of, I felt nothing, not even a bottom to bring my fall to a crushing end.

Dull, unending eternity.

There was no sway to the suffocating daze and no fight to alleviate it. Golden bits of my magic swirled out of reach. They searched for their spot within the puzzle whose image remained a taunting ghost to me.

The servants brought food, cut into manageable pieces, and pressed a cup to my mouth with the command to drink. Healers ran their magic across me. Days passed into nights and back without my acknowledgement.

Talk of how to cure me fluttered through the ajar door: More time and space, less coddling, forced walks, or bringing weapons to the room to train. It was as if they didn't notice clutching the blanket tighter exhausted any energy I'd sucked back in the hours of deathlike stillness.

Only at my mate's name did my heart break from the sturdy, weak rhythm.

"I'm not allowing him within this castle," Griffin said.

Amaury's shadow was cast against the cracked door. "Are you willing to sacrifice her life for your stubbornness?"

"She's burned out. Rest will heal her."

The mattress sagged beneath someone's weight, and I involuntarily rolled with it. A hand rubbed my shoulder. Amaury pressed a kiss to my clammy brow, though I didn't feel the warmth of his breath. I saw, but didn't feel, his bangs sweep across my forehead.

He pinched my arm. "You must leave this bed. Please, Kacela. If you value your life, get out of the bed."

The door creaked and death slithered through.

"Leave!" Amaury snapped.

"King Quillon sent for me." Pila's voice left me wandering through a maze without an end, chased by her polar sting. Her robes did not sway as she walked, but the shadows pulsed with her every step, coating her path in black. They distorted the snowy skin beneath her robes and blended with the wavering tattoos across her bald head.

"Leave," Amaury repeated.

She raised her black hand. Her ring finger was missing, the red of the skin like a drop of blood against the black shadows tingling around it. The red of her eyes sparkled like rubies. "I can help." Her voice was as icy as death and clouded the hole in my gut where magic once billowed.

A threat, not an offer.

Amaury blocked the hallway light from my face. "She's not strong enough."

Her consciousness flew past the patter of the mate bond, burrowing deeper toward my very core. She plucked at the sparks. I felt the shadows of the cave rising again, another tide to sweep me under.

Amaury pulled his sword from its sheath and pointed it at her throat, but the priestess of the Old Faith did not waver.

"Leave," Amaury commanded, "before I separate your head from your shoulders."

She pressed a blackened hand to the top of the blade and eased it down, away from her covered throat. "She will not die," Pila said, voice as slick as ice. "She has more to live for."

Two arms swept under me that night, or perhaps the night after. I hadn't turned when the door cracked open, casting my tomb in a low white glow. If death had arrived to whisk me away, I'd go silently. My only sense had been of Pila's swaying robes patrolling my wing. The elongated shadow sweeping beneath my door. Her presence like sticky humidity.

With me in his arms, Amaury climbed the stairs to the roof and took off into the night. I remembered flights with him when I was young. My love for the stars hanging above our heads. The tickle of clouds rolling down my cheeks. The city, it's lamps and torches, mirrored in the stars, winding around the gushing Vitient River.

I remembered it as if it were a painting I'd seen once.

When the city lights converged to become one on the horizon, hurried flaps became an even soar.

We stopped when orange replaced the gray dawn. Branches shaded where Amaury paced. Leaves fluttered onto my brow, scraped against my temples, and gathered in my lap.

When night fell, he left.

Abandoned, by magic and family.

I sank into the bed of leaves, and dew soaked through my clothes.

The thud of two sets of boots shook my breath. A tear slipped down my burning skin, dry from the night's flight.

Swiping away the tear, a callused palm cradled my cheek. Furrowed brows and curls like knobs of an oak branch blocked the embrace of the morning sun.

"What's wrong with her?" he asked.

"Burnout," Amaury replied. "Magic has a cost, and when it needs more than the wielder has, it takes from them."

"Why have you brought her here?"

"She needs you."

Easton's thumb brushed the flutter of my lashes. "She hates me."

"You hate her, but not enough to let her wither away."

He peered over his shoulder, though his hand did not retreat. "How long will she have to be with me before she is healed?"

"I don't know."

"The king—"

"I'm disobeying his orders by bringing her here. When I return, he could kill me for treason. You may hate her, and she you, but she nearly gave her life to close every crack within striking distance of your home. This is a small repayment."

Easton returned his gaze to mine, lips pursed.

"Fine." He jostled my hanging limbs, like those of a willow, into his arms. Wings unfolded to block the sun. His knees bent, and then he straightened. "Why hasn't she rejected the bond?"

Every finger ached and every nerve wailed at the clench of my hand around his shirt.

"Help." The word, hardened like a stale crumble of bread, tumbled out.

Widened green eyes snapped down. He curled me tighter to his chest, pressed his nose to my hair, and inhaled.

"If you reject her now, she will die."

His chest quaked around his exhale. "She will live," he declared, "and heal, until I can reject this cursed bond."

My heart floundered around the bit of hope seeping back to my gut, only to feel it wilt in my next breath.

Amaury nodded. "As long as she lives."

CHAPTER 16

I WOKE TO WARMTH and a clearing head. Muscles seized around each movement to press my cheek away from the pillow, but they moved all the same. Cool breeze flittered across my lips and soaked my tongue in lavender. Then, heat, like the steam of a tub, soothed the raised hairs on my arms.

Something rustled behind me, and I had half a mind to tell whoever disturbed my sleep to run off before I threw a dagger into their gut. The scent of pine robbed me of the threat.

My heart reared into my throat.

"You're awake."

The blankets twisted around my scrambling body. I whipped my head, kinking my neck in the process, to glare across my mate's tent at his bland stare.

My words fumbled with my memory.

"The healer wasn't sure you would," he continued, wiping the back of his neck with a towel. Sweat splattered his forehead and dampened his curls, darkened his shirt beneath his arms.

He peeled the shirt off and tossed it into a corner with a pile of equally rancid clothing.

Musk caged me in its pine-tinged grasp. The blankets, the

pillows, and the thin shirt I wore all smelled of him. I gathered the top blanket up to my chin.

Amusement quirked his brow. "I changed you, Kacela. Bathed you. Helped the healers attend to calls of nature. There is nothing of you I haven't seen."

"How dare—"

"I could have let you die." His words squeezed my breath.

"Die?" I hitched the blanket higher until its tattered edge tickled my lip.

"Do you not remember?"

"Remember what?"

He unclipped his belt and placed his swords against a rack with other weapons. A longsword leaned against an axe, its point buried in the pile of daggers and arrowheads.

Leaning against the edge of the steaming tub, Easton kicked off his pants.

I pulled my eyes from the contours of his torso and gloating smirk, instead assessing the rest of the tent. Every shadow I'd seen in my past visit gave way to more clutter. A frumpy pillow sat on a chair tucked beneath a desk stacked as high with papers and letters as Griffin's. A stool with uneven legs sat in another corner. There was a dresser with a door half-ajar, socks spilling out.

My memory raced, beginning at my last visit to Virian and meeting a dead end at the third crack. A whisper seeped through the wall, barring my memories.

Burnout.

"What happened?" My intended rambling, saturated with petty insults, stilled at Easton's content face. Splendor spread his lips into a knowing smile, as if it alone dared me to look down at his naked body drooping into the tub.

Water splashed at the rim.

"You don't remember."

I lost his gaze for a downward glance to where the water rippled against his torso. My grip on the blankets tightened and raised to shield the thundering pulse in my neck.

"You don't remember begging for me to take you back—"

"I would never!"

"Pleading with me to accept you—"

"Stop!"

"To protect—"

I threw off the blankets, unbothered by the sag of shorts around my hips and the thinness of the white shirt in my haste to reach the tent flaps. Easton's laugh chased me from it.

The noon sun welcomed me, as did a roaring fire and green grass scoured in leaves the color of my roaring cheeks.

"You're awake." Gil, the blond brute, sat on the log beside the fire. In his hand was a bowl of stew. The scent of caramelized onions and roasted mushrooms rose from it.

My stomach rumbled. I stared at the vessel in his hands.

Gil cleared his throat. "I can get you some."

"She can get it herself." Easton emerged behind me. His thigh brushed the back of mine. His breath scattered my hair across my shoulder. "Other side of the camp." He pointed over my shoulder toward a trail of smoke rising to the darkening clouds.

I turned. Our chests nearly brushed.

Water rolled from his shoulders to gather at the towel gripped at his waist.

I stared at a single bead in its course across ridges of pale scars littering his chest.

The mate bond erupted, weakening my knees. I wanted nothing more than to fold myself into the heat of his gaze. To give in to the urge to trace the water trickling down his torso.

I retreated a step and relinquished my bit of dignity, dropping my gaze to his neck. Another look at his clenched jaw and flaring nostrils would've sent me fleeing in search of food, even if it meant parading through Virian in my disheveled state.

"I…" but the words wouldn't come beneath his scrutiny.

A vein bulged at his neck, then his jagged breath released. "Gil, when you're done, grab another bowl. See if you can double the serving. She hasn't eaten in days."

The weight unfurled from my shoulders. Shame replaced it,

reminding me whose clothing I wore, whose tent I once again burst from.

Without another word, Easton returned to his bath.

I stared at the swaying flaps, hating the regret billowing within me and fighting the urge to beg for my mate's arms.

Fighting the urge to cry.

"We don't have more beds," Easton said as the dinner bowls were taken away by a young girl and both Gil and Berel retired to their tents. "You've been sleeping beside me for a week. Now, at least, I won't have to dress you."

I stared at the sizzling coals. Ash akin to Griffin's magic floated from them and gathered at my bare feet. The creases of the log I sat on no doubt were tattooed across my rear. I ached as deep as I could feel.

It all ached.

I couldn't pull myself from the spot, even to look around at those who strolled by.

"Amaury brought you." Easton sat beside me on the log. His leg brushed mine. The ache subsided.

"When?"

"A week ago. You extended too much energy closing the crack. He called it burnout." He offered me a water flask.

I sipped it. "I remember closing the third crack. That's all."

"I told Amaury I'd reject our bond when you were strong enough to handle it."

The world dropped from beneath me.

"I don't think you're there yet. Maybe in a week. Then, you can return to Kadea and stay away from me."

Crisp air broke the darkness blanketing me. It ushered in waves of blood to crash over and drown my screams. My fingers stuck to one

another as I scrambled to wipe the warm liquid from my eyes. More came to soak through my clothing and squish beneath my toes.

I slipped, and the world opened.

A shadowed skull yanked me forward with every wheezing inhale. It became a mountain and its eye became a cave. I tumbled into it.

Blood choked back my scream.

My back hit stone. My head rebounded off it with an echoing thud.

Spinning, I felt the accusations in their eyes and the pleas on their lips as if they were arrows aimed true. Each sank deeper than the last, riddling me with searing wounds. Wrecking me with jeers and taunts.

I shot up. Easton's arm caught me. His fingers traced the line of my jaw into my hair, where they anchored in the sweat-slicked locks, holding my gaze to his.

Moonlight breached a single tear in the canvas above our heads and haloed Easton in its glow. With his chin tilted up, he allowed the beam to catch his eyes and glow within them like the sunset on a rolling hill. Beckoning with every wavering breath.

I gripped his forearm where it stretched across my lap and matched my breathing to his.

The realization that we were not fresh from the war began in my toes, like stepping into a glacial bath, and traveled up to where our skin connected. Though it stung like needles, we were a statue frozen in eternity for those few breaths.

I choked and dropped my gaze. "I'm fine."

"You had nightmares the last few days as well." His fingers slid from my hair.

Brushing away his grip, I threw off the blankets and walked to the pitcher of water on the edge of his desk. Lukewarm, it did little to beat back the tide of heat rising in my gut from where the mate bond teased.

"What are your nightmares?"

"Being shackled to a Forterian brute." My laugh morphed into a cough, and I took another swig of water.

Easton scoffed. "Rather be married to a pompous lord?"

"You should have left me on the battlefield to die." I took

another swig of water to occupy my tongue from sprouting trifle insults.

In the darkness, I could make out only glimpses of the letters laid out on his desk. A name of another clan in the northern half of the continent, a chief's name Amaury would know, a seal torn in two.

"That is my usual nightmare," Easton muttered.

I peeked over my shoulder, feigning dulled interest. "Your nightmare?"

"A demon tearing you apart. And then me."

I turned back to the desk so he would not see the part of my lips. I drew in a full breath to calm the jump of my stomach. To unclench my jaw. "The cracks will all be closed soon."

Easton was still seated, as he had been when I jolted away. His back to me. I stared at the shake of his shoulders and where his fists knotted in the blankets.

"Did I wake?"

He glimpsed me over his shoulder.

"When I had nightmares over the last week. Did I wake?"

"No." He eased back into his bed and pulled the blanket above his waist. I set the water down on the edge of the table. My finger knocked a letter to the floor. It opened, but my curiosity died at Easton's sputtering sigh. "You spoke," he continued. "You begged not to go into the cave."

I stepped back to the bed and curled under the blankets, back to him. "Odd," I mused, "to have a fear of caves when I've never been in one."

"Perhaps it's what's inside the caves you fear."

I yawned. "Perhaps."

If Chief Daviat knew of my presence, he made no attempt to draw me from the small circle of Easton, Gil, and Berel's tents. None within the camp ventured close enough for me to hear their hushed gossip, though I sat on the log for the next three days, staring at the fire and soaking in the warmth of the sun before winter whisked it away. By then, though, I'd return to the magically warmed gardens of Kadea.

Something unsettled the camp. I could feel it in my bones. The burnout seeped from them, replaced by the decay of something. Yet, like my memories, I could not piece together the premonitions nor describe them.

"The mountain is angry," Gil told me at breakfast on the third day after I'd awoken.

"It's a mountain," I quipped.

"You are thick," Berel said. He sat across the fire, as far as he could scoot on the log from me. Letters overfilled the bag at his feet. He held two crumbled notes in his hands. "It is not just a mountain. There is innate magic living within it."

"Forterians do not have innate magic."

"You were less annoying on your first visit." Gil handed me a bowl of porridge. He wore a thin white shirt through which I could see every black line of his blessing, outlining and enhancing every major muscle. "Less high and mighty."

"Pompous." Easton emerged from the tent. "She hid it better before."

I didn't bother to argue with him. A few more days. My strength and the itch to leave the camp grew with each of their glares. Yet, I couldn't deny that I weakened in the hours Easton spent training, on patrol, or in meetings.

"We've seen shadows pouring from the caves in the mountain," Berel continued. He slid a nail through the next letter's seal. "Sound familiar?"

I scrunched my brow. "The king is not interfering with Sacrament Land."

"Then explain the smoke and raining ash." Gil stabbed into his breakfast with his spoon. The tattooed lines of his blessing flexed as his jaw clenched. They darkened with every pulse, stark against his pale skin as they ran up his neck into his blond locks.

I looked at the clear sky. "I know it's not him."

"How?" Berel demanded. The letters piled at his feet, his hand rested upon the dagger strapped to his thigh. His hair, like tangled string, fell over the Thinker Blessing on his brow.

My nostrils flared. "If he had been on the mountain before, he would not have struggled to enter Sacrament Land when I was with him. Whatever has poisoned your mountain, it is not Altun made. Find another to blame for your decaying society."

"Would you swear your life on that?" Easton asked.

I glanced at the knife on his belt. "My life?"

"That it is not your king causing this plight."

"I'd swear it on my mate's life."

Easton and Berel shared a look before the Thinker jumped from his seat, twisting on one hand against the log, and disappeared within his tent.

Gil scooped up Berel's forgotten breakfast and dumped the contents into his own bowl. "I hope you're right," Gil said. His voice sagged. "I hope it is not the king."

CHAPTER 17

"I CANNOT LEAVE if I cannot fight," I argued with Easton. "Going to the training fields will kill you. Chief Daviat is furious I hid your presence here, and your claim it is not the king affecting the mountain worsened it."

"It is not Griffin!"

He didn't look away from the work at his desk. "It doesn't matter, Kacela. You forced this clan to go against our traditions and made us a target. You're lucky to still have your head."

I slid from the bed. "You're awfully worried about me keeping my head."

"You keep your head so Amaury doesn't take mine."

My jaw twitched at the scratch of Easton's writing. "Is there no clearing nearby? Somewhere I can train without any knowing?"

His shoulders sagged. "Ask Berel. He'll take you out in the woods. Just leave me be to work."

I rushed to change into the smaller pants and training shirt Easton had acquired from some of the younger boys and hopped from the tent with one boot on. Berel sat on a log at the fire, sharpening a dagger. Though he worked at a steady beat, he titled his chin back to catch the sun's glow within his ebony skin.

"Easton said you could take me into the woods to train, so others wouldn't see."

One eye peeked open, brown as the planks across Kadea's northern water gardens. "I know a place."

We trekked an hour through tightly packed pine trees until we reached a clearing. It was twice the size of Easton's tent. Footprints had stomped the grass into yellow debris.

Berel dumped practice swords from a sack.

"Twin blades?" I picked two of them up.

"We're training in all forms of combat." He picked up a long-sword. "I prefer archery."

"Why? You can't shoot from the front lines."

Berel scoffed. He twirled the blade in his hands and motioned for me to attack.

My strength lagged my movements. I tumbled across my own feet, clanked my blades across each other, and missed openings. Berel played with me as Easton had. He picked at my hesitations and exploited my weaknesses, all with a blade traditionally wielded by Altuns.

"Easton lost to you," he scoffed when I flopped onto my back after an hour of battle, swords discarded.

I only had the strength to roll my eyes.

Berel squatted beside me. His breath came in gusts tinged with breakfast's oats. He pressed the blade into his knees, balancing on his toes with perfect stillness. "I do not need to smash at the front lines to prove myself useful in war. I am what you should fear: a warrior with a brain."

Dew from the morning seeped through my clothing to my drumming muscles. It drenched the call for war I felt when I picked up blades.

"I would give my life for Easton's," he continued. "You have a loyal mate who'd give his life for yours if you asked. Instead, you spit on him and us with your every breath. You're pathetic, and the sooner you recover, the sooner you foul another's life with your affliction."

I fought the tears gathering in my eyes harder than I'd fought him.

"Virian is to the north. Lord Lael's Estate is directly east."

I felt the chill of his words as I felt his absence and the choice he laid at my feet.

Easton was called away to a meeting after dinner, leaving me alone in his tent. Only the small lamp he left me lit the beige canvas in a soft orange.

I blew it out and relit it with my magic, shifting the glow to yellow. The energy building within me was like the gathering clouds of a storm. Darker and darker, they loomed.

Soon, I'd have enough for a downpour.

The tent reeked of my mate, no matter how often I beckoned a night breeze to ruffle the canvas flaps. Pines surrounded us, and the wintry air did little to cool the growing heat within the tent. Every moment sleeping beside one another was another twig on the flame. Another thread weaving through the mate bond to strengthen its hold.

Letters scattered his desk like fallen leaves. I'd seen Berel attempt to organize them once or twice, only for Easton to ruffle through the stacks, dispersing them once more.

The envelope seals were ripped, not sliced, apart. Their frayed edges were like a jagged wound. The letters were shoved back in with crinkled corners and smudges from oily fingers.

I pulled one from the middle of the stack. It'd been torn clear in half, only the bottom part was shoved back into the envelope.

> *Chief Daviat's temperament will hold back the youth. Keep Indiviar and his lackeys at bay in training. Remind them a move against Daviat is a move against yourself and threatens worsening conditions*

with many northern clans. No matter if it may
enhance his favor in the south.
    Keep your blades sharp,
    Raff

I paged through more letters. Lies of restricted movement and increased security to keep southern clans from sending their boys to the Sacrament. Inflammatory words meant to tempt revolt.

Lies, all of it.

I burst from the stifling tent. The night air reeked of pine. It ruffled through my hair as needles crunched beneath my bare feet and pricked at my heels. The trees bordering the camp closed in like a marching army.

I looked up to the midnight sky. Twenty years had not dimmed the dwarfed feeling of staring at the stars above Virian. The longer I glared at their twinkling taunts, the smaller I felt. Like I was no more than the girl hiding in a cabinet, wearing clothing sewn from sacks and sleeping on a lumpy pillow smelling of mildew.

I set off through the camp, twigs and pines making my trek like that up a mountain. The moon lit my path through the clumped tents and fires bursting with those who turned a blind eye to my wandering.

Only when I reached a tent at the western edge did I halt.

A red heart stretched across both entrance flaps. Tent flaps I once ventured from only once the camp slept. I stared at the light within it, wondering if the lamp sat atop a cabinet once concealing the life of an innocent child.

The tent flaps opened, and I was too stunned to break my stare from my mother's replacement.

"Oh," she said, straightening. She wore a dress without an apron and held a basket of clothing beneath her arm. The lack of torches cast her features in shadows, but her brown hair peeked from the shawl she veiled herself with. "I'm sorry, I didn't see you."

"No." I stuttered like my steps. "I'm sorry, I was wander—"

"You're General Easton's mate," she said, voice airy. When I said nothing, she nodded toward the nearby drying lines. "If you'll excuse me."

I watched the camp whore walk from the tent that could've been mine, wondering if her basket contained only her clothing, or that of a hidden child. If she, like my mother, woke every morning to shush a babbling baby.

"I knew your mother."

I spun to the elder I hadn't heard approach. His hand shook on the cane he leaned over. A white braid stretched down his shoulder, past his navel. He wore a simple beige shirt with a tattered collar and black pants tucked into boots either caked in or the color of mud. Around his eyes, a thousand creases scrunched together.

"Margaret. I called her Margie. You look like her, except the eyes. She had brown eyes."

"You're mistaken." I threw off his extended hand.

"I delivered you," he continued, following me as I marched back through camp.

Turning, I reached for the knife I always kept on my leg, only to grasp air. "You are mistaken," I repeated with as much venom as I could muster. Fury billowed with my magic. Its crackle raced up my spine into my ears. I kinked my neck to dispel it, but the agitation of tingling nerves remained.

His cane was a constant echo to my steps. "I warned her of what might happen when they saw you. I helped her make the plan when you were born. You'd only just disappeared into the trees when Chief Daviat shot her. She fought so you could live—"

"Stop," I pleaded, whirling on him.

"Amaury was meeting with Chief Daviat at the time. He heard Fleck report you. I told him which direction you ran, so he might save you. And here you are."

Despite the cramp in my gut and the iron cage of my ribs

immobilizing my lungs, I turned from a face that might've been familiar. "Your age had plagued your memory. I am no Forterian."

I forced myself to stride back to Easton's tent with my chin high and gaze unbothered by their whispers. The gossip of my mother's murderers. The accusations of those with her blood on their hands.

Who yearned to add my life to their tally.

I was an innocent. And they nearly took everything from me.

Hell-bent on returning without a break in my strut, I didn't see the rock until it struck my temple. Then, another whistled through the air and thudded against my shoulder. A third missed my nose, but the fourth crunched it and sliced the bridge.

I cupped the blood pooling from it and raised a hand to block the next throw. It sliced through my palm.

"Stop!" I demanded, hand leaking blood onto the trampled trail.

I caught the next attack and crushed it, grinding the dust into my stinging cut.

More ammunition thudded on the trail. I raised my glare to the young boys, no more than ten, hiding in the gaps of tents. They were a mix of blonds and brunettes, shoulders widened from training and chests marred in shallow scars from fighting. Warriors already. The dying fire cast half their faces in a yellow glow, the crackle of my magic cast the other half in near blinding white. It glowed in their eyes; the reflection of my magic tinged with their fear.

"Run," I growled. Their scampering feet kicked up clouds of dirt and scattered more pine needles across my trail. Their voices died, but their fear remained, dulling the scent of pine I could not rid myself of.

The lighting in my fingertips, still rough with the rock's remains, seeped beneath my skin.

"Terrorizing children?"

I rose to meet Chief Daviat's snarl.

My hand dropped the pool of blood from my nose. It splattered across my bare feet.

"You look well," he continued.

Warmth leaking from my nose coursed over my sealed lips and down my neck. I tasted it, as I'd tasted it on the battlefield. I smelled his fear, as I'd become accustomed to the tinge of my own.

"Kacela!"

I hated the ease with which Easton's voice carried through my nerves, smothering the sparks.

He approached from the path leading to his tent, Gil a step behind.

"What happened?" he demanded, reaching for my blood splattered cheeks. He cupped them. Blood collected on the curve between his thumb and finger. He surveyed my face, but I kept my glare for Chief Daviat. I stared at his hands, stained with my mother's blood, and remembered the howl of her pain battling the wind.

I'd atoned for my mistakes, each of the lives I'd sacrificed on the battlefield. Yet he stood at the peak of power without a slight to his reputation for the murder of an innocent.

"Nothing," I said.

Easton turned to his chief. "Did you see?"

"Children," he reported, "who drew more of your mate's blood than you could."

Where Easton's fingers chipped at the drying splatters on my cheeks, they stilled.

"You teach them no mercy," I said, drawing Easton's attention back to my wounds. "You think that stops at the training circle? Like you said, I'm lucky to still have my head."

Gil pressed at the jut of my nose. He traced the lines, as the firelight provided only shadows across my face. "Would you rather fix it with magic?"

Beside me, Easton jumped at my wince.

"It'd be easier if you set it first, and I can heal it further."

Gil spared a glance at my mate.

"Fix it," I snapped, then winced at the resulting stab of pain through my skull.

His thumbs traced the lines of my nose before snapping without a warning. The jolt raced up my forehead and down the back of my skull. I squished my cheeks, cracking the mask of dried blood.

I thanked Gil before pressing my palms to my nose. Eager magic raced through my veins. The pain dissipated, replaced by a numb hum.

"Your hand?" Gil asked, reaching for it.

I inspected the minute gash. It'd be as easy as taking a breath to heal it. Easy as lighting a flame.

Instead, I held it out for him to treat and wrap. For a brute, his grip was soft as a breeze. As considerate as a healer's.

I slipped into the tent and then the tub. The blood flaked into the bath, and that, too, I could have skipped away. It remained until Easton dumped it out past the tree line. He returned to a dark tent.

"What were you doing?"

"Exploring," I whispered, wet hair soaking the pillow.

"I told you—"

"I had to get space." I let my voice trail.

The bed sagged toward his side. "Berel told me he gave you the choice to leave."

I snorted. "Telling me the direction of an estate is not giving me a choice. I had no food. No water. I can hardly heal myself. Berel knew I would return."

His body warmth hummed closer. His breath crashed against my neck. "Did you want to?"

I didn't answer.

I didn't know.

CHAPTER 18

I LOUNGED ON EASTON'S BED, legs swinging off the edge. Two weeks had passed since Amaury handed me, in a burnout state, to my sulking mate. Easton leaned against his desk, Berel leaned against the tub, and Gil sat on the floor nearby. One lamp lit the tent and created wavering shadows across the scrunched brows of the Forterians. After a dinner filled with a stale silence interrupted only by munching, they'd ushered me into the tent, as Easton had every night since my run in with Chief Daviat.

"If not the king, then who?" Berel asked me.

I picked at the fraying thread on a blanket. "How am I to know? It's your mountain. Have your elders puzzle it out."

He rose and stomped to the bed to stare down his nose at me. The black thinker blessing on his brow, a crown of swirls and dots, seemed to glow in the low lighting, like a black silk ribbon. "They do not have an Altun brat who claims to know more about our sacred land than we do. Talk, before we march south and —"

"Berel," Easton interrupted, "she's too proud to fear your threats."

I hated how Easton's gaze seared my temple.

"Kacela, when you were on Sacrament Land, did anything feel off?"

Cocking my head toward my mate, I leaned back on my arms. His gaze shifted down slightly, and a pinch of red rose to his cheeks. The mate bond purred like a satisfied cat.

I shrugged. "I didn't recognize the magic, if that's what you're asking."

"It is not," Berel muttered, cut off by Easton's glare.

Gil spoke up. "Maybe we're wasting our time when we could be playing cards." He held up a deck he'd been shuffling. I'd come to enjoy the constant ruffling of cards around the fire and the giddiness in Gil's voice when someone challenged him to a game, then the calls of cheating when he lost.

"Very well," I sat up straighter. "You want more information about what I experienced on Sacrament Land, then I get information in return."

"No!" Berel snapped.

Easton crossed his arms. "What information?"

"I want to know about the clans. Griffin wants equality in all of them, but he understands little of Forterian politics and society."

"Yet rules with an iron fist," Gil grumbled from the ground. He fanned the cards together.

Easton pushed from the desk, stepped beside Berel, and bumped him away with his hip. He placed his hands on either side of my legs, thumbs brushing the seams of my pants. We were nearly nose to nose, too close to see one another's glares clearly. Heat shot where his breath trickled across my cheeks.

"I'm weary of your deals."

"No magic involved." I held up my hands, having to lean forward to keep from falling over. Our noses touched, but Easton did not reel. He held me in his gaze and the cage of his arms. I tilted my head and let my eyelids fall. "All on good faith, Easton."

Berel spat. "We're to trust Altun good faith?"

"No. I'll open the mate bond," I offered. "Easton will be able to see my memories as if they're his."

Without waiting for a reply, opened the bond, but only slightly. Easton's eyes bulged at the sudden onslaught, the flood of my emotions and the tinge of pain dull beneath the bandage on my hand. He stumbled back.

Without his proximity, my senses expanded to the entirety of the tent. Gil's flushed cheeks and averted gaze. How the left side of Berel's hair was flattened more than the right, and how he fingered the strap of the dagger on his belt as if he could cut Easton's attention from me.

"Very well," Easton nodded, both hands clasped on the back of his neck. "Show me what you saw on the mountain."

My mouth went dry. I opened the bond further to pull him into my memories.

His consciousness in my head, he watched Griffin and I trek across their sacred land where he'd fought for his life and blessing. Where he'd killed his comrades, childhood friends, and potential enemies for the black ink they all bore. He swatted at a bug that had been attacking my ears, as if they were his, and coughed past the smog as Griffin's magic fought off that radiating from the mountain.

The blizzard flashed around him, then the cave loomed. A black pit reeking of decay.

The memory tore from my grasp. Yanked by another.

I felt it as he did, the rancid shiver of deceit racing across our minds. It oozed from the corner of the tent, yet I couldn't find its source. A black veil fell across my psyche to subdue my magic. And though I fought, shadows submerged the sparks. Scraping claws raced through my memory and plunged deep, Easton and I shackled to it. Forced to streak through my memories until the shadow sliced one open and yanked us into it.

The door to the study creaked open. The light streaming in brightened the dull beige of the room, void of decorations and thus unused, and danced across the glass shards haloing my feet.

Nalin's beaming face peeked through. "There you are, sweetheart.

I've been – "

I hiccupped and swayed, the wine racing through my churning stomach.

I reared against the memory, still humming with pain from a year prior, and threw my magic up to shield Easton's view. The shadow tore the gold curtain away and stomped my effort away.

"Are you drinking?" Nalin sputtered.

I stared at my slippers, soaked with the remnants of wine from the bottle I'd smashed along with the smaller lavender vial once smelling of spoiled oranges. Nalin's polished shoes appeared in my vision, and I jolted at the hand he pressed to my cheek.

"Are you drunk?" The blunted words snapped my gaze to his. His forehead creased in a thousand ripples, pale skin with a grayish tint in the darkened study. "Kacy, you're pregnant!"

I retreated from his touch, arms crossing over my stomach. "Not anymore."

His face morphed then. Gone were the bright eyes of hope and mischief I'd come to pine over when tucked within the maze of the library or late at night, sneaking him past the hawk-eyed servants in my wing.

The general his father modeled him into returned with a glower of stone. "Kacela, what did you do?"

"I don't want to have children." I turned toward the stream of moonlight turned red by the tinted windows. "I took a tonic." I teetered, reaching for him.

Nalin snatched my hand in his iron grip and cupped my jaw in his other. "When did you drink it?"

I shook my face against his hold.

He skipped us, nearly causing my stomach to lurch and spew its contents across our feet. I landed in a tub, and at the touch of his finger to my shoulder, my stomach convulsed. The wine, tinged with acid, streaked up my throat and surged over my legs.

His hand pulsed again, and another wave rocked me.

Again. And again.

I muttered through a burning throat, "Stop."

He pressed a hand to my stomach. I palmed my eyes to block the blistering light filling the room.

"No!" His scream shattered the mirror in a spray of white mist.

I sniffled. "I didn't want to have a child."

The black veil over my magic thundered like a furious groan.

We tumbled from the memory. From my shame and the root of Nalin's malice toward me.

I sputtered to regain my breath around the lingering rot and heard Easton doing the same.

"What was that?" Easton demanded through a cough.

My shadow, cast from the lamp on the desk, laid out across the bed and thrashed. I sat frozen against its shove on my shoulders, pressing until my body arched. A soundless shriek burst from my lips. Spikes of vengeance, chilled as ice, pierced through my back and into the frenzied sparks in my chest.

Easton gripped my shoulder. The presence vanished.

I anchored to his wrists, the touch of his skin against mine washing the foul chill from my lungs. The air cleared, fresh with the fall breeze and pine scent of my mate.

"What was that?" Berel asked from somewhere behind Easton.

I raised my gaze to my mate, his eyes widened and nostrils flaring. His curls rounded off his brows and tickled mine.

"I felt it, too," Gil said. "I saw shadows—"

Easton's grip on my shoulder floated to the backside of my neck, and I let him guide my forehead to the curve of his shoulder, no matter the hurt to my pride. If only to hide the tear rolling down my cheek.

"There is something in the mountain," Easton whispered. "What does it want with you?"

I couldn't sleep that night. The shadows reached for me to finish the job their master could not. In the corners of the tent, they taunted me with their wavering.

Easton adjusted every few minutes, kicking off the blankets only to pull them back. Fluffing his pillow and beating it back down.

"It was a memory," I told him, my gaze on the thread hanging from a recently sewn patch of the tent's ceiling.

"That boy, he was with you at the celebration."

"I'd hardly call Nalin Tait a boy. His father is lord of the northern bluffs. They supply the kingdom with the majority of its army and obsidian."

He rolled toward me. "You were pregnant."

"About a year ago now. Griffin had considered marrying me to Nalin for years to solidify their loyalty. We were reckless. Young love," I snickered. "He hates me now."

"For a lady, you're not very good at politicking."

A laugh broke the tension in my chest.

I scrunched the blanket to my cheeks and twisted it around my leg. "I've never felt something so hateful." I failed to hide the shudder in my words. "Whatever was in that cave, it was not Altun, nor Forterian."

Easton opened his mouth, then closed it. He rolled onto his back, hands clasped over his chest. "We can take watches, if you'd prefer."

I threw out my magic to a small barrier around the bed, looking more like an eggshell than a golden dome in the candle-light. "No need."

I'd almost fallen asleep, my magic the cocoon of safety needed to clear my head, when Easton brushed the hair from my shoulder. His fingers stalled on my exposed collarbone.

"We could help one another," he muttered. "As you'd suggested earlier. There is something soiling the mountain. Amaury wants all Forterian females training. I can help you achieve that."

I flipped toward him, forcing his hand to drop to my arm. "You are not the ally I need, Easton. What can you do outside this camp?"

He eased closer. The mattress sagged beneath his weight,

threatening to tumble me into his naked, scarred chest. "I have sway in some camps, but none are eager to change. Not if the mountain is soiled."

"There may be more cracks on the mountain Griffin hasn't closed." I scanned the scars on his chest, down to where the blanket laid across his abdomen. "When I return, I'll persuade Griffin to investigate. If there is someone within it, Griffin is you're strongest ally."

Easton nodded. His hand crept downward, as if he meant to take my hand. "How will you give him information without him knowing I'm giving it to you?"

"I'll tell Griffin I'm pulling the information from you without your knowledge."

"Could you do such a thing?"

"It is easy. You have no mental barriers to protect your mind. I could take secrets from your head as I easily as I controlled you." I regretted the words as they crossed my tongue.

His eyes bulged.

I rolled onto my back to avoid seeing the emotions splayed out across his face like a map. His fingers slipped off my wrist.

"Learn to shield your mind, Easton. Then, perhaps, I'll be satisfied to have you as an ally."

CHAPTER 19

I SKIPPED TO THE MAIN GATES of the obsidian castle and raised my hands in response to the dozen guards training their crossbows on me from atop the spiked, obsidian walls.

The streets surrounding the southern entrance sprouted with late afternoon bustle. Vendors sold their wares to the wealthy heading to theaters and operas, their gaudy outfits matching the over-embellished horses pulling equally ornate carriages. Some eyed me, perhaps due to my armor, while others rushed to the street vendors lining the blocks. Those strolling close enough to see the alerted guards scurried across the road with their arms blocking their heads. A performer advertising for an acrobatics show moved his exhibition elsewhere.

The captain of the guards whirled on the soldier behind him. "Alert the king."

The gates swung open. Magic shimmered from them, and the guards parted down the middle for me to pass. My face was a confident mask, my gut a raging storm on the seas.

I entered the main hall, and moments after closing behind me, the door banged open. I spun, hands on my dual Forterian swords, only to instantly drop my mask and fighting stance.

Amaury braced against the door, eyes wide and chest heaving. His hazel wings reeled back through the slits in his armor.

"You came back," he whispered, a bite in his tone.

My courtier mask smacked back into place, stilling the raise of my brows. "Was I not supposed to?"

Neira stalled at the top of the staircase. "Kacy!" She skipped to the entry, then launched herself into my arms. I stumbled, my bones groaning at the hit. She prodded at my face as if she could squeeze answers out of my cheeks. "We've been so worried about you! Those brutes didn't hurt you, did they?"

"They readied her for war," Amaury muttered.

"Come." Neira wrapped my arm around hers and tucked my hand into the crook of her elbow. "Griff is in his study. He'll be so excited to see you!"

"Frustrated he'll have to delay the attack," Amaury said.

I turned to him, despite Neira's insistence. "What attack?"

"Did you believe we'd leave you with those barbarians?" Neira gave my arm a sharp pinch.

The doors to the royal study parted as we approached, and Neira ushered me inside first.

Griffin sat in his chair with hands folded atop the stacks of papers on the desk. The bags under his eyes had grown, but there was something there as he saw me. Disappointment? Only a flash, then his scrunched features softened.

He rose, stare never leaving mine, and glided around the desk. His shadows stepped with him, and only Amaury at my back kept me from retreating from them. Griffin embraced me. The shadows slithered up my boots.

I stilled myself from squirming in his grasp.

"Did you skip back?"

I nodded. "In small increments."

Amaury nodded to my weapons. A slender sword hung on either hip, a dagger rested on my thigh, and a smaller knife was tucked in my boot. All gifts. Equal to the quality of my mate's weapons. "Did he arm you before sending you back?"

I glared. Raised a challenging brow.

Amaury's pursed lips told me what he would not. He hadn't expected me to come back.

"He didn't send me back," I replied with a slight undertone of annoyance. "I left him."

"Sit," Griffin repeated, motioning to the chair on the right.

I stilled my hand above the backrest. Outlined in a nearly invisible, black aura, it tickled my palm. I eased onto the cushion and sat rigid, hands on the hilts of my blades and legs posed to pounce.

"Tell us. Everything."

I did. Somewhat.

The door cracked open in the middle of my explanation, and Pila slipped through.

I stilled, staring at her black robes and the swirling tattoos beneath her skin. They ebbed like my shadow had, snapping at those she passed.

"Do you see now why we wanted to break the bond?" Griffin asked softly, drawing my attention back. "Your talents are wasted in that camp."

I nodded.

"I think it's time—"

"Another waste," I said with a shrug. "But sure. Snap it."

The silence amplified Pila's stench.

"Snap it?" Griffin repeated slowly.

I felt his consciousness floating around my walls. Without reserve, I brought them down for him to see. He dug through my head, dove into my gut, and prodded at the mate bond.

I overlaid the truth with half-truths for his inspection, muddling them until Griffin gave up his prodding through my head. I had wanted to come back, even if not for the reasons he believed, and my loyalties had not shifted to Easton. He took the crumbs of half-truths I gave him without hesitation, as if he didn't believe me strong enough to deceive him. "You want it gone. Fine. Pila, snap it."

All eyes were not just on me but surveying me, as if at any moment I'd turn and attack the nearest person. I might've if

Pila moved closer.

I wanted to see what was under that black hood. If the shadows beneath her skin would dissipate in her death or curl around my blade. If she'd dye my blades red or black.

Pila stepped toward me, halted by Griffin's glare. Her consciousness floated along the connection already established by Griffin, tracing until it reached where the mate bond sat like a dull string waiting to be lit aflame. Her magic plucked it like a poorly tuned lute.

Griffin, without taking his eyes off the priestess, gestured for me to continue. "Why would it be a waste?"

"I can get into his head."

Pila's magic wrapped around the bond, testing the strength, curling it like a ribbon.

Griffin's head tilted and his chin raised, a predatory glean in his muse. "You're willing to extract information from your mate's head?"

I nodded, face inanimate. "He treated me like I was some horse needing its leg mended."

Pila's magic followed the bond to my core.

An involuntary shudder rattled my spine.

"Enough," Griffin snapped at her.

With her blackened hands up in surrender, she floated back to the wall.

Amaury stared at me, as if I were a puzzle he couldn't solve. "Easton's knowledge is only relevant if our goal is Virian. The bargain ensures their females are trained. What more could taking information from him do?"

"There are several meetings with other chiefs planned before the Sacrament. I can pull information on more than training traditions." I eyed Griffin. "I can plant ideas of rebellion."

Griffin tapped his desk, gaze narrowed on me.

"Did anyone harm you while you were there?" Amaury stepped closer to touch the chair, only to snap his hand away. "Do we need to have a healer look you over?"

Griffin's magic swept over me. "I had plans to return to

Sacrament Land in a week or so, to close more — "

"No!" Amaury snapped.

The king's eyes widened. The lamps in the room dimmed, basking us in dread.

"Fixing those cracks broke her." Amaury grasped my shoulder. "You nearly killed her."

Griffin stood. Black tendrils floated from the center of his back. They spiraled, constricting around Amaury.

"Put those away!" Amaury barked. His hand sat on the longsword at his left hip. "She's not strong enough to close the cracks on her own. Your mistake nearly cost her life."

"I want to help close the cracks." I stood, facing down the brewing storm of Griffin's magic. It spun closer, crawling up my boots. Though similar in color, his tendrils did not feel like wilting vines as the shadows on the mountain had. They did not reek of deceit. "There are more on Sacrament Land. The Forterians are sure it is your magic soiling their sacred land, and they mutter of rebellion."

Amaury, somehow ignoring the tendrils within a foot of his face, turned my shoulders.

The creases around his eyes multiplied, those around his lips thinned. His fingers dug into my clothes, as if he could anchor me to him with his grasp alone. His face had softened, and a small smile full of pride graced his lips. "The cracks will be closed, but you are not a power source to extinguish in one use."

Griffin's tendrils receded, only enough to stop the chair's rattling. "I needed her magic to close the cracks."

Amaury kept his gaze on mine. His grip tightened. "Then limit the number of cracks you close at once."

"I can — "

"You almost died," Amaury whispered, his voice rough as sand. "You were barely holding on, and anything could've killed you. Anything. I couldn't protect you." He looked over my shoulder at our king. "You offered to take her. You were responsible for ensuring she came home safe."

I gripped Amaury's wrist to pull his attention back to me.

"If you bring her back from closing the cracks like that again, Griffin," his voice shook, "I'll end you myself."

Before Griffin could respond, Amaury stormed from the room, dragging me behind him.

He yanked me to my chambers, easing the door shut. It'd been left exactly how I remembered it. The bed was made and my couch had a few books strewn across it. The stack of weapons I'd regained in the week prior were heaped by the wardrobe. With a flick of my wrist, I lit the fire. Warmth battled against the cool breeze floating through the open windows.

"You weren't supposed to come back," he whispered. I reached out with my mind past the doors. Only servants bustling about in the gardens and the halls.

He'd wanted me to stay away. Stay with Easton. Where he thought I was safe. Or safer. I'd scared him so badly he'd been willing to send me to the one place he'd promised I'd never go back to on a hope the magic of a mate bond would be enough to heal me.

"It was you." I gripped my blades. "I'd refused to believe you'd return me to the camp that killed my mother, but it was you!"

He dropped his gaze to my hands. "It saved you."

"You didn't know what would happen! "I stepped to him and shoved his chest. Amaury's face contorted, brows furrowing. I continued, pushing him toward the door with frantic, scraping hands. The first tear dropped from my chin.

Amaury forced my hands down and captured my upper arms in his grip. "You're okay," he said, stronger, almost like he had to convince himself of it. He stared at the next tear to reach my chin. It tickled where it dangled. "You weren't getting any better, and Griffin was starting to consider snapping the bond while you were..." his voice died. "I thought that would break you completely."

I threw his arms off. "It helped, but I had to be there, in that camp, where they killed my mother. For weeks."

He stepped closer. "I was trying to save your life."

Tears streamed down my face. I hated how they tickled my cheeks and lips, the salt gathering on my tongue, but I had to sell it, to convince him there was no emotion woven into my mate bond, that I could betray Easton, that I told him the whole truth. "You told me you took me from there for a reason, so I wouldn't be some dull wife to a Forterian, and then you hand me to him."

I watched his expression as he raised a hand to my cheek, swiping away a few tears.

"Leave," I told him. His features were a map I could follow through his thoughts. The pursed lips as he deciphered. Raised brows when he came to his conclusions. The narrowed gaze that scrutinized my every blink.

He turned, stopping with the door ajar. His hand, and my tears, fell. "Weeks ago, you couldn't move. You're alive. Hate me if you wish, but you're alive."

The door clicked shut.

I sank onto the bed. My braid came apart in my hands as I raked them back across my skull.

The mate bond sputtered, as if it had inhaled sand instead of kindling. A far-off darkness snuck its way back into the bottom of my gut. Waiting. Prowling like a hungry predator. As intangible as a shadow and reeking like a corpse.

CHAPTER 20

"WHO WHISPERS OF REBELLION?" Griffin made a note on the stack of letters piled nearly to his chin.

I'd hardly slept the night before, stuck between Easton's concern I would not uphold my end of the bargain and Amaury's knowing stare. I teetered on a line I wasn't sure still existed. It wouldn't if word of my stay in Virian reached the wrong ears, if Neira couldn't dispel the rumors of my Forterian mate like she'd promised the Taits she would.

"War-hungry youths."

"Amaury claims Daviat can prevent rebellion."

"Virian is his home, even if they have exiled him for his loyalty to Kadea."

"Virian is your home."

I scoffed. "It was my birthplace and mother's grave. That does not make it my home."

Griffin made another note. Behind him on a podium, his obsidian crown slightly obscured the single candle. One peak cast my face in a jagged shadow. The crow on one chair ear made the largest shadow across the far bookshelf. The red ruby in its mouth spun the pale light into morning orange.

"There was a presence within the mountain. Akin enough to your magic for the Forterians to believe you'd invaded their holy ground."

He made another note. "What did it feel like?"

"Like Pila." The realization was a gong in my gut, the words spewing before I'd fully acknowledged their truth. Only her lingering presence within the castle, charred and rotten, related the familiar stenches.

"She is a bonk, worshiping the Old Faith and the deities who once inhabited this continent. The mountain is older than their demise by thousands of years. It would not be impossible for one such being to still be hidden, shrouded from me by their cursed land."

"A being that can manipulate shadows?"

Griffin shrugged. "Perhaps."

"Should we investigate?"

"No."

I recoiled. "No?"

"They wish for their independence, then let them face the horrors of their land alone."

I eased forward. "And if it is a hostile creature, a powerful god, come back to reclaim the adoration of the continent? What then?"

Griffin's quill scratched to a halt. He sat erect in the plush black cushions of his ornately carved oak throne, eyes like sapphires atop a crown, glowing as bright as the ruby in the obsidian crow's mouth. "You are awfully concerned for the home you claim to hate."

"The Forterians are a shield against which our enemies break until one breaks them. Let us be the monster who crushes their autonomy and ushers in a new era of equality in our revitalized army."

His lip quirked. "What would you do, Kacela?"

"Easton has been speaking with other chiefs who voice concerns of a brute named Indiviar challenging Daviat for his position as chief. If given power, Indiviar will start the rebellion, and you will remind the Forterians a step out of line is treason against their kingdom. And that punishment for such an atrocity is death."

Silence sat between us. Whether he waited to collect his thoughts or provided me another moment to voice mine, I didn't know, and I feared to venture a guess. One misstep and the snap of the bond would be the end of my deal with Easton. The end of my push for equality in a society I claimed no favor toward. The end of feeling his mind at the other end, welcoming and warm.

I stood at the divergence of two roads. One led back to Virian, lined by pines. The other to the northern bluffs, to the Tait's fortress on the cliffs with the window framing Sacrament Land as a painting. A mountain best reserved for stories.

The silence beckoned, as did the narrowing curl of the king's lips, but I held my position. I waited, like a huntress with a snare.

"What will it take for Indiviar to act?"

"Remove Easton, if only for an afternoon." I told him of my plan, watched his sneer grow with every word, and accepted the glass of brandy Griffin floated to me with a swirl of his ashy magic.

I plucked it from the air. Ice clanked against glass, vibrating through my fingers like the deceit implanted in my deal with Easton from the start. If he'd known, if he'd suspected for a moment I had no intention of purging the mountain, I'd have lost.

Griffin floated his glass to mine. "Cheers." They clinked, and his floated back to his raised grip. "To the ruthless mastermind you've become."

I skipped Griffin and I to the heart of Virian War Camp. Our feet hit the ground, and I beamed at my first perfect skip. The fabrics of our world gave easily to my call, the slice I made in them widening for us like grand ballroom doors.

Griffin's hand slid from my shoulder. "Impressive," he said beneath his breath.

Easton stood nearby, and his brows rose. I hadn't told him, hadn't wanted to ruin the surprise. He followed Chief Daviat toward us, both their wings on display. The high noon sun seemed to breathe through the white of Easton's feathers, but Daviat's were a dull grey, like clay.

Beside him was General Indiviar. I recognized him from Easton's memories.

Ruggedly handsome, Indiviar nearly bested Easton's height. Two long scars ran the length of his face, from hairline to the angles of his jaw, ridging at his brows and creasing his eyelids. Black lines disappeared from his jaw and neck beneath the black leather of his armor. His hands remained on his swords while the others let theirs sway.

He inspected me as I did him.

Chief Daviat straightened. "My King, as always, it is an honor to host you. I will have tents cleared immediately."

"That is not necessary." Griffin raised a hand. "We are returning to Sacrament Land today to close any rifts before more harm comes to nearby clans."

I smirked at the flare of Indiviar's nostrils, infuriating him further. His swords twitched up, and his eyes surveyed the blades I wore on my hips, akin to his.

"You have come to observe the training, then. I can assure you," Daviat pulled his sleeve back to reveal the tattooed bargain, "it is being done."

"Kacela told me your general expressed concerns of my magic infiltrating Sacrament Land."

Chief Daviat turned to Easton. His fists clenched and brows furrowed, but Easton kept his gaze on me. I saw the threat in his eyes. Felt it beating at the walls at my end of the mate bond.

I let them fall.

Traitor, he seethed.

We are here to help. My sweet tone only tightened his grimace. I blocked him from my thoughts and shifted my consciousness to the open mind of the brute humming with rage beside him.

"If you can spare him for a few hours, General Easton may accompany us to see how we close the cracks and return to report my good intentions to cleanse the continent of demons."

Easton didn't meet his chief's glare.

"General," Chief Daviat snapped.

"Yes, sir?"

"You'll go. Return with a full report."

"Chief —"

"Full report."

Reaching into Indiviar's mind, I curled his grin. I primed him for an opening to move, as he'd planned for months. His fingers twitched on his blades again, but his bloodlust swung away from me. He side-eyed his chief.

Easton spoke behind a hand to Berel, who nodded and left the training circle. I glanced around for Gil, not seeing the boyish glee amongst the blond brutes plentiful within Virian.

"Apologies," Griffin said, gripping Easton's tensed shoulders, "skipping can be a rather unpleasant sensation."

Easton's squinting gaze snagged mine. "I know."

I strengthened the block on the mate bond, not to keep him from my mind but to garner my clashing emotions. The prospect of avenging my mother's murder pushed me through the fear of Easton rejecting the mate bond if he learned of my scheme.

We landed outside Sacrament Land. Stepping through the barrier was like jumping over a line of coals. The heat was nearly forgotten, but trickled upwards in warning that it could, if sparked, burn.

We trekked through the northern jungle. Easton held the pommels of his swords despite the attack of branches at his shoulders. He maneuvered around them and dipped, arms tucked tight, as if scared to touch anything.

"Are you sure there is a crack here, your majesty?" he asked.

"No," Griffin replied. "We experienced a blizzard during our last venture to the mountain, one uncommon of the Sacrament according to the royal commander. Despite the aggregate magic here, storms roll from beyond its borders. Whatever attacked us, remains."

Our boots crunched the first line of snow.

"Let your mind wander," Griffin instructed. His pressed behind mine, allowing me to guide his strength to the very peak and down again, swirling within each cave. I raised a veil between us, smoothly inching it around my psyche to keep him from the streaks of it venturing away. They crept through the caves, sliding across the rockiest terrain and surfing the raging Vitient River within the mountain's base.

Another presence joined mine, but not with the ashy residue of the king's magic. It felt frigid, as if I'd dunked myself into the Vitient. It rode the shadows beside the streaks of my consciousness, blowing me back toward the sun-warmed caves.

The slices of my mind rejoined the rest racing the mountain's southern edge toward the sand dunes where heat rose in visible curls.

Then a chill, not of snow, but of shadows on stone floors, hung above the mountain near the divide.

"Do you feel it?" I asked.

Following the sensation, we skipped again. One of my boots landed on the jagged rock of the base of the mountain, the other in tumbling sand, and I fought to keep my legs from flailing.

Easton bent over, heaving.

"It gets easier," I teased, but he didn't raise his head to meet my gloating smirk with one of his own.

"Kacela." Griffin's urging probes rapped at my walls. I dropped a section and spun my magic to him.

He turned to the rift of black wisps, like grasping hands, above us. I felt every stitch of my magic seep through the pleading wound between dimensions, yet I stared at my mate.

His knuckles turned white where they clenched his pants, and his neck strained against the convulse of his gut.

I reached for him and pressed even when he jolted. Peace flooded through my touch, easing his stomach's churn and the growing pounding behind his eyes.

He stood but did not brush my hand from his shoulder. His hand covered mine. Appreciation, warm as the desert, rolled down the bond. A trickle of traitorous regret answered.

We were no closer than we'd been for two weeks when sharing a bed. Bumping shoulders in the early morning hours, changing with only the thin flap of canvas to block the sight of skin, wrapped in one another's scents no matter how many bathes we took.

Yet, I felt closer.

He squeezed my hand, then forced it to trace the line of his armor across his chest and brought my fingertips to the prickle of his beard.

I thought he might raise my fingers higher, to the scorch of his lips or blossoming blush of his cheeks.

Released as the crack winked from existence, my magic slammed into me. I stumbled toward the scorching heat, caught by Easton's reflexes.

Griffin turned. He surveyed my cheeks, then Easton's lingering grasp.

"The general doesn't take well to skipping," I said, making no effort to shake him off.

"If he'd prefer to fly home when we are done, I will not take any offense."

Curiosity probed the mate bond. I brushed it aside and strengthened the wall between us so he would not sense the fear I had for what awaited him when he flew home. The removal of Chief Daviat would restructure Virian, and I didn't know where Easton and his friends would fall into the new hierarchy.

"Are there more?" I asked Griffin.

He beckoned to the mountain. "You tell me."

"What have you done?" Amaury met us at the threshold of the castle's barring wards.

"You should be falling to your knees to thank us," Griffin exclaimed. "We cleansed all rifts from the mountain."

My grin lagged within the exhaustion tugged at my shoulders like a thick cloak. Even the stretch of a smile brought an ache to my cheeks.

"Daviat is dead, killed by his own general," Amaury growled. "There was a revolt only hours ago."

Griffin straightened his tunic.

"Indiviar claims the title of chief. You have replaced a level-headed leader for a brash brute eager to prove himself as more than a barbarian. Do you know the repercussions—"

"Enough." Griffin's smile slipped away, his voice absolute as death. "These are my subjects. The new chief will learn, as the rest have, to bow to the kingdom's might." He walked past, and whatever guilt Amaury prepared to douse us in fell in his wake.

Amaury reached for me. I parried his outstretched hands. My neck kinked and feet pulsed with agony.

"My office," Griffin said, and strolled through the black, cobblestoned courtyard sheltered by crossbow wielding guards. Roses, once bordering the path, were crimson flakes beneath our boots.

Though burnout tugged at my coiling muscles, I prattled along behind Amaury. I focused on our footsteps. If I gave to curiosity and let my mind wander down to the mate bond, I'd drop the barrier and send my worry to Easton.

"We begin the next phase of our plan," Griffin said after I'd taken my seat across from his desk.

Amaury, seated in the other plush chair, snapped to glare at me. "Next phase?"

"Kacela is rather gifted at scheming."

"This was your plan?" The armrests groaned beneath Amaury's clamping grip.

My stomach cramped around the pride and shame at his

words. It'd been my plan that'd killed my mother's murderer and betrayed my mate's trust.

"Kacela will return to Virian in a few days. I need someone within the camp I can trust, and we need a peace offering to Indiviar if you wish to quell the rebellion by non-violent means."

Amaury jerked to his feet. "There will be no rebellion. I will go to Chief Indiviar and remind him of the bargain and the Great War's peace treaty."

Griffin scorned him with a gaze. "Your attempts to keep peace with the Forterians have faltered. Rebellion grows with every Sacrament and new cohort of blessed warriors on my land. I only hope one camp will be the price to stomp out any whispers of rebellion before they claim the mountain requires more than Forterian blood."

"There is no rebellion! No call for Altun blood." Amaury's palms slapped onto the desk, rattling a bottle of ink and quill. "And no need for a grand scheme to bring the Forterians to heel. They are not hounds to be leashed."

The look on Griffin's face told me he thought otherwise.

"We need someone within Virian to send word when the rebellion occurs," I said, standing to touch Amaury's shoulder. The dark bags beneath his eyes hung across rosy cheeks. I couldn't help but worry about how much sleep he'd been getting since my burnout. I nearly reached to smooth away the wrinkles beside his eyes. "They despise and fear you, so they will watch you. I lived within the camp for over a week before any were aware."

He rounded on me. His callused palms itched where they cupped my cheeks. The creases above his brows were a thousand ripples, the frown lines near his mouth each their own canyon. "Do not underestimate their disdain for you."

I eased his hands away. "I do not, Amaury. Easton's reputation is all keeping my head from a spike. What if they believe killing you will end the bargain, and you make yourself a target by entering their camp?" My thumb rubbed over his sleeve. Beneath, the bargain magic warmed. "Easton will protect me.

The mate bond remains along with his loyalty, whether he hates me or not. You once enjoyed helping me scheme. Please, now when I will do it with or without your assistance, help me."

Amaury sank away and back to his chair. "If you will progress without me, where do I fit?"

I explained, with Griffin's nodding to keep my spirits high and thoughts from the creeping burnout. It started in my toes and dredged the energy from my muscles with constricting pulses.

Griffin dismissed us with a warning to see a healer, whom Amaury offered to walk me to.

"I need sleep," I told him before skipping to my room, the magical wards giving as easily as a willow's leaves. I stripped my gear, tossed it into a corner, and doused the lamps. I'd nearly dosed off when the shadows in the corners seemed to breathe. They surged, step by step from their hiding places.

I kicked away the blankets and squished myself against the headboard, my magic dragging as if it were waterlogged.

I raised my hand and begged for the golden sparks.

Then, someone banged on the door.

Neira stepped in, the light from the hallway banishing the shadows. "You've done it." The ribboned skirt of her blood-red dress swayed like shredded muscle. The silver fabric weaved into her hair gleamed like a crown.

I blocked the light from my eyes. "Done what?"

"Ruined any chances of being Lady Tait."

My weary head puzzled through her words.

"With this new plan, and you spending time in Virian, the entire kingdom will know about your mate." She yanked at the blanket scrunched between my legs. "The Taits won't risk their reputation to take you. You've found your blade, Kacela, and you've blundered its use!"

She stormed out. The slamming of the door rattled a dagger from the shelf beside it.

I pulled my knees to my chest and placed my forehead atop them, then my brain caught up to her words.

The Taits would end the marriage.

Tipping my head back, I filled my lungs as if it were my first breath. My shoulders fell with the sigh, and I released my clasped hands from around my knees. I sank into my bed, spreading my limbs to take up its entirety.

I lowered the barrier on the mate bond enough to feel Easton's essence at the other end. He pulsed with fury and, to my surprise, physical pain. My relief danced across the bond to console him. The warmth welcoming me was as cozy as the plush blankets I coiled around myself. I lifted a hand, the one he'd caught to keep me from falling, to my lips, as if I still feel his touch. A faint smell of pine wafted off my fingertips.

The mate bond hummed, as if it knew the cage I'd escaped. As if it sought to pull me into a new one.

CHAPTER 21

I SKIPPED TO VIRIAN, Amaury clinging to my shoulder. We landed near the training rings, as Griffin and I had a week prior to be welcomed by Chief Daviat. He welcomed us again today, his head the first one I saw on the spikes beside the chief's tent. His graying hair hung in tatters across blue-tinged skin. Beside him was the Altun messenger Amaury sent to congratulate the new chief on his position. Hazed over eyes stared down at us. They'd broken his blood-crusted jaw, so he screamed long into death.

An act of rebellion. The first of many.

Beside the stakes, three of which awaited heads, stood a newly erected tent. No longer the same forest green as the others, but blood-red.

I dug my nails into the strap of the bag slung over my shoulder to keep myself from grasping my swords.

Amaury nodded forward, and I followed, half hidden behind him, gaze on his heels.

Chief Indiviar stormed from the tent, his advisors on either side. One a thinker, the other a brute. All their blessings were dimmer than Easton's, but not necessarily less powerful.

Easton emerged after. His snarl was split, eye black, chin bruised, and left eyebrow cleaved in two by a stitched gash.

I gulped back the surge of bile in my throat.

"King Quillon sends his regards," Amaury said.

I only saw males on the training grounds. No females or children meandered between nearby tents, stirred the large cauldrons of stew for dinner, or hung clothing on lines. The camp was void of laughter. The ringing of blades made it sound like a battlefield.

We stopped before the chief and his highest-ranking warriors, all of whom rested their hands on their blades.

I let my mental barriers fall at Easton's knocking. *How have you betrayed me now?* His voice in my head was a low hiss.

I brushed him off as if he were a fly. *This is not about you.*

"May we?" Amaury motioned to the tent.

The brute advisor held the tent flap open for us to enter. His bushy blond brows pulled taught and full lips pursed. He'd grown his hair past his ears in a straight line, making him look like a mushroom.

My mate trailed, a slight hobble in his step. We settled around the table, Amaury and I on one side facing the Virian warriors on the other.

In the warm glow of the midday sun beating through the blood red tent, Chief Indiviar's scars looked fresh as his advisors' new ones. A slice ran from the left temple to the right nostril on the brute. The thinker had wide set eyes, an upturned chin, and a bulging nose only made worse by the fresh Xs across his cheeks. The wounds were sewn closed but ridged and red, as if they were purposely not healing well.

"The king can keep his regards," Chief Indiviar said, flat palm smacking the table. "His messenger was disrespectful."

Amaury nodded with practiced calm. My temper excited the magic rumbling in my gut. It sloshed at the walls of the well it sat within, waiting for the command to rupture hearts and puncture lungs of arrogant warriors.

"My apologies. I'll ensure we train our messengers in proper

Forterian customs." Amaury dipped his head, then pulled a scroll from his belt. "King Quillon hopes this message is better received."

Chief Indiviar snatched it from him. "The king does not dictate our lives."

"This is no tyranny, and King Quillon does not plan to rule it as such. Your daily lives are your own, so long as you follow royal decrees."

The chief ripped open the seal and scanned it, his brows raising with each line he read.

I let out a snort of laughter. "Look at your hand." I nodded to it.

The seal he'd ripped off melted on his fingertips and meandered up his forearm. It formed the Quillon family seal of a raven cawing to the waning moon like a metal bracelet, then sunk into the chief's skin. As black as the brute blessing it overlapped, a physical reminder.

Griffin had said the bargain had already been transferred. However, he couldn't resist reminding the new chief of his power by delaying the tattoo's appearance.

I heard the groan of a bow.

Spinning, I grabbed the raised arrow aimed at Amaury's back. My magic sparked around the center of the bow, reducing it to ash. The arrow and bottom half of the bow swung down from where the stealth held the string. The feline claws tattooed on the backs of his hands flexed around the broken wood. He lowered it to his side, chest heaving and frown deepening.

"Killing him will do you no good," I warned. The ashy chips of the wood dug into my clenched fist.

"Kacela is correct. The bargain will remain until all born in this camp are given equal training and opportunity to participate in the Sacrament, or it will take every life until it is satisfied there are no more who can fulfill it. I hope this is the warning you need to reincorporate late Chief Daviat's training schedules."

Chief Indiviar covered the tattoo with his other hand. He

looked at the bag slung over my shoulder. "And what of her?"

"I'm staying," I told him. "As a direct line to the king to ensure training for females."

"And you?" the thinker asked Amaury.

"Merely the messenger," he replied.

The thinker crossed his arms and grinned, then winced and touched the stitches on his cheeks. "A bit below you, isn't it?"

"I'd say an adequate response for our king to send a messenger who would behead instead of be beheaded," I muttered.

Amaury's glare sliced through me. He then turned to the chief and raised a brow. A challenge.

The tent flaps ruffled. I turned, as did Amaury, to the incomer. A blond winged, older than Easton, stalled before us. He held a scrunched scroll in his hand and bowed. "Apologies. I was unaware we were hosting."

His gaze raised to me. His thin brows furrowed and even thinner lips pursed.

"Fleck," Chief Indiviar grunted. "You've returned with a response?"

The messenger's head titled, and his gaze flickered to Amaury, who stepped between us, demanding my attention.

"Your place is here now. Understand?" Without waiting for a response, Amaury threw open the tent flaps, unleashed his wings, and took to the sky.

I stared at his disappearing figure until the tent flaps settled closed, feeling once more like the girl he'd swept from the field, and whispered, "understood."

With tension sticky in the air like humidity, I turned back to the table of warriors.

Easton cleared his throat. "May I, sir?" he asked his chief.

Chief Indiviar had been poking at the tattoo on his wrist. He looked up. "Get out, all of you!"

Easton reached me first, though the messenger remained staring, his head angling back and forth as if I were a familiar face he couldn't place.

My mate put a hand to my back to steer me from the tent, the two advisors trailing behind. I readjusted my bag, feeling the messenger's stare like a second layer of skin.

"Girls training and with power," the thinker advisor cut through the tents behind us. "It'll be the children next, then the goats."

I glanced over my shoulder, relying on Easton's guiding hand to maneuver through the tents. The thinker jutted an elbow into the other advisor's gut, then fluffed his bangs from atop the blessing over his brow.

"Pity." I let my gaze rake over the thinker, down and then back up. By the time I scrutinized every freckle, his cheeks and neck beamed pink.

"Pity what?" he demanded, hands reaching for his blades.

Easton yanked my arm.

"To be blessed brains but not wisdom to speak with your mouth instead of your ass."

Easton reached for his blade.

"Baine, Callum. Leave us."

We reached Easton's tent, and the advisors wandered off without another word.

"You're trying to get yourself killed." He held a flap open. "What are you doing here?"

"Are you not happy to see me?" I stepped closer, so he'd have to crane his neck down to see my innocent grin and fluttering lashing.

Easton gripped my shoulder, then shoved. "No," he closed the tent flap behind us, "what did Amaury mean by your place is here now?"

I dropped my bag next to Easton's bed. The tent flaps opened, and my consciousness danced through the unprotected minds of Easton's best friends. I kept their glares on my back, focusing instead on the bed I'd spent so many nights in. The night I'd skipped into his tent, he'd slept in the middle, but now, the blankets were only ruffled on one side. "All the estates know of my Forterian mate. The king has no use for me if I cannot secure alliances through marriage."

"You were supposed to convince the king to deal with the intruders on our mountain!" Berel snapped. Paper fluttered together. Something wooden crashed to the ground.

I picked at a frayed blanket edge. "There are none. I searched while I was there."

Easton gripped my arm and turned me to him. Behind him, Berel matted down his frizzy hair and Gil rearranged the letters knocked from the table.

There was a softness within my mate's eyes, like new spring grass instead of emerald stones. "There was something. It wanted your memory. A very specific one."

The reminder came with a dry gulp. "Whatever it was, it's gone. Perhaps it came from a crack and fled back."

"When do you leave?" Berel demanded. He unclasped the dagger on his thigh, the sound echoing through the tent.

"Not for a bit," I tried to smirk at him, "maybe never. If I cannot secure Altun alliances, it is the king's wishes for me to convince Indiviar we are on the same side."

Berel kicked at the overturned stool beneath Easton's desk. "I'll believe you're on our side when the first female is blessed." Then he was gone, Gil following.

I rubbed my eyes with my palms, but the tinges of my mate's wounds were pinging at the bond between us. "When were you attacked?"

Easton stepped back. "When I returned from your expedition." The accusation was a bell in his tone.

I nodded. "They ambushed you to—"

"I let them ambush me to lull Indiviar into a false sense of security so I could remain as general. It was a test for us both. To see if he would take the full responsibilities of chief by defending his clan against any threats, even internal ones, and to see if I would fall in line behind him."

"Why?"

Easton kicked my bag into the corner. "Forterians follow the strong. Discard the weak."

CHAPTER 22

I SOUGHT OUT THE ELDER the next day during Easton's patrol duty. On the outskirts of the camp, he watched the females work through slow, methodical stances led by an unblessed boy hardly older than fifteen. Near, an audience of brutes prowled from the thicket of tents like cockroaches.

"Hello." I shadowed the elder from the midday sun.

"Kacela," he gestured to the girls, "a wonderful morning for training."

"Wonderful." I plopped beside him. His nearly white hair was braided and draped over his hunched shoulder. Dark eyes like the center of a storm peered up, his chapped lips scrunching his rosy creaks into a dozen creases.

"No weapons?"

I rolled away my glare. "No, your new chief prefers I remain weaponless until he can trust me."

My hand fell through where my sword should have been on my hip. I silently cursed the chief with every jitter I could not tap out against the pommel.

"You'll never regain your blades." His laugh dried into a cackle and then sputtered into a cough. "My name is Doyon."

I dug my heel into the ground. "You know my name."

"That is not all I know."

I twisted toward him. "If you —"

"Calm, child. I have never breathed a word of your existence, and I do not plan to break my oath to your mother."

I couldn't breathe past the lump in my throat.

"If you wish for your blades back, admitting to your heritage may be the first step."

"I'd rather they throw my blades into the Vitient."

Doyon howled with another sputtered laugh until it settled into a cough. "As spirited as her. Twenty years have not sapped your spunk."

"If they do not trust me now, they never will once they discover I'm not only a whore's daughter but also a half-breed."

"Some may call for your death. Half-breeds are not welcomed in many clans."

I managed a dry laugh despite the lump in my throat. "They've tried to kill me multiple times already." I ducked closer. "Do you know who my father is?"

"I only know he was not from this camp and your mother refused to say once she discovered she was pregnant."

I picked a leaf from the drying grass and itched at its brittle spikes. "How did she hide me? If she was the camp…"

He pulled the long gray braid from his back and began to redo it, deft fingers working swiftly. His skin was as dull as his hair, so thin it showed the blood vessels beneath. "Times have not always been so quiet, Kacela. Forterians are bred for war, and we will seek it even in our sleep. The camps have primarily been females and children for decades." He plucked the leaf from my fingers. "And you were a tiny thing. Born early, but I told her you'd be strong with a few months of good feeding."

I fought the tightness in my chest. "You were there," I peeked over my shoulder, but all gave me a wide berth, "that night."

"I did what I could." Doyon placed a leathered hand, marred with poorly sewn layers of scars, on my shoulder. "I know your mother would be proud of what you have done, and she would approve of Easton. He is a good boy, and a better leader."

"It doesn't matter." His hand fell when I stood.

Wrinkles tucked under one another at the ridge of his brow. "Kacela, it does matter. She gave her life—"

"The females are coming along. The king will be ecstatic with the work being done here. Soon, other camps will see the strength of doubling the warriors."

The look in his eyes, as if he wished to say more about my mother, stewed the discomfort in my gut. I was a match, seconds away from being struck.

Doyon's brittle voice followed me like the falling leaves across the field to the females working through stances. I took up wooden practice swords and fell into step at their pace.

Some glared, others paid me no attention.

I pressed into my heels and settled into the steady beat of my heart's battle.

They'd taken her from me, because of me. Because another saw her body as theirs and staked a claim destined to butcher my mother.

Some inched back to me after retreating. Curious to mirror my steps, how I felt my grip, the angle of my jaw, the pattern of my breath. With every move, every extension of the blade as if it were born from my arm, every sweeping step, I chipped at their hatred.

Some perhaps saw me as a leader instead of a conqueror.

It was a start.

"Were you going to drink all of that?" I asked Easton, pointing to the open wine bottle on his desk. He hesitated, teetering his gaze between me and the bottle.

"You went to train today." He offered the bottle.

I sank into the warmth of the wine in my chest, refusing to relinquish it until I'd taken multiple swigs. Tinges of strawberry clouded out the pine scent of my mate.

Easton gripped the bottom and pulled it from my lips with a resounding pop. His raised brow challenged me.

"I don't have many friends." I reached for the bottle again, only for him to snub me. "I would die of boredom sitting in your tent. And how am I supposed to give Griffin updates on the training if I do not see it?"

"I will give you updates to pass along, as I had before whatever plan you've hatched dumped you back here."

Again, he pushed my hand from the wine. I huffed, falling onto the edge of the bed. "Do you think I enjoy being in a camp of those who wish me dead?"

"You seem to." The wine bottle clinked on the desk. "If I asked you again why you are here, would you give me the truth?"

"What makes you think you don't already know the truth?"

Easton sat back in his chair and propped an arm on the desk. He studied me, and though each elongated moment stuck in his gaze felt like an eternity and the space between us like a chasm, I mocked his scrutiny.

"Half-truth," he finally quipped. "There's deceit in those crystal eyes of yours."

I raised my chin, and Easton fought the furrow of his brow. "Have you been looking close enough to tell?"

The swig of wine swirled in my gut with the challenge of his gaze. I was on my feet in the next moment, striding through the gorge of weariness between us.

Close, too close.

The dangerous line we'd toed had disappeared with my betrothal. Every action was now without repercussion, at least not one Griffin cared about.

His gaze swept downward from mine as I walked with an extra sway in my hips.

No challenge remained in his eyes when he spied my raised brow. Like a warrior marching to his death, Easton looked as if he knew he'd lost. His lips gasped opened, eyes fighting to widen. His throat bulged around a shoulder-tensing gulp.

I traced my nails against the desk, drawing his attention to where they fluttered from wood to the back of his hand. Leaning, I leveled our gazes. "Can you see what's in them now, Easton?"

Closer, until the huff from his nose battered my upper lip. Even then, I pressed.

Still as a statue, Easton awaited my assault. His fist clenched as my fingers traced the lines of his unsteady pulse. His stare held mine, though it wavered, as if wanting to make another downward sweep.

His mouth thinned, again searching for the words to rebuff me. When they didn't come, I dared closer to feel the warmth of his lips.

I smirked in triumph when his eyes fluttered closed and his free hand reached for my knee.

Then I was gone, twirling from his grasp and leaving him cool with the ghost of my kiss.

"Careful, General, you might've just let the enemy into your camp." I gripped the tent flaps, turning to flash him a victorious wink. "And your bed."

My victory was cut short by a soft body in my path and a squeal in my ears. I nearly tripped on Easton in my haste to retreat from whoever blocked my grand exit. His hand caught my arm. The warmth bottled up from our almost kiss exploded through the single caress.

"Here," I offered my hand to the mess of aprons and skirts floundering in the stale leaves.

"Do not!" She ripped the flap of her apron from her head. Her mousy hair, the same beige as her apron, tangled like thread across her down-turned eyes and heavy lower lip.

Easton stepped past me. "Saige, what are you —"

"She's sharing your tent?" Her banshee scream set me on my heals. Across the campfire's glow, Gil and Berel were on their feet. They treaded toward us, and I tried to clear my confusion by analyzing the small grin on Gil's face. If not nearly in the middle of Easton wrestling the girl to her feet, I might've laughed with the brute.

Easton dropped her arm. "She's my mate, Saige."

The way he said her name, twice, had my magic rearing. I rolled my shoulders back to force some restlessness from my grip, only to find it scorching to the surface with every second she stood beside him. I stared at where grass and leaves fluttered from her hand outreached toward him.

"She's the plague of Virian." She latched onto his arm. "She might as well have spat on you. She forced us to train even though we despise it, and today she made a greater mockery of us by training with us as if she's one of us. Defend our clan, Easton!"

"Enough!" I snapped. The air around me seemed to crackle.

Easton reached between us, chest turned to me. "Kacela," he said, voice low.

I stared at her grip on the shield of his arm between us. Power bundled and wove its way through my nerves, shoving and urging for release, demanding to shred the camp as it had once shredded the Tait library.

Too close. I was too close to an explosion of power.

She was too close. To me, to my mate, to the fury of my magic and the demands of the mate bond to protect what was mine.

Dragging my gaze to Easton, I hoped he could see the plea in my eyes. My power brewed like lightning within a storm cloud, but I could not pull myself from its intoxicating clutches.

Easton's curls rose, as if suspended by strings.

I saw Gil lunge.

The girl's eyes bulged and her fingers reached once again for my mate. His name on her lips was the flare my magic awaited.

I struck.

Two arms wrapped around my waist, hauling me into the dim shadows of the tent. Pine wrapped me in solace, my nerves and bouncing magic giving to the demand of the mate bond's pull.

The sparks redirected. They burrowed through my gut to the thin, magical bond between us. It twirled around it and speared through him.

I heard his gasp and felt the grip of his fingers on my waist. The other hand traced up my spine to clench in my hair. It was the anchor I needed to keep my magic from sweeping me out to sea.

I grounded in the feeling of him. His calluses snagging on my hair. His fingers uprooting my shirt to stroke the skin beneath. His breath cascading from my ear to shoulder.

With him as my guide, I reeled myself back.

"Kacela," he whispered when the sparks died. Only then did I realize the wrinkle of his shirt in my fists and how tight our bodies pressed. How my forehead stuck to his neck, the curve of his chest beneath my chin, the grip he had on my neck and hip. How I was caged against him.

And yet I couldn't release his shirt.

"Kacela," he repeated.

He forced separation between our chest to reach for my cheeks. His eyes were so near I could count the blue shards outlining his irises.

"Are you alright?"

My chuckle eased into a dry cough. "Altun magic."

His concern broke into laughter, full of relief. "Altun magic," he agreed.

I pulled his hands from my cheeks, digging my fingers into his wrists to feel his pulse. "I'm fine. Young magic wielders have been known to have outbursts."

"Caused by?"

"Emotions, usually."

My breath sputtered at the gleaming smile stretching across his lips. The glimpse of radiance in his smirk rivaled the sun. "Which emotions caused this outburst?" Then, his embrace returned. One arm wrapped around my lower back, and the other reached upwards. A palm against the pulse in my neck, fingers in the tuffs of hair escaping my braid, his thumb running the length of my jaw. "Are you jealous, Kacela?"

"Of her?" I demanded, voice airy. "I am not oblivious that

a high-ranking general may have his choice of girls within the camp. Trample around with whoever you wish, Easton."

I let him hold me and feel the stillness of the mate bond and fixed beat of my pulse as proof of my indifference.

His chin dipped. The shadows across his gaze darkened the emerald gleam in his eyes. "Bit difficult to do so when you share my bed every night, love."

"Find me another bed. Another tent would be ideal."

Outside the tent, commotion raged with Gil and Berel's pleas for peace. The girl screamed of an attack and bolstered the cries of children and threats of warriors. Yet Easton stared down at me. His thumb worked across my jaw, tilting it up. Higher and higher. Angling my mouth toward his gloating grin.

"Ironic," I whispered, "for you to lecture me about being jealous when you looked ready to rip the head from any who touched me at the ball."

His tongue darted out to wet his lips.

"I wanted to. I would have killed any boy who dared. You're my mate, not some namby's."

"I am nothing to you, Easton."

"You are nothing to the Altun lordlings as well."

My breath caught and the crumbling realization I'd been fighting off since Neira barged into my room threatened to douse the excited mate bond. I'd spent years postponing an arranged marriage only to have it finally ripped away by my mate, exactly as I'd hoped. Yet, the destroyed path left me wilting like a plant in winter's approach, and Griffin's promise to train my magic had died with it.

I'd be an unwelcome guest in Virian forever, no matter if I could convince fifty-one other Forterian clans to train their females.

His fingers curled in my hair, yanking my head back and chin up. Lashes flushed against my cheek, and his breath fell across my pulse. Easton snickered as his lips met my neck, and my traitorous heart squeezed. I let go of my fury and allowed my magic to seep back deep within me. I gave to the distraction of Easton's whispers against my skin, the curling of his fingers into my hip, the slight sting at the base of my roots. "You know, Berel and Gil have a bet going."

I blinked.

Easton nipped at the skin above my pulse. "Of who will fall first."

"A stupid bet. Are you so bored?" Though my nerves jittered with the aftermath of my magic's demands, Easton held me frozen with a few fingers entangled in my hair.

"Bored?" He shook his head, lips tickling my collarbone. "Intrigued. To hear an Altun brat beg."

His words were a blow I couldn't avoid.

Mine were as staccato as my breath. "I was raised in a castle, general. Begging for small favors is beneath me."

Easton's fingers crept further into my hair. "I enjoy your clever tongue, love." He retreated so our eyes met, the heat behind his stifling. Then, his head sank. His lips brushed mine. I reeled, but the hand in my hair refused to concede.

I could've snapped at him, given to the temper of my magic. Instead, I stilled against the shivers of his fingers unwinding from my hair and watched him back toward the tent flap. Only once he'd untangled us did I notice my hands held waist height, reaching for his retreat.

The smirking glint did not leave his eyes. "Clean up. You smell like charred remains. I'll handle the mob come for your head."

I reached for the tub full of steaming water, meant for Easton's bath, and sapped the heat from it. Dunking myself beneath, I cooled my nerves.

If only for the night.

CHAPTER
23

THE TENSION DIDN'T RESOLVE, not in the cramped cage of the tent nor in my daily updates with Griffin. My plan stalled with Easton's insistence on spoon feeding me information. If I could not engage with the females, I had only what I could pull from meetings I wasn't invited to.

I knew Berel's weariness of me was behind it, convincing Easton to meet my every move with a question or offered chaperone. If Berel could have smelled my every breath, he might've, just to see if it stank with deceit.

Easton didn't waste a minute of my growing agitation, prodding at each wrung out nerve. He was an ever-annoying presence, exacerbated by a revelation he'd known from the first spark of my magic through him: I'd fortified our mate bond with the redirection of my magic away from the blubbering girl. No longer a thin thread, the bond was like a ship's rigging.

Mental blocks between us gave to the slightest emotions, ravaging the bond with heated glances and ignored urges. He knew about each of my stolen glances at the blessing across his back, the urge to brush my fingers through his curls, and muddling effect of his scent on my thoughts.

But for every thought of mine skating across the bond, one of equal heat responded.

Still, all I had to show for my weeks at Virian were a horny mate and an impatient, disappointed king.

I needed something to appease the latter.

None reported of more rifts on Sacrament Land to allow us back onto the mountain. There were no whispers of rebellion, no matter how far I pried into their minds. I even walked the camp at night, desperate enough to hope a warrior might attack me and bring Griffin's temper back to his favorite targets.

My only source of relief was the daily trainings I'd goaded Easton into.

"Take it seriously," I spat at him, accepting the flask of water.

His brows raised. "Who put the stick up your ass?"

I glared back.

His head dipped and breath raised the hairs on my exposed neck. "You need to relax. Fortunately for you, I know just how to get that stick —"

I jabbed him with my elbow, causing him to lose his hold on his own flask and spill water across his head. Easton tipped his head back and roared with laughter, the water running down the columns of his neck, glistening in the afternoon sun. He tussled it from the limp curls against his forehead.

Another jab of my elbow to his gut.

"Dirty play." He rubbed the spot.

"Fight me," I barked.

"You want an actual fight?" Easton pointed his blade at my chest, dipped his chin, and grinned. "Don't complain when I put you on your back."

I tossed the flask outside the ring and retook the wooden handles of practice swords. The grips itched, too rounded for a comfortable grip.

Easton stepped into the training circle and it seemed to compress around us, as the tent did. He inched closer, sheltering me within his presence. I couldn't escape him without abandoning my plan. Every day near him was a demon cutting through the frontline of my emotions, picking at my shield until the gaps left from disdain and hatred were replaced with another less hostile. Until my actions reflected those warming sentiments.

We mirrored one another, then Easton straightened, staring at something over my shoulder.

I turned.

Chief Indiviar stomped toward us from his tent. His brute advisor, Callum, held a limp Doyon by the collar of his jacket. Baine, the thinker, trekked behind him, shadowed by a smirking blond winged.

With them, the crowd surged around our training pit, confining me within it. I kept my attention from their curious stares, but their mutters berated me.

At Callum's shove, Doyon hit his knees with a thud, then collapsed in the dirt. He peered up with a watery plea in his dark, beady eyes. Patches of red and blue marred his wrists, neck, and face. Blood puddled from his lips, soaking through the white tunic. His braid had been sawed off, tuffs of hair sticking to his cut-littered face.

Chief Indiviar unsheathed a sword and pressed it to the elder's neck.

I raised my blades to bat it away, but Easton's knocked them down. His arm stretched across my midriff.

"Grow tired of killing chiefs? Moving onto the elderly?" I snapped. My magic streaked down my forearms in golden bolts. The practice swords shattered in a flash of lightning. The charred remains stuck to my palms.

Baine retreated a step, eyes widening.

"I protect my clan," Chief Indiviar snarled back.

"From an elder who trained your finest warriors?" I would've spat at him if Doyon wasn't laid out before me like the prized buck.

"Who are your parents?" Chief Indiviar raised his sword, beckoning Doyon to lift his chin to keep from slicing his skin. Still, the old training master would not meet my gaze.

Doyon spat blood. "I'm sorry," he managed out, voice raspy and dry. "I didn't want to, but—"

I reached for his unprotected mind, soothing it. The crinkles around his eyes and above his brow softened.

Easton stepped forward, pointing his practice sword at the chief's blade. "Take your weapon off him. You've done enough." I may have shuddered from the authority in his voice if I hadn't been holding myself rigid to avoid tearing into the chief's sneer.

The messenger who'd interrupted Amaury, Fleck, stepped to Indiviar's side. His beady gaze surveyed me, then he smiled, revealing crooked, stained teeth. "You look like your mother."

I raised a brow, ignoring the sweat-amplified chill beneath my leathers.

"I saw you. Once, when you were just a babe. Stumbling from the cabinet, crying." His blond wings ruffled, rising. "I should have killed you both then."

Easton's presence rushed across the mate bond. I solidified the wall between us, and he slammed into it.

"Take your sword off of him," I ordered the chief.

Smirking with victory, he sheathed his weapon, then Easton motioned for a someone to help Doyon back to his feet and away.

With the space cleared before us, I stepped to Indiviar. Glaring up, I hoped he saw the promise of death in my eyes. "You could've asked," I purred, unclenching my jaw. "I would have told you of how my mother, the Virian Clan whore, hid me in a cupboard until the night she was murdered by her own chief."

Gasps punctured the silence of the camp.

"Your existence is a mark of shame on our camp." He rolled back his shoulders, the black inking seeming to come alive with every movement. "By Forterian laws, you should be put to death."

Easton took a half step past me and put his arm across my torso. His fingers curled into my hip.

The crowd around us muttered. I felt their agreements like poisoned darts. Their cries for my death amplified until I couldn't hear my own thunderous pulse in my ears.

My magic jolted between my fingertips. I tried to settle it. This would not be a massacre at my own hands. I'd never agreed to quell the rebellion for Griffin, only incite it, but they pressed closer and raised steel blades.

"Did your mate know?" Indiviar pressed, raising his blade to Easton's chest.

At the threat to my mate, my magic struck the ground. It lit the gleam in the chief's eyes and silenced the converging crowd thirsting for my blood.

All but Indiviar stumbled back. He stared down Easton. "We should kill you next for protecting a traitor."

"I am not a traitor," I said, voice unwavering. "I am one of you. Born in Virian to a Forterian mother. Raised under Forterian training traditions."

Stillness overcame the training yard. All held their breaths, wondering who would speak next and with what declaration.

"She's a Forterian warrior," Easton finished.

I bristled at my mate's proclamation, reveling in the moment I'd endured their hateful glares for. I trembled with my next breath, wondering what reaction would bring the rebellion. I began to reach out with my consciousness for Griffin.

Baine smirked. "And what would you have us do? Submit her in the Sacrament?" His face turned pale as the words lit a smile across my face.

"No," Chief Indiviar stated.

"It's my birthright."

"No female is allowed in the Sacrament." The chief's teeth were grinding.

"The Sacrament is open to all Forterians with adequate training to survive its tests." I withheld the triumph fluttering in my gut from my voice, instead allowing it to beam through my grin. "Denying me access to the Sacrament would violate the bargain tattooed on your arm."

Chief Indiviar's nostrils flared. He reached for the bargain beneath his armor. I saw the death promised in his snarl when it returned to me.

"Such violation would result in your death." I drew his gaze toward the spiked heads with a nod. "Do you think the next chief will put your head beside Daviat's?"

The crowd retreated, as if they thought I might strike their chief with my next breath.

"The Sacrament is in a little less than a month," I said, turning back to the center of the ring. "You can either forfeit your life or allow me to participate."

"You have magic. Unblessed Forterians do not. It would not be fair," Baine stuttered.

I peeked at the thinker over my shoulder. He blanched.

"King Quillon can block my magic again." I let golden sparks jump between my fingers. Awed, bemused gazes of the onlookers assessed me. They scrambled from me, as did their chief.

Easton's consciousness tapped at mine. *They're going to kill you.*

The words seeped through as both a warning and a glorious realization. I'd found a path, Virian as my trailblazer, to force the equality throughout all camps. To right lingering wrongs caused in my naive youth.

The dream of the battle returned, but this time I'd be stronger. I'd be better.

I'd found my blade on the frontlines, and within my greatest adversaries, I found my target.

They can try.

"Forterian." Gil whistled. "That's some secret."

Berel looked outright offended to share lineage with me. He matted down his hair, muttered something beneath his breath about damning the mountain, sent me a glare lethal enough to kill, and stalked from the tents with a bow and full quiver, knocking the deck of cards from Gil's hands as he did.

"And to be entered in the Sacrament. No one will help you. They'll all want to be the one to kill you." Gil scrambled for the cards, still smiling. He fanned them together with beefy fingers. "Are you ready?"

I uncrossed my arms. "No. I thought Amaury wasted his breath telling me how I wouldn't survive the Sacrament. I grew up in a castle. My survival skills include having a servant bring me food."

"Those can be taught," Easton said, voice as dull as his features. "We'll start tomorrow."

I mirrored Gil's small shake of head and widened eyes. "You're going to help me?"

There was no warmth in his eyes or comfort in how he stood, body locked rigid with hands folded behind his back. I awaited the argument he'd been sending down the mate bond since Chief Indiviar exposed me, yet, in the safety of his tent, he said nothing of the sort.

He shook out his curls, then avoided looking at me. "I've heard losing a mate is incredibly painful."

He ripped the floor out from under me with such a callous response.

"If you're worried about being hurt by my death, reject me. I don't need you anymore to remain here. I'm Forterian." I stomped to him and grabbed his arm to make him face me. "Rid yourself of me. I'm nothing to you, remember?"

"No!" Gil lunged between us, as if he could take the brunt of my words from his friend.

Easton placed a hand of comfort on his friend's shoulder, and I stared at it for a prolonged moment, wondering what it'd be like for him to offer my every worry the same sympathy.

"I'm not going to reject you." The world settled the jumbled mess within me. "Mates are not so easily given. I've seen many go their entire lives without meeting theirs, and though fate has been cruel to give me an Altun brat—"

"Part-Forterian brat," Gil reminded him, nudging me with

his elbow.

I gave him a small smile.

"A brat," Easton rectified, "I will not reject you so soon after meeting you."

I drawled, "How kind of you."

"You'll need to learn survival skills, and quickly. We train for years to survive the harsh landscape of Sacrament Land. If the boys don't kill you, the elements will."

I sat outside by the dying embers of the fire, past when Easton asked if I was going to sleep at all after my check-in with Griffin. The king had been ecstatic at my progress, seemingly forgetting the one secret hidden for twenty years could turn all Altun favors against his top commander. I waited for the fallout, the consequences and lecture on my carelessness. Instead, he beamed at the access to the secrets of the mountain.

Information he expected me to survive the Sacrament with.

The log I leaned against dug into my lower back, and the damp ground soiled the black trousers through to my numb skin. Dreary ache pulsed within each joint. The wintry chill reached the camp, and it'd remain in its grip for months to come.

"You're still awake." Berel dropped a deer carcass just inside the fire's glow.

"I am."

"Waiting for me?"

"No." I sighed, then saw his raised brow. "Yes."

"Why?" He unhooked a long knife from his belt. The first slice of it through the deer hide sounded like demons slicing through the front lines, a ripping of skin and plop of blood. My gut squirmed and my magic receded into its hiding place.

"You know." I dropped my gaze to the stick in my hands.

"I know many things. It does not take a blessed thinker to see through your deception."

"Oh?" I cracked a twig before tossing half of it over the humming red pit of coals. It caught fire in a blink, then went out with a puff of ash riding the smoke upwards.

Berel peered at me over his shoulder, though in the darkened clearing, I could only see the movement of his hair and the glowing whites of his eyes. "Easton has made it clear you aren't to be harmed. I'll wait until you look to add his blood to your hands, along with that of Chief Daviat, before I gut you."

My joints locked at the flash of his knife in the firelight.

"I'm not going to hurt him," I muttered, snapping the twig again.

"You would kill us all if it advanced your plans with the king." Like a phantom sweeping through the camp or the shadows of my nights, he stalked to me. His footsteps no more than a ruffling of dead leaves.

I didn't flinch when the tip of his knife pricked my chin.

I wanted to meet his fire with my own temper, but beneath his glare, I wilted. My shoulders caved, and the knife cut deeper. His glare told me to hold whatever argument I could flounder through. Only my permanent departure would scrap his anger.

"Do what you will within the camp. Mountain be damned, soil the Sacrament if you must to accomplish your king's tyranny. Leave us out of it. Leave Easton out of it. He's too good for you."

Blood dribbled down my neck. He returned his knife's slice to the deer, folding himself within the shadows.

I sulked into Easton's tent. The handful of water I dumped over myself to wash away the feeling of Berel's glare on my back sizzled where it trailed my spine.

Warmth welcomed me into Easton's bed, along with his mumbled, groggy voice. I waited for his breath to return to steady before rolling toward him.

I felt a hitch of heartbeat across the mate bond when I reached for his lip and traced the scar running through the corner of his mouth, then the ones making patchwork of his thin beard. I wanted to touch more, to feel the tangles of his hair through my fingers and trace the scars across his shoulders and torso. To see their tract, where they led to, and hear their stories.

I wanted to kiss him again and feel the demand of his hands. To have another stolen moment in the trees.

Instead, I flipped to my other side and curled my arms around my pillow, fluffing the smell of him from it. Pine wrapped around me like the ghost of his embrace.

Hating him had made my plans easier. I wanted to hate him, as much as I wanted to throw Berel's threat from my shoulders, but would I not have done the same for a childhood friend?

If I could consider any ally a friend.

A childhood friend instead of a dozen sons and nephews of lords and ladies who refused to do any more than dance with me, daughters and nieces who tolerated my presences while they gossiped amongst themselves. The relationships I'd always seen as beneath me, because Amaury had raised me to rely only on myself and the strength of my blade.

My only friend, once my betrothed, was now little more than a memory and a wish.

I crunched the pillow harder against my cheek, hoping that might banish the bitter loneliness.

Trifling matters then, to have a friend. Now, perhaps my death.

I wiped away a rebellious tear rolling across my cheek, but when the rest reached the pillow, their tracks crusted on my skin.

Maybe it would be better for him to reject me.

Rather a snap of pain now than an avalanche of misery later.

Better to be alone than hurt by those closest.

CHAPTER
24

I WOKE TO EASTON'S THUMB on my chin.

I kept myself from stirring to feel the warmth of his fingers for a moment longer, until the prodding became incessant.

"Stop," I muttered, brushing away his hand.

"What cut you?" The callused words hummed with outrage. He batted my arm away to rub his thumb against my sliced chin again, knocking off the scab, then it trailed upwards across the crisp remains of my tears. His eyes widened further.

I rolled from his grip and out of bed. "Probably from training yesterday."

If he saw through my lie, he didn't protest.

I healed the cut with a touch of magic. The tightened skin loosened, but my gut remained a tangle of knots.

As quickly as I could, I changed into heavier clothing to brave the wintry chill seeping through the tent flaps. "We need to start on survival skills, soon."

"Go start the fire," Easton ordered. "No magic."

I turned to protest, mouth running dry at his bare backside. The mate bond sparked from my side, and his shoulders tensed. Tearing my gaze from the vivid black lines of his winged blessing, curves of feathers streaking down his back along with a crosshatching of scars, I dashed from the tent.

The slam of bitter air relaxed the buzz of the mate bond.

A flurry of snow covered the fire pit. I stared at it with disdain.

Gil emerged from his tent, sending me a boyish grin. He unmatted his blond hair with a few rough scratched through it, then sheathed his dual blades. "Good morning."

I looked back at the fire pit. "Morning."

Gil stepped beside me. He fastened his coat up to his chin. The fur lining bunched around his neck, giving him the appearance of a long-haired cat. "I can start the—"

"I've never started a fire without magic," I whispered.

"It's easy. I can show you." He bumped his arm into mine.

I swallowed my shame and squatted with him. Gil walked me through each step with a gentle voice and soft corrections. Within minutes, with his abundant help, the fire raged.

"See? Easy." He thumped me on the back and stood. "I'll go get breakfast."

Once he left, I rubbed the spot sore from his pat and stared at the fire, feeling as warm from pride as my hands felt from the flames.

Easton emerged from his tent with a rope. "We'll go out into the forest later, maybe tomorrow. Today, I'll show you how to make a rabbit snare."

"I won't have rope."

Easton's coat was heavier than Gil's, lined with brown fur matching his hair. A tear on the side had been stitched back with dark green thread. When he turned, I saw slits in the back, allowing his wings to slide through, were lined with extra fur. "Outside resources are forbidden in the Sacrament, but that has never stopped anyone from carrying supplies in or having it dropped through the barrier in the week prior."

I took the rope. "And if I'm caught?"

"Death," Berel said, ducking through his tent's flaps. "The penalty for cheating in the Sacrament is a Forterian execution."

I shivered at the excitement in his words.

Easton shook his head. "They haven't put anyone to death in centuries for bringing in resources. We brought in an entire sack of weapons and tools. Even some food."

"We were not at the top of everyone's kill list. Chief Indiviar will take any chance to kill her before the Sacrament. She goes in with nothing but the leathers on her back." Berel kicked a log into my perfectly constructed fire. The rupture of red sparks lit his face in a crimson glow. "Unless you'd like to watch her limbs be ripped from her body."

The world seemed to crunch around me. "That's a Forterian execution?"

"It's the most extreme form of execution," Easton said, taking a seat beside me on the log. "It hasn't been used in over a century."

Berel shrugged. "I think the chiefs would make an exception for her."

I might've stepped between the two, despite the fear of getting singed by their glares, if Gil hadn't lumbered into the clearing with four bowls of what smelled like cinnamon oatmeal. I took mine before he toppled over with it.

"Vines can also work for snares," Easton explained through a mouthful of food, "or you can steal rope from others."

"That would mean getting close enough to get herself killed," Berel said.

I huffed at the reminder.

They disappeared after breakfast, though Easton left the rope for me to practice making snares in the tree line with. After an hour at it, I returned to his tent, knees damp from the blanket of snow and fingers nearly blue. Magic would whisk the frost away, but I wouldn't have it in the Sacrament. I'd have to tie my snares soaked and shivering.

I set a small ball of fire burning at eye level near Easton's desk and slumped into the seat. Despite his insistence on minimizing what I saw of trainings, he left his work on his desk for my wandering eyes.

I shuffled through what I could without disturbing the order or knocking the smaller notes to the floor. Beneath a bound stack of reports from a nearby clan, the top half of a torn letter peeked out.

> *Easton,*
>   *Deceit has many faces and comes as a wrapped*
> *gift in our greatest triumphs. This year's Sacrament*
> *will be no different. Each pole is desperate to thin the*
> *other's numbers, some seeking help from the bonks*
> *to gain an advantage. You are not the only clan*
> *fighting off war to withhold our peace.*

Someone kicked a log outside the tent. I shoved the letter beneath my shirt and threw myself onto the bed. Easton barged through the tent flaps a moment later. He spied the small ball of fire before his frantic eyes met mine.

"Pack, only the essentials. And put that out," he snapped.

The ball of fire fell as ash.

"What's going on?" I demanded.

He shoved a bag into my chest the moment my feet touched the ground. "There is a band of chiefs coming here. They say it is to address the camp's state for the northern region's Blessing Ceremony. I think, and Berel agrees, they've come for your head and to stop the female's training."

"The bargain—"

"Many would rather see our entire clan wiped from existence than allow the females to train, and worse, allow a halfbreed to lead the charge. Pack your warmest clothing."

Then, he was gone, leaving me with the letter burning against my stomach, a dozen questions, and an empty bag in need of filling.

The skip sapped the energy from me and I landed on my knees besides a hurling Easton. He wiped the back of his hand over his mouth.

"I'll never get used to that," he muttered.

"Is this far enough?" Ache crept into my bones.

"Where are we?"

"South, near the desert of Sacrament Land." I couldn't feel the heat of it, but the magic slinked from the mountain. It crept through the pine trees blocking out the harsh winds and first snowfall of the winter. A flake landed on my eyelash, melting when it brushed my cheek.

Easton nodded, pushing to his feet. I took his offered hand, and he hoisted me up alongside him. "Far enough for now."

"Which chiefs?"

His weapons clattered against one another as he dropped them onto the ground. From his larger pack, he pulled a tarp.

"Find firewood, as dry as you can."

"Easton." I grabbed his arm.

His shoulders fell, but he did not look at me. "It's cold, and it will only snow more. The sooner we can collect firewood to keep it dry, the more adequately we will be prepared for the next few days."

"If our lives are in danger, my magic—"

Easton spun on me, nails digging into my shoulders and nostrils flaring. He yanked me closer. "Your life will be in danger for thirty-eight days, from the elements and trained warriors. Better to test your abilities now with your magic as a reserve than learn your flaws when they kill you."

I stumbled from him and returned with two armfuls of brittle branches.

Easton had thrown the tarp over two low-hanging branches to create a shelter, and beneath it he'd rolled out the furs and blankets. I stared at it a moment too long, with my mouth slightly ajar, and Easton swooped close to take some of the branches.

"Don't worry, we won't be sleeping together."

I raised a brow, holding tight to my scavenging. "Where am

I sleeping?"

"You won't have a tarp or blankets in the Sacrament. You need to learn where is safe to sleep. Trees are a good option, caves if you're desperate, hidden in the snow if you have no alternative. You'll have to set traps to protect yourself in case someone or something comes hunting in the night."

The remaining branches slipped from my grasp. "Something?"

"Predators on the mountain, only wolves and bears."

My stomach cramped. "Only?"

"Clear a spot for the fire," Easton instructed.

"Only?" I insisted. "What used to be in the Sacrament?"

"You work, I talk."

I set to work sweeping the snow from a small patch outside Easton's shelter. It soaked through my gloves and numbed my fingers.

"Our ancestors fought the monsters crafted by our goddess, and before then, they fought her as well. Every kill in battle is dedicated to her, and every warrior lost during the Sacrament fuels her fire."

Easton handed me two flint rocks. The first strike created small sparks swept away in the breeze.

"Lean closer to block the wind with your body."

I did so, and the second strike created more sparks, but no fire. I tried again and again until my hands refused to hold the rocks, numb from finger pads to wrist.

"Harder," Easton smirked. "You did it with Gil's help. What's stopping you now?"

I bit my lip to keep a snide remark at bay and struck the flint again. I coaxed the resulting sparks with a bit of my own magic to send them dancing across the kindling. A tiny flame burst to life.

He stamped it out. "I saw that." Easton didn't balk from my glare. He stared down his nose at me, foot still in my stack of branches. "Do it correctly or return to Kadea and forsake your Forterian blood."

I raised the flint. "I can't light the fire if your boot is here."

"A boot on your fire would be the least of your worries." He dropped beside me, forearms resting on knees and quirked his head. His curls toppled over one another like thrashing waves. "If you cannot make a fire in a bit of wind, how will you survive rain or snow? You'll freeze to death long before anyone can slit your throat."

I could've shoved his boot away, brought a rain of fire down upon him and laugh at his charred smirk, but the truth of his words stung. I couldn't make a fire. Couldn't skin a rabbit even if I caught one. Couldn't survive in the wilderness by myself.

The name stung, but I was a brat. A spoiled, privileged brat raised in a sparkling castle that held more wealth in one room than any Forterian clan did.

With a full breath, I held out the flint. "Am I doing something wrong? Or is it a matter of persistence?"

He eased back, one hand bracing in the snow-sprinkled, yellow grass. "When you strike with the top, yank back the bottom." One of his hands wrapped underneath mine. "Strike it."

I did, and he yanked my bottom hand back. Sparks shot at the tinder.

"Now protect it with your hands and lightly blow on it. If it threatens to go out, more sparks."

Easton leaned closer to block the wind, and my cheeks burned as hot as the growing flame. Another spark and it spread beneath the stack of wood, bursting to life at the heart of the kindling.

"When did the Sacrament change?" I asked. "When did the monsters disappear?"

"After the Great War. Our goddess left, and we lost everything."

CHAPTER
25

I SPENT THE FIRST NIGHT in a tree a few yards from where Easton slept on a bed of furs, high enough to hide in the bristles from predators and low enough to jump down and run if someone spotted me. The next morning, we set snares for rabbits or squirrels and found the nearest source of water using moss.

I was a fair climber, able to reach higher branches and steady myself on narrower ones. I didn't mind heights to the point Easton mentioned twice I could be blessed with wings.

If I survived.

The last part always went unsaid, but never unfelt.

The day after, we practiced baiting enemies, both of animal and Forterian kind, into traps. I dug a ditch deep enough to set up spikes to spear through those who fell through the leaves I'd placed over top.

I had to avoid confrontation. Any fight with more than one Forterian would most likely result in my death.

Easton caught most of the food the first few nights, though my snares had some luck with rabbits. Enough to keep me alive. Not strong, but alive. On night three, I snared the plumpest rabbit I had ever seen, and he taught me to skin it in dim lighting. We cooked it over a smoldering fire.

"What if I cannot make a fire? If someone is hunting me and I must remain unseen?" I asked through a mouthful of dry meat.

"Then don't hunt. Find berries and nuts. They'll sustain you." He tore through his rabbit leg. "For the first week, it may be best to not hunt. You'll need to be constantly moving. The deadliest times of the Sacrament are the first week and the final night."

"Why the final night?"

"One last chance to bathe grudges in blood."

I peeked past my dinner at where he sat across the fire, back covered in his makeshift tent. "How many did you kill during your Sacrament?"

"Twenty-one."

I choked on the rabbit leg.

"Twenty-one?" I repeated, more to myself.

"I had a target on my back after I snubbed a few offered alliances in the years prior. One of the chiefs currently in Virian, Barin, attacked me before I found Gil and Berel. We had a plan to meet on the eastern edge, where jungle and desert collide. I was dropped on the opposite side of the mountain, and instead of going around it, I went over. Barin caught me at the peak. I left him there, nearly gutted. He came back for me the last night."

"Who else is at Virian? What other chiefs?"

"Chief Ran of Faveos. Chief Clodova of Rowera. Both from the south."

"What target do I have on my back because of you?"

Easton offered me another leg of rabbit. "You should be more worried about the target you've put on your own back. And your quest."

I furrowed my brow. "Quest? Amaury never mentioned a quest."

"Many don't. Each warrior's is sacred to them."

"Will you tell me yours?"

He nodded and gulped down a bite. "Gil didn't grow into his shoulders until he was at least fifteen, and Berel was never much of a fighter. I delayed my Sacrament until my twenty-fifth year to give them as much time to prepare as I could." He stared down into the dying fire. "My quest was to ensure they both survived."

"How did you know?"

"Some say it came to them in a dream or they accidentally completed theirs without knowing. Others had a gut feeling."

I tucked my legs up to my chest. The logs crackled in a bed of four days' worth of ash. I watched embers catch the breeze and spiral toward the overlaid branches blocking us from the moon's light.

"You were at my Blessing Ceremony."

I'd been about to leave the fire's glow to find a sturdy branch to sleep on when his words staked my rear to the ground. He peeked up, the curls parting over his brow.

I remembered, in the moment before Griffin skipped us away, how my breath refused to come and my nerves jittered like they were filled with lightning. How'd I'd been searching for something.

"I was in the back. I knew the moment I saw you."

"But you didn't—" My voice and gaze fell. The chill of the snow seeped through my pants and wrecked my body with shivers. I fought it, wrapping my arms tightly around my legs.

"I was sent to learn to fly on the northern bluffs a week later. Then, to the front lines. We have been at war since long before the demons attacked, with one another. Northern clans against the southern clans. If I'd have found you, I'd have left you to tend to Virian until I returned. Many didn't."

I raised my gaze to find him already watching me.

"I couldn't have done that to you. It was easier to convince myself you were safer wherever you were. You were a child."

"I was twelve."

Easton chuckled, then matted the curls back from his forehead. They branched at odd angles across his hairline. "Amaury would have killed me before letting me near you."

I kicked the cleaned rabbit tibia into the fire. "I'm sure the thought still crosses his mind daily."

We fell back into silence. Only the occasional howl of a wolf or the crackle of the fire interrupted the thoughts colliding against equally strong blocks on either side of the mate bond.

"What else did you lose after the war?" I asked.

Easton cocked his head.

"You once told me the Great War— "

"Blunder." Easton's tapped my blade's hilt. "You're Forterian now, even if only part. It's the Great Blunder, a botch in our history we dream of righting."

I pulled my hair from its braid, strand by strand. "You said it wiped your names from history. That your goddess left afterwards. What did the treaty truly take from the Forterians?"

"What does your history books tell you?"

"My royal tutors said the Forterians agreed to live under Altun rule, pay the tariffs, and build trade routes. In return, they'd be protected." My hair hung limp around my shoulders. I raked my hands through it to loosen the dirt and pine needles.

Easton brushed my hands away and began picking the sticky needles from it. "The treaty forced us to forsake our goddess and forget our customs and holidays. Only the Sacrament remains from what we once gathered for. "He curled a handful of hair through his fingers, then let them slide out. "When the Altuns learned they could not take our Sacrament without the land being consumed by plagues and droughts, they took our names. We are no longer marked by our lineage, only by the blood we shed on the mountain. Only our blessings."

I braided my hair as he spoke, in silence, even after his words flittered away with the fire's smoke. I stood and stretched out my legs. Earlier, I'd seen a tree to the north suitable for climbing and was set on making it my bed for the night.

"Kacela," Easton called from his bundle of furs. "I hope you do survive. The goddess may be gone, but that does not mean we forsake those with her strength."

I stood in a small stream branching off from the Vitient River the next morning, his words still ringing in my head and his scrutiny on my back. I'd discarded my socks and boots on the bank beside where Easton sat, rolled up my pants to my knees, and forced frigid fingers to lock around a sturdy tree branch sharpened at one end. My teeth chattered loud enough to scare off the fish.

We saw schools of them meandering through the shaded shallows, but as soon as I waded knee deep into the water at Easton's beckoning, they scattered. I waited, the waves slashing up my shins and seeping up my pant legs, for one to swim close enough to stab.

"Easy." Easton pointed. A fish darted through the shallows toward me. The wood of the spear itched at my grip.

I reared back, though Easton had told me a hundred times to only burst forward, when an arrow sliced through my shoulder. The spear dropped into water soiled with a spray of my blood. I ducked into the shallows. The current ripped at my now submerged thighs and arms, threatening to drag me toward our attackers.

Easton unsheathed his swords.

I clutched the wound and braced against the tide to stagger to shore. I stumbled, pinwheeling my good arm to keep myself from landing face first into the blood-stained, mucky shore.

Shadows moved through the dense pines. I counted three stalking us, then a fourth figure further back raising a bow.

"Duck!" I warned.

The arrow slice through pines, my world slowing to the half breath of its flight, aimed true and too quickly for Easton to move.

I screamed.

The arrow, a hair from puncturing my mate's chest, exploded in a spark of gold. Bits of my magic, intermixed with the splintered arrow, splashed over his face.

He twisted behind the trunk of a tree, swords at the ready as I scrambled to my own hiding place. Another arrow flew over my head.

I had no weapons other than the dagger on my thigh. Back in the stream, the hastily carved spear rolled with the tide.

They stalked closer, boots crunching snow. The rushing Vitient obscured their grunted commands to one another.

Easton lunged from his hiding spot to take the first attacker. Their blades clanged together, and Easton pivoted to block the second blow coming for his head.

I rolled from a blade stabbing through the pine needles shielding me. Bare of noticeable blessings, my attacker advanced. I parried his next attack with my small blade and rolled beneath his outstretched arm to stab my dagger into his gut.

Blood pulsed between his fingers as he pressed a hand to the wound. He glared at me and his eyes darkened.

Black tuffs of hair spurted from his cheeks, then down his neck and from beneath his sleeves. His nose stretched to a snout. His joints, each contorting with a sickening crack, rolled him forward onto all fours, long talons digging into the grass. He was more bear than fae, swords discarded and canines glistening in slobber.

A shapeshifter.

I scrambled toward the nearest tree, sliding beneath the branches to hide behind a wall of pines. The beast roared, shaking snow from the trees onto my head.

He barreled into me. We tumbled into the next clearing. His claws shredded my thigh and canines grazed my ear.

Squeezing my legs between us, I kicked with all my might.

He skidded away, claws scraping through the underbrush. A devilish grin overtook the fur-coated snout. He reared, then pounced.

I covered my head with one hand to protect from a blow and threw the other out to stop it. My magic leapt from my palm. There was a flash of blinding light, then something thudded on the ground beside me.

Warmth drenched my side.

Two hands gripped mine, prying my arms from my head. "Kacela." Easton eased me into a seated position, then up to my feet.

Any rational thoughts stalled at the sight of the shapeshifter. The fur receded into his gasping cheeks as he released his hold on the monster lurking beneath his charred, smoldering skin. Dulling eyes blinked once more before all life left, and the top half of his torso convulsed.

Then stilled.

Easton stared at the twitching lower half, cleaved clean at the waist.

"The others?" I clutched his hand.

Easton dropped to his knees before me. He pried my slashed pant leg aside to reveal the ribbons of shredded muscle beneath. "Dead. Except one."

"You," I swallowed past the shock, "killed them?"

He titled his head back to flash a grin, one corner of his lip hitching higher than the other. Sunlight speared through the trees to embrace him, as if called by his smirk. "I'm a decorated war veteran, love. Three newly blessed warriors are nothing to the likes of me."

I couldn't help the chuckle releasing the clench of my shoulders. "Cocky bastard."

"You killed one as well."

I stared at the two parts of the shapeshifter. With so few scars on his chest, he could not have seen much war. He may have been blessed only a year or two before.

Blood coated my hands. The metallic scent soiled my next breath. I itched at the blood drying in the creases of my palm. It gathered under my nails, and my palms turned a brighter pink.

Easton clapped his hands around mine. "Kacela, stop."

I raised my blurring gaze to his furrowed brow.

"My first," I whispered.

He rubbed his thumb over the back of my hands. "First?"

"First kill."

Releasing my hands, he shrugged. "Better now than in the Sacrament."

I tucked my hands tight to my chest. "I was trained to fight, Easton, not bred for war."

"Then you are more Altun than Forterian." He smiled, and his words were warm, as if he took comfort in them.

My shoulder began to ache through the dulling adrenaline. He probed the gash on my thigh again. Stabbing pain shot through where claws had made minced meat of my thigh.

I pressed a hand to my thigh, only for Easton to snatch it.

"Don't heal it." He held my wrist close enough for my knuckles to graze his chin. "We'll use it as a learning opportunity."

My hand sparked gold. "How about I rip your body open, and we use that as a learning opportunity?"

He dropped my hand and stood to poke my shoulder, causing a gasp. "You may deal with worse during the Sacrament. Come, there is still the last one to deal with, then I'll show you how to stitch your wounds closed."

"I won't have a needle or thread to suture," I reminded him.

Easton took a step, then tripped. Sprawled out across the forest floor, he grunted, "Mountain be damned." He flipped to examine a slash through his thigh. The flaps of his pants gave way to a thin slice pooling with thick, crimson blood. It rolled down his skin and sloshed near his calf, confined by the thick fabric.

I dropped to my hands and knees before him. The burning in my thigh became a wave of nausea.

"Let me." I held up a hand encased in a golden hum.

The warmth in Easton's cheeks drained. He reached to bat away my hands, but the blow was barely a brush. "Save your energy."

I shoved his hands away and slapped my hand to the sticky wound. Blood splashed up my arm and across my shoulder. The metallic scent clogged my nostrils and seemed to coat my tongue.

The golden magic traveled up my arm like a glove and squirmed into the hair-thin slice to find the severed vein. It pinched the two ends and melded them together, the action as natural as breathing. It made quick work of sewing his skin back together, each suture of golden magic pulling the skin taught.

Golden light pouring from the wound faded and I dropped my hand to the pine-needle-covered ground.

Easton's bright red cheeks stretched his scars into a half smile. "Thank you."

My lungs burned, the smell of his blood like noxious fumes within them. I watched his softened eyes survey my face and masked the pain streaming in from everywhere to return the grin.

We eased to our feet. He turned before I stumbled.

I threw up more blocks in the mate bond to prevent the trickle of pain from travelling across.

I could hardly start a fire or catch a rabbit, but this I could do. I could take a hit from a Forterian without the comfort of my magic.

Easton bent beneath a bush and plucked a green flower with a yellow stem from the warm of the roots.

"This," he raised it before me, "is the only herb you will eat in the Sacrament. No matter how hungry you are. This will save your life. Careful, it has slightly hallucinogenic effects."

It was bitter and flaky but dulled the pain enough for me to walk unencumbered behind Easton's elongated strides, back to the bloodied stream.

A Forterian lay half in the stream, the gash on his leg producing a red branch to feed into the Vitient. More blood trickled from the gash on his forehead, and some dripped from his fingertips.

"Kalman," Easton greeted, dragging him to a seated position.

"Traitor," he spat back, teeth coated in blood and brunette hair caked with mud. "Kill me already."

"Who told you we were here?"

He barked a laugh. "Many want to bathe the mountain in her blood."

Kalman's mind opened for me at the slightest touch. Animosity, so thick it left a singed taste in my mouth, wrapped around me. I batted it away to peel away the secrets laid bare for me, consuming them one by one until his memories were mine.

"Barin," I muttered, tracing a line of memory back to Virian. I dove deeper in search of Berel's name woven within it. He'd promised not to kill me himself, but the thinker was a threatened fox desperate for safety. I didn't care to imagine what other schemes he'd hidden from Easton.

When I didn't find a mention of him, I maneuvered along another thread of consciousness, where pacts and deals regarding my Sacrament bubbled with excitement.

Summoned by the bonks, the Old Faith priests of Beaddeon, bloodthirsty creatures were raised with my scent as their favorite flavor. Kalman's fear for those too close to their release on the final night sowed my own.

Give me your knife, I told Easton across the mate bond.

Why?

I want to send a message to Barin. I clenched my teeth. The barriers between us quaked against the waves of pain, its blur threatening my vision like a falling veil.

Easton gripped my shoulder. *Kacela, you may start a war you cannot fight.*

I have all fifty-two Forterian clans as enemies. I will not roll over and allow any chief to make a fool of me.

I felt the fight in his head, between protecting and supporting me, with a smaller voice arguing for the preservation of Forterian traditions. Finally, he relented with a chest-heaving sigh.

Carve this. I saw the symbol in his mind of two war hammers crossed over a flame. *It's hers. Warriors once carved it onto their shields before battle.*

As protection?

As a warning.

Across the branching streams of the stamina's blessing,

signifying his magically enhanced perseverance, I carved. His skin split like silk and blood rolled over his sides. It squished between the mucky shore and my toes.

"What is the warning?" I asked, watching Kalman stumble from us, a trial of blood soiling the fresh sheet of snow.

Easton sheathed his swords and turned toward camp. "Come, death awaits."

What little pain relief the pungent flower offered wore off on the walk back, and I stumbled through dizzying pain. A trail of blood marked the drag of my leg. I collapsed beneath the tarp, soiling the blankets in red blotches. The block across the bond gave, and my pain gushed like a river being released from a dam.

Easton stilled, rocks held above the awaiting tinder of the dead fire. He threw them down, causing a cloud of ash to mushroom from the fire pit. It caught the breeze and breeched my lungs in each heaving gasp.

My magic slinked from the depths, a tantrum-throwing toddler angered by being forced back.

Easton crawled over me, fingers prodding the gash on my thigh, then the slice through my arm. I flinched, as if his poking fingers were razors.

"Your magic," he blurted.

It rolled into a boil in my gut, but the stream of it reaching my fingertips did little more than warm them. Every yearn for more cost an extra breath, a spasm of my heart I couldn't keep steady.

The cool blanket of burnout pulled over my toes, then up to my knees.

My eyes rolled back. Away from Easton's demands. His words were muffled, as if my ears were clogged with water.

The agony in my arm and leg blended to one until all I knew was the pulse of pain I'd become.

Across the unblocked bond, Easton's consciousness darted to mine. It was the same blizzard of worry I'd felt from him after the Demon War, when he hadn't known my name but had plastered my face to every drop of fret tensing his jaw. *Kacela, stay awake.*

Not a command, but a desperate plea.

Reaching his mind was like swimming against a tide. *Kacy,* I muttered back.

What?

I felt his arms wrap around me, then something heavy laid across my legs and chest. The sting of pain gnawed deep into my bones.

Kacela, don't fall asleep. Stay here. With me.

Kacy, I repeated, hating how his use of my name was too similar to the sternness of Amaury's. *Call me Kacy.*

The fret knotting our minds together loosened, allowing in a bit of warm.

"Kacy," he said, but his voice was an echo down a dark tunnel.

CHAPTER 26

FINGERS SKIMMED MY FOREHEAD, toppling wisps of hair down my brow. His breath tumbled over my cheeks, and then he did it again: Fingers through hair, tucking it further behind my ear with every pace. Then breath, warm as a summer breeze, across my neck. Again and again, a pattern I matched my own breath to.

His other arm wrapped around my back, hand on the curve of my waist. My legs twitched against the tangle of his.

"Not yet," Easton whispered, lips skimming my hairline.

I eased back, releasing any protesting thoughts.

A slight hum left his lips. The song rose, and a ghost of a memory surfaced with it. I heard its echo in my cupboard, when mother prepared to release me into the morning to watch the stars disappear.

His embrace was as warm as the cupboard, beard as scratchy as the blankets, and shoulder a hard lump like my pillow. I curled his shirt into my fist. An anchor. A plea to stay within the sanctuary of his embrace.

I dragged my leg over his hip, assisted by his guiding hand, and shifted to press the bridge of my nose into his neck. His hand glided up my thigh, over my hip, and clenched the back of my shirt below where his other fingers splayed across my ribs.

His mind opened and the mate bond rejoiced like gossiping ladies. I pulled his consciousness across to mine. Not within, but as close as we were: Skin to skin and hands groping for a firmer hold, as if the next breeze fluffing the tent would rip us apart.

I cursed the next breeze, the shift of power within it, and the tart taste I knew better than my own magic. The demand of it, diluted by whatever magic protected the Forterians.

"Mountain be damned," I hissed, then untangled my legs from Easton's.

My forehead was cool when I pulled it from beneath his chin, my hands cramped while unfurling.

I eased away, averting my gaze to Easton's tent, the mess of our camping gear strewn across its floor, and a trickle of dried blood leading from the entrance to the bed.

His hands slid from me, fingers snagging on my shirt and waistband.

"Kacy," he said, still reaching.

"Nalin Tait is here," I replied, pulling my hair into a low bun.

Easton bounced off the bed before I did, snatching up his blades.

I skipped, blocking him from leaving the tent. "Don't." Hints of burnout burrowed in my bones, and I placed a hand to his chest to steady myself. I thought to snatch it back, but instead let it wander up to the chocolate locks curling around his ears. I smoothed them down so he did not look as if a gust of wind battered him from behind. "When I come back, you can tell me how we got back here and where the chiefs went."

His hand encased my good shoulder. "You want to meet him by yourself? You've been out for days." He leaned so close he could have brushed a kiss to my brow, then backed away.

I nodded and touched my injured shoulder. Beneath my shirt, a line of stitches held my skin together. My magic pulsed and healed the torn muscle and skin on both my shoulder and thigh. The stitches turned to ash and tickled my arm as they fell out my sleeve. Those from my thigh gathered on the top of my foot.

"I'll grab food for you." Then, he was gone, his rush to leave wrapping me in a pine scent. I let it fall around me, and only once I'd doused my senses in it did I emerge from the tent, dressed in my leathers and heavy winter boots.

The snow crunched beneath every footstep from the warmth of the fire toward the darkening forest. The towering pines, as large as the spikes on Kadea's castle, rebutted the afternoon sun. Snow piled in the paths through them, reaching to my knees.

"You could have skipped." His voice was a low grinding, no longer the sweet melody of a minor key.

"I enjoy the walk."

Nalin stepped from the wall of pines, feet hardly making a sound. He wore black detailed in white, his family's crest of a stalking leopard embroidered on the left breast. Its eyes, drops of ruby, sparkled from the silver swirls at his fingertips. His raven black hair, so stark against the trees, was a shaggy mess, hanging in juts across his furrowed brow. The same deep creases lined his eyes.

He took another step. His jaw tensed, and the magic swirling his fingertips jolted.

"Why are you here?" My magic boiled. More than steam reached my fingertips. Strikes of lightning as minute as thread arced from finger to finger, raced up my forearms, and cracked in my ears.

Nalin stared at my hands. "You're Forterian."

Not a question. Not a sneaking suspicion. A confirmation.

"Who told you?"

Nalin blinked at me. He shook his head, dislodging more of the locks. "You're entered in the Sacrament. It's all any estate can speak of."

"King Quillon and I—"

"Damn the king!"

I flinched at his outburst. Silver mist hovered above his

out-turned hands like a blizzard frozen in time. His magic's reflection sparkled in his near-black eyes.

"Nalin," I eased forward, "why are you here?"

He dropped his hands and dipped his chin. Not even the brightest of my magic could banish the shadows around his eyes. "To help you."

I took another step, sinking knee-deep in a snowbank. My magic flared. "I don't need your help, Nalin."

"You don't understand what you're doing, Kacela."

"I do." I gritted my teeth. "If my plan works and I survive the Sacrament, the Forterians will train all their youths equally. That is why I am here, Nalin, and it will be worth everything I've done."

Nalin dug his fingers into his hair, streaking it back. "Training females is Amaury's goal. Griffin has never cared for equality in the Forterians. He's allowed your charade because it gives him a chance to shed Forterian blood. If he could, he'd use you to destroy them entirely."

"No." I retreated a step. "You're wrong. Griffin needs the Forterians. He only planned to sacrifice one clan to ensure none step out of line, and now he doesn't need that."

He stormed to me, lips pulled into a snarl and eyes like the deepest sea caverns. His nails dug into my exposed wrists. "You think he'll stop even if you can convince all the clans to train their females?"

I felt like a child, dwarfed by his gaze and the trees, squished beneath a weight I could no longer carry. The truth of his words sunk in, and I didn't know anymore: Not why I'd come or what it was all for. What the betrayal of my birth would mean for me, for my mate, for Amaury, or for the king. Not what Griffin wanted, though I'd never truly known what that was.

"Then why allow me in the Sacrament? He could pull me from it easily."

"He needs access to the mountain." Nalin gritted his teeth.

I tugged at my arms still caged in his grasp. "He's been on Sacrament Land."

"With you," Nalin snapped. "You're Forterian. The mountain recognizes your blood."

"There is something in the mountain. Griffin can protect us from it."

Nalin yanked on my arms. His eyes widened and the wind scattered his hair across his brow. "You've felt it?"

"It attacked me."

"When? How?"

My golden magic attempted to shove his hands off, but silver mist battered it away from his grip. "Months ago."

Nalin yanked harder. His magic fell atop mine like a net, blocking me from it. "Why, Kacela? What did it want?"

I shrank back, stilled only by his unrelenting grip. Silver flurries tickled my nose and pricked where they landed on my cheeks. "It went through my memories."

He reeled me close enough to see the sparks of his magic reflected in his eyes. His nails pressed further into my skin. "What memory?" His words were as blunt as a blade.

"Of us," I whispered. "When I took the tonic."

Nalin snatched his hands away and wrang them out behind his back. He muttered to himself as he paced away and stopped with his back to me. His shoulders settled with a sigh. "There are greater stakes now, bigger than the king's greed and training the Forterians. The demons were only the start of a war this realm cannot survive."

"Realm?" I demanded, stumbling forward.

He nodded and kicked a bit of snow. "You can return with me. You have nothing to prove here, Kacela, and you'd be safe."

"The Sacrament is my birthright."

He stared at me for a breath, then looked past me toward Virian. With another sigh, he muttered, "I hope it is worth it, the sacrifice of this clan and of yourself. Good luck in the Sacrament, goddess knows you'll need it."

Then, he was gone. I breathed in air ripe with pine instead of tart cherries.

"Sacrifice this clan?" a gravelly voice demanded from behind me.

I whirled to Easton. He held his blades out, one pointed at me. His face burned red beneath the kinked curls strew across his brow.

"You meant to turn my clan into a lamb for slaughter? Why? For whose greed, Kacela?"

"Easton—"

He took one step, then stopped and straightened. His blade tips disappeared into the snow. "Berel warned me, almost daily. You were raised by them, so even if you were born to this camp, why would you—"

"Stop!" I clenched my fists around the sparking magic. "You don't know. You only heard that. You don't know what I've done for us. Griffin called a priestess of the Old Faith, a bonk, to the castle to snap our bond. Everything I have done since has been to preserve us."

I grasped my blades. My chest heaved for every breath. Heart fought to keep the blood from ringing my vision in red fury.

"Do not pull your blades on me," Easton said, voice low like a feline's prowl. "You are the enemy to this clan. To all Forterians."

I raised my hands from my blades and curled them, dousing the flickers of magic. "I made the king believe I would come here to spark rebellion, but my goal has always been equality for females. I did not lie to you, Easton."

"I don't believe you."

The words were a well-aimed dagger. I couldn't swallow past them. Couldn't pull them from my heart. Couldn't stop the pain gushing from his narrowed gaze.

"You're a traitor."

"To the king!" I shrieked, the cracking of my magic replacing the thundering of blood in my ears. "I lied to him to protect you."

His swords clanged back into their sheaths. "I can't unwind the lies you've told. I can't trust you to keep your word any more than I could months ago."

"Easton—"

"A traitor is a traitor." He turned on his heels and strolled through the snowbanks, returning to the warmth of the fire. Leaving me with the ice of his words.

That night, there was a cot in the corner of Easton's tent, and the next day, a hastily erected tent behind his.

Exactly what I'd asked for.

The night before the Sacrament, a winged from another camp delivered my leathers. Easton watched me pick at them in his tent since mine was too small to do any more than curl onto the cot. I was aware of his glare on my back, as well as Berel's, who'd insisted on following me around. Gil sat in the corner playing cards, giving me sympathetic half looks when I turned.

Easton dismissed them after my magic wove through the leathers for the umpteenth time. "I would tell you to go to bed, but I know you won't sleep tonight."

"Did you sleep the night before your Sacrament?"

"No." It was the most we'd spoken since he called me a traitor. I thought I felt a tinge of regret across the mate bond, snatched back by a glare.

I didn't face him, couldn't, just as I couldn't ask for his forgiveness, though I may never have the chance again. I'd damned myself, and if death was the price I paid to atone for the look on his face as he left me knee deep in the snow, I'd pay it.

I'd pay it a million times.

"I was in awe of you on the battlefield." I hadn't heard him approach, but he breathed down my shoulder. His body was a step from mine, shadow of his hand on my hip. "I'd already lost ten warriors, and you cut a demon down by yourself. I watched you sleep after you'd been healed, proud to be blessed with a strong mate."

Tears traced the curve of my jaw.

"When you beat me, I thought maybe I'd be lucky enough to keep you. I thought they'd have me thrown out at the ball. Then I saw you, and all the anger and fear washed away. You were there, safe. When I worked up the courage to ask you to dance, I was certain you would say no.

"But you didn't. I dreamed about your smile that night. Of how you'd laughed in my arms and the feeling of holding you. That memory got me through the nights without you." He sniffed. "I think I felt it when you were burned out. The mate bond was the thinnest thread. I feared if I leaned too hard on it, it'd snap." His fingers dared to skim my arm. "I can't trust you. I might still hate you."

His words, like a shove off a cliff, broke the world around me. I couldn't move, too terrified he'd pull his hand from my arm and let me fall.

"What do you want?" I counted my staggered breaths, shoved through a tightened chest, waiting. Ready to tell him every idiotic, self-sacrificing thing I'd do to have him pull me into his embrace and wipe away tomorrow's worries. How I'd burn down Kadea, if only to feel his lips on mine once more.

His other hand crept to my waist. An offer to pull me back from the edge. He guided my back to his breath and dropped his forehead to my shoulder.

"My soul has allied with yours," he rasped. "Come back. Just come back."

CHAPTER 27

THE LINGERING GHOST of Easton's embrace trailed my every lumbering step from the privacy of his tent. He'd held me all night, as if his arms alone could hold back time. The unhealed wound between us remained, tucked away for one night that might've been our last.

I rose from bed and dressed before he woke.

Easton walked with me out to the training field, where Griffin spoke with Chief Indiviar and his generals. I searched for Amaury amongst the winged, all with feathers on display.

Griffin caught my attention and beckoned me close. "I cannot risk allowing Amaury from the castle. Too many estates have demanded his death."

Because of me. He didn't need to say it.

My heritage had always been a well-guarded secret, one we knew would destroy Amaury's reputation if the estates found out he'd attempted to marry a Forterian to their heirs.

"Are you ready?" Griffin asked. I stared a second longer at the skies, as if Amaury would fly down despite the danger to his life.

The others, nearly two hundred trained warriors between

the ages of eighteen and twenty-five, cast sideways glances laced with horrid intent. They surveyed my steady knees and steeled spine for a sag of weakness.

I tore my gaze from a mother who was brushing the hair from her son's face as his father beamed at him.

"Yes."

Of the tens of thousands of entrants and high-ranking members of all fifty-two clans mingling outside the barrier to Sacrament Land, those who passed me glared and barked insults.

Among them were fifty-two clan chiefs whose egos we had to bend to my scheme.

"Chief Barin, there," Easton said, nodding toward a tall male with broad shoulders and a mix of scars crisscrossing his face. "Vertin Clan sees scars as strength."

"Did they promote Kalman?"

Easton's chuckle was slapped away by Chief Barin's glare. I lost the ease of my breath.

Only when a Sacrament entrant moved between us did his glare slide away from me. When I looked again, he was closer. Seven clans stood between us and them, then five, and then none.

Griffin stepped forward to intercept the scarred chief. He'd forsaken his crown, instead wearing only a black silk tunic and freshly polished shoes. The clear sky paled in comparison to the mischief in his eyes. And to appear here, before them all, without an army encircling him, spoke to his ego. To his view of them.

"It is an honor to have you here today, My King." Chief Barin dipped his head. His beady black eyes remained on me, shadowed by his brow. When he straightened, he swept a mangled hand toward me and said through a snarl, "I have been assured you will provide the block for the whore's magic."

Easton reached for his blades.

I held my breath to stop the churning of my magic, leaned around Griffin, and quipped, "Whore's daughter."

Griffin shot a flat look over his shoulder, but the sparkling within his eyes remained. "I will be blocking Kacela's magic to ensure the validity of the holy Sacrament."

Another chief barged forward. His black wings were frayed but held high.

Chief Teamet, of Flyeria in the north, Easton whispered in my head.

"What assurance do we have of this? Her meddling with unearned magic on Sacrament Land has already angered the mountain." His wings rose higher, casting us in their shadow.

Griffin raised a hand to block the sun peeking over the tip of the chief's wing, right into his eyes. "You lot are eager for more bargains."

"We've seen what your bargains lead to." Chief Barin nodded toward Easton. "No promise of mates assuming their rightful place will sway proud clans."

Griffin swept a hand back through his hair. I felt the change in the air. It soured in my lungs.

"No prize is worth the shame of a tattooed bargain," Chief Barin continued.

I searched for Chief Indiviar, but he'd disappeared in the crowd along with his advisors and the entrees from Virian.

"No prize?" Griffin raised a brow and quirked a smirk. "Not even your freedom."

"We are free," Chief Teamet barked.

"Autonomy then," the king said with a wave. "Your lands, all of it. I'll rework the entire kingdom, my estates included, to return the lands won—"

"Stolen." The word sliced like an arrow.

Griffin paused, hand still raised. He dropped it. "The lands previously held by your ancestors. The entirety, down to the last rock and blade of grass. Full secession from Kadea."

Fifty-two clans were silenced by my offered hand.

Chief Barin stared at it.

I raised my hand higher. "If you are confident in your warriors, then you have nothing to lose, and everything to gain."

Griffin swirled black ash in an upturned hand. "If Kacela lives through the Sacrament, every clan will provide defense training for females and train youths as equals. When they come of age, all will be allowed their birthright of the Sacrament."

Part of me, the Forterian girl who'd wrapped herself in her mate's arms the night before and prayed the sun never rose, bounced. She was calmed by the courtier raised in the shadows, knowing all actions were planned and every word a calculation in a grander scheme. She knew better.

Bargains were tricky, as Griffin once explained. A single change of tone, spin of phrase, or slip of magic could shift the bargain. Change the timeline. Change the outcome.

Chief Barin tore his gaze from my outstretched hand. "She'll have to complete her quest."

"Deal."

"Without assistance from anyone."

I twisted my offered hand into a raised finger. "Anyone outside the Sacrament."

Others joined the echo of Chief Barin's chuckle. "No one will help you." His grin smeared into a snarl. "You'll be the first dead."

"Then shake my hand."

They did, all fifty-two chiefs gathering to wish their youths the best in thirty-eight days of bloodshed. Griffin repeated the bargain for all: If I survived the thirty-eight-day Sacrament and completed my quest without accepting outside help, every clan would train their youths as equals. Failure to fulfill the bargain on either end would result in death.

Each chief walked from me marked with a pair of wings spanning from a nocked bow. I stared at the one of the last chief's arm longer.

"Amaury designed it," Griffin said, pulling back my sleeve to show the fifty-two-banded tattooed, marked with each clan's emblem, up my forearm. "He said Forterian female warriors were once called Archers for their deadly precision."

I squeezed his hand. "Tell Amaury I'm sorry." More of a plea than request, accompanied with the shame of tears threatening the burst through the dam holding back every sequestered regret.

Griffin returned the squeeze. "You'll tell him yourself in thirty-eight days."

A horn sounded. A brute from a southern clan stepped to me and motioned for me to spread my arms. Each participant was checked for weapons, and while others were briefly patted down, I was scrutinized.

I handed him my boots, stood in the bit of snow, and watched him shove his hand inside them. He motioned next for my leather armor and ran his fingers across every seam. Then he checked my undershirt and pants.

I hated the eyes of every enemy who'd be vying for my blood on the mountain and the greed of their chiefs wishing for my death. They scoured me where his hands had searched.

Even more, I hated the blush on Easton's cheeks and the furrow of his brow.

When the brute handed back my boots and I shoved my numb toes inside of them, something pricked at my heel.

I scrunched my foot and stared at the brute.

"Watch your step," he sneered, giving the nod of approval to Chief Indiviar.

Easton knocked at the barriers around my mind. *What's wrong?*

Nothing.

Did he—

Easton. Leave it. I felt his resentment, but the bargain said nothing of my enemies cheating. I held a blank stare as I laced up my boots.

Giving Easton one last tight smile, I stepped past him, across the wards etching themselves into the ground like twisting vines, and to the Sacrament barrier. It glowed a faint red where it touched the snow.

Come back, Easton whispered across the bond.

The entrants towered on either side of me, creating a wall to block out the noise of the onlookers pressing closer. I felt the shift in the air as the wards finished their crafting. The lack of magic was like dense fog rolling over my limbs.

I breathed calm into my thundering pulse, as I once did before entering ballrooms, when I'd allowed courtiers to escort me about the castle as if I were a sword hanging from their belt.

Before I'd found my own blade.

Another rushed breath and I might have sprinted back to Easton, demand he take me in his arms, and die there, life snatched by the bargain before any brute had a chance at the honors.

I took one more calming breath before I plunged into an arena without politicking or elegant smiles. No charm to sway sympathy to my side.

My only weapons were my fists and teeth and feet shaking in the cold.

Before me, the mountain beckoned, both as endless as the blue sky behind it and as abrupt as the blaring horn telling us the Sacrament had begun.

My Sacrament.

I stepped across the barrier with the other wide-eyed, blood-thirsty youths eager to prove themselves worthy of a blessing.

The sensation felt like skipping, but tighter, through a pin prick hole in the fabric of our world. I spun on my heels as it gripped me by the navel and hoisted, seeing my mate for one last time before I plummeted into darkness. With nothing to slow my descent, I closed my eyes and opened my mouth to scream.

But only shadows seeped out.

CHAPTER 28

MY FACE ITCHED. I opened my eyes into darkness.

No, mud.

Layers of it, both around and all over me, speckled with twigs and leaves, pricking my cheeks. With a groan, I shoved both arms beneath me, only for the mud to gulp those into its depths. It suckled at my legs as I reared back. Bugs invaded my next breath, and I coughed out what I could.

A great start to a month of trying to keep dry, healthy, and most importantly, alive.

I'd expected the lack of my magic after fighting Easton surrounded by similar runes. Its absence was like a phantom limp my mind tried to move. The silence in my gut sent a stab of pain coursing up my spine. Where Easton's psyche against mine had been like waves lapping at the shore the past few weeks, a void sucked me in like a riptide, submerging me in its silence. My lungs burned, as if his presence was the air I breathed and, without it, I was suffocating.

Screams expanded my senses. Hollers of glee and excitement, bloodthirsty demands shaking my spine. I searched the jungle for movement, waiting for a shadow to attack, listening to the leaves bristle and wind howl.

I rolled onto the solid base of a tree where roots pushed up through the muck. Steadying myself on top of them, I crept across their brittle bark toward drier, sturdier land. My feet hit the dirt. I waited for a noise to guide my escape.

The breeze tangled in leaves and creaked branches.

"There!" someone screamed.

I ran, bounding over the prodding roots and pits of mud, keeping to the solid tree bases.

I sprinted as fast and far as I could go, ignoring the ache in my legs and burning in my chest. The sun, shining through the heavy canopy, chased me. It rippled my shadow like a beacon to aid their hunt.

I cut left. My boots slipped in the mud. The prick on my heel became a stab, and the bark of the branch I spun myself around cut into my palm.

A red handprint remained as a new beacon.

I felt the breeze of an arrow flying by my head. Twenty steps ahead, I snatched it from the ground.

The jungle, with its stocky trees and low swinging vines, thickened. Spaces between trees lessened with every step. A bit further and I'd slip through their cracks, my pursuers unable to follow with their hulking figures.

A temporary fix. A welcomed relief.

Though they lost me, their screams pursued me into the vines beneath an overlapping canopy of leaves, strangling the light. Shadows met my every step, harmless for now.

When the darkness threatened to suffocate me and every unsuspecting root, limp vine, and fallen branch threatened to trip me, I settled into a light jog.

Their demands died, and my thundering heart relented.

I stopped to lean my back against a tree and catch my breath. The humidity of the jungle stuck to every breath. It wove into the sweat on my neck.

On my finger, I balanced the arrow they'd shot at me. It was well made and perfectly fletched with blood red feathers. This had not been crafted during the few beginning moments of the Sacrament. It'd been dropped in the week prior, ideally placed for those who landed near me.

I stuck the arrow in my belt.

As I walked, I searched for weapons. Branches large enough to be sharpened into spears. Jagged rocks for close range defense.

The branch I made my bed on for the first night was wide enough to hide me from below and the leaves low enough to obscure my figure from the sides. I carried up a few rocks stuffed in my belt and a club slicked with mud.

A few trees over, I'd set up a snare for a rabbit or squirrel with a vine I'd sawed off with the arrowhead.

I tore off my boot and shoved my hand into it to find the prick. Something snagged across the cracking skin on my finger pads. Then, a prick sank into my palm.

I pulled out a needle and tangled suturing thread.

The world converged. A single beam of light speared through the overlaid leaves, reflecting off the needle and blinding my left eye. A gift, the most beautiful one I'd ever received.

Then my mouth ran dry.

Clenching the needle, I waited for the bond to strike me down before I took another breath. Several seconds ticked by, and the tightening in my chest could have very well have bene my nerves as much as the bond's anger.

I stashed it back into my boot and shoved my foot in, adjusting until the prick returned. It wasn't help but a chance to sabotage. Either a prick in every step or a ploy to trick me in to break my end of the deal by unknowingly accepting help.

For the first night, with the distant hoots of other Forterians, constant snap of branches, and the itch of the needle in my heel, I did not sleep.

I found a stream by noon the next day and threw myself into it to escape the pests picking at the exposed skin on my neck and hands.

My snare caught a rabbit on the third day, and though I liked my sleeping spot hidden in the canopy, I couldn't spend a month in the jungle. The bugs berated me more than the jeers of gangs prowling like jungle cats, and though my quest may come to me in a dream, I couldn't count on being so lucky.

I walked for two days without spotting another, slept in trees, and itched the bug bites into bleeding wounds. When my thoughts wandered too far, back to Easton's warm bed and Amaury's messy office, the snap of a branch or wind rustling the leaves returned me to reality.

The Sacrament would only allow so much vulnerability. Would only give so many innocent snaps of branches.

Eventually, one would be death.

On day three of trekking toward the beckoning cold, my boots hit the jagged rocks of the mountain's base. I stared at its slopes, waiting for my enemies to reveal themselves as the demon rifts had.

I weighed my options. Begin the ascent and risk the cold or stick to the base and risk an attack.

A cave within walking distance up the mountain looked invitingly absent of bugs. I trudged on the jungle side, back and forth, for at least twenty minutes in each direction. Satisfied no one watched the line, I took one step onto the jagged rocks, then another.

The sun warmed my cheeks.

Snow littered the jagged rocks halfway to the cave, and a few steps later, I was up to my knees in frigid cold. I dashed the distance to the cave despite the uneven outcrops and burn in my calves. Flattening my back to its exterior, I peeked inside. I couldn't see to the back of it. No assurance that nobody lurked in the shadows.

Behind me, a crack of lightning lit the northern sky. The thunder rattled pebbles from the cave walls.

Caves, Easton told me, were ideal for getting out of the elements but not for sleeping in. If anyone stumbled upon me, I'd be trapped.

I didn't need the warning.

He hadn't felt the tug of the cave, nor had he seen the shadow wink from within. I'd lied to him before, and to Griffin. Whatever had come for me remained, obscured within the mountain. It didn't call to me with a song, but a rustled offer. A conniving promise of either my doom or salvation.

I went back out, made a set of footprints leading to the jungle, and trekked back through them, careful not to leave any trace of my direction. With no firewood, I sat down to eat the last bit of squirrel I'd saved from my earlier hunt. A rabbit sat beside me, uncooked and rotting.

If the storm didn't rage through the morning, I'd go out to gather firewood and cook my rabbit in the jungle before finding a new sleeping spot.

It hit after sunset. Thunder shook the cave. Lightning cast my shadow over the downward slope, banishing the advancing shadows.

I should have gone to the back of the cave to prepare for a shivering sleep, but the lightning called to me. Without it, I was not whole. Like a soldier returned without a limb, or a mother without her child. Not wholly me without it in my every nerve.

The fifth lightning strike cast shadows of rushing figures across my cave mouth.

I tucked myself around the first turn, where the lightning's blaze could not reach me.

"We got lucky boys," one of the intruders declared. "Don't find an empty cave too often."

I curled back around the bend of the cave, dragging the rabbit carcass along with me.

"You know how I feel about caves."

"Only the bonks of Beaddeon believe the Children of the Night haunt this mountain," the first snorted.

"Jorian's ma must've read him too many stories at bedtime," a third teased. "Who truly believes there is a thriving city of nightmares beneath the mountain?"

"All myths have roots somewhere, brothers," another replied, voice quiet as if he feared someone listened. "Virian reported wisps of black from the mountain for the past few months. If not the Altun King, then who?"

"In all the years of the Sacrament, no one has once reported seeing anyone living in the mountain. And how many do you think have camped in these caves?"

"Not all caves lead to Inmonte."

"And you think this one might?"

"Do you see the back?"

I clutched my rabbit and scurried toward the downturn of the cave floor, where it veered left into complete darkness.

There was a pause, then a huff of a sigh, before three shadows appeared too close for my jittery heart. I pressed my hand over my mouth to stifle my breathing.

They inched closer. Closer to my hiding space with the rabbit I held like a child clutching their blanket.

"It's back there somewhere."

Two of them returned to the mouth of the cave, but one stayed. The light from a lightning strike flashed around his blond locks.

I snapped my eyes closed as his gaze came dangerously close to my hiding place, and only after I heard his footsteps retreat to the mouth of the cave and the banter of warriors unafraid of the coming days did I open them.

Prepared for a sleepless night, I stared down into the darkness, feeling like something stared back at me, beckoning me within its maw.

The three boys, younger than me, fell asleep early in the night without any bothering to keep watch. One was slender and around my height, with blond hair like Gil's and a flattened nose. The other two were beefy, one with dreadlocks and the other with shaggy, black hair cut to his shoulders.

The thunder battering the cave obscured their snores and my rifling through their bags.

I hated them for what they had dropped into the Sacrament in the prior week or were able to sneak in on them. Two carried bags of dried and salted meats, daggers, wire, gauze, and extra clothing.

I slipped a pair of socks from the first bag and, from the second, I took a few strips of jerky.

Part of me, the soldier outraged at the loss of magic, yearned to bathe the cave in their blood. I could've slipped a weapon from their bag, slit their throats, and taken off with enough supplies to last weeks.

I pulled a plain dagger, hilt wrapped in black leather, from one bag and observed the reflection of a lightning strike across its blade.

The blond boy stirred.

I flipped the dagger into a reverse grip and crouched.

He rolled toward me, his arm slipping off his waist. His eyelids fluttered and lips spread into a half smile.

My gut churned.

He was scarless, as far as I could tell, and had delicate facial features. He was a child forced into war.

I eased back, my knees groaning at the sluggish pace, and returned the dagger to the pack. I slipped to the frigid shadows of the cave. Anger boiled in my gut and raged through my lungs to my every shallow breath. I dug my nails into my palms to pin back the bloodlust riding the rampant tide of my frustration.

Rolling my forehead against the cool, rough gnarls of the cave wall, I grounded myself. I sank to my knees and caved my body around a sigh. My bubbling rage simmered then settled, still as volatile as a volcano, yet tranquil as standing water.

Bloodlust seeped from my clenched fists. Shame replaced it with bitter claws in my chest.

When I opened my palms to catch the tear rolling off my nose, the mercilessness seizing my nerves galloped away on a breeze smelling of poppy.

It wasn't until nearly lunch the next day when they discovered my thievery.

"Who took two pieces of jerky?" one asked.

Their few accusations turned to jokes, and the jokes to wrestling.

I took advantage of their friendly brawl to explore the cave. It dropped off steadily until the light faded around the second bend. Loose pebbles threatened my every step.

Even if this tunnel led out, I wouldn't find an exit without the darkness threatening madness.

"I don't like the deal," one said. I peeked around the corner to see the blond speaking through a mouthful of jerky. "She shouldn't be here, but to offer an alliance to kill her? She is a Forterian's mate."

The one with dreads carved at a piece of wood with his knife. "Where do you think she is now?"

"I heard she was dropped in the jungle nearest Jude, Leon, and Mika. They were supposed to take care of her within the first few minutes," the blond said.

My throat closed in on itself and stomach gurgled around the strip of jerky. There was cheating greater than sneaking in supplies, and I, of everyone, couldn't partake.

The one with shaggy hair, his teeth crooked and eyes wide set, opened a water flask. "I ran into them on my way to meet you two. Jude said he had a clear shot until Leon stumbled into him."

"You mean War Chief Ran's son, Leon?" the second asked. Chief Ran, one of those who'd forced me to flee Virian to camp in the woods.

"He's only tasked with capturing her. He's not a killer," the blond said.

"Not a killer?" The one with wide-set eyes chuckled. "We're all killers here."

The blond snatched the piece of wood away. "He's not a killer. Besides, Envers is promised her death."

"Of Vertin?" The boy with dreads tossed down his knife. "How many deals did Barin make for that?"

The blond whistled. "Too many."

The next day, when I'd nearly resorted to eating the uncooked rabbit, they left. I bounded from my hiding spot. My legs nearly collapsed, having stiffened from two nights of sitting with them tucked tight.

The first mouthful of snow chilled my throat. The next calmed my gurgling stomach.

I sulked back into the cave, stopped by the gleam of the sun off metal.

A dagger. Set on top of a piece of jerky I finished in three bites.

I wanted to scream the impossible from the mountaintop. I let myself imagine how I'd wave the blade to all the chiefs, especially Barin. Proof I didn't fight alone. Proof there were Forterians willing to accept a future of equality.

I spent another week in the cave, hidden in the back in case more came through. A few did, stopping to survey it before retreating when they saw the never-ending tunnel. The back-less cave became my ally, as did the shadows within. They surged at each newcomer, scaring most away before nightfall.

In quiet moments, I pressed deeper inside. One step at a time, using the wall as my guide. The cave dipped and twisted and split, but never ended.

I felt eyes on my every wandering step deeper into the bowels of the mountain. They unsettled me, like the darkness. Yet, I couldn't leave it. Couldn't leave the shadow's hold. Something within it begged me to venture further.

After four days, I was convinced my imagination and growling stomach tricked me into seeing the cave as salvation. By the seventh day, I knew I had to leave. This cave would not be my home for the remaining three weeks.

It might have ensured my survival, but I couldn't just survive.

I had a quest to complete.

A mate to return to.

A point to prove.

CHAPTER 29

I STEPPED OUT of the safety of my cave, into a gust of wind threatening to knock me off the jagged outcrops of stone breaking through the blanket of snow. I clenched my jaw to keep my teeth from chattering.

With a makeshift club in one hand, arrow tucked into my belt, and the knife wiggling between my fingers, I set out across the barren tundra in the direction the trio had gone. Easton had said to avoid the boundaries of the different landscapes and the possible ambushes lining them.

I spotted one as I walked, and though he aimed his bow at me, I was too high on the slopes for him to see who I was, especially with my hair tucked into my leathers.

Two days after leaving the cave, I trekked the steepest slope of the mountain, where caves were few but juts of rock plentiful. Too high up the mountain to reach the rolling hills before nightfall, I dug myself into the snow within the jagged edges of an outcrop and built a small shelter.

The sun dipped past the mountain and night watched me wrap myself around my club. I wouldn't sleep, not with the snow soaking through my backside.

It'd keep me awake, at the very least.

Awake and alert, listening to the wind howl across the mountain.

My bones ached, and the wind chipped at my snow barrier. As it fell, chill air swelled within my cocoon. I blocked my face with my arms from the initial gust, but it was a continuous battering of wintry nips burning my cheeks.

I'd be dead by morning if I didn't fix the shelter.

Crawling from my little hole, I packed snow back into the crevice with shaking hands. The wind fought me. It blew away every handful of snow I gathered into the opening.

Then I heard it, shrouded in the echo of my frustration. A feral growl.

I didn't turn to see the wolf pack descending on me, but I smelled the blood on their snouts and their stale breath panting after me.

I stuffed my knife into my belt and ran.

If I could get to the rolling hills and outcrop of trees, I may have a chance to climb from their grasp.

The wolves rumbled down the mountainside. Their howls were like warning horns, their paws a steady war drum.

The slopes expanded before me like the never-ending desert to the south. They rolled, the white reflecting the waning moon's beam back into my watering eyes. No leap I took cut the distance. I could run to the horizon and still feel the shame of being mauled to death by wolves on my back.

My heel hit an edge and I flew over an outcrop protruding from the snow like a broken bone through skin. My arms pinwheeled and legs peddled against gravity.

I landed on my side, the club flying from my grasp, on a steep slope slicked with ice. I was like a tumbleweed, unable to slow my descent. My side cracked against another outcrop, and I spun from it on my back.

The world continued to spiral, the sliver of a moon waltzing around the stars. My fingers scraped the bare stone and dead grass marking the base of the mountain.

Searing heat sliced through my left calf. Blood sprayed from it, soaking my hands where they reached to brace.

I grasped splintered wood of an arrow, sticky and warm, protruding from my leg. In the moonlight, I only saw the vibrant red in the otherwise barren mountainside flattening to a green horizon.

Again, the wolves howled. Then whimpered.

Predators worse than wolves were on me before my next heaving breath.

A hand raked across my skull, ripping hair from my braid, and yanked my gaze back to see its owner's head haloed in the moonlight. His lips curled, revealing missing teeth.

I wrenched the dagger from my belt and aimed it for the hand entwined in my hair. It sliced skin, warm blood speckled my hands, and my captor jerked my hair.

Someone grabbed my hand and pried the dagger from it. Another tugged at the arrow tucked into my belt until it popped free, the head tearing at the seam of my pants.

A voice from further back demanded, "Get her up to the cave, Rory. Now."

The hand in my hair yanked. I clawed onto the wrist, scratching at the leathers and curling my fingernails into their grooves. Anything to alleviate some of the pain from my scalp. He hauled me back up the side of the mountain. Snow gathered in my collar, in the waistline of my pants, and in the tops of my boots. It melted within, locking me in a frozen second skin.

A parade of warriors trampled through the tracks of my thrashing legs.

Every jolt rattled the arrow skewered through my leg, and warm blood sloshed in my boot.

My back hit the hard rock of a cave floor and I rolled into the wall. My shoulder popped, and searing pain arched from elbow to neck. I curled onto my side and tucked my arms into my chest. A stab of pain met each labored breath.

One Forterian with ebony skin flashed a dagger in my vision, the one left by a member of the trio. He stepped before me, blocking my sight of the others with his broad shoulders. "Where did you get this?" He clutched my shirt, forcing my blurry gaze to his dull brown eyes.

As if I were a rag doll, he yanked me to my feet and slammed my back against the wall. Another wave of pain began in my shoulders and cascaded down to crash in my calf.

Five others circled me with weapons in twitching hands.

His hand adjusted, and I couldn't breathe past where he palmed my throat to trap me against the cave wall. I grabbed his wrist. My nails sunk into the exposed skin. I pressed onto my tiptoes until my calf gave. Then, I was slipping beneath the current, unable to suck in enough air to beg.

I'd failed.

Every scheme, betrayal, and moment proved me to be the Altun brat they despised. It all fell uselessly in the puddle of my blood. Weeks of living in their hate.

Adrenaline surged through me. With a well-aimed kick, I dropped him to his knees. Another, as white as the beaming moon, slammed his hand to my throat. Amber eyes, like a raging inferno, widened.

He stumbled from me, a string of curses raining from his blue-tinged lips.

I crumbled in heap. My forehead rolled through sticky blood.

The one I'd kicked stopped the others from advancing with a raised hand.

I eyed the nearest, one with ebony skin like the first but no hair. He angled his head left, raised a dagger from beneath crossed arms and tapped it against his chest over his heart, then pointed it at me.

"Where did you get this knife?" the first demanded, righting himself with a hand still cradling his groin.

"Why?" I said in a high, sneering voice from my hunched crawl. "Did it belong to someone special?"

He grabbed the back of my leathers, like a mother dog gripping her pup, and hauled me upright, then shoved me down onto his raised knee. His grip returned, preventing me from smashing my face into the stone.

The snap of my collar against my neck pulled another staggered breath.

"It's of Clan Wunort. You stole it."

"Maybe I killed them, too, before I took—"

He slapped me. My cheek stung with a slash of a blade he'd concealed in his sleeve.

"You don't know when to shut your mouth." His dark features scrunched. He eased me onto the balls of my feet. My nerves jittered, anticipating a sway in his attention, a potential opening to attack. One moment. All I needed was a lapse in attention to reach for my last weapon.

A sharpened rock in my belt pressed into my side, strengthening the tread of defiance I clung to.

His breath smelled of salted venison. "If you killed him—"

I spat in his face.

Then I cursed Easton for his advice to rile up any captor to the edge of a mistake. This one raged beneath a mask of calm logic withholding his temper. I saw the thunderstorms brewing in his eyes. His nostrils flared and jaw clenched. He looked as if he might kill me with just a glance, a power I thought only Amaury possessed.

He threw me down. My head thunked against the wall and my arm crumbled beneath my weight. I bit my lip to hold back a whimper. Blood swelled in my cheeks.

"Leon, Jorian's not dead. You'd know if he was," said the amber-eyed one.

Leon, who the trio had spoken about. Who one claimed wasn't a killer.

"He's got Abe and Gad with him."

Leon squatted before me. He pressed the blade's tip to the hollow of my throat. "Tell me what you know about him before I gut you."

I let the blood pooling in my mouth leak from the corners. It puddled near his boot. Something softened within his eyes and his rage was gone in a blink, replaced by guilt.

His shoulders slumped and he dropped his glare to the dagger, running his fingers across the metal hilt.

"He was alive when I took the knife a week ago," I rasped.

"How'd you take the knife?"

I drooled more blood. I should've said I'd killed them. He'd nearly beaten me to a pulp. A bit of worry until they found their friends would be nothing compared to the arrow in my leg. But my voice failed, and I collapsed in on myself, resolved to a small lie. "I stole it while they were all sleeping," I choked, the blood threatening to course down my throat. "In a cave I was hiding in."

Leon shot up and headed for the mouth of the tent. He pointed at the two stockiest, one with jagged scars across his round jaw and the one who'd dragged me up the mountainside by my hair, Rory. "Take first watch."

"And the girl?" Rory stepped toward me.

Leon intercepted him. "Don't touch her. Envers gets her."

"I don't know why—"

"Those are the terms. You don't like them, see what Envers has to say."

Rory threw his hands up. "Envers is a brute meant for the lines. He'll never be winged."

"Neither will you if I kill you now for not taking watch. Go."

Rory headed for the mouth of the cave, where the other already sat.

Leon assisted the amber-eyed one with building a fire while the one who pointed his knife at me paced before me. He had a sharp jaw, high cheekbones, and out-turned ears that looked like fish fins. His head inclined, coffee eyes light.

Not threatening, but curious.

I shoved myself into a sitting position and lean back against the cave. My skull ached as it rolled against the jagged points of the wall. Beyond the wisps of smoke and spiked cave mouth, the stars twinkled at me.

I took some solace in their insistent winks, unchanged from when I'd crawl from the cabinet in my mother's tent or sat on the balcony in Kadea to watch them fade in the sun's waking breath.

Tears slipped down my cheeks at the thought of Easton wandering through the crowd of survivors, searching until morning in vain with Amaury beside him. The hope glimmering in their eyes snuffed out by the gloating sneer of Chief Barin, his twin scars rising higher at the twitch of his grin.

Tears seared paths down my cheeks. I touched one but let the rest mix with the snow melting across my neck and chest.

Death was absolute, whether I died crying or fighting.

A hand touched my injured leg. I kicked with the other, only for it to be captured in a vice-like grip.

"Do that again and I tie you up," Leon said. "You're more trouble than you're worth if we have to carry you."

I kept my glare on him as he yanked out the arrow, rolled up my pant leg, and sewed the wound shut, ignoring my winces of pain at each needle stab. He smothered it in green paste and wrapped it with a bandage.

I motioned to my disfigured shoulder.

As he prodded it with his fingers, spikes of pain shot up to the base of my skull. "This will hurt." He reset it with a yank.

I clenched my teeth to mute my scream, yet all attention returned to me as I cradled my throbbing shoulder and blinked away the tears.

Leon crinkled something into my palm.

I recognized the yellow-stemmed flower from my time in the woods with Easton.

"Chew it," he muttered, picking up the supplies he didn't use. When I held it up to the fire's light and ruffled it between my fingers, he shrugged. "Or be in pain. But tomorrow, you're walking with us. If you fall behind, I'll let Rory drag you."

I munched on the stem. "Your threat doesn't hold much weight when I only see death in my future."

Those dull brown eyes swirled with tints of green, and I ached for arms that would never hold me again.

He looked like he wanted to say something, but the words

died on parted lips.

I held his gaze, chewing like it was my greatest act of defiance.

He sucked it another breath, then stalked away.

Leon hauled me to my feet before the sun entered the cave.

My every movement was like fighting a tight corset. The flower could only relieve so many stabs of pain in my ribs and the dull pulse in my shoulder, not to mention my calf where a new kind of demon fought beneath my skin.

Rory walked minutes ahead of us to scout, accompanied by a blond with a hatchet on one hip and dagger on the other. Directly before me, the one with scars crisscrossing his jaw marched, sneaking glances over his shoulder every few steps. Leon trudged at my side, with the remaining two following close on our heels.

The others created boot prints in the snow.

I left long rows marking my lumbering pace around the southern edge of the mountain. "Where are you handing me to my death?" I asked.

Leon looked down at me, lips pursed. "Other side of the mountain."

"And Envers gets the joy of taking my head from my shoulders. Why?"

"I don't question orders."

"You have to be curious."

Leon caught my arm when I tripped over a crop of rocks hidden beneath the blanket of snow. His grimace lightened then, downturned lips straightening and hand softening on my bicep.

I tugged my arm and looked away.

He continued, "Spoken like an Altun."

"I'm Forterian—"

A shadow blocked the sun's warmth from my other side.

"You were raised Altun. Your mother's lineage means nothing until proven in battle," said the amber-eyed, pale one with a stale frown.

Leon nodded. "You've embarrassed a war chief on his own lands."

"After he killed another—"

"Forterians follow the strong." Leon gave me another surveying glance. "I heard about the transfer of the bargain to Chief Indiviar. How?"

I shifted my gaze back to my red stained boot. "The deal was transferred when he took the title of chief. King Quillon prevented it from materializing on his skin until he broke the seal. Our king has a flare for the dramatic. "I fluttered my fingers for emphasis.

They jolted away, as if my magic sparked between my fingers.

"You still haven't answered my question." I meandered across the next crop of boulders, arms outstretched like a toddler.

"Killing you will be a badge of honor," amber-eyes muttered. His long, nearly white hair flowed over his shoulder and swayed near his hip. He was as ivory as Leon was ebony, able to blend in the snow like the northern foxes.

"This is Jude," Leon said, nodding to him, then jerked his head backwards. "And that's Mika."

I cast a glance over my shoulder. Wearing a bow and quiver over his shoulder, Mika sauntered along behind us, steps so light he hardly sank into the snow. The arrows in the quiver on his back bounced with him. He smirked, and the sun warmed his irises to gleam like molten copper.

"If it helps," Jude said, pulling my attention back, "I'd prefer to kill you now and be done with it." He barred his yellow stained, chipped teeth.

"You shot at me."

The arch of his brows smoothed after a breath. "In the jungle when we woke. I only missed because some namby tripped into me." He jerked his head back to his quiver, now with an additional arrow retrieved from my belt, his narrowed gaze giving to gleeful smile. "Thanks for returning it."

Leon huffed. "You were aiming to kill."

"A hit through the shoulder wouldn't have killed her," Jude grumbled. "And it would have prevented the last week on the slopes."

He looked forward at the looming mountains. Over the top ridge, a small black dot descended toward us. The slope steepened, my pace slowed, and Rory's predatory glances back at me got wilder until Leon sent him to intercept two figures stumbling toward us.

"We'll stop for lunch," Leon said as the sun broke the clouds above our heads. He sat beside where I collapsed. "Give me your leg. I'll check the wound."

His hands were soft as they unwound the bandage, wiped the green muck from each side, and re-bandaged it. I eyed the medical bag he carried longer than necessary, hiding complaints and threats behind grinding teeth.

His dull eyes followed mine.

"It's unfair," he said softly, but not shyly, "that many of us snuck in supplies but you couldn't. The Sacrament used to be a test of a true Forterian. Now, it's a place to hash out old grudges and eliminate competition."

"As a chief's son, I'd think you'd appreciate the thinning of competition."

Leon ran his hand, still tinged with green, through the thin tuffs of hair. A streak remained.

"As an Altun," Jude sneered from beside the small fire they'd started, "I'd think you'd appreciate the thinning of the enemy."

I held his glare with a blank stare. "You are not my enemy."

"Maybe not, but you are mine."

CHAPTER
30

I RECOGNIZED THE BOY they carried to the fireside. His disheveled eyes searched each of us before narrowing on Leon. Blood clotted in the wound around his neck, leaking only when he shuddered back from Leon's approach. It crusted into his dreadlocks and appeared only as a gleam against his dark skin. "I tried," he screamed, voice raw, "but he had ten others with him."

"Gad," another warned, helping him to sit. "Calm down."

Leon stalked, his fists tightened and back hunched, to him.

Gad raised a quivering hand to block Leon's glare. "We were hiding in a cave. I'd taken watch. I saw torches. It was Envers and the others. I didn't want to let them in, but Jorian said we had a truce, so we could share the cave for the night."

Leon squatted. His hand skimmed the dagger at his side. Jorian's dagger. "Where's Jorian?"

Gad's lip trembled as he raised his gaze to Leon's. "Still alive when they threw me out to die in the snow"

"Abe?"

He shook his head.

My stomach churned.

Leon turned away from the Gad's rambling. His hands clenched and released multiple times. His lips muttered curses combined with ideas as the chill of death wrapped around my throat.

His glare landed on me and, for a moment, I felt as if I was already dead.

He turned to Rory, the blond who rested a hand on his hatchet, and the last whose scar coated jaw looked like a yellow and orange quilt in the morning sun. "Go back and take Gad. We'll continue from here." Leon turned his attention to my rigid posture. "Our enemies have revealed themselves."

Gear was split, packs heaved onto backs, and Gad dragged back through our boot prints.

With only Leon, Jude, and Mika, I straightened. I pressed into the sure base of the outcrop. My leg ached at the thought of running, but my adrenaline would not release the fluttering hope of living.

"You have a plan?" Jude asked. He scraped his dagger against a rock he leaned against.

Leon huffed. "No."

"You sent away —"

"You said you'd follow me," Leon barked. He released a sigh. "I do not hold their loyalties enough to trust them with Jorian's life."

My curiosity staked me there. Jorian, who'd left his dagger for me, who'd feared a backless cave, who Leon cared enough for to forsake a pact made before the Sacrament.

Who may be dead.

"This is a treason against our clan." His eyes went to the other dark-skinned warrior. "Chief Barin has stuck his cock in our clan's affairs too many times. I won't allow him to turn our Sacrament into a joke."

Jude put his blade away, stood, and placed his fist over his chest. "I stand by what I said, brother."

"As do I," the other mimicked.

Leon, with a nod in acknowledgement, turned to me and

wiped away any chance of escape.

"Then we need a plan."

I was left beside the fire, hogtied. They marched far enough off for the wind to obscure their voices. Far enough they couldn't see me squirm and roll through the bitter snow. It stung my ears and nose, rattled my teeth, and melted down my leathers to soak through my shirt along with my sweat. I kept moving. I allowed the agitation at their weapons and gear, the hoax of a fair Sacrament, and the sham of a true test of a warrior's strength to fuel every wiggle toward freedom.

The heat wrapped around me first, lessening the snow's depth until I lurched across bare stone, then steam rose from me as I rolled into the desert dunes.

"Found her," a voice called, giddy.

I floundered a few more lengths before a hand yanked the collar of my shirt. It snapped the hope and breath from my lungs.

"Damn you, namby!" I shrieked.

"She's starting to talk like us." Mika twirled me around to grab the crux of my bound limbs. As if I were a sack, he lifted me and walked back up the clear path I'd carved into the snow.

Leon sat within its glow and skinned a rabbit. "You got further than I thought."

The outcrop he dropped me on sent a stab of pain into my cracked rib. I wheezed a shallow breath.

Jude leaned against the rock. The strike of his blade against it matched the thunder of my blood in my ears.

Each held a weapon. Each could gut me before I finished my next breath.

"My cousin helped drag Easton from the battlefield of the Demon War," Leon drawled, watching Jude's blade strike stone. "He told grand stories of his mate, the demon killer."

Mika raised a blade and slashed downwards. I flinched, only

for the tie between my bound legs and arms to give. I yanked my arms into my chest and kicked away. My back thudded against a rock.

Leon didn't wait for me to settle. His blade didn't lose its rhythm as he sawed through the rabbit skin. His eyes never raised. "I'll make you a deal. You help us kill Envers, and I won't kill you."

"Help how?" Sitting, I rubbed at my knees and shoulders where they'd been scraped against the stone during my attempted escape. Prickling cuts and deep bruises protested to my prodding.

Jude tapped his knife against the rock. "We need bait."

"I was wrong." Anger soiled my words.

Jude raised a brow.

"The Forterians may not be my enemy, but you are. Give me a reason besides avoiding an earlier death to help you."

Amber eyes blazed, and he stepped forward with his blade outstretched, only for the veins in his neck to bulge and lips to purse. Stuck, as if ropes tangled his limbs and held him from ramming his knife through my chest.

Leon stepped between us, hand on Jude's arm. "We have a plan to save Jorian. We can take the rest of his allies if Envers is lured from the cave."

Realization chilled like the snow melting at the nape of my neck. "You save Jorian while leaving me to die."

"Maybe not." Mika smirked, revealing perfectly white teeth.

"Our worries are less if Envers is killed," Leon continued. "We'll give you a weapon and loosen the rope so you have a chance to kill him."

Jude lurched again, catching himself with a hand on Leon's shoulder. Heat burned beneath the ivory of his skin and ridged veins pulsed at his neck. "Or we give you to him hog-tied and defenseless. He'll slaughter you without breaking a sweat."

I stared at the thick, green muck leaking from the bandage. "I'd never planned to die without a fight." The bitter chill in my lungs left on my next exhale. "If you'll give me a weapon, it's my best chance."

To survive. To prove myself a Forterian warrior. To return to Easton.

Leon stood and stretched out his hand. For long enough for Jude to huff, I stared at the extended truce. His hand was like a blade's hilt. A promise to fight, if only once more.

I clasped it and allowed him to haul me to my feet.

"Kill him," Leon told me, voice staunch.

My breath caught, but below that, warmth bloomed. A spark of belonging lit the pyre of doubt, reducing their muttered accusations and bellowed insults to ash.

I wasn't alone.

Not anymore.

Jude, of the three, seemed least trusting of me. He ignored me only because the rest of the plan satisfied the mountain's call for blood they all claimed boiled in their chests.

We found a cave near Envers's and waited for dawn to announce our arrival. Leon said it was safer not to approach at dusk in case his guards felt like testing their bows, but he'd only decided after watching me collapse against the wall of the cave and suck down half a water flask.

Mika left to investigate the depth of the cave. We watched him blend with the shadows until only his footsteps indicated how far he'd ventured.

He returned, checking over his shoulder every few steps as if the shadows surged at his heels. I watched them dancing between cracks of stone, groveling from the moon's light. "If there's an end to the cave, I'm not walking far enough to find it."

"Inmonte isn't real," Leon huffed. "All caves have backs, even if you have to walk a day to reach them."

"Inmonte?" I teased. "The fabled city beneath the mountain?"

Leon nodded. "A myth. There is nothing beneath the mountain except the Vitient."

Even if all three believed that, they only ever walked with their backs to the mouth of the cave as if our true enemy would stroll from the shadows.

I snatched the beef strip Jude offered as if it were a rabbit about to escape my snares.

"Calm." Mika chuckled. "If you eat it too quickly, you'll puke it back up."

The beef landed roughly in my stomach.

"The story," Jude tapped his knife against the cave floor, "of how you beat Easton to force Virian to train the girls, is it true?"

I tore another bite and nodded.

"How'd you do it? He's got at least a few stones on you, and twenty years. He's a war hero in the north."

I swallowed the rest of the strip. Deceit was poison amongst potential allies, even ones as fickle as these. "Amaury was at the camp under ruse of assessing losses after the war. When he came back, we worked through Easton's fighting style. Figured out the partners, found vulnerabilities."

Jude bent low, as if it'd keep his words from leaving the cave. "And then you—"

"Got him off?" An arched eyebrow accompanied the question.

"I heard it was in front of everyone," Mika whispered, gaze everywhere but on me.

My gulp of water snorted from my nose. "No. I skipped us out of the camp and then back."

Leon's scowled stayed on me. "You beat and embarrassed him, your mate, for what?"

I met his cold demeanor with my own. "I saved Easton's life from demons when he dropped, defenseless and injured, to the ground. In return, he told me to tend to his tent. He is my equal, and I am his. Everything I've done is to ensure he remembers that."

Leon tapped his sword against his boot. "He came back to

you? After that?"

"He understood the message it sent."

"You think he's changed from the warrior you first met?" Jude snorted. "He hasn't."

I met his challenging glare. "Then I am ashamed to have claimed him as my mate."

Jude lurched to his feet and excused himself out into the howling wind.

"Ignore him." Mika kicked at the dirt around a fire pit forgotten days ago. "He hasn't met his mate. He doesn't know the pain of being without her." When he met my gaze, I saw that very pain within his eyes. The loss I felt within my gut where the mate bond once hummed insistently with Easton's heated stares and nagging urges was like a snuffed-out fire.

The last bit of sun slipped from the cave. We couldn't afford a fire giving away our position before we'd set our own trap, so we curled up for a cold night of sleep.

A small blanket, no bigger than me and no thicker than a sock, soared into my chest. I looked across the cave to Mika, who tossed another to Leon.

"You met your mate?" I asked Mika.

He nodded and handed the third to Jude. "She's like you. Spitfire of a girl. Will kick my ass if I don't come back. We grew up together in Faveos. This is the longest we've ever spent apart." Mika leaned his head back against the cave wall. His eyes fluttered closed. "Do you feel it? The hollow ache of being separated from half your soul?"

I raised the blanket to my cheeks to feel its brush against wind-torn cheeks. Venturing to the void in my gut, I jabbed at it only to be sucked within its deafening current. I placed my hand over my stomach. My mouth ran dry, and I looked east toward the stars hanging above Easton's head. "Not as much as you. Easton and I aren't mated."

Mika stilled. "Why?" Ice crept through his warm tone.

With a shrug, I pulled the blanket over my shoulders and tucked myself into a crevice in the wall, facing the dancing shadows of the cave's oblivion. "What does it matter now, why we haven't completed the mating bond? If I die, let his burden of having a traitorous mate die with me."

Leon and Mika snored shortly after, but my thoughts flirted with the incoming moonlight and fears grew with the vibrancy of the stars.

I clambered to my feet and stepped to the mouth of the cave where Jude took the first watch.

"You'll probably die tomorrow."

Altuns did not contemplate their own deaths in castles and estates. They knew the end of their mortality would come with dragging feet. I'd never considered mine. I thought I knew what I'd die for, but that soldier had been smashed. Shards of her reflected back at me, the warrior facing her death. Though this time, I would not be fueled by a fear of dying. I was stronger than the girl stumbling into war with an oversized shield and lumbering naivety. I'd routed my own path to my grave.

The night sky was no different than it'd ever been. The stars twinkled as they always had and always would, yet in the prelude to my death, they were a standing ovation. "I know."

"You don't know us, or Jorian. You could make your last stand here against us and have better odds than tomorrow."

"You wouldn't kill me the moment I stepped from this cave?"

He forced a swallow and avoided my gaze. "If you don't die, Envers kills us. He'll probably kill Jorian as well. Messages must be sent."

The silence between us became stifling. I stared at the stars, waiting for the usual strength I found in them to come. "I've been told Easton is the best, both as a warrior and leader. If I ran now, you may not catch me and I may see him again. But if Jorian dies when I could have helped, I don't know how I'll face Easton. If I'm to claim my Forterian heritage, shouldn't I also accept the responsibilities as well?"

"Responsibilities?"

"To fight for every Forterian brother. To do what is right despite the risk. You follow the strong, and the strong do not run. They fight."

Jude observed me in the moonlight. "I heard you were a bitch."

I dropped my gaze and the frown holding my jaw clenched. "I've heard that, too. From Altuns and Forterians alike."

"You're sacrificing a lot."

"That's what Forterians do, isn't it? Fight, fuck, and die."

Jude slapped a hand to his mouth to muffle his snort. I joined him, though my laugh felt bittersweet on my tongue.

"I'm going to die on this mountain," I continued, voice softer, "but if my death can do some good for another, then I'll do what I can to delay Envers tomorrow."

"You're so sure you're going to die. What would Easton think of that?"

CHAPTER
31

THE CAVE HAD SUBSTANTIALLY WARMED, and a faint scent of poppy swirled around me. I went to tug at the blanket on my lap, only to grasp empty air. It'd disappeared. As had my weapons. And my clothing.

I stood in the cave, my bare feet frozen to the stone.

Not a cave with an escape, but a stone dome bigger than my room back within Kadea. All one room with different sections decorated to model a home. A plush couch sat against the wall to my left with a patch quilt draped across it, a bed with too many pillows was pushed askew against the rounded side, and torches were magically suspended above me, flickering their curiosity.

Enough weapons to outfit an entire platoon littered the walls.

I stumbled toward the couch, each step like sliding across ice. Above it, a longsword near identical to those carried by Altun soldiers was bolted to the wall. My knee hit the couch arm, and I tumbled forward, grasping for the backrest. I clutched the wrinkled fabric of the quilt.

Then recoiled, nearly throwing myself off my feet.

Skin.

Each patch of various skin tones, no larger than my palm, was painted with a victorious scene of bloodshed. Warriors brandishing weapons, killing one another, streaked in blood. The detail was too minute and perfect to be made without magic.

The beef strips staled in my gut. The salt reminiscent of the blood splattered across my helmet on the front lines.

I stumbled away from the quilt, passing a tulle veil separating the living area from the bedroom. My fingers curled around the board at the bed's base. Slender, curved railings of chalk white cylinders rimmed it, mirroring those of the ornate headboard.

It warped the longer I stared at it. Femurs linked in intertwining lines. A skull sat between some, while kneecaps connected others.

I snatched my hand from the bone bedframe.

"It's been a while," a haughty voice said behind me, "since I've been graced with the presence of a young female."

Holding my erratic breath, I spun on light toes to the speaker. Easton smiled, dressed in full battle gear. His curls hung over his brow, each scar on his chin was slightly raised, and his heavily hooded eyes watched the flicker of torchlight on my skin.

I gawked at the Easton before me, but it was not my mate. Not the one who'd asked me to come back, who my soul had allied with. This Easton was far more beautiful and elegant than the one I knew, with stronger cheekbones, sharper eyes, sleeker hair, and slenderer shoulders. Taller, as well.

He strutted to me with a million promises swimming in his burgundy eyes.

"You're not Easton," I stuttered, retreating. The back of my knees hit the bed. I felt a desperate urge of desire, like a sizzling wave rolling over me. My body reacted to it, and I sank onto the cushion.

Those shimmering eyes told me everything his muscular hands would do to me, how his full lips would love me. They outlined every moment of blissful eternity in the stone cage crushing around me.

My knees wobbled as the images flashed in my mind.

The fake Easton rolled his eyes. "No, sweetheart, I am not. You are far from your mate." His voice, though near Easton's, held a purr of lust. I wanted to curl into it and lose myself beneath its gentle caress.

He halted before me, lean shoulders blocking the glow of torches. I clenched my hands into the blanket on the edge of the bed. Only a sliver of air separated us, a shield to block the remembrance of how his blessing caved with every flex of his back and the warmth of his mouth on mine.

I held his gaze, scrutinizing his eyes. Not green. It rooted me to my spot like a gag forcing back down my desires.

He reached, running his knuckles against my cheek.

Fiery pain speared across my face and neck, its spikes of anguish thundering long after his touch disappeared. My legs seized, then buckled.

He caught me.

More pain.

Worse pain.

My body flared as if blistering fire coursed through my veins. Through every muscle, every unwilling breath.

I was dropped to the stone floor.

Time flowed without constraint as I wailed and cried, begging for the burning to subside. When it did, the dull taste of fear lingered.

Raising my plea to the imposter rekindled the burn in the base of my skull.

Fake Easton stared at his hands. I wanted to give him an Amaury-worthy death stare, but the energy had been sapped from my body, leaving barely enough to hold myself up on quivering palms.

His eyes flickered to mine. They no longer shimmered. They were midnight black inkiness akin to a starless sky, like dark embers waiting for a match to spark their rage.

"What are you?" he seethed.

My mouth dried when no answer came. I wheezed on my fear. The being before me shifted from the male I'd hoped to see again to a figure of fire armored in black plates.

I threw my arms over my head. "I'm a Forterian."

The fiery being howled. Pebbles raining from the ceiling caught in my hair where I clutched it.

Fire erupted in a half circle, trapping me against the end of the bed. I lunged to my feet and scrambled across it. I grabbed for the nearest weapon bolted to the wall, a sickle blade as curved as a crescent moon with a grip the length of my forearm.

The bolts gave. I spun to face the fire.

It stalled, every flicker immobile. Inside were faces and flesh and hair frozen in a fixed blaze.

"What are you?" I wheezed, holding the blade between us with both hands.

"I thought it obvious." The figure waved a morphing hand at the wall of weapons and quilt of skin. "Though maybe I've been imprisoned for too many centuries for your generation to remember me." It glared at the quilt of skin. "My symbol was on every Forterian shield. My name chanted as they marched into battle, knowing I only champion the strongest on the continent."

I gulped. "You're the Forterian goddess of war."

From within the immobile inferno's blue center emerged a female with bronze plating across her leathers, iron hammers the size of my head on each hip, and brass colored hair ribboning through her crown of fire.

Eyes like coals narrowed. "How did you get here?"

"I was sleeping," I muttered, suddenly very aware of how naked I was, "in a cave. I'm in the Sacrament."

The spark in her eyes was snuffed so quickly I feared I'd imagined it. "A female in the Sacrament? An anomaly for this century."

I nodded.

"How?"

I lowered the blade to one hand to cover my nakedness with the other, as if that'd stop her from looking. She smirked before twirling her hand, and a robe appeared around me. It, like the blankets, begged me to stay a bit longer. I fiddled with the silk ties to fasten them with one hand, aware of her growing smirk.

"There are no laws barring any worthy Forterian from earning a blessing."

A thin smile stretched across her blood red lips. "There hasn't been one in hundreds of years." She nodded to the blade. "Do you know those markings?"

The writing was like nothing I'd ever seen before, swirls and dots in a line down the handle.

"That's the ancient language of the gods. Only a direct descendant of a certain god could claim a blade within these walls."

I gaped at her. "A god? There are more of you? Those the priests of Beaddeon worship?" The ghost of Pila's claws raked down my spine.

"You think Forterians are the only ones to worship a god? There are hundreds of us, child." The torches above our head flickered. She leaned closer, eyes widening as if they could swallow me. "I see it now, the hints of your father peeking through your mortality. He is the one who trapped me in this wretched hole."

My mind still didn't digest what she was saying. "My fa—"

The bubble shook.

"Oh dear," the goddess shrugged, "that is your cue to leave." She threw her hair back across her shoulders, turned, and waltzed to the couch.

I raised the blade. "To leave?"

She eased onto the couch, her armor and leathers disappearing, replaced by a satin robe. "Why has he sent you to me?" She held up the quilt to study.

I took two stuttering steps, then felt a knot in my core being tugged away, akin to skipping. "Wait, your magic holds the Sacrament. Do you know my quest?"

"Of course. "She stroked a patch on the quilt.

"Can you tell me?"

A gleam lit the embers in her eyes. "It is the mountain you seek, answers veiled in shadows and deceit."

Before I could question her further, the world tipped and went black.

A hand shook my shoulder. Though the cave remained blanketed in shadows, the others padded about.

I patted myself over, relieved to find I was, in fact, wearing my leather armor. Leon offered me another flower for the pain relief, but I waved it away. I didn't need more hallucinations. I needed the same focus I faced the demons with.

"Let you sleep as long as we could," Leon muttered, retracting his arm as if I'd stung him.

Breakfast was bleak. The rising sun looked like a bruise on the horizon, a reminder of our day ahead and the blood we all might shed. Golden rays leaked across the cave floor toward where we leaned against different crops of the wall.

Though my stomach grumbled for more, the scent of salted beef tickled my nose. It's rough, dried texture brought me back to my dream, to the skin quilt draped across her couch.

A dream.

It'd been a dream spurred by the yellow-stemmed flower. The goddess of war, a feared warrior deity able to command the greatest army on the continent, trapped beneath the mountain like some weak damsel.

Leon approached after I'd set aside my jerky. He held a rope.

Jude stepped beside him. He offered me his dagger. "It's the smallest blade we have and your best chance to kill him."

I slipped it into my sleeve and raised both hands for Leon's knot work.

"If you lose it," Jude threatened, "you better die, or else, mountain be damned, I'll kill you myself."

CHAPTER 32

ENVERS STEPPED into the cave's mouth. The sun pinged off the blade on each hip and the dagger on his thigh. Its golden light staled across his tawny cheeks and appeared white in his umber, buzzed hair. His bulky shoulders took up half the cave mouth. His booted stomps rattled the dust and pebbles separating us.

Three jagged scars ran from his right temple to left earlobe, stretching to accommodate his sneer. He sucked in a deep breath through a crooked nose, as if he could smell the fear lacing my gagged screams.

"Leon." Envers swept into a low bow, lips curling around scarred gashes. His gaze flickered to me. "Whore's daughter."

Leon stepped between us and placed a hand on the dagger on his belt. "Where is Jorian?"

"If you are so in love with the namby, assign him better guards. Chief Yule will learn the war did not bring us all together. Not well, anyways." His voice was deep and breathy. A rugged handsome that'd already seen war.

"Release him."

"Faveos is enjoying strong alliances. As for the namby, he's safe. He shouldn't even be here."

"If you harm him—"

His scarred hand snared Leon's collar. "Back your threats," Envers shoved him, "or cower like your father."

A deep growl rocked the cave.

"Now get out." Boyish glee lightened Envers's tone. "Take those two and find another mountain side to piss off of."

Leon stopped at the edge of the cave, stared at me past Envers's shoulder, and raised a fist to his heart in a Forterian solute.

My chest squeezed and the rock in my gut slowly sank. I blinked, clearing my vision to ensure I was not mistaken.

I raised my bound hands to my heart and nodded.

Then he was gone, off to catch up with Mika and Jude to save Jorian. From there, they'd go somewhere safer, somewhere they could wait out the rest of the Sacrament.

Leaving the bloodthirsty brute to me.

The blade was warm beneath my sleeve. I rubbed my wrists back and forth to loosen the restraints further, ignoring where the rope chafed my skin.

Envers yanked at the ties of his leather armor, then chucked it into a pile by the cave mouth. His shirt went next. As he lifted it over his head, he revealed the crosshatching of scars on his skin. Like a map of his pain. They stretched with the pinwheeling of his arms. The arch of his shoulders popped a kink from his neck.

I averted my gaze to my bindings, feeling like I was intruding on a personal moment. The knife's tip reached my palm.

"Impressive, huh?" he asked, motioning to the scars. Envers pivoted to display the pattern decorating his back, swooping down its planes and along his shoulder blades. An outline for the Oracle to trace when blessing him with wings.

He squatted before me and yanked the gag out of my mouth. Hazel eyes, surrounded by scars instead of wrinkles, widened. His nostrils flared.

I spat, hitting him between the eyes. I had to rile him up,

break his focus so he wouldn't notice the blade until it was in his neck.

His hand, coated in scars from the fingertips down, yanked back my hair. He was so close I could smell tobacco on his breath. I could see the yellow stains on his teeth.

I shook at my bindings. The dagger's point nipped my finger.

He punched the scream from my lungs. Releasing my hair, he mused over his pile of weapons and armor, then selected a knife barbed like an arrow while I heaved in a shallow breath. "Chief Barin didn't want me to kill you right away. He wants your pain visible for all who see your body when I bring it back, as a reminder you may have been born in our camps, but you are not one of us." He sliced through the ropes at my feet. "We are not the same."

I kicked my legs free, aiming at his lower region. The hilt was nearly in my hand.

He caught my legs, tucking them under his arm. "Beg me not to kill you. "He crushed my legs into the ground with his knee.

I bit back my grunt of pain.

Eyes widening and face reddening, he punched me in the nose.

Blood gush from it. Its salty warmth pooled in my mouth. I fumbled with the blade. Closer, so close to falling into my grasp.

"I heard you were a talker," he barked. "Use that pretty voice now to beg for death."

My glob of blood-filled spit hit his chest and rolled down, landing on my pinned legs.

His snarl spread across his thin, cracked lips. "That wasn't very lady-like."

The barbarian's concentration did not waver. He pulverized me like a slab of meat, fists tenderizing my stomach, shoulders, and face. More blood, more aching and stabbing pain through every breath, as if they were threaded in my skin.

The dagger slipped from my grasp. It clattered on the stone floor.

My scream ripped through the echo of hits, vibrated through

the cave, and blared from the cave like a horn.

Like the turning of the tide, Envers receded.

I attempted to breathe against the crunch of my ribs and the ache radiating in my limp shoulder, where it jutted at an odd angle. My gaze narrowed beyond my control, one eye swelling completely closed. Blood puddled in my cheek, dribbling down my throat.

"Tell me, whore," he sneered from somewhere near, "who gave you this?"

I stared at hazel eyes rimmed red. Blood freckled his nose and cheeks. The hand he held up the dagger in was bright red, knuckles a blossoming purple.

My lips refused to form the words. My head split in two at the thought.

"This is a prized hunting knife of Clan Rowera. Jude's clan. If you have this—"

My good eye slipped closed.

His fist tangled in my hair and yanked. "Let this be his first warning."

Pricks of pain raided my skull at every saw of the blade through my hair. Then, immense relief, and the cycle continued. A single tug, the hacking of a blade, and then relief. Over and over. Each time I thought it was all gone, he found more.

I reached for it and felt the blade's rage on my fingertips. Blood spurted from them. It fell in warm rain across my brow. Blond hairs stuck to my sticky hands, tangling around my fingers.

He tossed me aside when finished. I rolled once and remained as he'd discarded me, limp and useless on my side. Pain seized every muscle, pulsing from my bones.

His resonating stomps faded.

My head rolled onto my sliced hand, where warmth flooded the pain. I crept my good eye open to find him, but he'd left me staring at the downslope of the cave. Shadows danced beyond and within my vision. They promised to swallow me whole.

I wished they would.

Then, something flashed within them. A streak of light in the deepest cavern.

My palms twitched against the stone. I pressed into my shoulder and rolled onto my elbow. The stone came away beneath my clawing nails, leaving a trail of scratches for Envers to follow.

I had to move.

Faster.

He'd return to an empty cave, and if the fear of Inmonte didn't hinder him as it did the others, no distance I could crawl would save my life.

A wave of nausea churned my stomach and sapped the adrenaline from my aching knees. I pushed again, reaching the downslope of the cave.

Death breathed down my back. I kicked off with a grunt of heavy pain leaching up my legs. My hips and shoulders took the brunt of each roll down the slope. I clenched my teeth to keep every wince cage behind them. The dirt, freezing from its shadowed grave, welcomed me with its grainy embrace.

Laid out at the bottom, staring at the ceiling with my arm twisted oddly, and awaited the pain to subside into numb eternity.

Nails traced my forehead. An adrenaline-laced scream burst from my gut.

"Don't—" a high-pitched voice said from further back, but it was too late. The hand dipped to my cheek and warmth flooded through my body from it. I arched against the sickening pop of my joints and itched where skin stitched back together.

"Damn it!" Envers shouted through the cave.

"Grab her," a deeper voice snapped, "quickly!"

"No," the other replied, voice even and secure. A hand, warm like sunned stones, wrapped my finger around something jagged. A rock. "He said not yet."

No sound came from my pleading lips to stop the shadows from abandoning me.

"Find us," the second whispered. "Find us, Child of the

Night, before it is too late."

I grappled with my voice to beg, but the warm presence disappeared and loneliness splashed over me like water. Their magic faded. I stared into the darkness, as if my silent demand would bring them back.

Children of the Night, hidden within the mountain's bowels. Come to my aid. Claiming me as theirs.

"Whore." Envers's hand curled around my ankle. I hardly felt the bumps of the slope against my back, exhausted by constant pain. The blinding light, a stark reminder I may never see another night, basked my swollen eyes in red.

He released my leg, and I maneuvered the rock beneath my sleeve. Through a slitted eye, I watched him kneel over me, his thighs caging mine between them.

He appraised Jude's knife.

Envers hitched it beneath my leather armor at the center, the blade tickling my navel. It slid clean through, dividing my armor and shirt with one slice.

My skin pricked where his gaze fell, then finger pressed. He dipped his fingers into the blood dribbling from my mouth, then marked a sticky line from navel to sternum.

Envers raised the knife again, and fear clamped my gut in its maw.

I smashed the rock into his right eye.

He lurched away. I pulled back for another hit.

Envers caught my wrist and slammed it into the ground beside my head. His glare was darkened by the thick patch of blood raining from the gash above his forehead. A drop fell onto my cheek. It slid down to my lips and across my jaw.

The rock rolled away.

He released my wrist and grasped my throat.

I clawed into his forearm, choking for every wheezing breath.

Envers trailed the knife down the line of blood, then balanced the tip above my navel.

He pressed.

My world narrowed to the knife searing me in two. The

pricks of pain, like a million needles, tunneling through me.

My screams turned to shrieks, then sobs, then hoarse barks.

His nostrils flared. His tongue darted out to wipe a bead of sweat from his lip.

He heaved in the scent of my death.

Seconds or minutes or hour ticked by. My blood pooled around where he staked me to the stone floor.

I fell, held in suspension above death by those hazel eyes. The warmth of my blood faded without replacement. With it went the feeling of my twitching toes and the scrap of my nails against my murderer's wrist.

My limbs thudded to the floor.

My eyes rolled back.

Shadows engulfed me whole.

I expected oblivion. Instead, I stared at the stunning female from my dream, her full curves on display beneath the thin veil of red satin. Brass hair cascaded over her shoulders and swirled across the bedsheets.

Her hand trailed from hip to shoulder, and I tore my gaze away to study the weapons on the walls. It was her magic rousing my curiosity, I told myself. The same magic she'd lit my skin ablaze with.

"There are many escapes from pain," she cooed, her voice rumbling like a melody of cellos. "I find mine here." Fingers inked black from nail tip to knuckle traced the swirls of bedsheet.

"He's going to kill me," I rasped, grasping at my clean stomach where I'd felt the pierce of Jude's knife. "Please, help me."

"I do not interfere with the Sacrament," she warned.

I staggered toward her. "Please." My knees gave and rang where they landed on stone. "There are always exceptions with magic."

Her lips twisted into a snakelike sneer. "Perhaps, if you

promise me a favor, I can reward you with a weapon of some kind."

I stalled. "What promise?" My gaze went to the bed.

"I do not make such deals," she snapped. "I want freedom from this cell your father trapped me in."

"I'll find a way," I stuttered, falling to my hands. I crawled toward her. "I'll free you if you'll give me a weapon to kill him. Anything."

The goddess swept her fluttered gowns from the bed. She waltzed to me, hips swaying like the breeze. "You are foolish to trade an eternity here with me for what, a Forterian? I am better than any mortal, even a king."

"I'd trade my life for the future of the Forterians."

She offered her hand. The sickle blade I'd taken from the wall before appeared in it. "It is a deal."

I took it.

The handle squirmed beneath my grip. Red lace tied around the pommel, liquified, and streamed down my grip, up my arm, and to my navel. I felt the warmth of the bond solidifying, as I had for the fifty-two clan crests on my arm. It was a weight, not on my shoulders, but like a sled I'd forever pull, dragging me back for every step I took.

I looked back to the goddess. Her coal eyes seemed to spark, a hint of dying flames within them. "Every life I claim in battle, I dedicate to you. Starting with his."

CHAPTER 33

LIKE BREAKING THROUGH the surface of water, I woke. My breath threatened to lodge itself in my throat. A breath would prove I was still alive and in pain. Still at Envers's mercy.

I tilted to angle my less swollen eye toward the cave mouth.

The knife in my gut, like a flag staked in conquered land, wobbled with my next breath.

Pain returned to my muscles and bones like a snake constricting its prey. My dried blood cracked around me. My every breath threatened to reopen the split veins. I stopped, only to catch the yelp of pain.

Then waited. If he were above me, he'd yank the knife and I'd be dead. Weapon or not, I'd be dead.

I ventured another glance. He sat in the cave's mouth, scarred back to me. Someone cast a shadow across him and the cave floor, nearly to me.

"Dead, all of them."

"Three killed eight of ours?" Envers demanded.

I closed my eyes and gave a small sigh of relief. The knife quivered in my gut, eliciting another wave of immobilizing pain. Red beads ran from where it kept most of my pain plugged.

"Yes. They let me escape."

Envers huffed, getting to his feet. "Go back, start giving the last rites. I'll be along shortly."

Hopeless relief. They'd escaped, but they would not be returning to save me. Leon had made it clear. My survival rested on my shoulders.

I jolted at the stinging reminder of a pommel against my palm. As the goddess had promised, the sickle blade was tucked beneath my numb leg, obscured by the flaps of armor and mess of blood.

Four breaths passed before Envers's fingers toyed with the knife's hilt. "I will deny you death until you beg for it."

I eased my thigh off the sickle blade to free it.

Envers leaned closer, the stale beef on his breath itching my nose. He jostled the knife upwards, along the sticky line he'd drawn, rekindling the burn as if its embers flared in my gut.

A tear trailed from the corner of my eye and across my temple.

"Open your eyes." His voice was guttural. The knife twitched left. Every scab acting as a dam to hold back my death cracked and fell, washed away by a fresh tide of blood.

I would not beg, would not allow another useless breath until he had his last. I looked at him, stared into his hazel eyes with roaring malice.

Envers flinched back.

I sprang, crunching around the knife in my belly to hook the sickle through his gut.

His eyes went wide as he stared at me in shock.

I stumbled to my feet, pulling free Jude's knife. My hand slipped in the blood.

More than adrenaline swelled, more than fury. Hunger. What fluttered through me on the battlefield defending my mate. What others claimed was the mountain's demand for bloodlust. There was no pain, not here. Not anymore.

"Beg for death." I yanked the sickle from his belly, slicing him open from the inside.

Envers hit his knees before me, mouth ajar and breath jagged. He grasped his belly as his blood puddled with mine, swirling as one.

Angling his head back, he had a settled gaze. A soldier who knew his fate. "No."

"Then we are the same." I swung.

His corpse collapsed as his head bounced away with squishy plops.

I didn't spend another breath staring at it. The goddess of war could have him, the brute that he was.

I pressed my hand to my bleeding gut and turned, limping toward the shadows. Coldness collected in my bones as blood spurted from the wound. Every step cracked open the clouts and brought me closer to death's door.

The darkness welcomed me. The chill of death shackled my joints.

My legs gave out at the top of the downturn in the cave. I tumbled down the slope, bouncing until the cave evened out.

"A bit further."

Snapping up, I searched for the voice like wind rustling dead leaves. Both a promise and a threat as intertwined vines.

Pressing myself up to my knees with my good arm, I began a three-legged grovel toward salvation. My eyes didn't adjust. A black blanket remained around me, wrapping me in its warmth. In comfort.

"Live," a smoky voice demanded. "Fight."

I shrieked at every length. Felt each second stretch for eternity, until even those faded into sobs.

Then, silence.

I had to live. Not me for, and not for Easton or Amaury.

Not for my mother, who'd given her life so I didn't one day hide my own daughter in a cupboard.

For something bigger than a single life.

For those silenced and squandered. For those who would

follow me to victory, not to their deaths.

I tumbled to the cool cave floor where no light warmed my neck, body refusing another movement. Ice spread through my limbs.

I wanted to scream into the darkness, beg to know how far was enough. When salvation would find me.

And then I didn't want to.

Didn't want them to come save me and return the warmth so I'd fight another day. I'd fought enough.

The sweet release of death, an encasing of nothingness, beckoned.

Within its current, I sank.

Death was warm, oddly so, and plush. It caved around me and swaddled me in a feather light embrace, almost as if I was floating within a thick sea.

I scrunched my grave in tingling fingers, dozens of pins pricking at my palms with every flex.

"She's awake!"

I jolted from the voice, my hand finding the curve of the bed. The facade floated away, and with it, my calm. I searched the room, but I was blind. Blackness encased me like a tomb.

"Oh, dear," she cooed like an overbearing mother, "she's panicking." Two hands, cool and wrinkled, caught mine.

I broke from the grasp with a jutting elbow and prodded at my eyes. "I'm blind," I croaked, blinking rapidly.

"No." She giggled. It was a victorious shrill. "No, dear, you are not blind. There isn't enough light here for above-grounders to see."

The stale air burned my throat and settled like water in my lungs. I gurgled past it, "Inmonte?"

"Yes child, you are in Inmonte. The first visitor we've had in so long, did you know? A pity, I think. Inmonte is quite beautiful. And the stars are wonderful this time of year. One day, you'll see them." She slid her leathery hand into mine. Squeezed it. "Ta, our best healer, should be here soon. How are you feeling?"

I brushed off her grip and craned my neck to hear the approaching steps.

"Oh dear, she's panicking again."

"Calm, Kilp," the deeper voice from the caves said with a full breathed sigh. "Give her a moment to adjust. She'll need it. He is almost ready."

"He?" I demanded, dropping her hand.

"Your father, of course." Kilp captured my wrists again in her velvety hands. "He was so delighted when you killed that boy with his blade. There's talk of a feast in your honor!"

I grappled with my thundering heart and the crashing truth. The goddess hadn't lied. My father was a god. A deity of insurmountable power, hiding just out of reach.

"She should dress soon, unless you'd like to present her to her father in a blanket." I heard light steps near the bed. A warm presence snuck toward me, the same that'd given me the rock in the cave. The healer I assumed to be Ta prodded at my stomach, then my shoulder.

"He presented her naked to that bitch. I'd be surprised if he noticed what she wore."

Ta snarled, "Hold your tongue."

Kilp giggled again, and what sounded like feet shuffling away faded until a door closed. "I'm too old for that lecture," she said. "If your father was going to smite me for comments on his behavior, he'd have done it by now."

I let my questions fall aside.

"Come," her grip returned, "let's get you dressed."

I clutched the blanket to my naked chest.

"My leathers were—"

Ruined. Cut apart like my stomach. Drenched in my life and discarded, same as me.

"New leathers," Kilp amended. "They may not match those now in style above ground. Only Our Savior, himself, knows how long we've been away from their fashion trends. However, they are well made."

She eased me into a scalding bath. The scent of lavender rippled from it and petals floated across the surface into my shoulders. I plucked one from my arm and mashed it to pieces.

I felt the smooth skin of my abdomen where not even a ridged scar proved my skirmish with death. Magic, like a second skin, coated my body. I welcomed its familiar restraint.

After the bath, she helped me dress. The leathers fit snug, moving as if a part of me. Better fitted than those made for me for the Sacrament.

"Now your hair, dear. I can grow it back."

"Shave it."

"Growing hair is very easy, will only take—"

I ran a hand across the jutting tuffs and through the stringy strands hanging across my temples. "Please, shave it."

As we left the chamber, she hooked her arm through mine. Kilp hardly came to my shoulder. She was round and teetered like a duck. We hobbled through the winding hallways, our footsteps covered by her ranting about the murals I couldn't see.

Each step was a shove against the current of darkness, even at the creak of stone doors and rush of stale draft woven with poppy.

Kilp hauled me the first few steps forward to break my dumfounded stall. Her hand released my arm as she whispered, "Ten steps, then stop."

The shadows yanked forward. Mutters and giggling of children shrouded my scuffed footsteps.

"My daughter." His voice, like the wind wailing off the northern bluffs, settled the murmurs of the crowd.

I stared up at where it came from and felt the shadows swirling like hounds circling their master.

"I apologize for the lack of light, but my Obscurions cannot bear any light not of my making."

I fought the stammer of my heart.

"What is your name, daughter?"

"Kacela."

"How is your mother, Kacela?"

"Dead," I choked out. The shadows flittered at my every word, snatching them before they'd left my mouth.

"Pity," he dismissed. "You resemble her. That is favorable. I am a horrendous sight for many."

Hesitant chuckles rippled from the onlookers.

"You've brought me a great gift by bloodying my blade. That begs the question of why you are on the mountain."

I scrunched my brow. "It is my Sacrament."

I heard the smack of stone, as if he'd slapped the ground, and felt the rumble of his growl like an earthquake. "My daughter, in the Forterian Sacrament to earn another's magical abilities. You look to soil your bloodline with her magic."

I wrung out my hands. "I did not know." The excuse felt like burning coals in my mouth, leaving behind the dried wrinkles of a burn.

"What good is her magic when you have mine?"

It was the question Amaury asked me a dozen times. Why earn a blessing when I was born with a gift?

"It is more than the blessing, father. I am here for a bargain." I yanked at my sleeve to reveal the first half dozen tattoos on my forearm. "If I survive, all Forterians will train their youth, despite gender. I do not fight for my life. I fight for freedom."

Thunderous laughter mighty enough to shake pebbles from the roof. They bounced against my bald head and nicked at my hands.

"My daughter, not only a warrior, but a spearhead against the Forterians and their wretched goddess. We must celebrate your accomplishments. The first female in the Sacrament in centuries! A feast, on the full moon."

I stared at the source of his voice, puzzling through the shift in his tone. Analyzing the power of his presence and the nagging hesitation in my gut.

"You will stay. Won't you, Kacela?"

"No," I balked before sense stalled my temper.

The crowd, once buzzing with excitement of a feast, hushed. Silence, like the shadows, surged.

"You deny my offer?" His voice morphed from demand to growl, something beyond mortal.

I grasped at the hilts of the twin blades strapped to my hips. I licked my lips. "I do not mean to offend, father, but the full moon is the final day of the Sacrament."

"I know the damned day!" His shadows wracked the room once more. I flinched, hands blocking my head as more pebbles plinked on my boots.

"My bargains —"

"With my enemy," he scoffed.

"You sent me to her while a brute pulverized me. Why?"

He did not respond. Stone groaned and the shadows shifted.

"You sent me to her." My tone soured. "Naked."

Gasps washed through the crowd like ripples in a still lake.

He clicked his tongue. "If," he emphasized, "I'd have sent you differently than the rest, she might have struck you down before you could plead ignorance."

"And then I took the blade off the wall."

"A feat only one of my blood could accomplish. I couldn't help you until I had proof the Sacrament held my blood within its bonds."

I rolled my eyes like a teenager scolded by her father. "Help?" I sneered. "I made the bargain, I shoved the sickle through my killer, and I crawled back into the cave while I bled out —"

"To my healers, who saved you," he gloated. "You are alive, Kacela, because I am merciful and overjoyed at the return of my only daughter."

I gritted my teeth. "I thank you, Father, for your regard."

If the shadows would part, I might've thrown the dagger in my boot at his laugh. The same pompous gloat Easton claimed wrinkled my every word coated my father's. But the power he radiated bounced off the walls and converged on me, squashing me like a bug beneath a heel. I strained against it to remain upright.

Another god, another being greater than Griffin, hiding in the mountain. Sheltered by the goddess of war's magic. These were the secrets Griffin yearned for when we'd planned my Sacrament. The reasons he needed for invading its depths to snuff out the threat to Kadea. The ruse he could overwhelm the Forterians with to bring them fully under his command.

The plan I'd set into motion.

"You enjoy making deals." My father laughed before his voice retook its gravely snarl. "Here's another. I'll allow you to leave these caves, with weapons and leathers, to finish your crusade."

"And in return?" I seethed, clutching harder at my blades.

"You will spend every night for the rest of your life with your dear friend, the goddess you've pledged your every kill to." All fever rattling my bones seeped from them. He was before me to catch my next breath. "Daughter," his voice felt like knives slicing my cheeks, "do we have a deal?"

I grabbed my sword hilts. "And if I refuse?"

"I'll release you into the bowels of the mountain where I keep my pets. They have not chased healthy prey in decades."

I raised my glare to the source of his voice. My heart plopped into my gut. "Every night?"

"Every night," he confirmed.

"Do we shake on it?" I deadpanned. The gasps of the crowd wouldn't scare me, not after all my father had taken from me. What he threatened to take from me.

"Put out your hand, daughter."

Shadows wrapped around my hand and forearm, encasing it from fingertips to elbow in wintry pricks. Power tenfold of Griffin's streamed from his grip through my body. Boiling chill raked above the mark of the goddess's bargain, doubling me at the waist.

"Do not disappoint me again, Kacela."

Kilp pressed my hand to the cave wall. "Keep your hand here. Ignore the first five breaks in the wall and turn left at the sixth. In a few hours, the sun will still be up. Wait until its descent to emerge."

She forced a pack onto my back and pressed a dagger into my hand. The etched grooves of the blade soiled with my blood dug into my palm.

"We toasted to you the night after you closed the portals to the demon realm on our mountain. Those are terrors even we of the night do not claim." Her nails dug into my arm, and she dragged me lower so her lips brushed my ear. "Return. You are a daughter of Inmonte. A Child of the Night. An Obscurion as much as a Forterian. You will not fail us."

I grappled for her retreating hand. "Fail you?"

"Go," she shoved me. "And come back when the time is right. Come back to save us."

CHAPTER 34

I STUMBLED ACROSS A ROCK as the wisps of light seeping from the cave mouth blinded me.

"Who's there?" Jude called. Maybe it was sheer dumb luck I emerged from the cave the four boys sat in, weapons at the ready. Or maybe Kilp was more devious than she seemed.

A sob broke from my pursed lips, but nothing more. I didn't dare come around the curve of the cave where sunlight would burn my closed eyes.

"Who's there?" Jude repeated.

"Kacy," I pleaded. "It's me. Kacy."

I flinched from the approaching stomps. Hands grabbed my shoulders.

"Kacela?" Jude's breath ran across my face. "What the hell are you doing here? What are you wearing?"

I chuckled, smiling as tears threatened to fall. "Long story."

Another breath hit my face. "You have my knife?"

I held up the knife Kilp gave me, eyes still closed. "Is this it?"

Hours later, my eyes adjusted to enough for me to sit beside them in the mouth of the cave and bask in day's remaining warmth. Jungle spread out before us, nearly the opposite side of the mountain from Envers's decaying body.

"You killed him!" Jorian's excitement tore open his healing split lip. His left eyes pulsed at each word, swollen nearly shut, and the bandage wrapped around his chest peeked above his shirt collar.

I nodded, taking another piece of beef from Jude, who'd warmed up to me since the return of his knife.

"I would've liked to see that!" Jorian said, elbowing Leon, who sat with his legs out and arms back, one tucked behind Jorian. "Doubt you could've done that."

Leon returned his nudge. "Watch it."

Whether or not they fully believed my hastily told story, none mentioned the lack of bruising or injuries, not even Leon after I'd denied his offer to re-wrap my leg. Explaining the midnight black leather armor with dyed gold patches and black dual blades was more difficult. Once I'd mentioned voices guiding me through the tunnels, all questions dropped.

Speaking of possible Inmonte dwellers was worrisome enough for Jorian. The others didn't seem to mind the bit of mystery.

"How long until the full moon?"

Mika stared at me for a moment, head cocked. "It's tomorrow."

I stared back, waiting for him to claim it all a joke and we had over a week, as we had when I'd killed Envers. When they all remained silent, I began to laugh. Bellyfuls of laughter rupturing from me like geysers echoed through the cave I wiped the gathering tears from my eyes. "We're done?" I'd spent over a week in Inmonte, unconscious and safe in my father's domain.

Jude's glare cut to me. "Don't say that! The last night of the Sacrament is the bloodiest. Desperation and insanity run rampant. Some have yet to fulfill their quests. Others just want a taste of the glory, and the worst ones try to start wars."

"What do we do?"

"We wait," Leon answered. "We wait it out and hope we've set enough traps outside to scare others away."

The sun crept away, as if teasing us for this one last night. The sooner it set, the sooner we'd be whisked away.

I hid my smile between munches of jerky. My quest was completed, my bones were reset, and my skin was fresh and unmarked. I'd return a survivor, an ally. The magic would drag me back over the line to the amused face of my mate, the relieved face of Amaury, and the furious faces of fifty-two chiefs before panic to arrange trainings set in.

If I made it another twenty-four hours.

The long day stretched into an even longer night.

The next morning, we tore through my pack from Inmonte. It was full of jerky and water flasks and new supplies, including herbs with labels on their stems. There were also poisonous leaves and healing roots, and other sundries.

"This would've been nice the first day," I muttered, replacing most of the equipment.

Jude snuck another piece of jerky out of it before I closed the pack and chewed with a gloating smile.

The day crept along.

We took shifts to watch the unchanging slopes.

"Maybe they don't know you're alive." Leon sharpened his knife with a stone from the pack.

"You left one alive, and Envers's body is in the cave. When they don't find my body rotting beside him, they'll speculate the rest."

I held in the last piece of information I hadn't told anyone, not even Easton. The information I drew from Kalman's mind. Chief Barin planned to ruin my final night with wolves or dogs or beasts, hoping I'd be celebrating my victory early and would be too relaxed to notice the pack of wild beasts hunting me down.

During Leon's watch, I sat beside him. The others were within earshot, but it was not their approval I sought. I watched the unchanging slope with him, feeling the chill of loneliness beyond the cave's grasp.

"I'm going to leave, "I said.

"What?" Jorian demanded.

Shadows veiled the horizon. "Envers was not the only monster Barin promised my death to. If I can make it to the tree line, I can hide until the moon pulls us out."

Leon's face contorted for a brief pause, then he returned to staring down the graying horizon, as if it might make the moon rise any faster. If I ran, I'd reach the tree line by sunset. Night may cover my scramble to find a sturdy enough branch, but even then, the shadows summoned by Barin's deal with the bonks could tear me from it. However, that was a sacrifice I was willing to make.

To spare their lives. My allies.

Jorian stood behind us, still in the safety of the cave. "You're not leaving!"

Leon raised a hand. "Jorian—"

"No, Leon. She was willing to sacrifice herself for us. She won't face Barin's monsters alone. If she goes, I'm following."

"It's suicide." Leon's face stilled despite the stomp of Jorian's boot.

I nodded. "It's my life or yours."

"You don't decide that," Mika said from behind me. "If you leave, I follow. I won't turn a blind eye to Barin's tricks any longer."

Their collective gaze on my back made my chest tighten further.

Jude stepped closer. "I always thought I'd die in the Sacrament in a bloody mess. Mountain be damned, nambies, one last fight in the moonlight may earn us enough glory for a song."

That pulsing power within me, the one that'd sputtered for months, exploded in a show of sparks and ashes, encasing me in the warmth I never thought I'd have. Not in the Sacrament. Not in any Forterian war camp.

Brotherhood.

"Sit your asses back down," Leon barked. "No one's leaving the cave. It's an ideal vantage point with unsteady rocks and a small mouth. It'll be easiest to defend if an attack comes."

His eyes shifted to me.

"I can't—"

"We won't abandon you. Not again."

"The longest night," Jorian said. He leaned against the opposite side of the cave mouth. Blood creased over his lips and soiled his fawn cheeks. In the dying light, his features were smooth, lacking worry lines of his comrades. He smiled, hands stained with only his blood. "Waiting for the moon to appear. She makes sure of it."

I nodded.

"I wanted to do more to help you in the cave." He sighed, ringing out his hands. "I saw you sleeping in the back. I thought I'd heard something earlier, but I didn't want to risk giving someone away if they were hiding. I waited until the others were asleep. I wanted you to have a fighting chance. It didn't seem fair, the deal. No help from outside the Sacrament. All of us brought in at least one weapon."

I grinned, meeting his hazy blue eyes. "Thank you. I only used it on Rory, but it gave me hope I wasn't alone."

"I'd hoped you didn't have to use it on anyone." He bowed his head. The curly locks of honey blond fell over his swollen eye. "None of us should have to. It's cruel, the Sacrament. It messes with our heads. It warps us into bloodthirsty warriors. I've seen the best go into the Sacrament and come out like Envers. I didn't want to enter. I have no need for a blessing, but Leon promised it'd be worth it." He turned over his shoulder to smile back into the cave.

I reached for his shoulder. "It will be."

"One more night and this is all over. I can curl up in my bed and sleep with pea—"

An arrow punched through his chest.

He fell into my arms, eyes reflecting the sun like a rippling stream. Before his next breath, the murky depths rose to swallow the vibrant light.

I searched the others' faces. They searched mine, as if the key to rebuffing death had been marred across my features.

Magic.

I reached for it, not caring I died for Jorian to live.

I reached and reached and reached, but it was like wandering a maze with no end.

Jorian coughed red. He tried to speak, but bubbling blood choked out the words.

Leon shoved me aside, and I tumbled away through the puddle growing around his fallen friend.

The sun disappeared with Jorian's labored breath and Leon's pleas for him to stay. To live.

He didn't.

CHAPTER
35

ARROWS RAINED on the cave mouth and craggy path leading to it. Mika darted between the rocks, mixing with the dusk shadows to fire the poisoned arrows back and buy us time. I crawled beside him and wedged any broken arrows into the cracks between rocks. The remainder went into Mika's quiver.

Minutes ticked by. The rap of arrowheads on stone lessened, then stopped.

Mika motioned to return to the cave.

After giving Jorian's last rites, Leon joined us at the front of the cave. Blood rolled off his armor. I flinched at every plop of it on the stone. Tear tracks stained his cheeks.

"I'm going to kill them," Leon stated.

Mika's eyes shot up. "Your quest—"

"The goddess be damned. I'm going to kill them all." His eyes scanned the three of us. Terror seeped from them. No longer a mourner, but a general ready for war, assessing his troops. "Do you have a numbers report?"

"Six." Mika reached out to give Leon's shoulder a squeeze though he shrugged it off.

"I recognized four from Virian," I said.

"One from Vertin, another from Flyeria," Mika said.

Leon's glazed gaze drifted to the jungle beyond the snow-coated boulders.

My knees knocked into one another.

Jorian had said the Sacrament turned the best of them into Envers. Had he, too, seen that look in Leon's eyes before and wondered how close he was to becoming a mindless killer? Who else had he seen on the cusp of breaking?

"I'm going to kill them," Leon repeated. "I don't expect any of you to—"

"You're thick-skulled if you think I'll let you walk out there alone," Jude stepped up to him and raised a fist to his heart. "I'm not losing you, too."

Mika placed his hand over his chest. "I follow you."

I stared at my right hand, already curled into a fist at my side, and raised it up before me. Jorian's blood cracked across my knuckles, lined my nails, and dyed my palms crimson.

I met Leon's stare and placed my blood-stained fist over my heart. "I follow you."

When the sun disappeared, I watched the clouds obscure the glistening moon, as I once watched the curtains before a play, jittery for it to begin.

"You good with a bow?" Jude asked.

"Yes." The quiver on my back was full. The arrows, their heads slathered in yellow poison, smelled like spoiled fruit.

Jude adjusted the strap on my shoulder. "In close combat?"

"In practice close combat." I shrugged off his fingers.

Jude's snarl set my stomach into aching knots. "Don't hesitate. They may not be demons, but they'll kill you just as quickly."

There were no bets on who would kill more and no light-hearted jokes. Only us and the suffocating silence in the wake of Jorian's death. I saw his boots peeking out from where Leon tucked him into the cave's bend, dusted and scuffed at the toes. A smear of his blood split the cave in two.

Jude ducked his head. "If I don't survive this, tell Easton I messed up. That I've regretted it with my every breath since. Please."

I snatched the bow from him. "You'll tell him yourself."

He didn't look convinced, but we had no time. Mika signaled our enemies approaching.

I grabbed Jude before he could step away. "Leon's quest—"

"Not to kill."

I watched Leon bend to a knee, resting his forehead to the hilt of his blades.

Jude followed my attention. "Jorian always claimed not to believe in the goddess or the importance of the Sacrament. I think it was a lie. I think he believed in the goddess more than the rest of us, and that he knew this is not how she wished for us to worship her."

"Easton told me the monsters disappeared from the Sacrament a thousand years ago. He was wrong." I fought to take another breath. "The monster didn't disappear; they just look like us now."

Jude offered his hand. "Survive," he said. I clasped his forearm, and he clasped mine. "This will be the first of many battles for you. For us."

"They're approaching," Mika hissed, voice as grim as the grave.

I held Jude's arm as he turned to fight. "Save Leon's quest."

Resolve settled his rising brow. He nodded.

I set myself before the cave's turn. A guardian over Jorian.

The bow creaked as I pulled the string taut, slicing through the silence of the cave.

There was no need to burrow into myself to find the soldier tucked away, begging to never fight in the front lines again. She was purged.

Replaced by a warrior bred for this moment. To live freely with every move of my own making. Here, with death's progression ringing loudly and the crunch of snow announcing their approach, I prepared my own ballad of death.

In their haste to reach the cave, they stormed through the poison-slathered arrows jutting from the rocks like reeds. The first to reach the cave's mouth fell, mouth foaming and skin-tinged green. His allies tripped over his corpse.

My arrow found one's throat before he could right himself, and Jude created an opening for Mika to finish the next.

I shot again, causing the fourth to spin into Jude's awaiting slash. They tussled against the far wall, blades discarded and fists thudding against leather.

Another arrow steered the fifth away from Leon's charge.

Mika finished him as well, and my arrow sliced through the final attacker.

Sobering disappointment loosened my grip on the bow. The fight ended before it'd began, and the warrior within me pined for more blood. The mountain's demand for death turned me toward the one remaining, pinned against the cave wall by Jude's dagger at his throat.

"Are there more?" he demanded. A line of red caressed the blade.

"Kill me." Our enemy spat blood onto Jude's thigh. I stepped to his side with an arrow coated in poison. He stared at it teetering between my fingers. The promise of death slipped from his eyes, replaced by paralyzing fear. The bags beneath his eyes smoothed.

So young. He looked so young, as young as we all were.

Young. Naive. And now, killers.

"There's more," he stuttered. "Hounds. I don't know what they are. They have your scent." Frantic eyes speared me with their quake. "They're coming. Please, they'll kill all of us. Let me go. I'll run."

"Kill him," Leon ordered.

"No," I said, pushing Jude's blade away from the boy.

Leon rounded on me, eyes alight. "He killed Jorian!"

"I didn't!" The boy squished himself into the wall. He shielded his face with clenched fists. His tone was an octave too high, his words drenched in desperation. "I promise. I shot above you. I didn't want to kill anyone."

Leon shoved Jude aside and pressed his sword to the boy's throat. Blood pooled as the edge nicked flesh.

"Leon," I whispered, "your quest. Jorian knew what it would do to you if you didn't complete it. If you became a monster like the rest. He saw the Sacrament for the bloodbath it is."

The tension slipped from his shoulders.

"Then what do we do with him?" Jude asked.

Before we could argue, a snarl ripped through the mountainside. I turned toward it, and as I did, the boy yanked the arrow from my grasp.

He lunged at Jude's turned back and sliced the arrow into the back of his knee.

Jude spun and sliced his favorite dagger through the boy's throat, adding his blood to the dried remains of mine on the blade.

The boy fell, eyes wide and hands at his throat, as if he could shove back in the blood cascading out.

Jude touched his leg. Blood as thick as sludge stuck to his fingers. "I'm fine." He wiped it on his thigh. "We have more pressing matters."

Bodies of morphing silhouettes slinked into the cave. Their nostrils flared and yellow eyes pierced me. My first arrow soared harmlessly through the shadows of the beast's neck.

"Hellhounds," Mika whispered. "The stuff of legends. Nightmares—"

"As were the demons, and we killed those." I threw aside my bow and the quiver, taking up my black blades. Four more pairs of yellow eyes appeared in the cave's mouth, glowing like the moon.

"Look!" Leon pointed with his blade past the lurking beasts. Behind them, the clouds parted and the full moon radiated with glory. Light beamed from it, highlighting my allies.

But not me. I remained in the shadows with the hounds, as if someone blocked the moon's salvation.

They passed the warriors to reach me, and the raised brows of my new brothers-in-arms worsened the panic swelling in my gut.

I blinked, and Mika was gone.

Leon threw down his blades and dove to Jorian's body. He disappeared with it, sucked out of the Sacrament by the moon.

I swung both blades into a leaping hellhound. It tumbled away. The shadows seeping from my blade's slices were like blood from a wound. The hound swayed, then melted into a cloud of black mist.

Jude grabbed my forearm. "Don't let go of me," he commanded.

Light encased him. I stared at his blurring face despite the growl of the approaching nightmares. A hound dove, and we tumbled from its grasp.

"Pull me out," I screamed at the moon from my bloodied knees.

Jude battered away another hound. We were up. Pivoting, I dropped a blade to clasp his forearm as he held mine. We maneuvered in circles, keeping four snapping hounds in our switching sights.

Sweat slicked our grips. I dug my fingers into the ties of his forearm guards.

I should've urged him to go, to escape the bloodbath before he found oblivion on the mountainside with me, but I could not pull my grasp from his. Not within the circling hounds.

Jude slashed away another. It retreated without the seep of shadows puddling like blood, as if Jude's blades hadn't sliced it. Not like how my gifts from the Obscurions had.

Realization dawned like the relief of the moon. I stared at his sweat-coated brow and the droop of his shoulders. Blood from his leg puddled at our boots. My heel slipped in it.

He stumbled with me, shoulder smacking into mine. Our arms kinked together. I met his gaze. It dulled with every second slowed in the eternity of my next breath. His face blurred and cleared, the moon battling with me to pull him from the cave.

He was going to die here.

Heavy tears blurred my vision. I yanked my arm from his hand. "Go!"

His eyes rounded. Hands grappled for mine. "Kacy—"

Then Jude's amber eyes disappeared, replaced by eyes the stale yellow of his teeth.

I spun from the outstretched, shadowed claws and slid beneath the beast lunging for me. My blade, raised above my head, severed it in two. A cloud of black shadows hovered above me for a breath and scattered in a gust of wind.

Spinning on my knee, I scooped my other blade from the ground and blocked gnashing teeth. Its claws raked past my crossed blades and through the leather on my arms.

Ice stemmed from each gash. It crept through my chest. Blistered down to my toes.

The hound snapped at me again, stale death exhaled in snarls. My arms screamed, shoving it across the cave.

Another sprang, and I skewered a blade through its neck. I scattered its ashy remains with my next breath.

The remaining two prowled on either side of me, herding me away from the salvation of the moon's beam. I waved my swords before them.

Both pounced.

I dodged the first and met the second's snapping jaw with a spinning slash. Black mist burst into my eyes and rammed down my throat.

Blindly, I stumbled from the clink of claws across the cave. I rubbed at my eyes with my knuckles, itching dust from them.

The hound snarled. Its nostrils flared and yellow eyes beamed. Spine rigid.

Settling my breath and blinking through the itch in my vision, I held my blades at the ready. One last beast between me and the end of this nightmare. Then I'd walk to the edge of Sacrament Land if I had to.

"Come on!" I screamed.

It stilled, head quirked as if it assessed me as more than prey. Then, it sprang.

Claws sank into my thigh. My swords punctured its chest as I fell back against the cave wall.

It crumbled, the shadows falling across me and then retreating into the cave.

Dazzling light eclipsed me. Magic cocooned my arching back and suppressed my cravings for more blood. A bright flash filled my eyes. The world squeezed around me, then released. Dried grass cropping out of grainy snow pricked at my hands.

I eased onto my hands and knees. With each cough, bits of shadows raked over my lips and soiled the patches of snow.

Mika's screams brought me from the pain burrowing in my thigh.

"Get a healer!" He cradled Jude's still form against his shoulder. Amber eyes, as dull as leaves hardened by winter, stared at the brilliant moon.

"No," I choked, crawling through the trampled field to them.

Magic, my magic, rushed back to me like a dog returning to its master. It embraced me within its well of power. It numbed the searing claw marks. Banished the ache from my bones.

I raised a crackling hand and rerouted my entire well of might into Jude's unmoving chest. Light pulsed beneath his chalky skin.

His heart clenched, and my magic sang through the swell of his lungs.

He lurched from Mika's grip, rasping out curses through a mouthful of blood.

Spying me out of the corner of his eye, Jude went silent. A snort scrunched his widened eyes, then his thunderous laughter dragged my heart from my gut.

"I hope this isn't death," he muttered, slapping his hand atop mine, "because you are the last one I want to see after I die."

I sat on my heels, staring at the golden strikes of lightning jumping from finger to thumb and crackling up to my elbows.

"We did it," I whispered to them.

The raucous screams for those not present brought me from the heave of our breaths and zaps of my magic. It prodded for attention like a child.

Jude clawed at my shoulder. "Did you complete your quest?" His voice held an air of panic I was grateful for, as if he expected the bargains to strike me down before my next breath.

I nodded. "Did you?"

He dropped his hand to mine, my magic branching to encompass it. "My quest," he settled the tremors of his breath, "was to keep you alive."

Mika stalled beside him, spurred to his feet only by desperate call of his name. He rushed to a girl who threw her arms around his neck and legs around his waist.

Leon, not far off, picked up Jorian's body and stumbled to a couple. He sank to his knees at their feet. Jorian's mother, sharing his complexion and high cheekbones, fell to her knees beside him. She gathered him against her, cradling his head against her chest as tears streaked her cheeks.

Her husband kept a stone expression of appraisement and gripped her shoulder.

Leon's apologies began as whispers. He stilled, the veins in his neck bulging and eyes widening. Grasping his chest, he heaved as if the weight of the mountain fell on his shoulders. A sharp cry splintered from his lips.

Jorian's mother held him closer, whispering in his ear as he convulsed and reached for Jorian's still hand.

"Leon and Jorian completed the mate bond a week before the Sacrament," Jude whispered.

Mate.

My head shot up. The empty vat within my gut filled with more than magic. It bounced and tumbled over itself to sprint down the mate bond toward Easton's tightly wound worry.

I traced the bond, silent and empty for so long, to his first staggered step toward me.

His green eyes were rimmed in red exhaustion.

"Go," Jude smirked, titling his head. "Explain to me later why you tried to kill yourself."

I wobbled to my feet. Then I was in his arms. Mine around his neck, my fingers knotted in his hair. He breathed in as if he could inhale me, and I held him tight enough to feel every groove of his armor, every tie holding it together, the clasp of his belt around his waist.

His wings cocooned around us. The white light of the moon glowed within them.

Safe. I was safe.

"You came back," he whispered against my shoulder.

"My soul is allied with yours, Easton. I will not lose you."

CHAPTER 36

THE BONE BLADE CLEAVED into my paralyzed muscles, resonating scalding pain.

Metallic blood coated the bite of bark clenched between my teeth. I wailed against it.

The blade, so thin I feared it'd break apart at each pass, slipped back into my skin, thundering like a raging storm, while I clawed into the table with chipped nails on blood-stained hands. My vision blurred. My lower back convulsed, and for a moment, I felt as if I were falling into a stream of lava.

I forced myself back into the final moments of the Sacrament, ground myself to that temporary pain to remind myself this, too, would fade with the memories. The pain dulled. My heart settled into the rhythm of war, eased by the memory of the yellow eyes of nightmares reincarnate.

The blade worked up my left shoulder, crossed my spine, and caressed my right shoulder.

Easton had told me not to guess at the markings, but my heart hammered with every swoop of the blade. Arcs at the top and points at the bottom. Each line solidified my suspicions.

Tears gathered in the corners of my eyes. A rebellious one

traced the curve of my jaw before it fell into a puddle of ink muddled with red swirls of blood.

The Oracle, an ashen figure draped in hoary robes, padded away from the table. As Amaury had always said, they smelled like feet. They set aside the sliver of a blade and gathered a tray with a bowl of ink, a mallet, and a chisel with jagged teeth already stained black.

Each tap of the chisel, depositing the ink into the fresh wounds, was a million pricks plummeting into my gut. I held back the zaps of my own magic begging to heal the blessing, enraged at the foreign magic rooting itself in my shoulders, abdomen, and back.

My body buzzed, torn between the two sources of magic refusing to mingle.

Again, the Oracle moved away. A hum of magic remained in the air around us. Ink dripped from the chisel onto the floor.

They gave a single ringing grunt. It was enough finality for me to sag onto the table, arms and legs hanging off the edges. Limp like a rag doll.

The bite of bark thudded on the dirt floor.

The Oracle popped open a new bottle of ink. It sloshed into the bowl. The chisel's tip clinked in as well.

I whimpered through each staggered step to the tent flaps, fighting the agony attempting to knock my knees to the ground. Clutching what was left of my shirt to my chest. I batted aside the tent flap. One of the canvas lengths ran across my back. Searing pain blinded me, but two arms cradled my reeling shoulders.

Not Easton. He'd been speaking with war chiefs when I'd gone into the tent.

Jude threw my right arm over his shoulder, and Leon took my left as Mika entered the tent.

"We got you," Leon said. The two hoisted me back through the gawking warriors. My friends' faces were both daring and proud.

I groaned in pain. "Tell me it's not a damn river."

Jude roared in laughter. "You wouldn't be a stamina. You couldn't even outrun us!"

"There was an arrow in my damn leg, you namby," I grunted.

"You know what it is." Leon's voice was soft. Secure.

I knew, but I wanted to hear it. Needed to hear it. To solidify my survival would be more than a start. It'd be a lethal blow to my opponents. To be marked as the best of all Forterians.

Jude pulled short of Easton's tent. I lifted my head to see my mate's raised brow.

"You'll have competition in the skies," Leon smirked before this voice dropped, "General."

It was Easton's turn to laugh. The pain scattered as Leon helped me into my mate's arms.

Jude was slower to release my arm, his eyes nervously scanning Easton's features. "General—"

"Dismissed." Easton barked before hauling me into the tent and a warm bath smelling of honey.

Perhaps my father took pity on me that night, or he'd forgotten about our deal. A dreamless sleep, void of scheming deities, awaited me.

Easton kneeled before me on his bed, hands on my neck and thumbs trailing across my jaw. "Your body will adjust when you first manifest your wings. It will hurt, but after this, pulling them from the blessing will be as natural as walking."

I clutched the blanket tight to my chest with both hands. When he'd been turned away, rambling about flight mechanics, I'd slipped off my shirt and shielded the bargains with a scruffy blanket from the foot of the bed.

"It'll also heal the blessing. The ink will settle into your skin, and the scars with smooth out."

The rigid scars would disappear, no longer catching on every shirt and blanket rubbing against them, but the pain of the bone blade slicing through my skin would remain in my memory forever. I settled my shoulders. Pain pricked inward from the ink, as if the mallet still beat into the wounds.

"Imagine having wings," Easton whispered against my brow. I rested my forehead against his lips. The tip of his nose huffed hot air onto my bald head, and I flinched, the lack of a barrier to my scalp still foreign.

"Can I pick the color?"

He chuckled. "No, love." Easton trailed his hands, as soft as feathers, across the pulses in my neck. His fingers tapped my collarbones, then he had my hands in his, untangling them from the blanket.

It dropped to my lap.

I froze.

"You should feel it happen first," he whispered, lips wisping my brow. Delicately, as if he believed I'd break, he cupped the back of my hands in his then raised them to his lips and laid a kiss upon each palm. He guided them along his sides to the center of his back, where the ink felt greasy.

Our gazes held. If I tipped my head and raised my chin, I'd feel his lips against mine again.

Humid magic seeped from his blessing like heat rising from dunes. A thin trace of poppy mixed with the pine scent of my mate. The tattoo raised for a moment, then feathers tickled my palms. They swelled against my hands until I could no longer hold them. His wings appeared, unfurling from his blessing as smooth as the drawing of stage curtains. They reached past the edge of the bed.

"Your turn," Easton prodded. His wings enclosed us, smothering the yellow light of the lanterns spaced throughout the tent. Within it, Easton's skin glowed golden, his eyes like emerald jewels.

I arched away from where the feathered tips tickled my spine, eliciting a tangle of pricks across my skin.

"I just imagine I have wings?" I curled my hands back into the blanket and raised them to my chest. "And they'll appear?"

He caught my chin between thumb and finger. "Find the

magic and use it. As one with innate magic, it should come naturally to you."

I closed my eyes to avoid looking at him. While my magic was burrowed deep in my gut, ribboning around the mate bond as if the breeze twirled it, the new magic lingered in my joints and muscles. It did not meet my presence with jitters, as my own magic did, but with a tepid embrace. I sank into it.

"The magic knows what to do," Easton whispered. He cupped my jaw. "Let it guide you."

My shoulders softened, the magic like a heavy cape dragging them down. Beneath my shoulder blades, it burrowed into my spine and stitched itself into every nerve, then bloomed. I arched against the swelling pain rippling back and up through my sides into my chest. Feeling like an inferno trapped in my muscles and bones, the magic rearranged my joints, popping them out of place, until it found a snug hole for itself.

I clawed into Easton's wrists and barked out a plea.

"Let it guide you," Easton repeated.

My spine felt as if were split in two. A thousand pricks around the ink, as if the Oracle continued to hammer the jagged chisel in the wounds, set my skin on fire.

I was both sweating and shivering, bracing against Easton's caress and arching away from it, writhing at the shifting of my bones and clenching still to avoid agitating the inking.

The magic went still, then it yanked, resetting every bone it'd nudged aside and realigning my muscles to its adjustments. I sucked in a raspy breath and fluttered open my eyes.

Easton smiled, his brow pressed to mine.

Silence.

My skin tightened over my shoulder blades and lower back. The feathers, manifesting, speared from the ink as if lined with razors.

Easton gasped. "Kacy."

My back bloated, crushing my organs and the breath from my lungs. I knocked away Easton's hands, hunched over, and shrieked into the furs scrunched between our knees. The pain swelled like a dammed river. It thrashed against my skin, threatening to burst if not released.

The bed shifted, and Easton ran a hand down my back as the feathers inched out. Each touch cracked the dam, letting the pressure trickle through.

I raised my head, released a shrill cry, and jolted my innate magic. It came to my call, surging upwards through every pore, shoving the pressure from my back in one gust.

Golden light filled the tent, then disappeared.

Drawing in a full breath, I sagged onto the mattress with my legs squashed beneath me. My hands dangled off the end of the bed. The crackling of my magic in my ears muffled his words.

He eased my legs from under me, lying me flat on my stomach.

Something heavy and soft settled across my back.

I rolled my head to the side. Gold clouded my vision. Reaching to dismiss the lingering magic, I instead felt feathers.

Easton kneeled before me. He cupped my cheek and kissed my brow. "They're beautiful."

Golden wings.

Pressing onto my elbows, I raised the wings as easily as I might raise my arms, suspending them above the bed enough for the draft trickling through the tent flaps to ruffle them. A shiver jittered through the new nerves, sheltered by the feathers, to my spine.

I clasped Easton's hand between mine and yanked him close enough for our noses to brush. "Teach me to fly." I raised my wings higher, imagining the wind sweeping them back. I could soar through the clouds, race the sun across the sky, and silence the taunting of the stars with my own place amongst them in the clear night skies. I could go anywhere, even off the continent, if I caught the right breeze.

"Soon." Easton toyed with the feathers over my left shoulder.

I lurched to my knees. "Tonight."

He rolled his eyes. "We have dinner plans tonight."

"What if I flew to dinner? Imagine the look on Barin's face." I clenched his hand harder.

Thunderous laughter burst from him. His warm breath skittered across my wings.

I sucked in a cool breath to calm the rising heat in my neck and cheeks.

"You'd be more likely to barrel into him." He smoothed down the ruffled feathers. "It'd be impossible to learn so quickly. Then again, you've accomplished multiple impossible feats." He smirked. "What's one more?"

I sprang from the bed, teetering beneath the new weight of my wings, and reached for Easton's outstretched hand for balance. As soon as I grabbed it, he curled his nails into my palm.

"What are those?"

I followed his gaze to my stomach. Even in the shadows cast by our wings, the tattooed deals gleamed as if smeared with grease. He stared at the blood red tattoo of hammers crossed above a flame, veiled by shadows hanging from a black mountain above it.

He dropped my hand. "More bargains? From whom?"

I snagged the shirt draped across the bed and slipped it onto my arms. "We had very different Sacraments."

Easton grabbed the shirt as if he thought I could yank it on over my wings to hide my shame from him as I had for the past week. "You haven't told me anything about your Sacrament. Or your quest." His voice softened. "Haven't mentioned why you returned minutes after the others or with a new set of blades and leathers."

Yellow eyes flashed through my memory.

He reached for my cheek, but I turned to deflect his touch.

"Kacela, I survived the Sacrament as well. If there is anyone you can talk to—"

I swiped away a tear gathering in the corner of my eye. "I was hunted, Easton, like a wild animal. You may have gone in with grudges and enemies, but I went in as an Altun invader.

The sole enemy." My voice, so meek, was nearly a plea.

Easton dropped his outstretch hand, nodding.

"You told me to come back," I whispered. "I came back, no matter the cost."

I forced down the red wine, ignoring the tinge it left on the other's mouths. It gathered in the corners of Chief Indiviar's lips and rolled down his chin. When he swiped it away, it stained his fingers. I clamped my jaw shut to hold back the rising bile.

"I'd think you'd be proud to have the first blessed female in centuries come from your clan. A badge of honor," Amaury said between sips of wine. He blocked me from his head with newly made metal barriers.

Chief Indiviar's glare swung to me. "Pride does not fix the disarray in our clan."

"Your warriors sharpen and clean their weapons on the battlefield," I remarked. "They cook their own food and wash their clothing."

"When war demands it," Chief Teamet of Flyeria snapped. His black wings were on full display, as were the other winged in the tent, including Amaury.

I adjusted against my chair, not used to the weight of my golden wings or sitting in a backless chair to accommodate them.

"If these changes are too trying for any of you, I am confident another will gladly take the bargain on your arm," Griffin continued. He sat at the head of the long table, dressed in his finest tunic of black and red. He'd thrown his black cape, embroidered with his family seal on the back and lined with red-dyed fur, across the entire chair. Heavier bags hung beneath his eyes, and his features were narrower and cheeks hollower than before.

"That's interfering with clan business!" Chief Ran, Leon's father, slammed his hand into the table. He was the same ebony as his son, but had shorter hair buzzed into intricate waves above his ears.

The king observed some specks in his wine. His ashy aura pulsed from him, thin enough to go unnoticed by most. I felt it on my hands, my neck, my cheeks, and, most unsettling, within my feathers. "If your actions threaten my rule, I am at liberty to deal with you as I see fit, according to the treaty."

Silence.

"Very well," Chief Yule of Wunort, Jorian's clan, grunted. "The blessed warriors will care for their weapons and armors. They will not learn to cook and clean. It will not be worth the effort."

Griffin mused, "Equality does not come with the snap of your fingers."

"Teach the boys," I said. "Those who have completed their Sacrament will keep their own weaponry. Young boys and girls will have the same schedule. They will train together."

Easton raised his wings higher. "The new generation will be the start of our equality. For all clans."

"The new generation must be ready for the war you will ultimately call us to die in," Chief Barin snapped. A new, bright red scar, cresting above his raised brow, was sewn shut with thick, brown thread.

With another swirl of his wine, Griffin leered. "When war comes, all must answer the raven's call, Altun and Forterian alike, to defend Kadea."

"The sooner you start," I said, "the larger your forces will grow. Imagine how other clans will cower when they bring their males forward for the Sacrament and you have double the participants? When your females make quivering nambies of top entrees."

Chief Indiviar's nostrils flared. "How did you survive the Sacrament?"

I sipped my wine to flush the rock from my throat. Mimicking Chief Indiviar's arched back and gritting teeth, I locked my gaze on him. "I was hunted. Tortured. Nearly killed. I found allies. I fulfilled my quest."

Easton pressed down the bond. His touch cooled the boiling rage I sheltered behind a stone mask. I allowed his presence to swirl in the pain-laced memories.

With a jerk, he withdrew.

"What was your quest?" Chief Teamet set aside his food. The other chiefs leaned closer, causing the table to creak. They glared like vultures waiting for a lame deer to die.

I took another sip of wine. It itched my already dry throat. Raising my wings slightly higher, I leaned forward.

"I survived on my own for weeks, though I had no more than the leathers on my back while your boys brought in weapons, tools, and food. If I can do that," I turned my gaze away to stare at my swirling wine, "imagine what a league of highly trained Archers could do to those who underestimate them. You can lead them, or you can watch your boys be killed by them."

I left soon after, the little bit of meat I'd eaten threatening to follow my claim out onto the table. Easton trailed me.

"You're right," he said within the safety of his tent after helping me retract my wings into the blessing. "I don't know what you went through."

Like he had the night before the Sacrament, he eased himself to my back with a grip on my elbow and wrapped the other arm around my waist.

I remained still as stone. My chest tightened, scared to release the words forming on my tongue.

"My quest was to go beneath the mountain to find answers." I shifted, and his head raised from where it rested on my shoulder. "I met the goddess of war and the god who trapped her beneath the mountain. They each took their delight in toying with me, and I can't decide whose touch was worse."

I turned in his grasp and raised the edge of my shirt enough to reveal the hammers. Easton stepped back, allowing the wintry air to raise the hairs across my skin. "She gave me a blade to kill Envers, if I promised to break her from the prison." I lifted it above the mountain. "And he let me leave the mountain, fully healed, if my consciousness returns to her prison every night in my dreams."

"For how long?" he asked.

I dropped my shirt. "For the rest of my life."

His brow dipped. "Why?"

"When you're immortal, life is boring enough to toy with mortals."

Calluses scraped against my cheek as Easton's thumbs flattened the growing bags beneath my eyes.

"Do you believe me?" I didn't know how to tell him I didn't believe myself, as if the entire thirty-eight days had been a fever dream. A manic illusion my sanity needed to remain intact. Much of it I attempted to puzzle through in my nights on the goddess's couch, ignored by her.

He pulled his lip between his teeth. "Kacy, you suffered —"

I pinwheeled an arm through his caress and pointed at the black blades hidden in the tent's shadowed corners. "Then explain the blades and the armor. I crawled into that mountain with what I thought was my final breath. The Obscur — Children of the Night, they exist. They are down there, ruled by a god of shadows and deceit."

Easton grabbed my shoulders, forcing my flailing arms back to my sides. "Kacy, I believe you. Give me a moment."

I threw his grip away.

"Why?" he demanded. "Why do gods care so much about you?"

I stammered back from the accusation in his tone.

He ran a hand through his curls, matting them down. "Kacy, are you not wondering the same?"

I let my sigh fill the space between us. I'd wondered it every moment in the silence of the tent. Why hadn't my father found me sooner? What good did locking me in a cage with his greatest enemy do?

Did he have anything to do with the war Nalin claimed would purge the continent?

"Yes, of course I have."

Easton cupped my jaw, drawing me closer with each breath. I slipped my hands beneath his loose tunic to feel the curve of his back and the greasy lines of his blessing. I sank into his embrace, as I had sunk into the blessing magic reforming my body to accommodate the wings. I breathed in his pine scent as if it were the air I needed, no longer suffocating in his absence.

"We'll figure it out." His breath rained over my mouth and nose.

I strained on my tiptoes for the warmth of his words, curling my fingers into his sides. "Together?" I whispered.

He nodded, then, against my lips, he whispered, "Together."

"Are there more?" I asked the goddess, taking my usual seat on the couch. "Like me? More children of deities?"

"I never had any." She threw her brass hair off her shoulder. "But yes, many. Hundreds within the first few years we arrived. Our offspring are born with a portion of our magic. The stronger the magic, the more recent the birth."

My own sparked in my gut where I lay beside my mate, though my mind could not reach it. "My magic—"

"Might be strong enough to shatter this prison, if you were not so dull-witted."

I balked, then ran my hands across my legs to settle their trembles. "Can you teach me?"

"To kill me like your father wishes?"

"You're a god. Can you be killed?"

She huffed, throwing herself back onto the bed. "We are not truly all-powerful, immortal deities like you worship us as. We are stronger, yes, but mortal beings trapped in this dimension after a long war ruined our home. Some of us found the transition easier than others. Some, like myself and your father, preyed upon the admiration of inferiors. It wasn't until our half-fae offspring grew that we learned they inherited our magic, and even then, some didn't care about soiling our strength with your mundaneness."

Like Easton had, I fumbled with the new information. It worked at the puzzle of my birth, moving new pieces to light and creating the semblance of a potentially continent-shifting realization.

Altuns were children of the gods.

"Unfortunately, even if you could find this place, you do not have enough of your magic to break it."

I lurched forward. "What do you mean?"

"There is a block in your magic. What you have now is a small portion of what lies within you. You are, after all, the direct descendant of my kin, even if he is a lesser being. You could be immortal compared to all others, and you will be your father's greatest weapon in the coming war."

My thoughts stumbled. "Coming war?"

"As the dimensions orbit one another, we come within touching distance of my home. When it does, a portal will open and those we fought in the last war will attempt to infiltrate this world."

"Why?"

"My home is ancient, and while we may be immortals compared to you, land can only take so much destruction until it morphs into that of nightmares. I fear ours has done just that."

"We have to stop it!"

Nalin's warning sprung back into my head, his pungent fears and promises of safety. Neither he nor his parents could have known what not even Griffin could guess at.

"There is no stopping the will of fate, idiot girl. The war is coming, and you will all perish within it."

I stood, fists at my side. "Not if you help us."

She scoffed, "Why would I do that?"

I swallowed, not having an answer.

Then, her chamber shook more violently than ever before. The smell of burning flesh, then ash overlaying the usual poppy, burst into the prison.

"Do you feel that?" she cackled, and a sickly sweet smile

spread across her porcelain face. "An intruder, knocking down your walls bit by bit—"

Stabbing pain in the base of my skull sent my knees to the ground. I hunched over them and blocked my ears with my palms. The pounding continued.

But she was wrong. The walls protecting my mind were not knocked down, they were razed to smoldering debris.

The goddess's cackle radiated through me.

A black cord speared my heaving chest. It yanked me through my memories. The voices swirling in my head snickered at every ounce of pain, stretching them out through eternity.

Demanding the secrets of Inmonte, the magic of the mountain, the whereabouts of the goddess.

Then oblivion.

And silence.

CHAPTER 37

MY ENTIRE BODY ACHED. I pried open my eyes.

I was no longer in Virian, instead in my bed in the castle. The duvet was as warm and fluffy as I remembered, the pillows soft like clouds, and the mattress like a mother's embrace.

I could've stayed there forever.

If a hoarse voice hadn't woken me.

"Orders are strict. No visitors."

"I'm her mate."

Easton.

"King's orders. No visitors."

I tripped over the duvet in my haste to reach him and slammed into the obsidian floor which reflected my disheveled expression back at me. The duvet tipped with me, throwing the pillows in every direction and making a mess of the water glass on the nightstand.

The doors were thrown open. Easton stood within them, hands outspread like his wings. Behind him, both guards were in an unmoving heap.

I kicked away the blanket and reached for him.

He ran a hand down my back. I clutched at his shirt, fastening myself to him.

I opened my mouth, but he silenced me with a shake of his head.

Easton dropped his forehead to mine. *It is not safe within these walls.*

My head pounded at the effort to respond across the bond.

There's something here. Something as strong or stronger than the king. I don't know what, but I know when he is in my head. This is worse. Like it's looking for something. There are spies in the walls. You must –

"She's awake!" Griffin called from the doorway, stopping only a moment to observe his unconscious guards. Amaury followed his king with downcast eyes, Neira waltzing in behind him.

Her painted red claws reached to embrace me.

Easton turned, shielding me. "Get out!" he snarled. "You had no right to do that to her!"

"It was a matter of security," Griffin seeped through gritted teeth.

Can you get us away from here?

I felt it then, something else within my head that did not belong. Not the heavy ash of Griffin's magic, but something lighter, like smoke billowing from a pyre.

Griffin's cheerful smile seeped back. "You're safe here," he said to me, eyes twinkling with dark delight, "you've always been safe here."

I gaped at him. "You went through my memories?"

"We had to," Neira cooed.

Beneath Griffin's sour grin, a monster lurked. It'd clawed its way to the surface, draped in black and red silks, tattering the soul beneath with unyielding, sharpened talons. This was not the king I'd known.

I stared at Amaury. He stared at his shifting feet.

"You've met the goddess of war?" Griffin asked. "And you found Inmonte. I'd always believed it was there." His smile slipped away. "You've given us the perfect reason to attack the mountain. I'm so proud of you."

But those weren't eyes of pride.

I'd seen that look. In Easton. In Leon. In Envers.

The gleam of passion. Hunger. War.

"You saw —" my voice died.

"Everything." His gloating smirk seized my gut. "Except through the darkness of Inmonte."

Neira's lips curled into a sinister smile. "It's only a matter of time before we see it, in full daylight."

Amaury shrunk back further.

Griffin scraped at the walls around my mind. I whimpered as they tumbled. Easton tried to wrap our minds in his own walls, but the king made quick work of those as well.

"The daughter of a god, under our noses this whole time!" Neira cackled. "And all those bonds she holds the Forterians to. We'll storm the mountain within the month! And then —"

"No!" I shouted, fighting to kick Griffin out of my head. He held strong, tendrils swaddling me. "Get out!"

Calmness forced itself on me. I fought as it leaked into every open crevice exposed to him. I felt naked, as naked as I had been the first time I'd met the goddess of war.

"She needs to rest," Griffin said, voice radiating with his command. "She'll come to her senses soon. This is, after all, the future we envisioned! We're so near to destroying the Forterians."

"No!" I screamed.

Tendrils constricted, stilling my mind.

I couldn't move, couldn't talk, could hardly breath as he squeezed tighter. My hands fell from Easton's shirt, my legs weak as I struggled to stand.

Easton turned, eyes wide. His hand went to my cheek, and though I felt the scrape of his calluses against my skin, I could only stare at him with widened eyes.

"There are easier ways for us to accomplish what we want, Kacela. If you cooperate, we will win this war before it starts."

Neira advanced.

I wanted to tell them this wasn't the war to fight. Tell them the goddess's warning, of a war requiring Forterians and Altuns to band together. Another realm whose rift could threaten our lives more than the demons had.

The words pressed at lifeless lips.

"What are you doing?" Easton demanded. His hands went to the swords on his belt.

"You're going to get hurt," Amaury warned.

"You're hurting her," Easton seethed. "She trusted you, of all of them, to protect her! You're going to stand there as he forces her. After what she's been through? After what she's done to help you?"

Griffin sighed. "This is what's best for her."

Easton pulled his swords.

Neira was faster. She reached out a hand and a flare of red shot from it, spearing through Easton's chest.

I felt the pain flood the mate bond. Blood spurted from his lips.

I screamed. An actual scream. Golden light ripped through Griffin's hold on my mind, searing the closest tendrils with strikes of jagged lightning. The windows shattered and my magic batted Griffin, Neira, and Amaury away.

It was like overcoming the first peak of a mountain, not truly knowing the extent of the range until the light illuminated it. The block within my head was no wall, it was a dam large enough to contain an ocean's rage.

It splintered.

Then exploded.

What I thought had been the wealth of my power was beggar's change.

I lunged for Easton's falling figure, illuminated in gold. The released magic encased us, more than I'd ever known surging from my gut. I drowned in the power of it, attempting to push my way to the surface to gain a sliver of control over it and redirect the cascading waves into Easton.

The mate bond grew weaker. The light faded from his eyes.

"My soul has allied with yours," I said against his forehead. "Please come back."

His head rolled back onto my arm. Hand dropped to the floor.

Another scream tore through me. I pressed my hand to his chest. Light engulphed the room. The mate blond gleamed in it, strengthening, repairing itself all the way down to Easton's chest. The connection grew until the bond was no longer a braided rope. Instead, a steel chain.

His consciousness gushed over the gap to my mind. He wrapped his entire being around every part of me.

Easton heaved in a breath.

The light faded, receding back into me in pulses.

My mate stared up at me, eyes as vibrant as ever and lips quirked. I wiped the blood from them with the sleeve of my shirt.

"You came back," I whispered into his curls.

Griffin staggered from the wall.

Neira stiffened beside him, her pretty face warped into a familiar snarl. The tyrant king's power reached for me, but I would not bow to his suffocating demand for submission again.

"I knew from the moment Amaury landed with you asleep in his arms," Griffin growled, wiping at a cut across his forehead, "how much power you had."

"You knew," I glared, voice flat. "You put the block in."

"Of course." Griffin's eyes softened. He opened his palms and ventured a step. Black tendrils danced in his fingertips. "You could've killed people." His voice softened. "Your magic is uncontrollable. The block was a necessity."

I swelled my magic. "When were you going to tell me?"

"Kacela—"

"No!" I snapped. "When were you going to tell me how powerful I was? Answer me!" My magic surged, a golden tendril striking Griffin through his throat.

His eyes widened as he grasped at the golden tendril connecting him to my hand. His mouth gaped around the lies. "Never," he finally managed with a gasp. "You would have died with that block in."

Amaury appeared in the window he'd been thrown through, his hazel wings speckled with blood. He landed between me and Griffin.

"You knew," I accused him.

"No," he whispered, eyes pleading.

"Don't lie to me," I seethed, another golden tendril striking through his throat.

"I didn't know," he said with surprising calm, shoulders slouching.

Kacy, what are you doing? Easton's voice washed the rage from me.

The golden tendril at Amaury's throat fell like mist.

Amaury never lied to me. He'd hidden things from me, things he thought would keep me safe if I remained ignorant, but he never lied to me. He always tried to protect me.

Neira lunged toward her mate.

I shot out a net of gold, which wrapped around her and threw her back against the wall, trapping her there.

"I should kill you," I snarled.

Kacy.

"You nearly killed my mate!"

Neira smirked, her court-like appearance surfacing. Calm and collected, as if she should be swirling a glass of wine in one hand as she ran a finger down Griffin's shoulder with the other. "Mates can be replaced, darling."

Guards rushed into the room. With them was Lord Tait, dressed in black with his estate's silver detailing. His dark eyes widened, my golden magic reflecting within their whites. Silver magic, akin to Nalin's, danced at his fingertips, and he mouthed, "go" before slinking toward the king.

I had to skip us. Somewhere. Anywhere.

Griffin's voice was a creeping calm. "I'll make you a deal—"

"I'm tired of deals!" I screamed, feeling the tattoos on my

body vibrate as if they'd been called to the surface.

Griffin licked his lips. "Not a magic deal."

Easton's hand tightened on my thigh. He tried to push himself up, but his arm buckled, and his head landed back in my lap.

"I can see how you care for your mate. It's heartwarming." Griffin's magic shattered the net trapping Neira. She landed gracefully and brushed off her silk skirt. "I'll let him return home as my emissary. I'll allow him visits."

I reached my gold around Easton, blocking the black tendrils from encompassing the ground beneath us. The tendrils fought for control, spinning around us. Sparks flew where they collided with my golden magic, sending pin pricks of pain to my chest.

Amaury drew his sword.

He angled toward the tyrant king, his lip twitched into a snarl.

"And me?" I dared. I reeled my magic back beneath my skin, away from the glare of the king.

"You'll stay. I'll strengthen the block. We will need your access to the goddess of war. You can train with Amaury. The same freedom you had before you met," his eyes cut to Easton, "your mate."

"That wasn't freedom," I seethed. My magic hunkered lower. It prowled like the leopard on Lord Tait's tunic.

Amaury's shoulders tensed.

Neira broke through the three lines of guards. A red aurora wrapped around her every step, fluttered through her hair. She elbowed Lord Tait away, and he jumped as if he'd been burned. "These walls are impenetrable. Surrender, darling, and save your mate."

I'm not leaving without you. Easton tightened his grip on my leg.

Amaury caught my stare. He nodded.

I held my breath.

He lunged past the guards, plunging his blade into the

tyrant's stomach.

Griffin raised his glare to his commander. His closest confidant. His pawn.

The king's fingers, encased in black tendrils, curled around the blade. Blood ran down its length.

Neira's red magic speared into Amaury.

I screamed.

It dragged him from his feet, and his back arched in with a sickening crack. Beneath his skin, blazing red surged to his wings and exploded.

Feathers rained on us, soaked in blood.

My lightning sank into Griffin, weaving through his consciousness. The plans and alliances he'd made over the last six months were laid out for me like a grand feast. They surged, becoming as much mine as they were his.

Blinding silver light encased the room.

I blasted through the nearest wall with my magic, shredding the black tendrils struggling to maintain their hold.

A small hole, no bigger than a shield, appeared. The wards of Kadea gave like fluttering curtains to my magic's demands, parting for us to skip through.

The next barrier, one of fire, relented at my plea.

My back hit the wall of the cave where I'd made my final stand with my Sacrament allies. Easton landed beside me. He jolted to his knees and captured my shoulders in his hands. His lips flapped, but his words were lost in the ringing in my ears.

Where I gripped my mate's wrist, I felt the drumming of his heart. A steady war chant.

My battle cry echoed through the mountain and spilled from the holy land.

A warning once known to all.

A promise to my enemies.

Come, death awaits.

ACKNOWLEDGEMENTS

My thanks for my debut novel are endless as writing the book was only the first (and maybe easiest) step to publication. First, to my parents who lectured me about writing during classes but still bought me new notebooks to fill with my stories. To Brett for understanding "do you want to game?" is actually code for "I want to write", to Sarah for reading the first draft and pointing out very obvious plot holes, to my sister for bragging about me to anyone who will listen, to my friends who supported me through the editing process, and to my D&D groups who kept my imagination alive. Whether you all knew it or not, you helped bring my dream of being a published author to life.

All my gratitude goes to the team at Fedowar Press for seeing the potential in my draft despite it being 30,000 words too long. D.W., thank you for not only choosing my manuscript from the pile but also every minute of work you've put into it since. Renée and B.K., your edits not only improved my book but also me as an author. Thank you for helping improve my craft ten-fold during this process.

You only ever get one debut novel, and I'm glad you were all a part of mine.

ABOUT THE AUTHOR

Molly Adaza discovered her love for words in middle school and spent the majority of high school and college classes switching between taking notes and writing, much to the annoyance of professors. Her favorite stories include complex magic systems, dragons, and strong female protagonists.

When not writing, Molly can be found on the soccer fields, playing Dungeons & Dragons, or hidden away with a book. Originally from frigid Minnesota, she currently enjoys the warm weather of Atlanta, GA where she works as a public health consultant.

Find out more about Molly Adaza on Twitter or her website.

WHAT'S NEXT?

There's always new speculative fiction brewing at Fedowar Press. Visit our website and sign up for our newsletter to be sure you don't miss anything.

www.FedowarPress.com

www.ingramcontent.com/pod-product-compliance
Lightning Source LLC
Chambersburg PA
CBHW020402260626
47156CB00007B/2204